Rhea Hawke: Galactic Enforcer

# Metaverse

## Book 3: Splintered Universe Trilogy

By

## Nina Munteanu

### PIXL PRESS

**Starfire World Syndicate**

# Metaverse

### Copyright © 2014 Nina Munteanu

**Cover Design and Typography: Costi Gurgu**
**Interior Design: Nina Munteanu**

**Published in Canada by Pixl Press**
**an Imprint of Starfire World Syndicate**
**2545 Edmonds St.**
**Delta, BC Canada V4K 1M9**
**http://pixlpresscanada.blogspot.ca**

Library and Archives Canada Cataloguing in Publication

Munteanu, Nina, author        Metaverse / by Nina Munteanu.

(Splintered universe trilogy ; book 3) "Rhea Hawke: galactic enforcer". Co-published by: Starfire World Syndicate.

Issued in print and electronic formats.
ISBN 978-0-9811012-7-9 (pbk.)
ISBN 978-0-9811012-2-4 (kindle)

I. Title.

PS8626.U68M48 2014        C813'.6        C2014-901361-
2                                         C2014-901362-0

For Kevin

## Acknowledgements

I consulted the wisdom and science of many authorities in the areas of space exploration and habitable zones, AI, biotechnology, sleep biology, neurobiology, and ecology. The most notable source was NASA. Any mistakes are mine, not theirs. Thank you, Costi and Vali, for creating an impeccable cover of a character that lives. Gratitude also goes to Dawn Harvey, who narrated the trilogy as audiobooks and breathed life into Rhea. Karen, as always, thank you for the obvious, but mostly for the subtle and intangible.

This trilogy was so fun to write. Thank you, my readers, especially those of you who eagerly followed the books and reminded me that you enthusiastically anticipated Rhea's next adventure. Here it is!

# Praise for *Outer Diverse* and *Inner Diverse*:

"Nina Munteanu is … a master of metaphor … a creator of fantastic worlds and cultures. She combines her biological background with the infinite possibilities of the cosmos and turns an adventure story into a wonderland of alien rabbit holes … Rhea Hawke, is a fresh and multi-faceted heroine."
> — **Craig H. Bowlsby**, author of *Empire of Ice* and creator of *Commander's Log*

"… A rollicking science fiction plot with all the trappings … Hawke is a maverick in the Wild West tradition, up against the world … a genetic mystery with lethal powers."
> — **Lynda Williams**, author of the *Okal Rel Series*

"Nina Munteanu creates a human future on the edge of chaos, and a multiverse that flows back and forth, one universe feeding into another…Munteanu illustrates her love of diverse ecosystems, richly describing complex alien eco-webs. Rich descriptions of biodiversity populate her narrative, making the alien environment feel real, feel close, engage the senses. She evokes in the reader a desire for exploring the miraculous diversity of life…"
> — **Speculating Canada**

"A magic carpet ride of adventure that not only reaches deep into the folds of the Universe, but also into the depths of the soul. In this superb tale, Munteanu has woven a tapestry of events that had me spellbound to the end!...I am enthralled with Nina Munteanu's style of story telling and I have just become her newest fan!!!"
> — **Tricia Burns-Rodney**, Goodreads review

"Rhea Hawke is a Galactic Guardian, and I love to say her name. Her name alone let's you know that there is a bad ass super hero of a woman on site. I can picture her boots, her great coat, and her side arms. I want to be her when I grow up."
> — **Amazon review**

"Strong science fiction with action and intrigue… wonderful world building with fascinating aliens and planets, along with detailed weapons, missions, errors, and blunders."
> — **Martha's Bookshelf**

"…A well-written book, with a tight plot and lots of interesting ideas and events that maintains interest from start to finish."
> — **Amazon review**

"Powerful and brilliantly written, exceptional in style and detail. Humorous and witty this is a master work of metaphor and science fiction."
> — **Vanessa Rottner**, author of *The Diva Files*

"Through the empty arch enters a mental air blowing insistently over the heads of the dead, seeking new landscapes and unfamiliar accents; an air bearing the odour of a child's spittle, crushed grass, and the veil of Medusa announcing the unending baptism of all newly-created things…"

Federico Garcia Lorca

## PROLOGUE

You see the Gate on Borrias, its orifice shimmering with sudden life, vibrating with scintillating color. Scores of small spaceships the shape of elongated teardrops burst through the Gate. They fly low over the planet's surface then arc up into the blackness of space. Dread grips you even though you are only vapor, watching without eyes, feeling without a body. You know what they are and where they are bound. *Nihilist* suicide ships bound for your home.

...Is this real or is it a *dust*-dream?...

...You are commanding one of the ships...at least you feel his body. Feel his heart throb with adrenalin and his short shallow breaths wheeze with fearful exhilaration; you see his sweaty hands, human hands. You feel them tremble with the thrill of terror as they maneuver the controls in the fervent grit of a fanatic.

The ship has just jacked the particle stream, and you recognize the Iota Horologii system. The massive red giant, Iota Horologii b, lies ahead. The pilot maneuvers the ship alongside four other squad ships and they head in formation toward the far side of the gas giant where Iota Hor-2, her home, loyally orbits in quiet serene beauty. It looks so much like Earth. Your trembling thoughts breathe through you like a silent wind.

The pilot barks over the holo-com to the command ship: "Our squad is approaching target," he snarls. You hear the response: "All other squads are in position at designated targets." You know them: Gleise-12; Moner 7; Beleus; Ogium 9; so many others...Earth... "Commence attack."

The pilot's thrill of anticipation surges through you like a storm as the obsessive iron will of duty grips you. You see your hands—the pilot's hands—readying the instruments for lethal trajectory; for a crash landing. The console, once set, locks so the pilot cannot pull out in a last panicked moment of recoil. Upon impact each of the five ships will detonate a particle bomb that will engulf the planet in lethal radiation. It will kill all life.

The ship locks into its deadly trajectory. You feel it abruptly list into its suicide angle. You see several of the other teardrops ahead of you in formation. They will impact on the ground first. Their particle bombs will cause such a forceful explosion that several ships will detonate in the upper atmosphere, ensuring maximum radiation coverage. Total annihilation. This is far worse than your MEC could ever be. This has to be a dream, you reason.

You scrabble at your own terror and anguish, elusive like vapor, but swirling about you in a perfume of horrible inevitability. How can you stop this atrocious thing? You are a ghost without form or substance, without a mind to bend another's. You feel the pilot's abject fear. He fears death; yet he agreed to this mission. He thinks of his little brother...his two dead parents...of the small town he grew up in...

If this is a dream, you think, now is a good time to wake up. You do not wake up.

Iota Hor-2 rushes toward you. One of the ships explodes prematurely in a blinding white flash; *Athena*, the orbiting defense/research space station struck it with a missile. Your ship shudders briefly but punches through the debris. Within moments it and the other ships are beyond *Athena*'s range and far too close to the moon's surface for the *Athena* to risk another shot. Four ships; four particle bombs. More than enough to unleash a deadly radiation that will devastate an entire planet and all life upon it.

You see the ground rushing toward you in pulsating garish color.

NO!

You're knocked by a deafening smash in a blinding white flash and searing heat. Something hard and molten tears through your chest. Blood spurts up into your face—

—*Rhea! Breathe!*—

—I bolted awake with a gasp, hunched over my console and chest burning with excruciating pain.

"Breathe, Rhea!" Benny shouted as Huey nudged me hard.

I jerked back in my pilot's seat, seizing in panting breaths, and forced myself to look down. My death-white hands clutched my grey top in fisted balls. My top was dark with sweat but I saw no gaping wound. No sheen of blood. I shook like a leaf in a gale and my heart beat a furious drum-role. My face...I lifted a trembling hand and touched my face, wet and covered in something warm. When I drew my hand away I saw blood and flinched.

"Oh, God!" I moaned and felt the onset of convulsions.

"Get a blanket!" Benny shouted to Dewey, lingering by the cockpit hatchway.

Huey poked my arm with a needle and Dewey returned with a blanket that he threw over my shaking body. I heard myself moaning and couldn't stop.

"It's just a nose bleed, Rhea," Benny soothed. "You had a bad dream. That's all. Huey gave you a sedative. Your heart's racing like an old *cobra* motor." Then he commanded more sternly, "Breathe deep or you'll hyperventilate." I concentrated on taking in several deep breaths and felt myself calm down. As I regained my composure, Benny added quietly, "Must have been a really bad one. You went AWOL on us for a moment there."

"AWOL?" I said shakily. "What do you mean?" I'd stopped shaking but felt the blood still flowing from my nose and brought my hand up to cup it. Huey handed me a tissue. I took it and pressed it to my nose.

"I mean everything stopped. Your heart, your breathing. Your brainwaves. *Everything.*"

I gathered the blanket around me with a frown and got up shakily to my feet to wash the blood off my face. I was reminded with some alarm of *dust*-shakes. Then again, it might have just been my reaction to the dream. It had really shaken me, it was so real and horrible. Ever since I'd been *dusted*, I suffered more nightmares. And more nose bleeds.

A residual effect, I thought as I bent over the sink in mid-ship and glanced in the mirror at my face. It was peppered with blood. I rested my gaze briefly on my eyes, glittering like emeralds in the sunlight. That was happening all too often also. It was as though I still carried dormant *glitter* inside me, waiting to emerge with its accompanying hysteria, shakes and pigment-glow. The *glitter* was real enough.

That terrifying vision had been too vivid, I reflected soberly. Too real to be just a *glitter*-dream. Had the *glitter* let me tap into a possible future? Or was I just worried about it? I shook off the morbid thoughts with a long exhale and continued washing the sticky blood off my face with cool water. More like fear of failure, I reflected. That was my hallmark.

"Once you've cleaned up, I want you in the infirmary for a few tests, Rhea," Benny said.

I nodded, rubbing my face and splashing water on it. "Good idea," I agreed and wondered with some dread what was happening to me.

"Rhea," Benny said with renewed urgency. I looked up, face dripping, heart pumping. "Bastion's alive."

## ONE

I kept my gaze on the Eosian guard on the roof of the Med-Facility as I dove with powerful Khonsus wings toward him. His back was facing me. He had no idea what hit him. I knocked him down with my massive beaked head, then shifted back to my more agile human form and rolled to the ground as he scrambled to his feet. I leapt up and stunned him unconscious with my MEC. It was the only thing I carried except for the backpack slung over my shoulders that contained my clothes; otherwise, I was buck-naked.

"Jag!" I hissed out through the mouth-com embedded in my tooth. I'd noticed the goggles on the guard I'd knocked out. "They're wearing security glasses!"

"Don't get seen, then," Benny said over my ear com. "And Hurry! They're already alerted with that guard down."

"Yeah. Right." I pulled off an elastic that I'd secured on the butt of the MEC and single-handedly tied back my long hair with it. Then I scurried to the other corner of the roof, to the exit door. No time to put my clothes on. The second guard was stationed there, of course. It was in the middle of the day and we came face to face, both of us startled by the other. I had the advantage; he stared at my naked body before he noticed the MEC. By then I'd shot him.

"Damn! He got a good look at me, Benny."

"You're already in their system, Rhea. They'll ID you in a minute and send for reinforcements. You'll have to be incredibly fast."

I nodded and wrenched open the door, hearing the third guard racing after me. I turned and shot as he got within range. He toppled with a clatter of his side arm. *"The difficult is done at once, the impossible takes a little longer—*French proverb," I quipped.

"I know, Rhea. I'm counting on it," Benny said, then added as an afterthought, "Maybe you should have gone in the front door like I dissuaded you from doing."

"Thanks," I snarled and entered the building. "Okay, I'm in. Where to?"

"Bastion's on the third floor. But I detect auto-security at all exits, including the one you've just entered. Plus a security man on each floor and one in front of Bastion's room."

"Okay. Tell me how to get there."

Benny directed me down the best route. It was only three hours ago that Benny had informed me that Bastion was alive. How he'd managed to survive the Q-bomb I couldn't fathom. I'd half-suspected that it was a trap to lure me in, but Benny had assured me that Bastion was indeed alive. Benny had penetrated the Med-Facility's security surveillance and had seen Bastion.

"Rhea," Benny said urgently. "They've just identified you and have called in the Guardians."

I hissed my response and bolted down the stairs, thoughts returning to the communication Benny had intercepted earlier. It had been both wonderful and disturbing: wonderful because it revealed that Bastion was alive and in the Med-Facility; disturbing because the com was between a *Nihilist* and a Guardian—obviously one of Ennos's men. They were discussing how to finish Bastion off. The collaboration of a law officer and a terrorist was truly frightening. The Guardians had been alerted by the inverted Q-bomb, which was a particular signature of Eclipse hits. It wouldn't have taken them long to make the connection to me and then instruct the Med-Facility to put on extra security. Only, they hadn't counted on Guardian traitors and *Nihilists* getting there first—

The door below flew open with a bang. Three Eosian guards spilled out onto the stairs, shooting. I whirled and pounded up to the next floor as beta particles sang over my head; one guard was better odds than three, I thought, as I emerged through the stairwell exit on the sixth floor. The guard at the exit was expecting me but not my MEC. I burst out shooting and caught him as he raised his weapon. He fell with a thud. I raced down the hall to the exit on the far end and bolted down the stairs to the third floor, hearing my pursuers clattering behind me. More shots zinged past me from the stairwell and I felt a sharp sting on my left arm.

I hissed out a curse and threw open a door into a narrow corridor with my good arm. I looked down at my bleeding arm. They were using Class D *nokerig* pistols, ancient ballistic weapons with projectiles that festered in your body wherever they embedded. Although it hurt like chaos and bled copiously, the bullet had only grazed my arm, I noticed with relief.

I fumbled into the outer pouch of my backpack and pulled out a smart band-aid then quickly applied it to my wound. As I did, I heard distant shouts and urgent commands in the north and west stairways and knew that I would soon be ambushed.

"Benny!" I bit out. "I'm on the third floor. What do you see?" Benny had locked onto the security system and could follow the particle-tracking grid.

"Five men on your floor so far. I see you; they're coming toward you from the west wing...and the north wing. Bastion is in Room 313. Three guards are between you and Bastion. You should see them any minute."

"Of course," I breathed out and pelted down the hall toward them, pointing my MEC out ahead of me.

"Rhea!" Benny cried out. "There's someone in Bastion's room! And it's not a doctor or nurse!"

My heart slammed. "Vos?"

"I think it's—oh, no! They found me, Rhea...I think they're—"

Benny abruptly cut off and I took in a sharp inhale. They'd shut him down. I was on my own; so was Benny. I rounded the corner before they did and met three Eosian guards face to face. Startled at first, they grinned, aiming their *nokerig* pistols at me, and advanced in unison to form a wall of dark blue and purple.

I turned and fled, hearing them scramble after me. I dropped the MEC and rapidly shifted to a blenoid as they rounded the corner, then leapt at them with a ferocious growl. One Eosian shot. It went wide and all three turned and fled. I shifted back to my human form, hair flying loose now, scooped up the MEC then dashed after them and picked them off as I ran to Room 313.

I wrenched open the door.

An Eosian man stood over someone in a bed—I couldn't make out who but I presumed it was Bastion. At my entrance the man turned. He clutched a knife poised over Bastion's sleeping form and, seeing me, hesitated only a moment. I shot him with my MEC to no effect—a Vos. He grinned and turned back to the bed and plunged the knife down.

I leapt. We collided and knocked the bed aside. The knife caught the bed, not Bastion, who stirred from his sedated sleep. The assassin lunged out at me with the knife. I twitched out of his way and swung out with my MEC. It caught him in the head and knocked him out. He slumped against the bed and crumpled on the floor, knife clattering beside him.

I rose to my feet behind the body of the *Nihilist* and swiftly locked the door. When I turned I was looking straight at Bastion. He stared down at his would-be assassin then looked back at me, suddenly grinning with astonishment. That grin warmed me all over like hot soyka.

"Rhea!" he gasped. "You're..." He grinned like a boy at Christmas. I looked down at myself; I'd forgotten I was stark naked.

With an embarrassed grin, I bent to pull my clothes out of the backpack and hastily dressed, avoiding his eyes. After cinching on my tool belt and holster, I tucked my MEC into it. It was my last MEC. I'd lost the previous two, the first was destroyed along with Rashomon; the second was currently with Ka. The last article to go on was my Great Coat.

He gasped again. "You're a Guardian Enforcer!"

"Well, not exactly," I said with a crooked smile. Then I pointed at him with my finger in a casual gesture. "You're alive." He looked as though a *delta* class *shadow* freighter had hit him. His battered face was severely bruised and swollen in places and tracked with numerous small cuts. Benny had listed his injuries to me before: cracked and broken ribs, concussion, bruised vertebrae, torn knee ligaments — which had to be reconstructed — and lots of cuts and bruises.

Bastion wore a goofy smile. "I don't know what happened. They said the book you gave me might have had a bomb."

I nodded soberly with an apologetic half smile. "Sorry. It was planted without my knowing. But why aren't you dead?"

"Is that why you didn't come back?"

I nodded. "I'm sorry. If I'd known..." I trailed and lowered my gaze.

"Well, it was you who saved me...in a way," he said. I jerked my face up to stare at him. He grinned at me. "I heard you...saw you in my mind on the street behind my store. You'd dropped to your knees and cried out my name as if you were in great pain."

God! He'd had a vision of my reaction—before it happened!

"I dropped the book on the counter and ran," Bastion went on. "Literily ran. Luckily I did. The blast sent me flying anyway and knocked me out. But I'm alive," he ended with a self-satisfied grin.

Could it have been Serge? Had he planted the déjà vu into Bastion to leave his store and go out back? Had he done it for *me*?

"Who's *that*?" He pointed down to his assailant with a confused expression of dread on his face. "He was trying to kill me, wasn't he?"

I felt my lips tighten. I formulated what to say and raked the hair back from my face. I stuttered out something as I flicked nervous glances at the door and windows.

Then I saw it: a blue-green slime, seeping under the door. Q-gel! They weren't taking any more chances with me. Q-gel had nano-bots inside it that could be programmed to detonate within a specified distance from a specific object. I had no doubt what specific objects the bots were targeted for.

We had seconds. I leapt onto Bastion, seizing him as he yelped, and rolled us off the bed toward the window. We thudded to the floor and I winced at his cry of pain. Calling forth an invisible burst of Badowin strength, I heaved the bed onto its side in front of us and pushed Bastion gruffly down just as the gel ignited with a loud ear-splitting bang.

The blast threw the bed against us and together we collided into the far wall as the windows shattered. Shards of tiny glass rained on us. Bastion squeaked then whimpered.

"You okay?" I asked once I'd gotten my breath back. My voice sounded like I was underwater and my ears were ringing.

He nodded, grimacing tightly with wide eyes. I saw blood trickle out of both his ears and felt a warm flow down my left one. The blast had probably burst our eardrums. We were lucky, I thought, that it hadn't done more.

"Come on," I said, pushing the bed off us and scrambling

to my feet. "This is our exit call." I lowered my hand to help him up. He just stared. All around us, embedded in the walls and the far side of the bed were thousands of knife-like spicules. Dozens would have impaled us had we not been shielded behind the bed. Bastion shivered.

"Come on," I urged.

He didn't move. He just stared at me.

I bent down and forced my voice soft, "We need to go...Serge," I forced out his first name. That seemed to do the trick. His eyes met mine and he took my hand then rose shakily to his feet. I helped him limp to the window and pointed down. "That's where we have to go," I said.

He recoiled. It was three stories to the ground with only a few bushes to break our fall.

"You can do it," I said. I knew he could. Problem was, he didn't know he could. He was a Vos and had likely touched a Khonsus or other alien capable of flight. And like me, he'd likely tapped unknowingly into that form and others during his innocent life. I grew impatient and shoved him closer to the window. He stiffened and reared back like a horse facing fire. Bastion certainly wasn't Serge. This man was a meek and mild bookseller, terrified because people were trying to kill him for no apparent reason. He was actually the normal person, I decided. I felt sorry for him, sorry that I'd burst in on his normal world and drawn him into this one. But I had no time right now for sentiments. "We have no time," I snarled, glancing at the door. I could already hear sounds of men trying to get in. "Jump!"

He stood his ground, stubbornly refusing. Then he let out a low fearful moan and shook his head.

I pursed my lips and said, "I'm sorry."

He blinked at me. "For what?"

"For *this*!" I swung hard and struck him in the face with my fist; then winced as he dropped like a metatron weight on the floor. That was the second time I'd done that, I thought, shaking my hand from the pain of the impact. Only the last time it was the other Serge. I hastily undressed and stuffed my clothes into my backpack then shifted to a Khonsus and gathered Bastion into my arms. I flew out the window just as I heard the crash of the door being blown open.

Aware that I might be attracting undue attention, I landed in the nearest park and stowed Bastion's unconscious body under a juniper bush. I then shifted to my human form and quickly dressed.

I threw glances around me in search of some vehicle to escape in. Bastion was in no shape to run or do much of anything, especially right now after I'd belted him. Then I spotted it; a small *peewee*, parked a block away on the side of the road. The small two-seater resembled an ancient Earth motorcycle, except that it could fly. I pelted toward it and, after a brisk glance over my shoulder, straddled the vehicle and jimmied the starter lock then kick-started the engine. The vehicle stuttered on and I drove it to the bush where I'd stowed Bastion. I leapt off and pulled Bastion out from under the bush. After struggling with his dead weight, I finally got him, still in his pajamas, in the back-supported passenger seat and seat-belted his slumped form in. I jumped in the pilot's seat, grabbed his limp arms so he was leaning against me and secured his arms around my waist by lashing them together with chord from my pocket. Then we were soaring up just as several Eosian guards ran up to us, waving *nokerig* pistols and shooting.

*Nihilists* had perched themselves on the roof and caught my *peewee* in a salvo of torpedoes. I veered us out to sea but not before one grazed the vehicle. I felt the hard jerk to the right and craned to look over my shoulder. I noticed to my dismay that a green cloud of hesium fuel was spraying out of the fuselage. But we'd at least cleared the distance they could shoot. I had no idea where I was going, except that it was far from the Med-Facility and the city.

For now I spotted no pursuit. That would change quickly, I thought, glancing down at my options. We were heading out to sea toward a long string of islands. The Beleus Sea shimmered in the sunlight with mercurial hues of lavender, deep purple, aqua green and blue. So different from the oily seas of Horus, the Beleus Ocean was extremely clear, reflecting the shifting light of the planet's atmosphere in an exotic glitter.

Bastion stirred, head still lolling against my shoulder, and I reached behind me to jab him awake.

"Where are we?" I said gruffly. "We're low on fuel." I didn't tell him we were *losing* fuel. "And we need to land somewhere fast...and safe!"

I had to give him credit; he sobered fast and unfastened his hands then leaned forward to point to our left, toward a cluster of extremely tall islands. "There. Go there, to the Broken Islands. They won't find us there."

That was what I needed to hear. I veered hard to port and heard Bastion grab my waist again and moan out some expletive at me. I glanced over my shoulder and found him glaring at me and rubbing one hand over his sore jaw.

"Sorry," I muttered. "You weren't going to jump."

"What'd you do? Throw me over?" he asked in a sarcastic voice and felt himself gingerly.

"No, I just changed into a bird and flew you down to this vehicle that was waiting for us," I said, meeting his sarcastic tone.

He remained silent. The truth is always more bizarre than any made up story, I thought dismally.

We were fast approaching the tall island spires. Hundreds of them dotted the iridescent sea. It was obvious to me that we'd reached the Broken Islands. And good thing too, because the engine began to stutter. It spluttered and whined as if in objection as I gunned it. Then I hiked in my breath as we went into a silent glide.

"Are we—" Bastion stopped himself.

He decided that he didn't want to know; unfortunately I didn't have that luxury. *It's not enough to know to ride; you must also know how to fall*—Mexican proverb. Ok...here we go...

I grimaced as my hands fought the wheel to keep the nose of the *peewee* up. We were plummeting much too fast for a comfortable landing. I caught sight of a small island with a sand beach, and thought it would provide a softer landing than some of the other near-vertical rocky islands nearby. I steered us there. The island sat on a shallow sand shelf that then dropped into the deep indigo-blue abyss of the Beleus Sea. It resembled a coral cay.

"Hang on to something!" I yelled and steeled myself for a hard landing.

The beach rushed toward us. Then we hit. The collision threw me forward with an involuntary shriek and slammed my head against the windshield. The *peewee* skidded with a high-pitched squeal then finally stopped, throwing me forward again in an explosion of breath. I panted in relief and took quick stock: apart from a throbbing ankle and head, I felt fine. Bastion wheezed out his breaths and announced that he was okay too. He was already injured so I honestly couldn't tell where he'd been additionally hurt.

I struggled out, wincing as I landed, and blacked out for an instant. I then helped Bastion off the vehicle and braced him, limping hard, toward a low marine bush. After he let himself collapse under the bush, I pulled out my MEC and, after setting it to metalloid, seared a large hole near the bottom of the *peewee*. Then I tapped into my Badowin strength and heaved the vehicle across the sand into the water.

Bastion called urgently, "Don't go in the water!"

I turned to him and saw genuine alarm on his face. I turned back to the water.

He instructed, "The tide is rising so the *peewee* will slide down the shelf eventually."

I stood on the beach and watched. Sure enough, the water lapped up and the waves carried the *peewee* out. It slid, filling up rapidly with water, then burbled down over the shelf I'd seen from above and disappeared.

I turned to Bastion. "What do you mean, 'don't go in the water'?"

"It's toxic. It'll burn your skin if you stay in it too long."

"What?" I stared at him. "You mean we can't swim back?"

He shook his head at me with a wan smile. "Not unless you want to turn into a kreslid fifty meters out."

I glared at him. I didn't want to know what a kreslid was. "I wish you'd told me that *before* I sank the only floatable object we had," I bit out.

"Sorry...." He gazed at me like a wounded tappin.

I relented, feeling like an ogre as I met his lambent eyes. I sighed and limped over to the bush then crawled under it to get beside him. "We'll just have to wait for a ship or another *peewee* or something to rescue us." In truth, we had another way to get off the island, but I'd discounted it for now. I hoped I wouldn't have to use it and reveal what I was.

"Won't be a long wait," he said, idly scratching himself.

I thought immediately of pursuit and looked around. Seeing nothing, I turned to him and noticed his glum expression. "Why is that?"

"This is a tidal island. The tide's out now. I told you the tide is rising. The whole island's going to disappear in a few hours."

I stared at him and felt my face tighten again. "Why didn't you tell—" I cut myself off. It wasn't his fault. I blew out a long exasperated breath. In truth, I probably couldn't have landed us safely and without considerable injury anywhere else. Those rocky cliffs would have been suicide, I concluded.

I'd have to show him what I was. And the slightest chance we had of possibly being more than friends would evaporate.

Bastion was staring at me. I felt his eyes boring into me as I looked out to sea. I finally turned to him. He gazed at me with dark lustrous eyes and I felt an aching pull in my chest. He looked just like Serge. He *was* Serge. Serge Bastion. What had I done?

"You're bleeding, did you know?" he said and pointed to my head. I noticed that his hand was trembling.

"No, I didn't." I gingerly touched my forehead with my hand. A rather large lump had reared itself at my hairline where I'd struck my head against the windshield of the *peewee*. Locks of my hair were caught in it and sticky with flowing blood. I removed my hand and looked at it. It was covered in blood. Feeling an urgency to stem the flow, I fumbled in my Great Coat pocket for a smart band-aid. I found one then dropped it in my shaky grip.

Bastion snatched it from the ground. "Let me," he said

with gentle firmness.

I nodded my acquiescence. He pulled off the outer wrapping then leaned over me and pulled away the hair sticking to the wound, grimacing and wincing when I did. Our eyes met briefly and a thousand words might have passed between us. I blinked and looked away. He finally got the band-aid on and watched it stitch itself on my cut. Then he scrambled back to my side and faced the water again.

"Is this what you do for a living, then?" he asked me without taking his gaze off the water. "Chase after bad guys, then get chased back by them?"

I smiled wryly. I'd never looked at it that way. "Yeah," I answered, drawing the hair from my face with my hands as if to tie back then letting go. "I guess so."

Bastion frowned thoughtfully, still looking out to sea. When he turned his gaze on me, his eyes burned. "Why are they after me? Why do they want to kill me?"

I stared at him and blinked, then swallowed. We stared for a long moment until I replied, "Because of me." I looked away. "They think you're my...I'm sorry." I noticed that the tide had risen considerably since the time I'd looked before. I didn't think we had three hours even and prepared to tell him the truth about me, about him and the big bad world out there.

"That's okay," he said, surprising me with the softness of his voice. I'd expected him to be bitter at me for bringing him into all this. In fact, he drew closer to me, until our bodies were touching. I suddenly knew what he was thinking; I could smell it. I wasn't sure what I felt, except confusion. He added, "I'm honored that they thought I was that important to you."

I looked away and almost sobbed. It was complicated.

"You never intended to meet me on Scandia, did you?"

My gaze flickered to him in surprise then I looked away as quickly. "No," I answered in a dull voice. He was pretty smart, I thought. Of course he was; he was Serge Bastion.

"You were trying to protect me...or something..."

"Yeah." My throat felt dry and I swallowed down my guilt.

We sat in silence for sometime after that, both gazing out to sea and watching the water rise until it was lapping at our feet.

I scrambled out from the seaweed bush. "We'll have to move to higher ground, even though it makes us vulnerable to pursuit. But we're more likely to be rescued that way too." Getting picked off by a *Nihilist* tracker was preferable to dying a slow toxic death in the waters of the Beleus Sea. Of course, I wasn't going to let either happen.

I helped Bastion crawl to the highest point of the ephemeral island then parked myself on the sand beside him with a brief glance at him. He smiled sadly at me.

I looked away, gazing up and around me. My ears strained for any air vehicle sound; hoping for one and dreading it at the same time. Meanwhile, Bastion, who was resigned to his fate, sidled up until he was snug against me. I didn't begrudge him; I'd put him in this position in the first place. He was just a token in a war between the *Nihilists* and me. And he was going to lose, one way or another. I was going to ruin his beautiful world. I'd already invaded his peaceful life and brought *Nihilist* destruction with me. His innocent, safe world would never be the same.

I turned to him, eyes stinging with guilt, and leaned into him, steeling myself to tell him the awful truth. This wasn't how it was supposed to happen, I thought. I must have looked terribly miserable because it was he this time who offered a smile of solace.

"Rhea," he whispered, face leaning close. "You know...when you first stepped into my store four months ago...I thought you were the most beautiful person I'd ever seen."

I just stared into his thunderstorm eyes, feeling his breath on me, and inhaled raspberries and musk. I'd thought the same thing when I'd first seen him...Serge, that is.

"If this was another time or place...do you think we might have...would you have..." he trailed; he couldn't finish. Perhaps he couldn't bear the answer. I didn't answer; I kissed him instead.

He was stunned for a moment. Then he kissed back, first

with his lips then gingerly with his tongue. Sweet and sorrowful, he wasn't quite like Serge, but enough like him to bring tears to my eyes. He wrapped his arms around me as if to protect me from the sea creeping toward us and I closed my eyes as he lay me down beneath him on the sand. He thought we were going to die and was living that thrilling moment of passionate surrender.

But, we weren't going to die. I'd thought of a way off the island; it meant revealing to Bastion what I was and, finally what he was—putting an end to our friendship. But it would get us off and save him. I simply had to strip then shift into a Khonsus and fly us away. Why was I waiting?...

I gasped out a laugh: he was helping me strip already, gently helping me shrug off my Great Coat. As the coat slid off, I saw his eyes dilate with feral desire. His hands traveled over me like a man who'd found gold, tracing every line of my torso with reverence. Then, like a taut spring released, his hands dove with sudden urgency beneath my top to touch skin. He traced a fiery caress up to my breasts and I trembled with maudlin yearning then raised my bare arms to accommodate him as he franticly pulled off my top. In his careless move he rubbed against my injured arm and I winced. But he didn't notice in his daze of passion and let out an exultant moan at the sight of my bared breasts.

Once the top came off my face he kissed me fiercely on the mouth. My lips parted, letting him in, and I lamented a little that it was moving too fast, too urgently. But I told myself that I'd done this to him; teased him to distraction then brought him here and forced his hand. I owed him this...maybe myself too...He fumbled with my trousers as I, surrendering to the moment, slid my hands beneath his pajama shirt and folded my arms around his bare back—

We didn't hear it until the vehicle was nearly upon us because it had come from behind the large rocky island beside us. I felt its shadow on us and heard a familiar engine. I pushed Bastion off me with a gasp and we both squinted up. My hands scrambled for my MEC. Then I recognized the ship and froze: Benny!

"Are you ready to leave or do you need to kiss some more?"

Serge! I seized my top and threw it back on then surged to my feet. It was Serge's voice on my ear-com. How could that be? Why had he come back? I felt giddy like a teenager, and not sure why. Confusion and embarrassment raged through me and I realized that I was shaking.

Benny landed, kicking up sand and grit. Bastion and I shielded our eyes with our hands until Benny powered down. Then the hatch opened and Bastion's twin—Serge—stepped out with a great big smile. His smile crested over me like a Vancouver ocean sunrise and I beamed back at him.

Ω

Serge stood calmly like a tourist, dressed in beige slacks and a loose dark brown collared shirt, open a few buttons. His hair, tussled as usual, was cut shorter than last I'd seen it but the shadow of a young beard remained; his moniker. He climbed down the ladder then turned and met us on the few meters of beach that remained.

We must have been an interesting sight, holding onto each other for support: me in full Guardian clothes with my twisted ankle and bandaged head; and Bastion, bruised and battered, barefoot in his pajamas and favoring his torn knee.

Serge gave me a fond smile. Then his eyes twinkled. "I hope I didn't interrupt anything important."

I felt the blood rush to my face in a fierce blush. I opened my mouth to say something. I wasn't sure what I would have said because Bastion said something first. Staring at Serge, he burst out, "You're *me!*"

"Not quite," Serge said, smirking with amusement and glancing at me. I returned him a crooked smile. "And you'll love this, Bastion. I have someone else to meet the two of you," he said, looking privately amused then glancing pointedly at me. Grinning like a scoundrel, he turned to gaze over his shoulder and called, "Darling, come and meet our guests!"

I felt a sudden ache in my heart at his words and gave in to petulant anger to shield my dismay. *Our* guests! If anything, they were *my* guests! Someone emerged from the back. I'd already guessed from his words, but I still drew in a sharp breath as I stared at my inner diverse copy.

## TWO

"What?" Bastion grinned in astonishment. He looked from me to my copy, dressed in a flowing dark blue dress with revealing décolletage. "There's two of *you* as well?" He laughed with pleasure. I hadn't seen him this happy since he'd first seen me.

"This is V'rae," Serge said with a proud smile. "My betrothed."

Had he said it protectively or had I just imagined it? It also took me by surprise and I felt the ache inside me tug my smile down. Funny how I hadn't considered the nature of their relationship until Serge had mentioned it. Betrothed? I'd half-assumed that they were already married, having lived together for five years. Then again, I remembered how he'd referred to her as his girlfriend, not his spouse....So, when did he pop the question to her? Just now, before meeting us?

Serge reached for my arm to brace me. I shook him off, pointing brusquely to Bastion. Serge grinned at my impatient scowl then helped Bastion to the ship as I painfully tried not to limp behind them. Once aboard, Serge and I collided in our instructions to Benny. We stared at one another haltingly then Serge nodded acquiescence with a gracious smile.

"Take us out, Benny," I said. "Get us out of orbit. I'll take it from there later."

"Okay, Rhea. Glad to have you back. And, thanks, Serge for the rescue," Benny added. Leave it to my ship to do me one better. I hadn't even thanked Serge yet for rescuing us. Benny instructed Bastion and I to report to the infirmary to check our injuries. After that, we all met around Benny's small all-purpose table.

"Where will you take me?" Bastion asked as we all settled into seats around the table. Serge had just confirmed the danger of taking Bastion back to Beleus City.

"Benny suggested Scandia," Serge responded. I felt Bastion's eyes suddenly on me and tried to ignore him. "It has a very small but tight human colony in a mixed open galactic culture. And the native Scandi are a very friendly but quiet people—except when you give them blesspepper wine. They're really into the arts, I'm told; so, I'm sure they'd welcome a book-seller with your breadth of knowledge there." He flashed a grin. "Books are making a come back, I'm told."

Suddenly reminded of his precious books, Bastion paled and grew agitated. "What about my books? How will I get them? I can't just leave them! They didn't all get toasted in the blast." He'd turned to me at his last words. This was the jittery side of Bastion that I'd never witnessed in Serge. And personally didn't care for.

Before I had a chance to respond, V'rae patted his hand lightly and interjected, "We'll get them for you. We can discreetly arrange movers. Probably that Sporian firm, *Bolodo Galactic Movers*. They're reliable and quiet. Do you have them in this diverse?" She turned to me as Bastion, mollified, eyed her with admiration.

I nodded and couldn't help the smile that tugged at the corner of my mouth. I found myself glancing at Serge the same moment he glanced at me with a similar smile and quickly looked away, flushing. Feeling suddenly awkward, I rose and said, "I better do my regular ship's diagnostics and telemetry with Benny. Make yourselves comfortable. There's a soyka maker there and a Grade B food synthesizer over there," I pointed them out then turned to leave.

"You and I need to talk strategy," Serge said, rising quickly to his feet. "I'll join you, if you don't mind."

I nodded curtly, not sure how I felt, and we left Bastion

and V'rae in enthralled conversation about books and literature.

Serge didn't waste any time. As I sat myself in my pilot's chair, he glanced at me intently and before he even sat down, said, "So, what are you up to, besides making out with my double—"

"Listen, Serge," I cut him off, face heating. I'd resigned to calling him Serge, somehow unable to use his proper name. "Why did you come back? I thought you had important things to do in your own diverse."

"Okay." He nodded. He didn't look offended at my rude interruption or officious tone. "Sure, you deserve an explanation. It was mainly V'rae I was concerned about, Rhea. It turns out that the best way for me to take her out of the equation in the inner diverse was to bring her here." He looked smug for a moment. "I figured that I could do two things at once: help you here in the outer diverse with more pressing matters and keep her safe. So, here we are."

"That's smart," I admitted, turning back to my diagnostics.

"You don't look too happy about it." His voice sounded disappointed, almost hurt.

I turned to look at him directly and fought hard to keep from glaring. "I just wasn't expecting you, that's all. Thanks, by the way, for the rescue." I realized that I didn't sound thankful but that was the best I could offer. For some reason I felt miserable.

"No problem," he said with a tight smile, looking a little subdued. "Like I said, that's why I came back. To help."

I didn't bother to answer and we were silent for a long time. I found myself thinking of A'ler and wondered how I was going to break it to him. Now that he was back I had a responsibility to tell him of her fate. I continued my diagnostics with Benny, feeling Serge's gaze on me. I hadn't realized how tense I'd become until he finally spoke, and I released the tension in a flinch. "So what's next? Where were you planning on going—after we drop off Bastion, that is."

I turned to him and expelled a long breath. "Two more weapons facilities are currently in operation, pumping out a fleet of ships. The *Nihilists* intend to send a ship equipped with my MEC technology to every major human colony in the galaxy at the same time, a simultaneous strike. They expect to have enough ships built in..." I checked Benny's readouts. "Less than a month, now."

Serge stared at me with dismay and concern. He stroked his slightly whiskered face and frowned. "Do you know where the facilities are?"

"Not yet. But I think we're out of our league on this. There are only two of us, Serge."

He waved a hand at me in exasperation. "But what about your Guardians?"

"They're not my Guardians anymore," I reminded him with a surly look. I felt my face tighten as my neck tensed with the truth. I couldn't tell Serge everything. I settled for, "I don't think they're going to be very helpful."

"Why not? I know you're still a wanted criminal but didn't you get a message out to your boss?"

I stretched my head back to relieve the tension in my neck and sighed out. "It's complicated. Bureaucracy and such," I hedged and rubbed the back of my neck. "The bottom line is we can't count on the Guardians. So, I have a plan..."

He looked hopeful and rose abruptly. To my surprise he got behind me and moved my loosely bound hair aside and began massaging my back and neck.

"Chaos, you're tight," he remarked as I leaned into his kneading hands. His powerful hands were exquisite as they teased each tight kernel of knotted muscle into loosening. "So, what's the plan?"

It was a plan Benny and I had hashed out before I'd visited Bastion. It wasn't one of my favorite plans as plans go, mainly because it meant returning to the last place I wanted to go: Earth. I sighed out my resignation to it and said between grunts of painful ecstasy, "The fourth person on the Eclipse/*Nihilist* hit list is a human Gnostic priest named Raphael Martinez—"

"Yes," Serge interrupted me eagerly. "I know a little about him. He set up the Hermetic Order. They run a sanctuary temple on Upsilon 3."

I nodded and thought with an inward wince of A'ler. "For his advanced students," I said. "But he spends most of his time on Earth, running a seminary/retreat in the Eastern Townships of Québec. We'd be doing him—and hopefully us—a favor by visiting him on Earth and warning him about the Eclipse contract on him."

"How's that?" Serge said in a puzzled voice.

"Benny and I checked out this guy," I said. "He's amassed the largest force of Eosian guards in the galaxy. An independent army, with no affiliations to anyone except Martinez and his Hermetic Order. Martinez formed a Special Operations Unit who call themselves the *Orichalkon*, after the durable alloy the Epoptes supposedly made for the Eosians during their heyday in Atlantis. The *Orichalkon* consist of five elite squadrons, the *Cadmus*, *Odysseus*, *Prometheus*, *Perseus*, and the *Daedalus*. Each squadron is an effective fighting unit of a hundred supremely qualified men."

He stopped massaging for a moment. "What are you saying? That we should try to get them to help us?"

"Yes, that's exactly what I'm saying. I'm just aiming for two of the five." I turned to face him. He looked thoughtful. "We need help, Serge. We've got two weapons facilities we have to find and destroy within a month and we have to find Ka—the *Ancient One*—and stop him."

Serge straightened in a jerk. "Ka's the *Ancient One*?"

I nodded. There was so much I hadn't yet told Serge, I realized. "My grandfather," I added and watched Serge's eyes widen at me. I didn't tell him about my abysmal failure to stop Ka the last time I'd confronted him and I'd left out the other wrinkle: the Vos spy in the Guardians was my boss. I'd deal with him myself, I thought.

Serge seized my shoulders in his hands again, forcing me to look forward. I winced at his overly forceful knead with a squeak of pain. "Sorry," he apologized. "It sounds worth a try, Rhea," he said simply, leaving out so much. There was a great deal we hadn't shared; I wasn't sure where to start and instead said nothing. Serge was quiet for a few moments, obviously ruminating about my revelations. He finally said, "What do you think of this Martinez guy?"

"He's like any spiritual leader, flaky but decent, I guess. I'm sure we can convince him, especially once he learns that the *Nihilists* intend to exterminate all humans." I didn't include why I considered Martinez flaky. Serge would find out soon enough. Martinez was also reportedly breathtakingly handsome. Something else I didn't bother to tell him.

Serge stopped his massage and came beside me, scratching his stubble absently with a frown. He leaned against the co-pilot's chair, folding his arms across his chest, and crossed his long legs. "How are you going to convince him? He isn't just going to hand over his army to us on a say so."

"We have the documented hit list I can show him. I'd go in under a pseudonym, of course. And I'm counting on your diplomatic skills for the rest," I said, letting a crooked smile curl my lip. I didn't tell him about Martinez's strange appetites but I managed to consider that V'rae might serve a very good purpose, after all. Presented as twin sisters, she and I would pose a pleasant oddity that the Gnostic priest might find tantalizing. He had a peculiar obsession with twins apparently.

"Here, give me your foot" Serge said, kneeling on one leg like a squire waiting to be knighted. His hands dove under me and pulled out my left leg even as I tugged back with a nervous laugh. He won and quickly had my gravity boot and sock off. "Hmm, still a little swollen," he said, glancing up at me with a mock stern frown. "I heard you refusing the drugs Benny offered. You should at least let him administer a muscle relaxant." Serge began to massage my ankle and foot and I nearly gasped. It was painfully exquisite. Just having him touch me was wonderful enough. "They call him a prophet," Serge said in a scoffing tone.

I nodded with an affirmative sound between stuttering breaths. "He predicts the coming of the *Suntelia Aeon*, a catastrophic End of the Age." I shrugged at Serge's doubtful look. "Well, if the *Nihilists* get their way, he might not be so off the mark—at least for this diverse, anyway." I raised my brows at him and he acknowledged my point with a sober nod and purse of his beautiful lips. I continued, curious of what Serge would make of the prophecy, "I think Martinez means it metaphorically, though. He prophesies that the destruction of our old world will be signified by *the joining of twin soul-mates who will herald the coming of a New Age.*"

Serge snorted out his disbelief and shifted onto his other knee, still massaging. "He's just a sex nut and a chaos-raising naysayer." So, he *did* know about Martinez's quirks, I thought, feeling a repressed smile tease the corner of my mouth. Serge frowned. He shook his head. "The guy's as spinny as P923. He's a blenoid, flaked out on plock nectar, Rhea." Then he leaned forward, pushing his face so close to mine that I could see my own reflection in his stormy eyes. "I heard this weird story about him: when he's on Earth, Martinez does a monthly pilgrimage into the *vishna* mixed forest. He wanders off alone with nothing and doesn't return until days after—usually naked, flushed and beatific. That's when he spouts off his epiphanies and predictions." Serge gently put my sock back on my foot. I trembled at his caress, disappointed and relieved he was finished. Then he gently pushed the boot back on and straightened. "That prophecy is blenoidshit, Rhea. The guy's just spinning tales to lure in more suckers to his cult and brainwash them with *dust* and that erotic tree."

"Probably," I muttered. But I couldn't help feeling a dark foreboding and wasn't sure why. "Thanks for the massage."

"Don't mention it." Serge gazed out his porthole for a moment, then turned back to me. "You're okay with this? Going back to Earth, I mean? You've never been back, have you? Not since..." he trailed, noticing my expression.

I'm not sure what that expression was, but I swallowed down my agitation and nodded in silence.

"Okay, good," he said with some finality. "Good plan. I'll tell V'rae." Then he left me to my thoughts of Earth, no longer my home, and an ambitious plan to inveigle an eccentric neurotic to part with two of his precious squadrons.

Ω

It took a few days to get to Scandia and we all felt some relief at escaping our cramped quarters to enjoy some fresh air and sunshine. By then my ankle was much better and I hardly felt it when I walked. I'd taken Serge's suggestion and let Benny give me some medication for the swelling. The bump and cut on my forehead had also healed enough that I could take off the bandage. Bastion's injuries took a little longer. V'rae, who turned out to have a great deal more patience than I, had helped Benny nurse Bastion back to health. She and Bastion had hit it off immediately.

Scandia was a bio-engineered planet with a very favorable climate, whose seasons swung comfortably from ten to thirty degrees. Benny informed me that the current temperature was 20ºC as we made port in the Saabi Galactic Skyport.

We accompanied Bastion, hardly limping now, into Saabi, one of Scandia's main cities, and were greeted by the locals with friendly courtesy and a healthy curiosity. The spaceport was located in the center of town and we emerged from the port into a bustling open market, thick with shopping Scandi. Raising my hand to shield my eyes from the bright sun, I paused to listen to the banter and cheerful calls of shopkeepers selling their wares amidst the gaggle of shoppers and the distant singing of street buskers.

The Scandic people resembled Veniks, though only in the general reptilian look of their outer appearance. Unlike the large and oafish Venik race, the Scandi were lean and small in build with lithe and elegant lizard-like bodies and faces. Their eyes were also far from indolent. Scandi eyes resembled those of humans; just a pair of them and with a sharp and lucid gaze. They also dressed much more tastefully than Veniks, in flowing brightly colored clothes. The Scandi shirt, for instance—stylishly worn by the proud men—was copied by nearly every fashion designer in the galaxy. The Scandi were renown for the brilliant and tasteful dye mixtures and patterns they rendered on their fine materials. Seeing many of the patterns elegantly worn by the tall slim women, I was reminded a little of the serapes of the Africans on Earth.

At the sight of us, Scandi moved out of our way and bowed or curtsied in welcome.

Delighted with this hospitable welcome V'rae curtsied back and introduced herself to various shopkeepers on the street as she drifted from stand to stand, curiously eying the merchandize. When she spotted a book dealer, she seized Bastion's arm excitedly and pulled him over to it. The two of them gaped over the books like children at a candy store. My gaze gravitated to Serge, who glanced back at me and we smiled wryly to one another. I noticed how easily V'rae took to speaking their local dialect and envied her skill. She had somehow understood the Scandic passion for bargaining and was presently haggling over the price of a book she'd apparently chosen to buy for Bastion. The shopkeeper shouted excitedly then laughed as V'rae gently shamed and flattered him in quick succession.

Serge came beside me. "Don't you like to shop?" He looked at me curiously and I saw his eyes gleam in amusement. I smiled back with a shrug. He was feeling left out too.

"I never have the time," I responded honestly. "Unless it's a part for Benny, of course," I added, grinning sideways.

"Nothing ever for you?" he teased, sidling to a stall and glancing at the merchandize. As I joined him, he purchased something from the shopkeeper then turned to hand me a chocolate bar. "Not even chocolate?" He grinned.

I let my half-grin blossom into a full one and gladly took the bar from him with a laugh. He hadn't forgotten my penchant for sweets. But why should he? V'rae shared it.

As we followed V'rae and Bastion—she, introducing him to the finer points of Scandic culture as her artistic eye observed them—Serge and I silently ate our chocolate and gazed around us.

I noticed that the buildings were somewhat primitive and simple looking, one to two-story structures constructed with local and natural materials. But the Scandi made up for their humble structures with what they put inside them, I concluded, catching glimpses of opulent interiors through windows and open doors. This was more in keeping with their elegant though brilliant attire. The Scandi were a simple though proud people with an expensive taste for material things. Renowned throughout the galaxy for their exacting and creative material manufacture and design, the Scandi lived a simple life of elegant pleasures, enjoying the arts and literature. I thought Bastion—and V'rae—would fit in very nicely here.

Once out of the market, Bastion was tasked with finding himself a place and some employment. V'rae, already finding her way around the locals, offered to help.

I took advantage of the stop to buy some parts and do some minor repairs and maintenance checks on some of Benny's systems. Serge offered to accompany me, explaining that he was pretty handy with mechanical things. We ended up spending most of our time in the Spaceport hanger inside Benny while V'rae accompanied Bastion in his search for a temporary home and arranged for the Bolodo movers to retrieve his belongings and his books.

Despite her potential usefulness as my twin in gaining us an audience with the Gnostic priest, I was still half a mind that we should leave V'rae behind with Bastion for safety reasons. But Serge wouldn't have it. Was he being possessive again? He'd probably noticed what I'd noticed on our way here; that Bastion was infatuated with her. I'd caught them several times looking rather cozy together and wrapped in deep conversation. I'd been forgotten by the wayside. Apart from a slight blow to my ego, I didn't mind. In fact, it was a relief. I felt a little sorry for Bastion, though. He seemed fated to fall for the wrong woman—twice. V'rae was Serge's betrothed, after all.

I tried to reason with Serge as we both hunched over Benny's holo com, fixing the resolution of its read-out. "We just don't know what we're going to run into out there," I asserted. "It would be a lot safer for her here, on Scandia. No one would know she's here. Bastion is a gentleman and she enjoys his company."

"I said no," he said forcefully and straightened to glare down at me. I began to think it was more than possessiveness he felt; was it guilt perhaps? After what had happened before, he wasn't going to let her out of his sight, I concluded.

"Listen," I softened my voice and stood up to face him, "I know what she means to you. I saw the two of you right after it happened, when you were taking her to the ambulance; she was in a coma and you were…in anguish. I incarnated there. After I was absorbed into that place-time, after I witnessed the music of the spheres and saw the galaxy in a way I never have before. As a soul dispersed."

"What?" His face twisted in agitated confusion. "What are you talking about?"

I smiled wryly. "Remember the time you dreamt that we were having raunchy sex back on Benny when you were recovering from the Kappa wound? Well, we were."

"*What?*" His eyes widened and he stared at me. "But I wasn't using the transmitter. I couldn't have absorbed you. You couldn't have gone there without it."

I grinned my big Cheshire Cat grin, keenly aware of its affect on him. "Well, I did. It was utterly beautiful."

"But…that's impossible!" he said vehemently, close to startled anger. I almost winced at his reaction—it wasn't what I'd expected—and let my grin falter. "I've never heard of anyone doing that," he added. He leaned back and stared at me, first frowning in hard contemplation then eyes growing wider with conclusions. His eyes finally narrowed at me and he breathed out, as if to himself, "What *are* you?"

I recoiled from his look. God, everyone was asking me that, I thought, and dropped my gaze to the floor. I was beginning to wonder myself. I'd already discovered that I was part Eosian, thanks to my mother's whoring, then part Vos thanks to my grandmother's whoring…What else was I?…

I turned back to the holo com, feeling his eyes burn into me. I didn't pursue my argument and let the matter die.

Ω

Bastion said his hearty goodbyes and wished us well on our mission. After hugging me like I was his sister, he turned to V'rae and I noticed him blush like he used to do with me.

After a pointed glance at Serge, V'rae promised to help Bastion set up his bookstore once he got them through the galactic movers and was settled in. Bastion flushed with pleasure at this and we left.

We hastily gathered a few more supplies and a few frivolous delights, thanks to V'rae and her penchant for chocolate. Then we left, feeling the pressures of time. I instructed Benny to set course for Earth and we settled in for a few days, again crowded aboard a ship built for two but meant for one.

With Bastion gone, V'rae found her time appreciably expanded. I think she hadn't realized how much of her time Bastion had occupied as Serge and I argued our strategies and researched possible locations for the other two weapons facilities. As a result, V'rae seemed to gravitate to me, following me around—perhaps out of boredom—and tried to help. Whether I wanted her to or not.

I still found it hard to look at her, yet my eyes often drifted in furtive glances to my look-a-like. She was a magnet, pulling at my fleeting gaze. I wanted to study her but felt embarrassed. She had all my features, the slightly aquiline nose, full lips, high cheekbones, large eyes and dark expressive brows. I noticed the same small birthmark on the back of her neck and a small scar on her left temple just like mine. I'd received it during a mountain bike cross on Jarrid-9 when I'd hit a loose rock and flung myself over the handlebars at high speed. I was certain that she hadn't gotten hers the same way; she didn't strike me as the extreme-sport type. She even had a slight scar on her right hand; like the one I'd gotten on Sekmet. Did she have all my scars? I wanted to check her right knee where I'd received a J-shaped scar from a *Whip* race on Gemini-2. Or the jagged scar on my left buttock that I'd gotten from a Venik slave trader's dool blade. Did she have my puncture marks along my right thigh from the blenoid attack? I knew she had the scar across her waist from V'mer's knife slash; I had the very same scar from the same episode.

Despite being a spitting image of me, there were enough subtle differences for an observant person to notice. Apart from the obvious differences in dress and comportment, she wore her hair shorter than mine. It fell shoulder length and slightly longer than my own short mop that I'd crudely cut with the same knife I'd used to kill Bondar on Sekmet; only hers was neat, lustrous and parted to the side. She used nuyu makeup and always adorned her flowing dresses with tasteful jewelry or shawls. I found her generally softer, more even-tempered, much friendlier and openly compassionate than I would have described myself. She was certainly less aggressive and had the patience of a diplomat. It seemed, I reflected at length, that I'd gotten all the rough-edged emotions and left Vrae with the soft ones. We were like twin sisters and I was definitely the *dark twin*.

Serge was clearly infatuated with her. He practically fawned over her and I felt close to disgust at his obsequious mannerisms. I'd have cuffed him if he'd done that to *me*. That might have been one of the reasons he wasn't with me, I considered soberly.

Ω

I tried to steer away from them but in Benny's cramped quarters I inevitably ran into them often. I couldn't help noticing how Serge and V'rae never argued. They never once seemed to bristle with any tension. Even at the best of times, when I shared his apartment for a short time in Neon City, Serge and I squabbled and bickered over the smallest of things. He and I had been through so much together. We'd saved each other's lives. We worked well together, usually sensing what the other needed without words, and complementing each other's strengths and weaknesses. We just couldn't get along.

He and V'rae appeared made for one another, I concluded, catching them laughing and cuddling mid-ship. Everything they said to the other seemed to either amuse or delight. And the other always seemed to be in agreement.

With Serge and I it was altogether different.

Ω

During a routine check of communications, Serge noticed that I'd received a holo from Euaimon, confirming a Code 8 on my question. He turned to me. "What's a Code 8 and what's your question? I thought you and he didn't get along."

"Euaimon?" I looked up from the service chamber I was cleaning. "We don't. He's just saying that they're stuck in a bureaucratic stand-off regarding the processing of my MEC design."

"What?" he exclaimed. "You gave the design to both Ennos *and* Euaimon?" His face deepened a few shades and his eyes burned into mine. He waved his arms in exasperation. "You might as well have handed the design over to the Galaxy-Mart, for creon's sake! Am I the *only* person you haven't given it to?"

"Ennos never used it, so I thought..." I trailed, thinking he was stuck like a holo-loop on the design. Surely we were well beyond that stage. "I thought Euaimon would do the right thing with it, get it out to the other Guardians...so they could do something about the situation, not just hide their heads in the sand and hope it would all go away..." At least Euaimon was making some cautious moves, although I was disappointed with the little progress he'd made.

"And is he?" Serge challenged me.

I decided to handle it as a rhetorical question and dropped my gaze back to what I was doing before he'd interrupted. Even Euaimon had been cautious in revealing everything, hence the bureaucratic red tape. We were still on our own. Serge made an exasperated sound and I felt his sharp gaze on my back as I resumed my cleaning. All the more reason to convince Martinez to give us some of his men, I reasoned, feeling my face heat at his obvious annoyance with me. And I still hadn't told him about A'ler.

Ω

Despite my attempts to avoid V'rae, Benny was a small

ship and I found myself often in her company. I began to think she sought me out. In any case, we ended up having some interesting conversations. During one of my lunch breaks, she joined me, setting her plate of sushi next to mine, and took a seat.

"I hope you don't mind but, out of curiosity, I was just researching your ship's holo library about your family and there isn't much...."

No, there wouldn't be, I thought thankfully. I wanted so much to ask about her mother...and her father. I suddenly realized that I could find out who my father was by finding out about hers...and hesitated. Maybe I didn't want to know.

"My grandmother, U'dia conceived my mother without...a father," Vrae said with a lopsided, almost embarrassed smile. "We still can't explain it. She insists she had no relations and no implant or anything like that. Only a very erotic dream with a beautiful man she'd loved in her dreams."

"Ka," I said. "My grandfather. He was my grandmother's mate in this diverse." My apophus-grandmother, Diana Wood.

"But didn't you say that he exists in this diverse only? Our mothers were conceived ten years before the Gate was created. If Ka is the *Ancient One* then he was trapped in your diverse since old times. There was no Ka in the inner diverse."

"I know."

"You think..." Vrae began then faltered with a frown. "I don't know what to think."

I offered, "I think your grandmother soul-drifted into the outer diverse and joined corporeally with her other soul...*my* grandmother, Diana Wood...made love with my grandfather then returned pregnant, like my grandmother." I should know. I'd done something very similar: joined V'rae to fend off Serge's murderous brother, V'mer, and returned with the same wound she had received. I'd also made love to Serge that fateful night before V'mer attacked V'rae, over and over again in my soul-drifting recurring dream.

"Good God..." V'rae breathed out. She appeared a little naïve, but nice and sweet. I could easily imagine her charming the arrogant Serge and turning him into putty. V'rae peered into my eyes with a child's curiosity. "Is that…possible?"

"Yes." I gave her a wry smile. "I did it. With you…when V'mer attacked you."

"Oh, sweet Jesus," she murmured. "You're right. V'ser told me too." I still had a hard time thinking of Serge as V'ser. "Of course!" she continued gleefully like a child. "I did it too, with you…in the frozen lake on Uma 1!" Her spontaneous joy made me smile. I realized that I really liked her. Not because she was me, but because she was *her*. Her innocent and joyous spirit was infectious; even on me. I soon found myself laughing alongside her in unalloyed enjoyment. V'rae's eyes lit up. "Speaking of…do you think that Jesus was…and Mary…" she trailed.

I smiled sideways. "Puts a whole new spin on Immaculate Conception, doesn't it?" Then I felt sudden misgiving. Had I burst V'rae's bubble? Serge had mentioned that V'rae was a devout Christian and believer in God. Unlike me. I kept foundering between tremulous belief, disillusion and truculent disbelief. None of them felt right and I envied V'rae's simple unfettered faith in her God. *My* God was…invisible. *Call on God, but row away from the rocks—Indian Proverb*, I thought to myself.

"Why did you do it?" I ventured hesitantly. "Why did you soul-drift into me? You didn't know me."

"But I knew about you and about your capabilities. V'ser had told me. I knew what you might do for us, for the two diverses and for humanity…" Then she looked curiously at me and smiled sideways. "Why did you save *me*? It's not as though I'm an important warrior or super-detective who'd make a difference in either world. V'ser told me that you got the same wound I did. You could have been killed or ended up in a coma like I was just as easily."

I smiled and looked down. I couldn't answer. I'd done it for *him*. The man I loved…*her* fiancé. "It was the right thing to do," I finally said, looking up at her briefly. I swallowed down my emotion and looked down as quickly. I couldn't say more because my throat closed.

"You did it for *him*, didn't you?" she said softly.

I jerked my head up and stared into her hazel eyes, shining with understanding. She smiled with genuine warmth. Did she know the full extent of my feelings? Then she slid her gaze from mine with a self-conscious grin and confessed, "I think he finds me boring. You're much more exciting—"

"More like irritating," I cut in.

"I'm a one note aria and you're a complex symphony—"

"More like a grating cacophony," I corrected her and blurted out without thinking. "It's *you* he's in love with." *And you he wants to marry*, I added privately.

Her gaze returned to me with challenge and she startled me with her reply, "Are you sure?" We stared at one another, twins; the same, yet so different. What did she mean? Then her eyes sparkled with silent laughter. "There's a little of me in you and a little of you in me, don't you think? So, he must love us both."

I laughed out a half-sob and I found myself hugging her.

## THREE

Martinez had taken up residence in an old Catholic seminary just outside a derelict town in what used to be the rural Eastern Townships of Québec. I thought it apt that he chose a theological school for his Gnostic teachings.

As Benny entered atmosphere and circled down, I gazed through my starboard porthole at the familiar landforms and water masses of Earth. It was a lot greener than the last time I'd seen Earth through my view port aboard the shuttle that had taken me away from my home. Since the Eosians had colonized the planet thirty years ago, Earth had reverted mostly back to wilderness. Eosians were master ecologists who had honed their healthy symbiotic skills with nature into an art.

The planet, Gaia, was certainly healthier and happier now that her ancient prodigal civilization had returned. These former

Atlanteans had brought back the wisdom of millennia about living in concert with and through nature's arcane powers. They'd torn down humanity's great cities and replaced concrete and glass with natural organic, living materials. They'd uprooted the roads and bridges and introduced their native scree, an intelligent giant raptor, as transportation. They'd let nature absorb the massive agricultural fields and clear-cuts, to harvest and recycle her bounty in beneficial ways. They planted their native tree, the *vishna*, everywhere. They'd restored the natural environment from the ravages of strip mines, oil fields and gas plants and replaced them with their non-intrusive crystal technology.

I gazed at the endless rolling hills covered in a lush purple and green carpet of young *vishna* and native trees. It was a monument to a simple and gentle life, a respectful pantheistic life. I could have wept; it was so beautiful. But it wasn't Earth anymore....

V'rae wept for me. She and Serge had come beside me to watch once we'd entered atmosphere over North America. She said in a wavering voice, "It's so beautiful...but it isn't Earth anymore." Then she burst into tears.

I stared at her, stunned for a moment, until I remembered that she *was* me. Why wouldn't she feel the same way? She was the same as me...except for one thing—she had Serge. I threw a fleeting glance at him as he soothingly caressed her wet face with his hand. He thought he'd come back to help me; did he realize that he was torturing me instead?

"They've turned it into another Eos," Serge said soberly. "Look at all the *vishna* trees. There are probably more *vishna* trees here than on Eos."

*Eros*, everyone called it, I reflected. I'd read somewhere, or perhaps Benny had told me, that the *vishna* flower produced an exotic aromatic oil that aroused senses of well being, particularly sexual well being, and heightened libido and virility. A lot of good that would do me, I thought with a cursory glance at Serge and V'rae holding hands.

I eventually caught sight of the large estate with its

sprawling vineyard beside a fair-sized lake and pointed it out to them. "There it is, *the Solstice*."

Serge settled into the co-pilot's seat beside me and V'rae stood behind him, arms wrapped around his shoulders.

Martinez's estate, *the Solstice*, was an island of lavish order in a green frothy sea of mixed wild forest. The derelict farming town of Granby had been demolished and absorbed back into nature since the Eosians had taken over as Earth's new custodians. I could barely make out a criss-cross pattern of lighter greens in the forest mosaic that betrayed where old foundations and roads had previously lain not far from the current estate. Martinez's estate was one of the few human-built structures that the Eosians hadn't torn down and replaced with their symbiotic organic structures or left to natural and enhanced regeneration.

This had been apparently out of respect for Martinez's previous role in the *L'Ordre de l'Arbre Sacré* and his current role as leader and teacher of the Hermetic Order, which employed a considerable number of Eosians.

As I circled Benny down, I had a good look at the old four-story school, built in a "U" shape with extensive courtyard and ancillary buildings. Apparently more of an aesthetic than an ascetic, Martinez had surrounded himself with beauty. His property was impeccably landscaped and manicured, displaying several gardens, and roadways arched with old overhanging oak trees and lilacs. Martinez had the Victorian-style seminary re-designed in 207 SGT by an architect from Ogium 9. Practically gutting the original structure, and leaving only one wing and section as classrooms, he'd spared nothing to re-create the opulence of a pre-20th Century religious architecture with vast, multi-storied halls for entertainment and dancing, a concert hall for live music and a large refurbished lecture hall.

Serge shifted uneasily. "Are you sure about this, Rhea?" he said with a sober glance at me. "I've heard stories...."

I'd heard them too, stories that Martinez was just a charlatan, luring fools eager to part with their riches into his cult to pay for his fancy estate and using the powerful perfume of the *vishna* trees and *glitter* to run a brothel to feed his unusual and diverse sexual appetite. Serge had obviously been doing his own research or talking to Benny.

To my silence, he added more heatedly, "They say he's running a jagging harem cult there, for creon's sake!"

I frowned at him and saw V'rae look puzzled and clutch his arm. "Well, be that as it may," I returned coolly, "he's on the hit list and we still have to warn him. Plus he does have the largest and most capable independent Eosian guard in the galaxy."

His brows came together. Then he bolted forward, bumping past my shoulder with his face so close to mine I could feel the heat coming off him. His arm brushed mine to touch the navigation screen. "I really think we should reconsider and—"

V'rae seized his other hand and pulled him back. "Let her land the ship, V'ser," she commanded quietly. "We're here now." She was right and Serge knew it. He straightened with a sigh and I started to breath again. Then we were being hailed and I got on with the task at hand. "Strap yourselves in," I instructed once I'd been given the go ahead to take port in Hanger B, below the seminary. After a long intake of air, I took us down.

Ω

As I opened Benny's side hatch door, a blast of humid air hit my face and carried on its jet stream the complex scent of home, undercut with exotic. I inhaled it with mixed feelings and felt instantly clammy in the oppressive heat.

A young acolyte with pale skin and long hair like a girl— he couldn't have been more than fifteen—met us at the hanger entrance. Dwarfed by two surly Eosian guards who flanked him, the boy fidgeted as we descended from the ship. The bald-headed guards loomed over him in imposing black uniforms. I tensed, noticing with dismay that they illegally carried Class B side arms holstered to their thighs: the extremely accurate narrow-barreled Long Gun. I'd purposefully left my Great Coat and MEC stowed safely aboard Benny, wishing to appear anything but an Enforcer, and now yearned for a side arm. The Long Gun was made by Bodek and Lamb and had been used for years by the Guardians.

But when Guardian Enforcers started trading open enforcement for stealth operations, accuracy was exchanged for secrecy, and the Long Gun was abandoned in favor of the smaller and less obtrusive *pocket*. I'd suspected that the huge surplus of Long Guns had made their way to the slipstream, particularly the Eclipse run; I now knew where they all ended up and found it a little disconcerting that the guard of a Gnostic order traded with Eclipse.

I studied the boy. He was dressed in a light blue cambric textured shirt and loose beige slacks. He surveyed us out of large cobalt-blue eyes in a girl's soft face of innocence. Wheat-colored hair tumbled in waves down to his shoulders. I threw a sidelong glance at Serge. He hiked his brows at me and I mirrored his look. Martinez was training them young—and pretty.

The boy greeted us in flawless English with a lilting French accent. "*Bonjour.* Welcome to *Solstice.* I am Jacques. You are *Monsieur* Bastion?" he addressed Serge in a girl's voice; his voice hadn't yet broken to that of a young man's. He'd given the name its French pronunciation. He glanced furtively at V'rae and I, then followed with a nervous nod of acknowledgment when he caught us watching him. His nervous, though indolent gaze gave me an unsettling reminder of Sekmet. I studied the boy's intensely blue eyes and wondered if he used *glitter*.

"Yes, I'm Bastion." Serge leaned forward and shook the acolyte's hand, as was still the custom on Earth. "We're hoping for an audience with Master Martinez to discuss a matter of urgent importance to all of us."

"I understand," Jacques responded, nervously glancing again at V'rae and I and licking his lips. "*Mon Seigneur* is a very busy man, as you must know," he said with halting breaths. "During the morning he is at private meditation, then he teaches classes all afternoon. He will see you but only briefly at the gala this evening."

I exchanged a glance with Serge. He gave me an imperceptible shrug. It was already late afternoon.

"This way." Jacques swept his hand toward the large estate and led us down a cobbled path lined on either side with scented lilac trees. V'rae fell in beside Serge, slipping her hand in his.

I trailed behind, casting my gaze around the estate, as the taciturn guards followed behind. I noticed several other boys about the same age as Jacques and dressed like him, tending the grounds. They cut the vast lawns with push mowers or edged with hand-shears. The Earth I'd grown up in was abuzz with the urban murmurs of mechanized living. This place was a sanctuary where nature, tamed by the devoted labors of humans, celebrated its bridled beauty.

I listened to the gentle clip of shears amidst the mellifluous chirp and flute of birds and the rustle of leaves in the warm breeze. The scent of lilac breathed over me, stirring thoughts of home.

I caught Serge glancing back at me with furrowed brows of concern. Then Jacques looked over his shoulder at us to continue and Serge turned forward.

"I've been instructed to take you to the west wing where you can freshen up, rest and change into something more suitable for the gala event," the boy said. "We have clothes you can wear." He gave himself the permission to appraise V'rae and I more carefully and let his eyes rest on me with a kind of grimace I interpreted as mild disgust. I decided that he'd deemed my grubby flight slacks, top and jacket particularly unsuitable.

As we followed the young acolyte with the mauve-skinned Eosian guards behind us, I couldn't help thinking: if they knew that we were Vos, would we have been received so cordially? I felt a chill run down my back at the thought of our thinly veiled deception.

Once inside the main building, Jacques led us to the west wing, down a large ornate corridor lined on one side with a column of Greek-style sculptures and large plants. I recognized the entrancing Venus de Milo and David among many others. The opposite wall was adorned with splendid early-period Earth paintings—grand landscapes with voluptuous nudes. I wandered closer and recognized the work of Nicolas Poussin, seventeenth-century French painter: his *Midas and Bacchus* and his *Echo and*

45

*Narcissus*, languishing in sensuous poses. I saw V'rae craning like me in appreciation to get a closer look at another painting. Our eyes briefly met and I knew what she was thinking: were these originals, appropriated from the now defunct Louvre and other once-famous museums? We had both studied art and could appreciate the value of these works.

Jacques took each of us to a separate room and the guards stationed themselves between the rooms. I was last. "These are change rooms for the gala," he explained breathlessly. "*Si vous exigez n'importe quoi—*" he began in French then shook his head, blushing, and repeated in English, "If you need anything at the gala please ask one of the acolytes—we are all dressed as I am."

"Thank you, Jacques." Then I added just as he took in a deep breath to continue, "Jacques, what is the gala?" I'd obviously rattled him by interrupting his routine speech.

"It—it—" he stuttered with a blush. "—It is a daily event at the estate for acolytes, members and honored guests, and those who wish to be chosen." Chosen into the Hermetic Order, I assumed, and was about to ask for clarification when Jacques plunged back into his speech with a halting breath and I didn't have the heart to interrupt him again: "There is a bath and shower and all manner of beauty products for you to adorn yourself with. You may choose any of the dresses hanging in the closet; they are intelligent and will adjust to your body perfectly," he said, glancing down my body with another blush. "The door on the other side of the room leads directly into the gala hall where you will meet your companions…and *Mon Seigneur*," he ended with a long bow.

I'd caught an inflection, a note in his voice when he mentioned Martinez. Was it fear or reverence? I wasn't sure. I decided to quiz the boy: "Jacques, what do you know about the *Mon Seigneur's* prophesy of the *Suntelia Aeon*?"

Jacques visibly trembled. Again, I wasn't sure if it was out of fear or exaltation. His eyes sparkled and he gazed unsteadily at me, as if I had something to do with it. Then he gushed like a gossip, "I was outside, mowing the lawn, when *Mon Seigneur* emerged from his monthly forest pilgrimage. Of all the times this time he was *merveilleux, mademoiselle. Il semblait comme un ange.* He...was...*magnifique!*" It was definitely not fear, I decided. The boy's face told me everything. His flushed cheeks, slack mouth and dilated pupils painted a face of intense desire. "*Mon Seigneur* went out with nothing but his clothes and returned with nothing but the prophesy on his lips, *mademoiselle,*" Jacques continued, blushing fiercely but obviously enjoying the topic. "He had been with the *vishna* tree, the ancient spirits, for three days, feeding on nothing but their nectar and their love...they always undress him so he appears naked before them, like the first man before God. Then they copulate with him and he receives the blessing —"

"*Copulate?*" I cut in. I was sure I'd misunderstood or that Jacques had used the wrong word. A tree copulating with a man? I felt a smirk slide on my face.

"That is how he joins with the ancient soul," Jacques said matter-of-factly. That struck a chord with me; my great grandmother had apparently *joined* with an Epoptes through the *vishna* tree. I'd never bothered to inquire how. "*Mon Seigneur* has taught us this, *mademoiselle.* That is how the priest receives the blessing and the ancient knowledge. *Mon Seigneur* arrived that day with his most incredible prophesy, the *Suntelia Aeon.* He looked like...eh...*comme un ange, comme Dieu,* with light surrounding his magnificent body...his eyes were like jewels sparkling in the sun..." And suspiciously like *glitter.* "...and his face was like the sun itself, bright and full of love and not of this Earth."

I studied Jacques's dreamy eyes for a moment and wondered with growing discomfort just what kind of school this Gnostic priest was running. "Jacques," I asked, "how will I recognize *Mon Seigneur* Martinez?" *With his clothes on, that is,* I thought wryly.

He looked at me flustered again then said pointedly, "*Mon Seigneur* will recognize you. *You,* especially, *mademoiselle.*"

"Because we're twins?" I guessed with an indulgent smile.

"Just you, *mademoiselle.* You're different from the others," he blurted out with a fierce blush and stumbled on in a giddy voice, "You have that *other* beauty *Mon Seigneur* taught us about. The beauty of the rose. *La beauté d'Eros. C'est voux q'il va choisir ce soir.*"

I stared at the boy and felt my face heat. I'd been singled out. But for what? And what did he mean about *the rose*?

Jacques blushed and stared at me with a look beyond the innocence of his age. "*Bon chance* with the choosing."

"But I'm not here to be—"

He'd already turned and left me at the door.

I entered the room, noting that it was one of the original classrooms of the seminary, but refurbished considerably with elaborate wallpaper, wainscoting, ornate furniture and additions like a washroom with an antique bathtub.

"Jag me," I whispered with a slanted smile and breathing in that giddy essence I'd first inhaled upon landing here—*vishna*, of course. I yearned to pamper myself.

My eyes fell upon a rich tapestry that depicted Michelangelo's Sistine Chapel scene with God in his celestial cloud, stretching his finger out to bring life to the reclining Adam. I stood for some time, eyes fixed on the seductive scene, and stirred with uncomfortable feelings of arousal. I focused on what I'd learned in art school: that the nude celebrated the body as a beautiful creation of God, in whose image we were created, and was both a reflection of humanity's yearned redemption and a reflection of what humanity still lacked. I certainly felt lacking right then and turned away with a gasp.

Feeling suddenly grubby and exhausted, I decided on an old fashioned bath and stripped then ran the water. I almost fell asleep in the bath as hot steam, scented with exotic oils, swirled around me like the caress of a devoted lover.

Once out and dried, I wandered languidly to the dresser, enjoying the freedom of being naked. I looked over the jewelry laid out like in an expensive store and the vials of nuyu for all manner of treatments from blue skin to green hair or purple lips. I postponed that decision until after I'd chosen the dress. I wandered to the tall oak wardrobe and opened it. I breathed in. There had to be at least a dozen gorgeous gowns there for me to choose! Each one exquisite and, I surmised, original. I fretted over every one; I hadn't worn a dress since that disastrous tryst with Jesse when I was eighteen; we ended up in the back of his *viper* then I never saw him again. Dresses and I didn't seem to get along, I thought, stroking a bright red frilly one of crepe de chine…not my color, I decided.

I finally chose a tourmaline green gown of satiny silk. It was a simple though elegant design; a form-fitting top with *bateau* décolletage, a side slit to mid-thigh and a plunging, studded-lined back that made up for my modest front. Its elegant lines appealed to me, as did the rakishly low glittering back-line. I hesitated, thinking I was too daring, then thought of Serge and put it on.

I fussed with my dress and my hair and face. Even my shoes. I found that I was more nervous of what Serge would think seeing me in this than in meeting Raphael Martinez.

I tried to relax by reviewing what I knew about Martinez: he was human, but his life had not been an ordinary human's life and it had started with a very abnormal birth. His Spanish mother had apparently borne him without a father. That foolish claim had been her downfall; the Order of the Sacred Tree accused her of desecrating their consecrated *vishna* tree and debasing herself generally with other's mates. She was run out of the province with her baby in tow. Because she had initially given everything she owned to the order, she left with nothing and soon fell into abject poverty. The boy suffered through it all: the sordid one-room apartments that stank from harsh disinfectant, pesticide and smoke; cheap drugs for food; and a moody mother who cursed and cuffed him out of hand. Apparently she took in her clients while he, with no place to go, watched in quiet torment.

Then at the tender age of five, on a tryst off planet in Virgil City, he witnessed his mother and her lover melted in front of him. He'd never given the Guardians a good description of who had done it and I hazarded that he'd been too frightened, thinking that he'd somehow been responsible. Children did a lot of that; I'd know, though my guilt was definitely warranted. The Guardians guessed that a jealous client had followed her to Virgil City, known for its discreet trysts, where a wealthy client had taken her.

For Raphael Martinez, though, it was a second chance at life. After the horrifying incident, the Ngu, who trained him in informatics, unofficially adopted him. When he was fifteen, the same year I joined the Galactic Guardians, Raphael returned to Earth to run the farm his mother had abandoned when she'd joined the Order of the Sacred Tree. He studied Hermeticism and pursued his Gnostic beliefs. His good looks, intelligence and charismatic manner quickly earned him a place as a public spokesman and eventually one of the leaders of the movement. By age twenty, when I was barely out of Guardian school, Martinez was already a known spiritual leader, had formed his own sect, the Hermetic Order, and acquired a huge following, not in the least a sizable Eosian guard devoted to the protection of his assets—the other reason we were here.

Now Martinez was an accomplished Gnostic mystic and Eclipse wanted him stopped, preferably dead. I thought of what Ka had told me of Martinez while I travelled with him to Uma 1. His words had moved me to pity the boy. He'd had it far worse than I had. Apparently his mother abused him, perhaps blaming him for all her misery and suffering. It was his so-called immaculate birth that had caused the stir in the first place—and what stirred my curiosity now.

I'd botched my hair for the third time when I decided to let it flow loose over my shoulders. I then snatched a pair of long diamond chandelier earrings and downed a vial with just a marginal dose of nuyu, adding subtle color to my eyes and lips; just a touch of eye shadow and lash thickener. After slinging on a pair of strappy high-heeled sandals, I left the room with my heart in a knot of nerves.

# FOUR

Before I even saw the gala hall, the enticing aroma struck

me like a MEC wave as I opened the door to the sounds of laughter and flirtation mingled with music. It was that same unfamiliar fragrance I'd inhaled when we'd first disembarked and the same one that had filled the air in my change room. The *vishna* trees, I guessed. Once I let my other senses take over, I saw a spectacular gala hall, three stories high with frescoed ceilings and adorned with cream brocade walls and towering mirrors. Sparkling chandeliers hung from the vaulting ceilings.

A quartet of Sporian musicians, arranged at a second-story balcony, chimed out classical 19th Century music on genuine instruments of that era and the hall brimmed with a cheerful crowd, mostly human and Eosian. They were all lavishly dressed in formal gowns of all styles and colors for the women and smart textured suits, mostly tuxedos, for the men. I noted that the guests were young—my age or younger—as they swarmed in lively conversation and laughter.

Young acolytes dressed like Jacques flowed among them, carrying silver trays of tall-stemmed glasses with sparkling drinks and hors d'oeuvres. Only the few mauve-skinned Eosian guards, dressed in imposing black uniforms and posted near the doors, appeared immune to the heady atmosphere. As I scanned the hall for Serge and V'rae I noticed the preponderance of touching and fondling among the people. I watched an older man stroke a young man in an obvious bid for intimacy and have it returned in the form of a light kiss.

A young acolyte, no more than twelve years old with long flowing sandy hair, pushed a tray of milky-colored drinks toward me with an awkward but friendly grin. He stared unabashedly at me with *glitter*-bright eyes. I helped myself to one of the glasses.

"Thank you...Emile," I said after a quick glance at his nametag. I swirled the slightly pungent smelling milky drink in my hand. I raised an eyebrow of curiosity. "What is it?"

"It's *félicité*," he responded, showing some surprise that I didn't know.

I thanked Emile again and he nodded curtly. "*De rien, mademoiselle*," he said then bade me well and continued demurely on to another customer.

*Félicité*…bliss. I suspected that it was really *glitter*, judging from the sparkling eyes and beatific smiles of those partaking. Standing alone in the crowd, I peered down at the milky fluid with narrowing eyes. As if I wasn't light-headed enough with *vishna* vapor coiling through my nostrils.

I hastily found a place to leave my drink and continued the search for my friends. Martinez had surrounded himself with rich opulence and beauty—making up, no doubt, for the sordid poverty he'd suffered as a child. Men and women congregated along the far walls around the great tables filled with platters of food and colorful drinks; their savory aromas mingled with the *vishna* in a complex perfume. I noticed the same bowls of purple *vishna* petals on every available surface like those in my change room; it explained the ubiquitous scent.

I saw Serge first. He stood with his back to me in an olive-grey Italian suit that flowed like a caress over his tall muscular build and long legs. He was helping himself to a drink at the bar, not *félicité* I noticed with relief.

When he turned and caught sight of me, he suspended his action and stared, eyes widened into deep lustrous pools. They sparkled like a boy's. He'd never seen me in a dress before, much less one like this. My face burned as a stirring exhilaration surged through me. I felt my heart beating fiercely, as I gazed at his handsome face, ardent eyes storming into mine. He'd shaven and combed his unruly hair back and was grinning at me like a boy who'd just won a prize. His grin was like dawn breaking and I couldn't help grinning back like a fool as I approached.

"Rhea!" How did he know it was me and not V'rae? "Chaos knows how much I missed that Cheshire grin of yours," he said with unexpected cheerfulness as I reached him. God only knew how much I'd missed wearing that grin, I thought. I then wondered at his words.

"Doesn't V'rae grin?" I laughed uneasily.

"Not like you," he beamed and pulled me by my arm to turn me for a better look. "You look dangerous," he added as I turned for him, amused at his reaction to my bared back. He startled me by sweeping his arm around my waist to draw me close. As if to claim me. I drew in a halting breath and flushed with the thrill of his touch. Then I threw him a warning look to hide my embarrassment. Of course he would choose those words: as though I was hiding a *pocket* pistol under my dress. I *was*, but he didn't know that. Playing with the *Herkimer* diamonds lining my plunging back-line, he shocked me with unexpected words of rapt appreciation. "You're beautiful in that dress."

"It isn't very good at concealing a weapon," I confided with a crooked smile, trying to ignore the heavy scent of musk and strawberries that surrounded me in a dizzy haze.

"That's the whole point, *cherie*," he grinned, amused, and hugged me close. "But I wager you've managed somehow."

My smile opened into a broad grin and I leaned into his touch, daring him to find it.

"You should wear dresses more often." He ran his hand along the line of my gem-stoned hem, fingers brushing my bare flesh down to where the small of my back flared into my buttocks. He teased the bottom of the brazen v-line. My skin shivered with pleasure into goose bumps—

I suddenly thought of V'rae and broke off from his hold, face burning. I was still recovering when he abruptly straightened like a schoolboy caught smoking and aimed a beaming smile past me.

"You look ravishing, my love," he said, gazing past me. I turned and caught V'rae approaching us with a languid stride and a warm smile. I was forgotten as Serge moved instantly beside her, giving her a loose hug and a light kiss on the cheek. She'd chosen a peach-colored silk georgette gown, gathered at the shoulder and over the bust with a tight waist that then flared at the knee to a froth at her feet. The strap at her one shoulder was adorned with coral beads the same material as her teardrop earrings. She'd pulled her hair back in a braided chignon that leant elegance to her look. I noticed that she'd used more nuyu than I had and it suited her.

I swallowed down my own feelings as I watched them snuggle together and kiss. It was still weird watching 'me' with him, even though she wasn't me.

"I'm sorry if I'm late," she said with an apologetic smile. She was holding a glass of half-drunk *félicité* in her hand. "I fell asleep on that comfortable bed. Then I couldn't decide what to wear, everything was so beautiful." V'rae turned to me. "I love that dress! You're gorgeous in it!" Then she giggled with realization. "Am I allowed to say that? Or is it terribly Narcissistic?"

Without thinking, Serge and I exchanged a glance then broke out laughing.

"Shall we go look for this prophet?" V'rae suggested impatiently and slipped her hand into Serge's. They set off into the crowd. He reached out to snatch me along but I twitched out of his grasp and walked a few paces behind them. I had no time to contemplate the oddity of our threesome because Martinez entered and the room instantly transformed.

Ω

Some people add their presence to the ambience of a chamber; others create that ambience. Martinez was definitely the latter. Although he entered without ceremony, everyone somehow knew. People turned and the hall hushed for a moment in acknowledgement and reverence. I caught many a besotted gaze at him, particularly from the women. And I knew why; he was breathtaking to behold.

Martinez swaggered in, shadowed by an insipid younger man. Martinez turned to kiss the man on the mouth then gruffly dismissed him. He then leisurely cast about the room like he owned it, which he did, nodding cheerfully here and there to a few chosen guests worthy of his attention. I had a moment to study him before he noticed us.

He was not what I'd expected. I don't know what I expected, actually. Perhaps something like the ascetic Father Uriel. I'd forgotten that Martinez was supposed to be exceptionally good-looking. Given his history, I'd imagined him as a socially awkward, slightly introverted man with keen eyes and a kind mouth, lank mousy hair and a gangling walk. Raphael

Martinez was nothing like that. He was handsome—no *beautiful*—and bore himself like a god. For a Gnostic priest he appeared far from humble. He had a slightly husky build, standing taller and more muscular than Serge. Curly locks tumbled loosely down to his shoulders like a golden river, framing a face of perfection. He was the most beautiful man I'd ever seen.

I thought him more splendid than Barbariccia's perfect face and body; more compelling even than Serge's quiet depth and dignity. His long thick eyelashes swept down in a dark wave when he blinked and his hair shone like a molten field glowing at sunset. He was beautiful beyond perfection; his beauty glowed with an ethereal quality that seemed to surround him like a halo and drew me in like a moth to fire.

I know that I gaped because I had to force my mouth shut and caught Serge's silent glare at me. I decided that Martinez's flawless face was nuyu-mediated. Few men partook of nuyu; Serge, for instance, elected to display his few blemishes along with his rough stubble in a natural style. But Martinez was obviously a man of fancy and statement. And it occurred to me that he was more than a little vain. Where Father Uriel had given off the quiet energy of wisdom, Martinez spoke his energy loudly—in his swagger, his piercing gaze and the clothes he wore. He was dressed in casual but stylish jet trousers of impeccable fit, a loose-fitting jade silk shirt, in the Scandi style, that flowed open at his chest, and Italian loafers without socks. He wore little jewelry save a gold chain hanging on his neck and a gold watch.

Within a moment he spotted us and strode over. It was then that I noticed his eyes. Were they violet? Not quite; they changed with the light. Mercurial like the oceans of Beleus, his eyes shifted in the light, reflecting shades of lavender, deep purple, aqua green and blue.

When his gaze brushed mine I felt my breath give out and my face heated with sudden embarrassment at my reaction. I thought I'd seen his eyes flicker with gold, as though a whole galaxy sparkled inside them. I felt inexplicably drawn into them with an uneasy though familiar sensation of belonging and a disquieting desire.

I shook off the unsettling feeling as Martinez sidled over to a vase of red roses and plucked out a single red rose with his left hand then strode purposefully toward us. I stiffened with alarm. Was he the *Nihilist* agent, *the Rose*? I'd pretty much discounted A'ler; the *Ancient One* wouldn't have thrown her into the desert if she'd been his agent. Then I reminded myself that Martinez was on the hit list, one of the reasons we were here. I thought again; so was Ka, and look what he'd turned out to be. Was Martinez on the hit list also as a decoy? In which case our mission was destined to fail miserably.

Martinez reached us and I was grateful that he focused on Serge, giving him a solid handshake of greeting with his free hand. "You're Bastion," he said in a rich unaccented tenor voice, giving Serge's last name its French pronunciation. "I recognize you from your communication with Étienne, my secretary. I've been expecting you."

Somehow I knew his inane remark about expecting us meant more than what appeared on the surface. As though he'd anticipated us long before Serge's communication. My heart raced with an unreasonable thrill, as though he'd aimed his remark at me, personally. That was hubristic drivel, of course. He wasn't even looking at me.

"A pleasure, Mister Martinez," Serge said with a respectful nod, despite what I knew he thought of Martinez. Serge turned to V'rae and me. "These are the sisters I mentioned, Veronica and Rebecca Hall, from Iota Hor b." He swept his arm first to V'rae at his side, still holding his hand, then to me with a cursory glance.

"Ah, the twins! Splendid!" Martinez swept into a low bow to V'rae and took her hand to kiss in the ancient Earth tradition. "*Enchanté, ma belle Veronique,*" he said to her with an open smile. "*Vous êtes jolie, mais votre jumeau, elle est puissant avec la beauté d'Eros, n'est pas?*"

My heart raced. Had I interpreted him correctly? *Your twin is powerful with the beauty of Eros.* He meant *me.*

Then Martinez let go of V'rae's hand with another bow. She blushed, laughing softly at words she didn't understand, and murmured a response that I didn't pay attention to. Neither did Martinez who was already turning to face me.

I only realized that I was holding my breath when his eyes alighted on mine with something besides simple cordiality. A look of sharp recognition seemed to pass between us as I caught a tantalizing whiff of lilac, cottonwood and musk. It was not unlike what I'd felt when I'd first met Serge, only more intense, dark, and far more uncomfortable. I quivered, though imperceptibly, and bridled in a sharp inhale as I felt a lightening spark between us. The shock of it set my heart pulsing between my legs and I involuntarily licked my lips in a shuddering wave of desire. *You have that other beauty...la beauté d'Eros*...Surely I'd imagined the spark. I passed it off as "stage-jitters" and perhaps the heady and seductive *vishna* perfume that surrounded me.

Martinez had not apparently felt anything. He remained composed as he appraised me with an enigmatic smile. Who—*what*—was he? A human, of course, I answered myself. With incredible eyes. Why did I think there was more to him? He wasn't a Vos; I smelled no shape-shifter essence in him like I did with Serge and V'rae beside me. But there was something else in the aroma he gave off that I couldn't pin, something elusive that lurked like a shadow over me.

"And you would be the dark twin," Martinez noted, taking my hand to kiss.

I felt that strange energy pass through us again and rudely pulled my hand away, letting my voice take on an edge, "That would be me." I realized too late that he'd referred to my dark dress, not my personality.

But he didn't let my bad-mannered response offend him. He said in flawless French with another bow, *"Enchanté, ma belle mystère."*

*"Mon Seigneur,"* I responded softly, bowing my head to him, in turn.

Then he glanced up at me with that same intense look of eerie recognition. *"Votre soeur, elle et très gentil; mais elle n'est pas votre soeur. Puis je pense que vous n'est pas que vous semblez."*

I stiffened and felt my heart beat quicken. I'd understood,

as V'rae and Serge hadn't. Was that why Martinez had chosen to speak French to me? But how would he know I understood? Serge and V'rae looked on, as I gazed at Martinez with an even expression, not giving anything away. *We weren't sisters and I was not what I seemed*, he'd said. What did he know? What had he guessed? And why did I feel so exposed? He was a Gnostic priest, a wise man and a prophet. But he held a rose in his hand and he also gave off a strangely familiar and terrifying energy that made the hairs of my neck rise. An energy that tapped into a murky place inside me that I didn't even know existed.

"*Vous croyez, Mon Seigneur?*" I challenged, letting him know that I'd understood his words. "*Seems...I know not seems*, my lord." I found myself quoting Shakespeare. "'*Tis not alone my...visage...that can denote me truly. I have that within which passeth show.*"

"Indeed!" he said and stared for a brief moment then threw his head back and let out a deep laugh of unbridled amusement. "Ah, the old bard. You must visit my library...*O, wicked wit and gifts, that have the power so to seduce!—won to his shameful lust the will of my most seeming-virtuous queen...*Hamlet, I believe," he ended with a smirk. "And please call me Raphael. What I meant," he continued with a terse glance at Serge and V'rae who were watching our exchange with interest, "was that your energy is very strong and complicated. *La beauté d'Eros s'assied sur votre épaule...*Rhea Hawke."

I stared. He knew who I was!

In my peripheral vision I saw Serge stiffen and search the crowd for an ambush. Apart from several faces turned toward us to hear our exchange, there appeared no Great Coats—yet. V'rae looked blissfully unaware of intrigue or danger as she watched our exchange with *glitter*-bright eyes. I caught Serge's brief glance at me. He shrugged but looked concerned. Was Martinez challenging me? Calling me out? Were twenty Guardians—or Nihilists—waiting for us outside the hall? I thought of the *pocket*, strapped to my inner thigh—

Martinez seized my hands again. After my initial rude gesture, I felt reluctant to remove them, though I noticed Serge looking askance at me with dark miserable eyes. Martinez pressed the rose stem into the palm of my right hand and closed his hands over both my hands—trapping them with the rose. I winced at the sting of the thorns and snapped my gaze to him like a puppet. His eyes smiled with something more than amusement. Who *was* he? His touch alone seemed to control me and I felt the horrible thrill of recognizing that he was an oxymoron: a cruel priest.

"The most exquisite thrill lies where pain meets pleasure, don't you think?" he said. "That ragged edge where the expected meets the unexpected in the wilderness of our souls yearning for connection. Like this rose…"

I glimpsed the crowd pressing closer, and barely made out the shocked reactions on people's faces, as they watched with rapt interest. The rose obviously symbolized something in this gala and I feared I knew what that was. I let one eyebrow rise slightly and said evenly, "*He who wants a rose must respect the thorn*—Persian proverb."

"Indeed!" Martinez let a crooked smile slide on his face and went on, "Don't worry, Rhea—may I call you that? And please call me Raphael—I won't reveal who you are to anyone," he said quietly. "I didn't realize you had a twin sister, though," he ended still keeping his eyes on me and not bothering to glance at her. And I didn't have to ask him how he'd figured out which of us was Rhea Hawke. His eyes twinkled as he said softly, almost reverently, "*Vous êtes belle comme un ange…*"

I almost recoiled and quipped, "*A beautiful thing is never perfect*—Egyptian proverb." In truth, *he* was the angel, I thought, caught in his compelling gaze, hands trapped in his tight grasp, warm blood slick in my hand.

"The prick of the thorn is not unlike the first prick of another rose," he continued, clutching my hands in a flaming grip, "drawing warm virginal blood from its delicious red petals." The crowd pressed closer to watch our exchange. "*Vous savez bien que la rose êtes un anagram pour l'Éros*….Rhea, your energy is not of this universe."

He pressed my hands harder. The pain from the sharp thorns digging into my hand was nothing compared to what I was

swimming in, I decided. *A drowning woman is not troubled by rain* —
Persian proverb. I swallowed down my uneasiness and tried to
pull away without it looking obvious. Perhaps Raphael had
picked up some signature of my journey into the space-time
region between the two diverses, when I'd been absorbed and
transmuted into simple energy-matter. He was a mystic, after all,
a spiritual man...Ka had sensed it. Or perhaps Raphael was just
blenoid-shitting me with meaningless poetry like Serge had done
so long ago when we'd first met. Raphael pinned me with his
liquid eyes and I had to make a concerted effort to still my breath.
They swirled in successive shades of violet-indigo-puce, drawing
me in like a drowning sailor tumbling in the currents of the Beleus
deep seas.

"*Personne peut me résister, surtout vous, mon ange,*" he said.
"*Parce que je suis Dieu; vous êtes commes mois... nous sommes
pareils...*you're one of us," he ended and suddenly eased his grip.
With the release, I seized in my breath —

My heart slammed. I felt that same energy flare between
us, through our hands and our eyes, welding us together. This
time I was powerless to stop it. It pulsed through me in throbs of
incredible desire. And in his violet eyes that bound me in a
perverse embrace, I thought I saw sparks of pure gold flashing
like magic dust toward me, blinding me with lust. My heart beat
in excited terror as the brief moment stretched into a kind of
eternity where only he and I existed, naked in our desire.
Everything else — Serge, V'rae, the room — disappeared into a
drowning swirl of disparate sound and texture. It was not a déjà
vu like I'd experienced when connecting with the inner diverse.
Nor was it a vision, like the many I'd had since being *dusted*. This
was acutely *real*. Extremely erotic. And terrifying.

Time stopped.

Ω

I felt I was everywhere at once; yet nowhere. But with *him*.
It was not unlike my experience of disintegration during
absorption, yet different, and more frightening. As though

orchestrated by something with a will beyond my own.

I felt Raphael's essence embrace me and awaken intense arousal. He entered me in pulsing waves like icy hot fingers stroking my molten core. Throbbing breaths seized in me and I felt myself erupt with a moan as a cloying darkness gripped me...*The night hides a world, but reveals a universe*—Persian proverb, I sang as overwhelming emotion engulfed me. Then I was tumbling down that dark hole...

...I saw a young woman...my great grandmother—I don't know how I recognized Genevieve Dubois but I knew—she lay broken, dying, atop a *vishna* tree, surrounded by the murky waters of the igapo flood...And above her, surrounded by a haze of gossamer light, stood a double of herself! An angel, an Epoptes, in her form. I watched the two of them make love then my great grandmother shuddered with her last breath and the Epoptes merged with her dead body. The starship captain who'd left for Eos over 200 years ago was not the same person who'd come back. My great grandmother was an Epoptes!

## FIVE

My eyes bolted open with a shudder to Serge's face. He bent over me, his face tight with anguish. I inhaled his intoxicating fragrance, of a young forest in springtime, and felt safe. I sighed out a long breath and tried to smile up at him. I wanted to reach out and pull him down close to me but my arms wouldn't move. In a rare moment of tenderness, he gently stroked a wayward strand of hair from my face, fingers lingering over my cheek, and met my gaze with quiet relief.

"What happened?" I asked in a hoarse whisper. I was lying on a soft couch, covered in a blanket, in a quiet room full of old books. The rose Raphael had given me was still clutched in my tight fist. I stiffly opened it and gazed down in a daze at my punctured palm, sticky with congealing blood.

"You fainted," Serge said tersely with a scowling glance at my hand. He straightened, his look of concern dissolving into a ruminating glower. "...Among other things," he grumbled to himself.

V'rae sat down beside me and handed me a wet cloth for my hand then offered me a glass of water. "You fainted right in front of Mr. Martinez," she added as I sipped the water then gave her back the glass. V'rae took my cold hand with her warm one and gently washed off the blood. "He was so embarrassed. I think he blamed himself, Rhea. He caught you as you fell and didn't want to let go but Serge pried you from him and brought you in here." She glanced around her briefly. "It's a library of some sort."

Vrae continued to prattle as Serge watched me in brooding silence. His brows furrowed.

"Can you sit up?" V'rae finally asked me.

"I think so," I said shakily. I set the rose aside and pushed myself up then felt the onslaught of sudden renewed dizziness. "No, not yet." Taking a deep breath, I lay back and swallowed several times to keep the waves of sickness from rising. V'rae propped another pillow behind me and wiped my brow with a cool cloth. I shut my eyes again.

"Stay there," V'rae said comfortingly. "You're still very pale."

With a burst of impatience Serge surged forward and said brusquely, "What happened, Rhea?"

"V'ser!" V'rae turned a sharp rebuke on him. "Don't be so gruff. She needs to rest."

But I understood his urgency and when our eyes met, we exchanged a silent question. "You never faint," he said bluntly.

"I know," I murmured and caught V'rae watching me with concern.

Serge looked suddenly uncomfortable. "You're not—" He cut himself off, unable to say it.

I laughed, and then swallowed down more dizziness. "No, I'm not," I assured him. He needn't have worried. It wouldn't have been his...we hadn't been intimate in a long time.

"Then what?" He glowered. "I saw something happen

between you two. What was it?"

If I didn't know better, I'd have thought he was jealous. I ran my hand blindly over my face, feeling its clammy coldness against my flushed cheek. "I don't know," I said honestly and closed my eyes in concentration. I kept them closed as I continued in a wavering voice, "I think I astral traveled with Raphael...or something...to the past, to Eos...at least that's what it felt like...." When I opened my eyes both V'rae and Serge were staring at me. I didn't want to contemplate the vision Raphael had somehow induced in me and what it meant. Had he fed it to me in some kind of hypnosis? More importantly, was it real? Was my great grandmother an Epoptes?

I remembered the stories told by the Order of the Sacred Tree. They claimed that Dubois's daughter was a messiah, born of an Epoptes and an Eosian. Was it all true? "I can't explain what happened. I think he's a lot more than a human Gnostic priest, though."

The awful nagging question lodged and throbbed in my throat: everyone—A'ler, Serge, Bas...kept asking: *what are you?* Now I had a possible answer and it terrified me. I shuddered at what it meant.

V'rae misread my reaction and placed another blanket over me.

"With *Raphael*," Serge repeated the name as though it tasted bad in his mouth. "Is that what you call him now?" He paced the room like a lion. "I warned you about this place and about him. We came here to warn Martinez of the *Nihilists* and then to solicit his help. We did neither and he already knows who you are. Along with that Eosian army of his. Do you think they'll help us now? It's no secret what Rhea Hawke thinks of Eosians, never mind what she's *done* to them," he said sullenly. I thought it cruel of him to bring up my unfortunate history that way and prepared a retort but he rushed on with his tirade: "We're lucky they didn't lock us up right when we disembarked. This feels like a trap. Think of Ka—he was a Schiss priest. Look what he turned out to be. And Martinez, what did he just do to you? He creeps me out, speaking French all the time. Then that stuff about the *prick*..." Serge made a rude gesture. "I'll tell you what I think of that prick—"

"V'ser!"

Serge glanced fleetingly at V'rae with an exasperated sound. Then he looked back at me with a scowl. "What did he mean by 'you're one of us'? And what were you doing with all that Shakespeare-quoting and damned French and all those jagging proverbs?"

"She does it when she's nervous," Vrae offered. "It's a way to guard herself…"

I frowned at her. Really?

"I do it too," she confided with a funny smile. *"What a fool does in the end, the wise man does in the beginning*—Italian proverb."

Serge shook his head at V'rae and scowled. Still scowling, he turned back to me. "And what's with all this 'my lord' crap?"

"We're in Québec, and it's his *title*," I retorted, throwing my gaze up at the ceiling. I started to feel defensive. *"Mon Seigneur."* I purposely ignored his more unsettling question… *vous êtes commes mois… nous sommes pareils …you're one of us…*

"He's full of bombast, if you ask me. Too arrogant. And too damned good looking. We should abort, while we can."

"What?" both V'rae and I said together. I pushed myself up past V'rae's restraining hands and, wrapping the blankets around me, overcame my giddiness to stand. "Raphael isn't Ka, Serge. He's next on the hit list and we need his help. So what if he knows who I am. So do you. What's dangerous about that? It's not as though he's a *Nihilist* or a member of Eclipse. The hit list proves that." I didn't mention that I'd had my own doubts, especially when he'd handed me that rose.

Serge faced me with blazing eyes. I knew he was angry. I could feel the tension between us rise like heat off a volcano—poised to erupt. "You don't think there's any danger?" he scoffed with a grim smile. "Well, look at you."

"I just fainted," I objected. I pursed my lips in frustration. Already those unnerving impressions had faded and I was certain it had all been my giddy imagination as I blacked out from lack of food and oxygen. "I haven't slept or eaten in two days. That's all."

I quickly looked down, avoiding the flashing rebuke in Serge's eyes. He and V'rae had suffered as little sleep and food as I had. If anyone had fainted it would have been V'rae. I was probably more fit than she was.

"That's not what you just said," he retorted, hands waving dramatically. "Astral travelling to Eos and back...with *Raphael*." He gave me a frosty look. "That man did something to you. You acted like you were having a jagging orgasm, for creon's sake!" Serge burst out.

I flushed in sudden embarrassment. V'rae looked away, confirming Serge's observation. I suddenly remembered what Raphael had said to me before he revealed my true identity: *La beauté d'Eros s'assied sur votre épaule*...the beauty of Eros sits on your shoulder...Even the boy, Jacques, had said it: *You have that other beauty Mon Seigneur taught us about. La beauté d'Eros.*

"This place, with its jagging *vishnas*...It's subverting our minds, turning us all into brainless..." He didn't finish. Was he going to say sluts? At least he'd included himself in his invective. Then he made an impatient gesture. "Anyway, you look well enough now. Let's go—"

"No!" I'd said it more sharply than I'd intended.

His lips pulled back in a tight grimace. "Rhea, we're not staying here," he said brusquely, moving forward to take my arm. I shook it off and backed away. He moved with me. "It's too dangerous. He knows who you are. In case you've forgotten, you're a wanted criminal with a record of crimes as long as my arm. He's probably got Guardians waiting right outside that door. Now, *come on*," Serge commanded.

His chest puffed out like a damned aristocrat. He was so unreasonably overbearing. My anger flared.

"You idiot!" I yelled. "You're not my boyfriend or my father to order me around!" He visibly flinched at my retort and blinked. "What right do you have to advise me?"

He looked taken aback at my outburst. I caught V'rae glancing back and forth between Serge and me with a look of mild bewilderment. Had she never seen him this way? It was normal for us to quarrel, I thought with dismay. Serge drew himself straight and said quietly, "But I am your friend."

Deflated, I let my anger drain from me but felt continued resistance. My face involuntarily heated at what I was thinking: was I so adamant because of my dedication to warn Raphael and seek aid from his Eosian guard or because I simply longed to see him again?

Taking advantage of the silence, V'rae said, "Rhea, Master Martinez asked to see you in any case once you'd roused."

"*Don't*," Serge snapped, then lamented and cleared his throat. "Listen, there's something blenoid about Martinez. I don't like him. I really don't trust him." Serge might as well have said, 'I don't trust *you*.'

I started to laugh. Serge shot me a dirty look. "You don't *like* him?" I bit out, letting defensive anger give my voice a sharp edge. "Since when does anyone I'm dealing with need to meet with *your* approval?"

He lurched forward to within a foot of me and I felt my chest rise and fall in heaving breaths. My chin rose high to meet his stern gaze. His thunderstorm eyes blazed into mine with the same kind of passion he used to display before he kissed me. It set my face on fire. "Since you haven't been making smart decisions, that's when!" he bellowed.

"As if *you* have!"

"At least *I* didn't make an idiot of myself, moaning out an orgasm in front of a hundred strangers—"

"I *didn't*—"

Reprieve came in the form of the lyrical chime of the crystal communication device as it assembled itself into a holo. Raphael's solicitous face appeared. Serge hissed out his breath and muttered something, probably a curse.

"I hope all is well with Rhea Hawke?" Raphael said with a kind smile of inquiry.

"I'm fine, my lord," I said, purposely using the title that infuriated Serge. I slid the blankets off me and stepped forward with an eager smile. In fact, I was quite fine. My heated quarrel with Serge had brought color back to my face and cured my giddiness. My energy had returned and I no longer felt light-headed.

Raphael looked genuinely relieved. "Good. I'm glad." He let his gaze drift down me in appreciation. "I feel partly responsible. You've not eaten. Would you care to join me for supper in my patio?" Then he added, as if in afterthought, "Your sister and her boyfriend can partake in the gala hall. I'd rather have you to myself, Rhea," he brashly added with a gleaming smile. "Am I not correct in assuming that it was your idea to make this excursion? And that's *your* ship in my hanger, isn't it?"

"It is." I nodded.

"Then you and I can discuss why you've travelled so far to see me, while your friends can amuse themselves in the gala hall." I saw his eyes dilate and my cheeks instantly flamed. "So, how about it? Will you join me?"

"I'd be—we'd be—delighted," I answered without turning to Serge and V'rae for agreement.

I heard Serge grumble another curse under his breath and ignored it.

"Wonderful," Raphael said with a warm smile. "Your sister and friend are free to dispose themselves of all the food and drink we have to offer and they may use the quarters we've provided them should they wish to rest. I'll send one of my acolytes to escort you to my private patio." Then his image disappeared and the crystal mesh disassembled back into a loose lattice on the table.

"More like a Guardian escort to your doom—"

I cut Serge off with a gesture and turned my head. *"Don't,"* I warned in a hiss. "We came here to do a job and we're going to do it."

*"We?* Now who's the idiot?" he scoffed. "Are you sure that's what you're after?" he challenged. I whirled and glared at him. He glared back at me with fierce eyes of misery. "I saw how he looked at you." And I at him, he could have added. "Don't do it, Rhea. It's a trap. And you know it." I turned for the door. "For the love of Creos, Rhea," his voice exploded in exasperation. "He's a depraved Frenchman—"

I spun around to face him. "He's a Spaniard, you idiot,

not a Frenchman!" With that I turned and made for the door, forgetting in my eagerness to prove Serge wrong that I was meant to wait for my escort.

He seized my arm to restrain me. As I twitched angrily out of his grip, he said in a softened impassioned whisper, "Rhea!" It compelled me to turn and face him. His face was tight with concern. "I thought I saw you...disappear for a brief moment just after your eyes went...strange...when he put that jagging rose in your hands and held them."

My heart slammed. "What do you mean?"

"Serge thinks your eyes got little lights in them," V'rae came beside us, startling me. I'd forgotten she was there. "Not like *glitter* but sparkles. V'ser asked me if I'd seen them but I was facing the wrong way, looking at Mr. Martinez. But, for what it's worth, *his* eyes seemed to sparkle too. Maybe it's the lighting in the room," she offered.

I found my gaze back on Serge and stared at him, trying to hide my fear and recognizing his. We both knew it wasn't the lighting in the room. What was I turning into? What was Raphael? *My twin*...He and I obviously shared some connection. *Nous sommes pareils...You're one of us.* Serge had noticed it too. Was that what bothered him? All I knew was that I had to find out the nature of it. Since I'd set foot on Earth, I'd felt a strange energy that seemed to bind me to this mysterious man. Even young Jacques had alluded to it. I had come here on a mission but somehow I was already part of Raphael's mission, whatever it was. Serge couldn't possibly understand. I hardly did. And there was the irony: to prove Serge wrong—that there was no trap—I had to willingly walk into it.

Serge finally let go of my arm. "Don't do this, Rhea," he pleaded. "We can slip out the back door...find some other way, a safer way to warn him...get his help..." Our eyes locked for a long moment. He gauged my resolute expression and his face abruptly hardened. "All right," he bit out sharply and pushed me gruffly toward the door. I stumbled in astonishment. I'd never been the recipient of his violent temper before. "Go then! Go have supper with him. It'll be your last. He'll betray you to the Guardians. *We'll* be somewhere else. Have him to yourself and I wish you joy of him."

With that last angry outburst, he seized V'rae by the hand and pulled her with him to the other door. I watched them through my peripheral vision as I straightened my dress with shaky hands and slipped into my high heels. V'rae was resisting and whispering in low tones to Serge, while glancing at me with a frown of concern. He answered gruffly, flashed a last irate glance at me then dragged her through the doorway and I was left alone with my excited terror.

Ω

It wasn't a long wait, twenty minutes at most, but it seemed endless, as I fretted about my decision, mind swinging madly from anger and brazen confidence to abject fear...What if Guardians were accompanying Raphael's man? I was just thinking of bolting when the door opened. I flinched and spun around. One of the young Gnostic acolytes, a boy dressed like Jacques and not yet old enough to grow facial hair, bowed to me. His baby face, long lashes and straight sable hair that flowed freely down his back, looked youthfully innocent. But the intense liquid eyes that gazed steadily at me under bushy dark brows was anything but innocent.

What *was* Raphael running here? Was he molesting young boys under his tutelage? Drugging them all with *glitter dust*?

The boy was alone at least; no Great Coats accompanied him, I sighed inwardly.

"I'm André," he greeted me in a child's voice, lambent eyes searching the room. "I've come to take you to *Mon Seigneur's* private patio to have supper with him, *mademoiselle*." Then he rested inquisitive eyes back on me. I guessed him at twelve or thirteen years. He was barely out of his childhood; yet I felt myself appraised sexually by adult eyes. "The others, they are not partaking in the gala?"

I smiled tightly at him. "No, André, it seems not. They've

69

left. It'll just be me." I straightened and brushed my leg against the *pocket* strapped to my other leg. I could face the danger on my own, I decided. I didn't need Serge to rescue me this time.

"*C'est bien.*" André bowed again, dark eyes surveying me. "*Mais, voux êtes pret pour la nuit?*"

"What?" Had I interpreted him right? *Was I ready for the night?*

"*Ah, pardonnez mois,*" he said, blushing. "You may wish a shawl...for later..." he drifted off.

I hastily dug out a crepe de chine shawl from one of the drawers. André then opened the door. I inhaled the complex haze of a hundred competing perfumes and heated bodies, punctuated by the sweet *vishna* fragrance as he led me back into the great hall where I'd fainted only moments before. Crowds of people still milled about. The revelry had progressed in a certain direction. Many had formed couples and were fawning with arms draped over each other in open intimacy. Others cheerfully laughed and drank or cuddled close over the lavish food table. I caught a few ardently kissing here and there.

Acutely aware of the veil of Eros that hung over the beautiful crowd, I couldn't help briefly feeling like I was back on Sekmet, being led to some ominous assignation. Raphael had elevated our once intended brief meeting at the gala to an extended supper engagement in his private patio. That was surely a good thing. Then why was I shivering? I immediately thought of the boy's remark. As I entered the gala hall I cast furtive glances for Great Coats. I saw only the black uniforms of Raphael's mauve-skinned Eosian guard, eying me with sideways glances of abstract curiosity.

Within moments of my emerging from the library, heads turned and my face burned as I felt a hundred eyes on me. They were far from friendly: furtive looks of disdain, scornful glances and a few glares of open contempt. Mostly women but some men. I quickly understood that the daily gala was a ritual and they'd hoped to be chosen by the Master for his evening of pleasure... *C'est voux q'il va choisir ...voux êtes pret pour la nuit* ...But I'd supplanted them tonight; *I* was the chosen. I dropped my gaze to the marble tiles and followed André out of the gala hall, wondering what I was walking into. Serge was right; Raphael was not what he seemed. But then, neither was I.

## SIX

André led me out of the lavish hall, down a large hallway. I gazed at the brocaded walls and vaulted ceilings that arched like mountain peaks straining for heaven. Tall stained glass windows let in the evening light. More ancient paintings in gilded frames hung on the walls below the high windows, dappled by slanted shafts of early evening light. They were mostly nude portraits by early-period Earth artists. I recognized several curvaceous nudes by Renoir, and other nudes by fellow Impressionists, Degas and Gauguin. There was Manet's *Le Déjeuner sur l'herbe*, Courbet's *the Reveil*, and *The Turkish Bath* by Ingres. All beautiful and stirring me in all the wrong ways right now. I could not help feeling that I was walking in an ancient church — and desecrating it with my base thoughts — as my steps echoed down the marble-floored hall.

"You are enjoying *Mon Seigneur*'s art collection?" André said, startling me out of reverie. I'd gravitated toward Leon Louis Cassel's seductive depiction of the youthfully erotic *Nymph carried by a Satyr*.

I swallowed and turned to smile at the boy. "Yes, they're beautiful. Tell me, André, how did *Mon Seigneur* acquire them all?"

"Through auctions, *mademoiselle*, when they dismantled all the museums around the world. *Mon Seigneur* got them for very little." André moved and pointed to another artwork, a sketch on parchment. Splashes of pencil and watercolor depicted a nude reclining in sensual abandon, her legs generously outspread and her arms thrown up in careless waves that covered her face. She was a sublime portrait of sated intimacy. And highly erotic. "She's my favorite," André added cheerfully. I glanced from the original Rodin sketch to the boy beside me and saw his eyes caress the art; explore it all over with loving penetration. I realized that this twelve-year old acolyte was no longer a child. As if reading my mind, he added, "It makes me wish I was older, a man *avec un coq aussi grand que Mon Seigneur's*."

I blinked at him in astonishment. My mind refused to consider the darker implications of what he'd divulged. I crouched to face him directly, heart surging with compassion, and placed my hands on his tiny shoulders. "Oh, André." I smiled sadly, grieving his robbed innocence. "You're meant to be dreaming of playing ball with the other children, not *this*." I swept my arm at the hall of Eros. "This shouldn't be your reality, your truth."

"Yes, *mademoiselle*, but '*Art is a lie which makes us understand the truth*'."

I stared at the boy who'd just quoted Nietzsche to me and felt humbled. I then saw his *glitter*-bright eyes dilate as their gaze drifted down my bosom. I hastily let go of him and surged to my feet.

As André blithely led me toward a large filigreed oak door at the end of the hall, my mind conjured the soporific faces of those in the gala hall. So, this was how the humans who'd remained on Earth coped with the Eosian's interloping weed, the *vishna*. Only the Eosians, who'd lived for millennia with the *vishna*, remained relatively immune to its effects. Eosians were, however, lascivious my nature; perhaps a result of commingling with the *vishna* for so long. I thought this as I observed the taciturn Eosian guard who sat behind a small table by the oak door, looking rather imposing despite the fact that he was reading a book. Once André deposited me in front of the guard with a smile and wave of farewell, the Eosian glanced up at me, betrayed recognition with a slight grunt and frown of his hairless brow, then stood and opened the door. It led outside. He waved me through then closed the door behind me without a word.

## SEVEN

I stood on a flagstone patio in a colorful courtyard. I felt the warm sun on my face and a hot breeze stir my hair with the heady scent of familiar and strange. Despite the time of day it was still hot. The slabs of grey stone in the patio lay embedded in a lattice of thick moss. I glanced up at the brilliant azure blue sky then let my gaze drift outward. I faced a garden of trees, shrubs and ground cover, profuse with flowers and the sweet fragrance of home...and something else, quite tantalizing. The *vishna*, of course. I searched for purple leaves and flowers and saw a profusion of them; the *vishna* whose aromatic oil aroused all one's sensuality.

I caught sight of Raphael sitting beside a large table on the large patio. He was pouring some red wine into a tall-stemmed glass. A rich cornucopia of colorful fruit, meats and breads lay spread on the table before him. He'd changed into a pair of beige cotton shorts, sandals, and a pale yellow cambric shirt, short sleeves revealing the dark tan of his biceps. He looked relaxed...and utterly beautiful. Raphael looked up as the door closed behind me.

"You're alone," he said, looking pleased. I didn't move as he rose and came forward, eyes glowing into mine with a strange conspiratorial eagerness. Raphael's heady scent of lilac, cottonwood and musk swirled around me, clouding my faculties. I breathed him in as he took my hand gently and guided me with a tender smile to a chair at the table.

I didn't want to be here; yet I wanted it more than anything. Damn that Serge for making me angry. I might not be here, alone — terrified of what I might do — if he hadn't been such an idiot.

Raphael sat me across from him at the table. It was laden with fresh fruits, bread, wine and pastries, some of which I hadn't seen since I'd left Earth. There were strawberries, mangos, raspberries and watermelon; a dozen kinds of cold meats; hard cheeses and creamy blue brie, and flax seed bread so fresh I could smell the yeast; and real butter. I scanned the pastries with a watering mouth. They included an inviting chocolate torte with butter icing, bright lemon squares and macaroons, toasted just right. I stared and let an unabashed grin bloom on my face.

Raphael laughed. I felt drawn to him like a magnet. As his shoulders shook in laughter, the golden curls of his hair rippled in waves like a river of honey. To my startled surprise, desire pulsed through me in waves of heat.

He helped himself to a strawberry and slowly bit into it, casually watching me ache for him. I recalled the time Serge had surprised me with a bowl of fresh strawberries. I realized that it was mostly because of my quarrel with Serge that I was here, alone, with Raphael and my unreasonable desire for his magnificent body. I thought of all those pretty acolytes. Was this a trap and was I in danger?

Raphael poured a second glass of red wine to pass to me. "I'm not what you expected, am I?" He surprised me with his question as he passed me the glass. It was what I was thinking.

I accepted the glass and drank. "No, you aren't," I said softly, feeling the rich smoky wine burn down my throat.

"Not like Father Uriel at all, eh?" His eyes crinkled with amusement at my expression. "Father Uriel was quite taken by you, especially that you understood French." So, that was how Raphael had known I spoke French. I felt disappointment in Father Uriel. Had he deceived me? I'd convinced myself that he'd been ignorant of my real identity and had not thought him capable of dissembling. "He still thinks you're that animal ecologist," Raphael added, vindicating my belief in the Gnostic priest. "But I recognized who you were from his account and description." Then Raphael raised his glass to me, eyes flashing. "Here's to beauty…in all its forms…"

"…And imperfections," I added and took another drink, eying him over the rim of the glass.

The sun beat down like a heat lamp and I surrendered to the pleasant though drowsy effects of the wine and sun on my face. No Guardians appeared and I began to relax, thinking I might yet convince Raphael to help us. I leaned back in my chair and took in my surroundings again, deciding to enjoy the experience of being back on Earth. The garden in the courtyard sang with a wild chorus of chirping and twittering songbirds. It swelled my heart to hear them. Perhaps this was still enough like home....

We sat in relative silence. Mostly, we sipped our wine and listened to the birds and the rustling of the trees in the fragrant breeze. And I ate. I ate with gusto, thoroughly enjoying the simple Earth foods I'd not had since I was a child. Raphael watched me eat, languid eyes stroking me under a dark wave of lashes.

I'd found my appetite and ate with considerable hunger. The fresh air, the enticing aromatic breeze and my own surging remembrances of bygone Earth fed my soul as I fed my body with pleasure. I decided that I had time to broach the subject of why I had come to see him. No harm in enjoying myself a little first, I thought.

I was biting down on a juicy mango, when Raphael leaned back, stretching his torso, and in a sudden impulse, removed his shirt and shook his curls back into place. I inhaled sharply and almost choked. Feeling distracted and hot, I focused on why I'd come: to warn him of an impending assassination attempt on him by the *Nihilists*. And to solicit the aid of his renowned Eosian guard.

But the words of warning never emerged. As I drew in my breath to speak he said, "So, what do you know of gnosis?"

It was a perfectly logical question to ask me but I'd somehow forgotten that he was a priest. I contemplated a moment before answering, "I believe it's the philosophy that teaches that God is within you and is known by direct experience. I think that's what gnosis means." My eyebrows rose in inquiry. Had I passed his test?

He nodded with a look of satisfaction. "That's a good description. Yes, knowledge of the heart, insight about the spiritual nature of the cosmos, everything that surrounds us and lives through us." He leaned back and took a sip of his wine, letting a smile tease the corner of his mouth. "I'm told you don't believe that Epoptes exist..."

Who would have told him that? My face heated. I couldn't answer. I suspected he was one.

"Why wouldn't you think that way?" he replied for me. "With the exception of their so-called transgression when some descended and procreated with humans, the Epoptes have remained invisible, living 'above' everything. You've a scientist's mind. You need proof, right? But we only have stories...like the *Great Experiment*. According to the current mythos, the Epoptes and the Vos orchestrated the *Great Experiment*, the "Awakening" of Humanity. It was agreed that humans would be permitted to evolve into *portals*, to witness and directly experience God, using what 'can not be imagined' through the Vos and what 'can be imagined' through the Epoptes. Only, the Vos broke the agreement and betrayed the covenant...they left the Epoptes with a task they were not willing to fulfill in their elevated angelic state—to sacrifice the bliss of heavenly enlightenment and remain in the world to teach others, like Buddha and Jesus."

"What had the Vos done?" I asked.

He waved his hand dismissively. "They deserted the Epoptes after debauching the natives."

That wasn't the version Ka had shared with me. The way Ka told it, the Epoptes, who were matter and energy manipulators and, happy with the Eosian super-race they'd created, reneged on their bargain with the Vos and severed the link between inner and outer diverses. According to Ka, it was the Epoptes who had done the debauching—creating the Atlanteans. Then they deserted the Vos, causing what Serge had called the Great Rift. Despite what else I thought of my dissembling grandfather and of Serge I thought this made more sense.

"So, it came to pass that Shemhazai, one of the angels of high rank, led a sect of angels in a descent to earth to instruct the primitive humans in righteousness," Raphael continued his story.

Righteousness. That was a strange definition for lusting after females. I thought of the passage in *Genesis 6* that my mother had read to me: *the sons of God saw the daughters of men that they were fair; and they took them wives of all which they chose.*

"Gnosis teaches us to know God through experiencing

Him," Raphael said. "It's time for gods to walk among mortal beings again, Rhea, to teach them through intimacy to directly experience God and return to the *pleroma*."

I swallowed and considered that Raphael's demented interpretation of gnosis sounded very sexual. Or was it just my twisted mind under the influence of this place?

"You know that the teachings of my order include *duende*...."

I gave him a puzzled look. "It does?" I'd thought that the concept of *duende* had been the sole purview of the Vos. I'd only heard Vos mention it: Ka, Serge, even Bastion, who didn't even know he was a Vos.

"There is a wonderful quote by one of my country's great poets, it goes like this: *Angel and muse approach from without; the angel sheds light and the muse gives form....*"

The Epoptes of the outer diverse, I thought and recognized the poet, Lorca.

"*...But the Duende, on the other hand, must come to life in the nethermost recesses of the blood.*"

The Vos, I thought.

Raphael interpreted differently: "It is a call for intimacy, *mon ange*...intimacy with one another...but especially intimacy with the Epoptes, *les anges de l'universe....*"

He'd stolen a Vos-embraced concept, duende, and perverted it for his own use, I considered.

"It is a call for the Epoptes to return."

I changed the subject. "You call your estate *the Solstice*. Is there a story behind the name?"

A smile teased the corner of his mouth and his eyes licked me with a burst of lilac, cottonwood and musk. "No story, really. Winter and summer solstice mark the cycles of the seasons from death to living in constant renewal. It simply represents the soul's transformation by descending into chaos in order to be reborn." Then his lustful eyes sparkled with streaks of gold. They played in his eyes like stars coalescing. "So, too with the heart. It must descend into the chaos and depravity of carnal lust before it can find true love."

I turned toward the vineyards that I could just make out through the opening of the courtyard. It was an interesting precept he brought up, considering his own history with depravity. I forced myself calm and, holding up the glass he'd just refilled with red wine, I tried to change the subject again. "Yours, no doubt?"

He smiled lazily, dark eyes penetrating me as his hand stroked the narrow end of the bottle. "It's a *Pinot Noir*. In the summer the vine swells with firm, fleshy grapes that thrust out in a lusty profusion, plump and bursting with sweet nectar. Their flavor lingers...though with an after-bite. Do you like it?"

I nodded and dropped my gaze to take another sip. "It's lovely." I heard the hoarse undertone of desire in my voice and licked the wine off my lips.

"Its bite arouses the taste buds."

He teased the mouth of the bottle with his finger, sliding it in and out. I felt a hot throb between my thighs. He leaned forward with a burst of lilac and musk and said fervently, "You must take it in the mouth with the passion and devotion of a connoisseur."

I bridled in a gasp then mentally shook off the erotic trance.

I was about to mention my mission, when he said, "would you like a tour of the grounds?" He abruptly rose and put his shirt back on. He reached a hand out to me, inviting. I rose and took his hand, delaying my mission.

## EIGHT

Raphael walked me in silence through the garden. It was bathed in the exotic scent of *vishna*. We left the courtyard, which opened into a vast rolling landscape covered in a mosaic of purple and green. I inhaled the sweet-boggy fragrance of maple and beech, undercut by the strong scent of *vishna*.

We stood for a while in silence as I took in the pastoral scene and the smells and sounds of home. Raphael broke the spell by seizing my hand again. He stole a mischievous glance at me. "Come." He led me down to a marshy lake that reflected the brilliant blue of the sky and gold flecks of the sun. I could already smell the slight fishy odor of the lake's microscopic inhabitants, algae and the like.

"This is Lac Boivin," he said. "Bass and carp live in it."

"Do you ever fish?"

He gave me a rakish smile. "Only when it's worthwhile."

I noticed several wooden benches along a path beside the cobbled beach of the lake. Raphael led me to one, inside a copse of beech trees hidden from the seminary, and we sat down.

I watched the lily pads slowly rock with the lapping waves of the lake and thought to broach the topic of assassination. I was just drawing in my breath to tell him why we had come when he stood up with a lazy stretch.

"I'm in the mood for some skinny dipping!" He pointed to the lake with a conspiratorial smile. "No one will see us," he added, glancing toward the seminary; we were hidden well enough in the grove of trees from any casual observer. I watched where he swelled beneath his shorts. Biting down on my lip, I desperately wished that Serge and V'rae had joined us. I was in too deep. What did Raphael really want? I was certain now that he'd agreed to an audience with us entirely on my account. He knew who I was. Was it just a tryst or was it more?

Before I could brace myself, he'd reached over and pulled me to my feet. In one smooth motion, he shrugged off his shirt and stepped out of his shorts.

Jacques was right; he was magnificent. Raphael probed me with his eyes and reached out to undress me. I let him slide off my dress and inhaled him. His slender fingers trailed down my arms then my sides and hips, stirring an aching need. My dress fell and pooled around my feet. Before I had a chance to realize— or care—he'd gently unstrapped my *pocket* pistol from my inner thigh and flung it casually on the grass, as if it hadn't surprised him.

I stepped out of my shoes and we stood facing each other. His hands glided over my buttocks and rested there. Why did I feel like I was betraying Serge? He wasn't mine to betray. He was betrothed to another. Damn him anyway, I thought; then I lost myself inside Raphael's liquid gaze.

Ω

His eyes sparkled gold like a sea at sunset. They seized me in a burst of lilac and musk. They entered me and I gasped, feeling a deep probing throb that touched my molten core. My knees trembled as a hot cresting wave broke over me and I moaned out my come, pulsing wetness.

Oh, God! Perhaps he *was* a god! He'd drawn out an orgasm from me with just one look!

Raphael laughed then pulled me up against him. He slid one hand between my thighs and stroked me into coming again. My knees buckled. He scooped me up with his arms, unleashing a boy's laugh, and carried me effortlessly to the lake. I breathed him in, intoxicated with the smell of vishna, lilac and strawberries.

He splashed into the shallows and lowered me onto the sun-heated cobbles. I lay back, cool water lapping my legs and buttocks, knowing I'd secretly wanted this all along. He lowered himself on me as I arched up to meet him. Then he slid inside me in a clean swift stroke to my gasp of pleasure. We slithered over the hot rocks, feeding our vortex of passion. I reached out to grasp his blond locks to press him against me, but he abruptly sat up, filling me deeper. Like a blade of ecstasy. He drove deep and wide, coaxing out my wails. They poured out of me until I felt his waves of climax. I rode them and released my come in keening sobs to his shuddering moans. Wave upon wave of come surged out of me, lapping over him in a great tide.

I reached up for him but he remained aloof, sitting on my wet thighs and gazing down at me with a blissful smile.

It was only then that I realized he'd never once kissed me. And I understood what I'd missed the most: Serge's honest, ardent kisses. No, that was just the beginning of it. I'd missed all of Serge, giving in to him with all my heart and soul. On the outside, Raphael was perfect. His perfect beauty radiated like heaven's gold, pulling from me a perfect desire. Serge wasn't perfect. But I found myself yearning for that imperfection and what made him so endearing to me: the bracing rasp of his unshaven whiskers against my skin; the thrill of his fiery, sometimes awkward passion; his goofy lopsided smile when he knew he was wrong but refused to admit it; his unalloyed belly laugh when I did something stupid; the way he stroked his stubbled chin when he was thoughtful or confused; his tremulous hand on my body and look of boyish doubt.

What had I expected with Raphael? To soar on a sparking arc of gleaming light? Or a fireworks explosion of epiphany? I'd heard the stories of souls joining with the Epoptes, in the form of the wise erotic *vishna*.

Raphael withdrew and rose to his feet, hair backlit in a wild halo of curls. Whatever else he was, he certainly appeared as magnificent as a god. "You've been searching for me all your life just as I've been waiting for you since I was five," he said with insane certainty. "I'm your destiny. *That* is why you came, *mon ange*...and why I let you..."

Oh dear God... was that true?...

"That is why you'll stay here with me and why your sister and her boyfriend left you. They booked a flight on the next shuttle..." He glanced at his Rado watch. "They're gone."

I swallowed down the disappointment that lodged in my throat. Somehow I hadn't believed that Serge would abandon me. Then I recalled that he'd left me before to secure V'rae's safety. I'd foolishly and selfishly insisted on placing us all in danger. I suddenly realized that it was his concern for her safety that had driven him to quarrel with me in the library. I was truly alone.

$$\Omega$$

"Welcome home, sister..."

It sounded like a Sekmet sentence.

I sat up and stared at him, heart beating fast. "You called

me *sister...*"

He squatted down in front of me so his face was inches from mine. Heavy lidded eyes blithely smiled at me. "You and I are twins," he said. "We emanated together and we belong together."

I felt my body stiffen at the sudden thought of his prophecy... *the joining of twin soul mates who will herald the coming of a New Age.* It was just like Raphael to have the hubris to apply his own prophesy to himself.

"Caen and Akhana," he went on, "power and love; me and you..."

I'd studied a bit of the Gnostic teachings before coming here. The Gnostic Aeons came in male/female pairs called *syzygies.* Raphael was likening us to the twin angels, Caen and Akhana. When an aeon emanates without its partner aeon, the result is a *Demiurge,* a creature that should never have come into existence. Was he afraid of being that?

"We shared the same experience when we were five."

"I wouldn't say *exactly* the same," I ventured, neck tensing. He'd *watched* the deed; while I'd *done* the deed—

"I melted them too."

"*What?*" I recoiled from him and blurted out, "You killed your own mother?"

"She was a whore," he said. A dark cloud suddenly passed over us and I felt a sudden chilling breeze wick the heat off my wet back. Our histories were uncannily similar, except for one very important thing: I'd killed U'clid in a rage to save my mother; Raphael had murdered his mother in a rage to end her tormenting him. I remembered feeling that way about my mother too; but later, much later, when it was time to forgive her.

I studied Raphael, squatting before me and I suddenly saw the child, lashing out at the mother who never loved him. She'd flagrantly brought her strange men—and women—into their one-room apartment and forced him to watch. I thought of the boy crying quietly in the corner as his mother laughed, cursed and stripped and had sexual intercourse with stranger after stranger—in front of him.

He misunderstood something in my expression. "Your mother was one too…I know," he said tenderly and took my hand to lift me to my feet and lead me into the lake. Perhaps he hadn't misunderstood, I considered, letting him. We waded in waste-deep then he stopped and gazed deeply into me, tenderly wiping the tears I hadn't realized I'd shed. I thought I saw gold glinting in his eyes. His torment had been so similar to mine, only worse and so undeserved. I'd felt his pain just now; as he'd understood mine like no one else could…I considered that maybe he was right; perhaps he *was* my destiny and we did belong together: twin souls—though not soul-mates—linked by some absurd macabre fate, under the watchful approval of these sentient old souls, these *vishnas*…Serge had V'rae, after all. I'd come here for this as much as anything else. For my release.

Overwhelmed by compassion, I leaned up to kiss him.

Ω

He kissed me like a boy at first. Unresponsive and afraid—was I the first woman he let kiss him?—Then I felt the thrill of his heated response as his arms folded around me, pressing my breasts against him. He opened his mouth and took me in, embracing me with his tongue. My hand slid underwater and I felt him stir against my stroking grip and swell in waves. He moaned and trembled with desire. I guided him to me and he found me ready, pulsing for him. Kissing me hard, he surged inside me like a wave of light, literally lifting me off my feet, up out of the water—

The world vanished—Lac Boivin disappeared, the Earth dissolved—and I felt Raphael inside me, piercing through me in pulses of brilliance. His heart beat with mine. His sighing breaths matched mine, our bodies melded and dispersed into a synchronous fluxing energy. I was a particle surfing the revolving waves of curved space; I was a galaxy, the ouroboros, pouring my energy in the heat of motion and revolution; I was the Sufi whirling dervish dancing my tribute to God; I was a blazing fire,

83

clearing a forest in the cycle of succession, preparing for rebirth; I was love in all its facets from sacrifice to lust. I was God—

He withdrew suddenly and I tumbled back, splashing, to where I stood, facing him. I was back in Lac Boivin on Earth. Raphael seized my arms to steady me and looked at me with stern compassion. "You go too far each time, *mon ange*. At least this time you didn't faint. Take your time, young Epoptes." He gazed at me with wise, ancient eyes.

He'd called me an Epoptes!

"You have a lot to learn," he continued. "Eventually you'll be able to transmute matter and energy without needing an orgasm." He laughed and pulled me close to him. "We are kin to the ancient souls of these trees," he waved up to the *vishnas* that surrounded us. "They've gifted us with the powers of sight and transmutation." He smiled like a boy. "Epoptes are mutable creatures of energy, able to manipulate wave particles in any way we choose. Not the limited powers of the Vos, who must physically connect with their target to shape-shift; we intuitively understand the nature of all matter and energy, because it is all part of us, given to us by the ancient souls. We can control the weather, for instance, or the motions of a planet," he went on. "Our own form, of course. But like any soul we seek the familiar, a place of equilibrium—hence the form you've taken on, Rhea, which your soul has chosen. You've chosen to look the way you do, *mon ange*."

Just like Raphael had elected to become the most striking human being in the galaxy, I thought.

A manic smile spread across his face as though the sun had come out from behind a cloud and he tenderly touched my cheek with his wet hand. "You know what I am, don't you?" he said gently.

I nodded and wondered if he'd been "immaculately" conceived, like V'rae's mother, by a soul-drifter. My words stumbled out, "How? Who?"

"In a way your great grandmother was as responsible for my coming into being as she was yours. The *vishna* trees, *mon ange*," he said hoarsely. "Your great grandmother brought some back to Earth from Eos and three of them ended up in Québec with *L'Ordre de l'Arbre Sacré*. My mother helped run the order for a while until the Vos attacked. Even then she was terribly promiscuous and disobedient." A dark cloud passed overhead. "Someone once saw her naked and masturbating against one of the trees," he ended in disgust. Then he let his scowl dissolve under a roguish smile and stroked my hair with wet hands as the sun returned. "You might have noticed the allure of the *vishna* here. It gives off an oil that acts as a powerful aphrodisiac."

Yes, I'd already noticed.

"My mother gave in to her curiosity and insatiable desire," he went on. "She defied the edict of not touching or climbing the tree. She climbed it and when she reached the top she was overcome by lust and joined with the Epoptes through the *vishna*." He gave me a bitter smile. "I arrived nine months later."

So, Raphael's mother *had* told them the truth, I thought, remembering the story. She had conceived without a mate, a human mate, that is. I remembered the live-dream I'd had of my great-grandmother's erotic experience with an Epoptes atop a *vishna* tree. Was it the same? I thought not. According to my mother, Genevieve Dubois had earlier *joined* with the *vishna*, apparently enacting some taboo on Eos that had angered Azaes, who later became her mate.

"*Through* the vishna?" I asked, staring into Raphael's violet eyes.

He grinned and I thought of the monthly pilgrimages he made into the forest, emerging naked and glowing in the aftermath of intimacy. "Yes," he said, gently stroking my hair. "The *vishna* is an ancient soul, within which an Epoptes can reside. Each *vishna* tree produces millions of blossoms and each blossom is its own being, capable of independent movement and thought. When you climb to the *vishna's* crown, thousands of blossoms give up their lives by detaching and swarming around you, and caressing your body in a love dance of death."

I was reminded of the terrible snakes of Horus and their terrifying love dance of death—*my* death—and the apophus transformation I'd barely escaped. I wanted Raphael to stop but I stood transfixed, and saw my reflection of terrified arousal in his dark pupils.

"They sacrifice themselves, *mon ange*," he breathed out, eyes pinning mine in a penetrating gaze. "For love and wisdom. They flutter over you in a tender embrace, covering you in a purple mantle of sweet wet nectar…then they *enter* you—"

I caught up my breath, heart pounding between my legs.

His eyes sparkled as if filled with stars. "Once inside, they whisper their ancient wisdom to you in a deep exquisite dance…then they melt into an intoxicating molten soup that bubbles up and through your whole being like hot steam…" What was he doing? I felt as if I was lifted off the lake and was floating in an alien sea, drowning but not caring. Raphael's voice crested over me like a wave. "Then, just as you come apart like a million pixels of a holo-painting, their whispers coalesce into a singular reverberating shout—"

I gasped, pulsing out my come.

"…And you experience an epiphany." He smiled beatifically at me, hands gripping my shoulders to keep me from sinking into the water. "I understand a little why my mother was obsessed with the *vishna* tree," he said, returning to his earlier sullen mood. "*Joining* with it is the most incredible sensation one can bestow upon oneself. It is an honor above all else that requires invitation. That is why she desecrated the tree, herself, and the Order, with her action. She did it uninvited, out of greedy lust."

I wondered how different Raphael's actions compared. How did one get invited and had *he* been invited? "Why aren't you an Eosian, then?" I managed to ask. I thought of the myth of the Epoptes descending to Earth thousands of years ago and laying with the human females to create a new race, the giant people of Atlantis. They became the Eosians.

Raphael shrugged, hands trailing down my back to caress my buttocks. "I think because it was a true joining with the *vishna*. Just like the human form of your great grandmother did two hundred years ago." Yes, she'd returned to Earth as an Epoptes. Raphael lifted a rogue hair off my face and said quietly, "And speaking of...you now know what you are."

I nodded tremulously and swallowed.

"You're an Epoptes, Rhea Hawke. Like me. Do you know what that means?"

I didn't know what that meant. But my heart sank with a sudden loss and it startled me to recognize what it was: I'd plummeted even farther away from Serge. I was an Epoptes, mortal enemy of all Vos. I was suddenly reminded of that liquid thermal art at the place Serge had taken on Iota Hor when we'd first met. Where the Vos lay in supplication under an Eosian's blade with that beautiful Epoptes leaning over him in cruel satisfaction. My mother had that same surreal beauty, though blissfully ignorant of what she was. I suddenly thought of Ka and my grandmother. Like my grandmother, I'd followed a different path, and chosen my appearance accordingly. It then came to me: "But I'm a Vos too."

"I know," he said. He pushed away a wet lock of hair from my face. "But what little there is of that base lot is overshadowed by the brilliance of your Epoptes heritage, Rhea. Legend suggests that we were once the same," he continued, acknowledging what Ka and Bas had said earlier. "But the Epoptes are far more evolved than the Vos. Vos use that limited concept of *duende* as their precept; they burn with intuition, spontaneity, and impulse. They are a dark fast burn, but we are a slow and everlasting glowing light. We gleam with the ethereal light of intellect, logic and knowledge."

I wasn't sure how I felt about that. I was both Vos and Epoptes. How was I supposed to reconcile these two?

"Vos aren't connected to the ancient souls like we are, *mon ange*," he went on. "They know nothing of the *vishna* or the migratory trees. They bungle their intuitive way, ruled by the forces that run through them; we understand and rule those forces—climate, gravity...sexual desire..." His eyes flamed into mine and I flushed despite my growing unease. He grinned like a boy and kissed me hard. Then he pulled back with a boyish laugh. "Think of the never ending possibilities, *mon ange*...never-ending sex...spontaneous orgasms...all day, all night with *me*..." He grinned, perfect teeth glinting. I couldn't help thinking of someone else. "The Vos are primitive children next to us."

I remembered Ka defaming the Eosians because they could not hear the music of the spheres. Eosians, in turn denigrated Humans who then ridiculed the Rills...and so on it went down the pecking order...when would all this petty prejudice end? I then reminded myself that I had gladly subscribed to that very pecking order not long ago.

"The Vos are the fallen angels, while we rule still."

Funny, the Vos had called the Epoptes the fallen ones.

"They have only a limited understanding of the world that runs through them. We *are* that world."

I stared in astonishment, grappling with the concepts he described. With what I was.

But he wasn't finished astonishing me. He seized my face with wet hands and said fervently, "Marry me, *mon ange*! You'll be the rose for my seed."

Ω

Before he had a chance to kiss me again, the words burst out of me as I broke from his grasp, "The *Nihilists* want to kill you!"

"What?" He looked puzzled and frowned at me.

I'd stopped him, thankfully. I'd finally said what I came here to say. And with that outburst, I'd broken through my trapped sexual daze.

"You're on their hit list. I came to warn you, Raphael. *That's* why I came."

He smiled at me like I was a child. "*Mon ange*, you still don't understand. There's no reason why they'd want to kill me. We're working together, after all."

"*What?*" My heart raced with alarm and I stumbled backward, losing my footing and almost falling backward into the water with a splash. Raphael caught me by the waist and steadied me. I managed to pull away from him again and edged my way to the shore where my gown lay. "Why?"

"Because for now we're on the same side. Neither of us wants the gate open so the Vos can enter and defile this diverse. Once the *Nihilists* have served their purpose, I'll let my loyal soldiers extinguish them." He meant his Eosian elite guard, the ones I'd coveted. This was truly ironic, I thought: Serge, V'rae and I had come to solicit Raphael's elite guard to fight the *Nihilists*; while Raphael had planned all along to use his guard to exterminate them. The only difference was in the timing. And the purpose. We wanted them to prevent species annihilation; he wanted them to clean up afterward. I saw his beauty shrivel before me as his smile opened to a cold grin of triumph.

"The Guardians won't let you," I said.

"You know so little, *mon ange!*" He said cheerfully and blurted out, "The Guardians won't stop us. Your own boss will make sure of that." He laughed at my expression. I'd fabricated the surprise—he'd just confirmed my suspicions. But it did explain why Eclipse still had a contract out on Raphael. It was likely that Ennos, in his inimitable way, had kept the deal with Raphael a secret from his own people to play the game both ways. But that raised another question: was Ennos a Vos *Nihilist* or an Epoptes acting to root out his own revolutionaries?

"For now the *Nihilists* are useful to us," Raphael said as I advanced steadily to shore. "They have a plan to get rid of the gate permanently." I knew about that plan. Sadly, it involved a weapon of my own making. And the annihilation of all of humanity. Raphael went on, "I've cleverly agreed to send my two best squadrons, the *Odysseus* and the *Daedalus*, to help direct this glorious feat." He grinned like a fox.

I knew why. His guard, well placed, would just turn around and kill the *Nihilists*, who thought them allies. It was clever. And mad. I shivered with anger. "Glorious? You call killing every human glorious?"

"You're so naïve, *mon ange*," he said, following me out to shore. "You're clinging to a race you don't even belong to. Remember, you're not human. They've outlasted their usefulness and will soon be extinct, like the *fisk* and the house cat. You're an Epoptes. We'll take their place and become the most beautiful race in the galaxy." He seized my hands. "Your duty is to stay here with me, *mon ange*, at my side, on your beloved Earth where you were born…where you belong. We'll be married and you'll be my queen of the New Age. You'll create for me a new race of beautiful human-like Epoptes. We'll repopulate this precious Earth with a wondrous race of galactic rulers…*Ma beauté d'Eros…ma reign…*"

He was mad and I had to stop him. I stumbled out of the water and furtively searched for the *pocket* he'd dropped in the grass. There it was!

"You're an Epoptes," he repeated, following me out of the water. "Do you know what that means?"

I didn't. I shook my head, inching toward my crumpled gown. Toward my *pocket*.

"Our offspring will be the first pure Epoptes to walk this Earth since Genevieve Dubois did over 200 years ago. The children you'll bear for me will be Epoptes, like us, Rhea. Beautiful children…like me…"

"*Beauty without virtue is like a rose without scent*—Swedish proverb," I said with narrowing eyes.

He ignored my insult and continued, "It will mark a new era when Epoptes come out of the trees to create a new galaxy of rulers, with Eosians as our trusted soldiers. Do you have any idea how many Epoptes are so desperate to come out and live like you and I do?" He waved a sweeping arm over his estate. "Each *vishna* houses an Epoptes soul, hankering to be free. The day will come, *mon ange*, when you and I will announce ourselves as Epoptes. First you'll bear my child—the one I've just seeded you with. Then we'll make our announcement and show the others that we needn't abide by their foolish old-fashioned edicts. We'll show them a better way, complete the work your great grandmother began when she came to Earth. Epoptes will then walk the earth, free to live openly, to love each other unrestrictedly, and to rule wisely."

Rule who? Who would be left after his genocide? It was then that I fully understood: Raphael was one of their fallen angels—as was my great grandmother—a renegade Epoptes who was defying their edict of non-interference and invisibility; fitting the mold of those who'd come down in the first place to fornicate with the yielding humans, who no doubt thought of them as beautiful angels. Raphael wanted Epoptes out in the open, to fill in the niche left by the Vos. A spoiled god who wanted everything. The bastard was planning a revolution, on the heels of his genocidal war I'd so kindly made possible with my MEC technology. In a world without humans.

I darted and seized my *pocket* pistol from the ground then pointed it at him. "I'm sorry, Raphael. I can't let you do that." My hand was shaking. I wasn't sure I could pull the trigger. I hadn't tried to do this since I'd failed to shoot Ka.

"Now, *mon ange*, is that any way to treat your king, the father of your first child?" Raphael glanced down from the pistol in my hand to my face and smiled. He was so beautiful, like an angel. How could I shoot an angel?

"*After the game, the king and the pawn go into the same box* — Italian proverb," I said in a shaky voice.

Unafraid, he stepped forward; eyes flashing golden sparks in a penetrating arc. They struck me like lightening and I shuddered in a breath, knowing that my own eyes flashed back in loving caresses. Our eyes crossed and clashed in a voluptuous duel. I lost. Amid this blazing lover's dance, incredible desire seized me in an incapacitating embrace. Aching for him with an urgency I could hardly bear, I dropped the pistol from my limp hand and fell to my hands and knees, struggling to keep from crawling toward him.

Thunder clapped as dark clouds scudded overhead and it started to rain. It pelted us in waves. All I could think of was how beautiful he was. How could I think that? But he was, I decided, watching him approach and unable to retreat.

Then I came to a startling realization: Raphael still lived his childhood misery. Great Epoptes that he was, he'd remained a child. And, despite having surrounded himself with riches and beauty, he lived a life of miserable debauchery and self-torture. He'd become his mother; as I'd become mine.

Serge was right. This was a trap. I got off Sekmet; I wasn't sure I'd get off Earth. Serge had helped me get off Sekmet. God, I wished for him now!

Then I felt the cold sharpness of metal beneath me and realized that I'd landed on my *pocket*. In an instant of clarity, I dug it out from under me, aimed and pulled the trigger.

He jolted and pitched forward. He fell over me. I pushed him off me and scrambled to my feet. Blood welled out of a hole in his chest. He stared at me with glazed eyes of disbelief. The violet in his eyes shifted to aquamarine then a dark leaden blue-grey of an Earth ocean.

His hand reached out to me, shaking. "You can't do this…" he stammered out like a hurt boy in a child's game. The rain had abated to a soft sheet of mist. "You're my twin…my *queen*…you're an Epoptes—"

I pulled the trigger again and he fell back. "I'm also a Vos," I said.

To my astonishment, he opened his eyes and rose to his feet. Thunder crackled and I saw lightening flash in the dark sky behind him. The rain pounded on us. It sluiced down his smooth chest. Blinking rain out of my eyes, I stared at the two wounds I'd inflicted on him; they were already healing!

"*Mon ange*," he said with quiet control, rain dripping off his long lashes. "I'm an Epoptes—"

I suddenly understood: "So am I."

My eyes seethed and I sent a shaft of pure energy at him. I'd caught him off guard and his utterly beautiful body lit and melted into a mass of liquid flesh that toppled to the ground in a steaming pool.

I stared at what I'd done. I'd melted him, by simply willing it. I brought a hand to my mouth in stunned horror and stumbled back into a fall. I sat hard on the ground with a grunt.

I thought of the trauma Raphael had suffered as a boy and had never fully escaped in manhood. He'd been so beautiful and vital outside yet so ravaged inside. Had I finally released his soul? God, forgive me!

A dark sickening thought splintered through me: I'd just done the bidding of Eclipse again; I'd killed the fifth person on their hit list—

A commotion close to the house shook me from my grieving trance and I crouched, looking for Eosian guards. I went to grab my soaked gown then snatched Raphael's shirt and shorts instead. They would serve me better, I thought, as I pulled the wet clothes on and cinched the belt tight. Leaving my awkward high heeled sandals, I elected to go barefoot and, with a swift snatch of my *pocket*, I was about to sprint into the forest for cover when a dark thought inspired me and I glanced down at Raphael's clothes hanging loose and wet on me. My gaze drifted to what was left of Raphael, an unrecognizable pool that already seeped into the lake in the weeping rain.

Blinking the raindrops off my eyelashes, I gave in to the fearful thrill of my mad plan. There was still a way to get Raphael's Eosian guard to help us.

## NINE

I sprinted back to the courtyard where I'd heard the commotion. As I rounded the corner into the courtyard I caught my breath and bridled in a sharp inhale. Serge!

I felt a sob well up with his name on it and cleared my throat in a gurgling utterance: "Se-so...."

Four Eosian guards stood on the patio, restraining him. My first thought—unalloyed joy that he'd come back for me!— was swiftly followed by pity at his state. He'd obviously struggled and suffered a beating. His cheek was grazed and bruised and one eye was swollen shut. Blood ran down his chin from a split lip and another runnel flowed down from a gash somewhere in his hair. He was having a hard time standing; the guards were holding him up more than restraining him.

I channeled my intense emotions into a gruff response. "What are you doing, Ampheres?" I addressed Raphael's head of security in a commanding voice. "He's one of my guests." I tried to ignore Serge glaring at me through his one good eye.

"Forgive us, *Mon Seigneur*, but we saw that you were...eh...busy with her—on—in *le Lac*—" Ampheres cut himself off, clearing his throat. "We caught him spying on you so we took the matter into our own hands." And luckily they did or they might have seen me kill Raphael with my eyes. I'd thought we were hidden from view but obviously, from the tone of Ampheres's voice, they'd seen everything. Serge, whether he realized it or not, had saved me again. I was Raphael now, thanks to my Epoptes ability in transmutation. Right down to his voice, inflections, memories, knowledge and his DNA.

"Did you have to beat him?" I challenged, trying to dampen the emotions that crept in my voice.

"He resisted and attacked us."

I nodded, forcing the pity from my eyes as I gazed at Serge's bleeding mouth. "Leave us. He and I need to talk."

Ampheres instructed his guard to let go of Serge. He almost toppled but made an effort to stand and held himself straight. As Ampheres turned to leave with the others, I added, "Oh, Ampheres, tell Eumulus I wish to speak with him on a matter of great urgency. And have Étienne attend me right away."

Once they'd left, I waved casually to a seat at the table I'd shared a meal with Raphael earlier. The food had been cleared away prior to the rain. Serge gladly took the seat, looking like he might fall any moment. Soaked and bedraggled, he sank into the chair.

"Where's Rhea?" he demanded.

I couldn't tell him. We were being monitored and it was critical I maintain the pretense that Raphael was still alive. Then there was the matter of revealing my true nature to Serge; I knew what he thought of Epoptes.

"I'm sorry for the misunderstanding, Monsieur Bastion," I said steadily. "But you understand the precautions we have to take for someone of my stature and you were acting rather suspiciously." I let my eyes flicker to the field mag hanging off his neck.

"Where is she?" Serge insisted, pushing himself forward with a surly expression.

"She's...waiting for me at the lake, enjoying a swim in the rain." I threw the soaked gown on the table. "She won't be going anywhere without *this*," I added. It was important to explain Rhea's absence to the monitoring staff. I had to keep up the appearance of us being lovers, and stay in character with Raphael's lascivious habits. His staff fully expected Raphael to occupy himself with me well into the night. Point in fact, if I hadn't melted him, that's exactly where we both would have been still.

"I'll be rejoining her momentarily," I said. "But I needed to see what was happening here. You've interrupted us, Mr. Bastion." I swallowed at his reaction and unbidden tears welled up. I hadn't expected to see such misery on his face. I brushed away the tears with an explanation, "she's so utterly beautiful," and thought of Raphael's ethereal beauty. I cleared my throat and quickly added, "She's explained everything to me and we've made an arrangement. You will have two of my best *Orichalkon* squadrons at your service for as long as you need. They're from my Special Operations Unit, headed by Autochthon and Elasippus, two of my best men."

His eyes lit up despite his inner misery and I felt a little better for my deception.

Just then Eumulus came through the door into the patio. Unflinching at the rain still misting down, he approached us in a long cowboy stride. He was a hulking man, even for an Eosian, and I recognized him as Raphael's SOU general at arms. I stood and greeted him with a firm handshake as Raphael and he were accustomed to doing. "This man, Serge Bastion, and his friend, Rhea Hawke, require our services, Eumulus. The lady is my beloved friend and requires our special attention. Two of your squadrons will be placed at her command until she dismisses them, understand? "

He nodded to me. "Yes, *Mon Seigneur*," he said with a bow and a cursory glance at Serge.

"You are to have Autochthon and Elasippus assemble their *Daedalus* and *Odysseus* squadrons immediately and meet Officer Hawke and I at Hanger B." I then explained everything to him and he nodded quietly to it all. We talked of arrangements with vehicles and supplies—to be acquired post haste—as Serge looked on in bewilderment and, I thought, a little shame. He truly hadn't expected this kind of magnanimity from Raphael. He was right; he was getting it from *me*.

Once I'd dismissed Eumulus, I turned back to Serge. "Now, if you'll excuse me, I have a lady waiting for me in a lake. I suggest you wait for her in Hanger B, where an escort of my best SOU guards are waiting to serve you."

He stumbled to his feet with a nod. I wanted to reach over and hug him and tell him everything was all right.

The young insipid man I'd seen kissing Raphael at the gala came through the door: Étienne, Raphael's secretary. He hesitated at the door, less inclined to get wet, then loped toward us in a gangling gait, all lean muscle, with the awkward eagerness of youth.

"You'll be in charge again, Étienne," I said. "I'm leaving with my beloved." I caught a look of shock on Serge's face that was mirrored on Étienne. "You must run the school in my absence. I don't know when I'll be returning or quite where I'll be. We must maintain communication silence because of the secret nature of our journey. So, you must simply wait for me to contact you."

Étienne swallowed down his terrified disappointment then stared awestruck with sudden realization. "Is she the one, then, *Mon Seigneur*?"

Veiled beneath his outer joy I saw misery. He looked worse than Serge and I understood that he and Raphael had been lovers. Raphael must have confided in him about me, *his twin...his queen*. And, of course, Etienne knew the prophecy: *the joining of twin soul mates who will herald the coming of a New Age.*

I impulsively took his hands in mine and pressed them with a nod. "Yes, Étienne," I said in a shaky voice. "She is that...and so much more," I ended, wondering with the stirrings of discomfort how our 'twin-joining' would *herald the coming of a New Age.* Was it ironically in me killing *my twin*? Étienne pressed my hands back with a compassionate nod then let go. "I am so glad for you, *Mon Seigneur*," he said ardently. "I wish you great happiness."

"Thank you, Étienne." Then I dismissed them both with instructions for Étienne to take Serge to the infirmary to tend his wounds. Serge shuffled out like an old man through the door and was met by an Eosian Guard.

Once the door was shut, I raced out of the courtyard, hoping to beat Serge to the hanger. As I ran along the grove of lilacs, their fragrance overwhelmed me with grieving thoughts of Raphael. Out of the dozens of murders I'd committed as an Enforcer, it felt as though this one had been my only murderous act; it was the only one I'd committed while my soul was awake.

Autochthon and Elasippus and their squadrons were already at Hanger B when I arrived. It was a sight to behold; all these men standing here at my bidding.

I scanned the Eosian guard, row upon row of tall young men, mauve-skinned in jet-black, all standing at attention—and caught an anomaly. A pale-skinned lad, a human with flaming red hair stood among them. There was no mistaking, he was one of the guard, wearing the smart black uniform and standing proud among them, only two heads shorter. A young lad, no older than Jacques. I wondered how he'd escaped Raphael's harem.

The squadron leaders stood at attention in front of their squadron of fifty men each and saluted me as I approached. Both were fairly young for superior officers—I guessed they were in their twenties—but appeared extremely competent. Dressed in jet-black uniforms, they looked incredibly fit and were, like most Eosians, very good looking. The taller lankier one, Autochthon, met my gaze with honest eyes and almost smiled with the eagerness of new adventure. An idealist, I thought, he looked sophisticated and cerebral. Elasippus, who was huskier in build with the barreled chest of a man who liked his food and drink, wore a more complicated expression, not as easily understood. Rougher looking with dark calculating eyes, he looked like the older of the two and was no doubt gauging the mission. It was he who stepped forward and reached his brawny arm out to grasp my hand in greeting. *"Mon Seigneur,"* he said in a gruff basso voice. I took it and felt his firm grip, returning an equally firm one.

Autochthon stepped forward and came beside Elasippus to shake my hand. "Eumulus gave us instructions and all is in readiness, *Mon Seigneur,"* he said in a cultured tenor voice.

"Good." I nodded. "Thank you for assembling so quickly at such short notice," I began. "You will be serving under the command of former Guardian Enforcer, Officer Rhea Hawke. My beloved." I paused to let that sink in before continuing, "I will let her explain what is needed of you. Some of you may know of this lady's queer reputation, particularly to do with Eosians. Do not believe the rumors about Commander Hawke. She is not that person."

*She is not that person.* And I truly believed that. I was not that person any more. Sekmet, Serge, my apophus grandmother, even Raphael had irreparably changed me. They'd taught me that I could no longer blindly hate anyone for what they were on the outside. I knew too much about how deceiving appearances could be, my own included. "Commander Hawke is embarking, with your help, on a very dangerous mission that will save all humans and anyone who believes in freedom from fascist oppression in the galaxy. You will accord her all the respect you can. Is that clear? Because when she returns—and I expect her to return to me unharmed—I want to hear no complaints. Understood?"

"Yes, *Mon Seigneur,"* they both said in unison.

"You are forbidden to communicate with anyone unless expressly agreed upon by Commander Hawke. That includes anyone here, even me. From this moment onward, you are hers to command and you are to remain in communication silence." Then I smiled and added, "Good journey. Now I'll just tell her good bye...and..." I grinned out of the side of my mouth. "...Leave her a little gift of my love...then she'll speak to you herself."

I strode into the hanger and once out of their vision, shifted back to myself and cinched in the belt of Raphael's shorts. I'd forgotten the gown on the table. After waiting a few minutes, I emerged and felt my face heat as a hundred and two Eosians stood at attention, facing me. I felt acutely aware of my state of disarray. My hair was still wet and plastered over me in tangles. I was barefoot and wearing Raphael's clothes. The inference was all too obvious.

"Men," I began in a steady loud voice as I noticed Serge hobbling toward us from the mansion, "First of all, thank you for agreeing to this mission. As Raphael—*Mon Seigneur* told you, it is dangerous and involves stealth, cunning and courage. Much is at stake and I appreciate your willingness to help humanity and Eosians alike in averting a tragic war and saving the galaxy from an enemy oppressor."

Serge skirted us to enter the hanger as I forced myself to continue. I couldn't gauge the expression on his face as our eyes met briefly. I then drew Autochthon and Elasippus aside to speak with them only. I pressed them on the urgent need for closed communication; I was after all still a wanted fugitive. We discussed secret codes of communication, particle-stream pathways and rendezvous points. Both men responded with alacrity and respect and swiftly demonstrated their skill and experience. Autochthon was quick with challenging questions and solutions and Elasippus provided some ingenious ideas. I was already impressed. It was no wonder this Eosian guard was coveted by many. When all was said and done, I finished with, "In freedom, then, shall we go?"

Both officers saluted me. I winced inwardly and made a point of saluting back. Then they broke formation and headed for their ships in Hanger C.

## TEN

I entered the hanger, looking for Serge. My heart beat like a hammer. There was no sign of him. Where was he? He must have literally heeded Raphael's bidding and decided to wait for me inside Benny. Taking in a deep breath, I headed for Benny's hatch and climbed the ladder.

When I entered, I found Serge, stripped to the waist, and leaning over a basin in the infirmary. He was washing his face. At the sound of my footsteps, he stopped and stared at me, dripping. His face told everything, a complicated storm of shame, anger, torment, and—yes!—terrible yearning.

I approached him in hesitant steps with a tremulous smile. Had I hurt him too much? Shamed him too far? It wasn't as though I was *his*...

I didn't know what to say, so I asked a question I didn't want to ask: "Where's V'rae?"

"Safe in a shuttle, bound for her beloved," he said, miserably. *Her beloved*? I had no time to register what he meant because he quickly added, "And what about yours?"

My beloved? My one and only beloved stood right before me. But I understood who Serge meant. I drew in a shuddering breath. "Dead," I said shakily and saw his eyes widen with shock. "I killed him—"

He grimaced. "With your *pocket*?"

I didn't answer and let his thoughts lead him where he wanted them. The truth was too frightening. And with it I started to shake uncontrollably at what I'd done, what I was, and all that had transpired.

He took two large steps and pulled me into his arms in an embrace. His compassion opened my emotional gates; I wept openly, shuddering against him as he murmured sweet meaningless utterances in my hair, "*Cherie...ma cherie....*" He stroked my wet tangled hair gently and whispered, "What have you done...."

"No one knows," I finally stuttered out. "Because I—"

In a flame of musk and strawberries he cut me off by slamming his mouth against mine. Startled at first, I let myself melt into his kiss and kissed back, our tongues embracing; I'd craved this with him since the moment we'd landed. The one man I truly loved was in my arms, kissing me.

Warm in his wonderful embrace and glowing in his delicious kiss I felt the surge of unencumbered desire. This was so different from what I'd felt with Raphael; *my* choice, *my* desire, for the man I loved. I leaned into him with delirious joy and felt him stir in response. He pressed me against the bulkhead, hand urgently sliding beneath one of my billowing shorts legs. I fumbled his belt and zipper open. One hand was already down his loosened pants, grasping his swollen manhood, as his hand found the wet heat between my legs. I seized in my breath and thought I might come right then—

He broke off suddenly with a hoarse gasp, as if he'd fought himself to do it, and I gasped out my own disappointment. He pushed himself off me gruffly and I recognized disgust on his panting face as he stared from me to his hand, now shaking. "This place is *disgusting*," he said, mouth in a tight snarl. "I hate what it's done to...us."

I backed away. After a convulsive swallow, I pushed out hoarsely, "I'm so sorry...." I couldn't say more. I wasn't sure what I was apologizing for...except that we were dishonoring V'rae...and Raphael? Then I rushed to the cockpit to get away from him.

"Benny, get us started," I said, my voice cracking.

"Okay, Rhea. Nice to have you back."

"Thanks. Nice to be back," I sobbed out. I drew in a deep breath to gain command of my voice and added more steadily, "Benny, get those scrubbers going full tilt." I wanted every last oily drop of *vishna* aerosol out of here as fast as possible. I fisted away my tears then leaned my elbow on my pilot's chair rest and let my head sink into my hand. I closed my eyes with a long exhale. Then snapped them open as Serge came beside me—he'd thrown on a shirt—and sank into the co-pilot seat, belting himself in.

I cleared my throat and made ready to take off, signaling Autochthon and Elasippus with instructions on trajectory and formation. They acknowledged and we set off.

I piloted Benny out of the hanger and we soared into Earth's atmosphere again, flanked by two of the most competent stealth-fighter squadrons in the galaxy.

I took a last glance down at the familiar coastline, though considerably greener than I'd last remembered it, and maneuvered Benny into the blackness of space and into the particle stream, followed by my Eosian escort. I was glad to be out of the visual field of that blue-green planet. Earth was not what it used to be; but then neither was I.

Only once we were safely in deep space did I turn the controls over to Benny and glanced over to Serge, seated beside me with a sober look on his face. He was doing his best to ignore me. Then, without a word, he brusquely unbuckled his harness and went aft. I busied myself in a brief communication with both Eosian commanders; we agreed to meet aboard Autochthon's flagship, the *Elyssia*, once our little fleet achieved orbit around Tau c in the Tau Gruis system, our agreed first rendezvous.

I stretched in my seat and listened to the murmuring thrum of Benny's environmental system. I heard the buzz of the soyka maker and pushed myself off my seat to join Serge mid-ship.

"So, you got what you came for," he said coolly.

I nodded and wondered why he'd come back...V'rae was *bound for her beloved*, he'd said...Was it possible that he'd actually come back for *me*? "You came back," I said quietly.

He was silent for a moment, measuring out one of his additional ingredients. "After I saw V'rae safely off with a man I'd paid good money to stand as my double. Yeah, I came back," he said coolly. "But the guards spotted me as I was watching you."

I blushed, thinking of my sexual tryst with Raphael on the shores of Lac Boivin. Tapping into his gloomy mood, I let my anger spike. "You were *spying* on me?"

"Not spying!" his words exploded, eyes now blazing into mine. He waved his measuring spoon in the air. "For creon's sake, Rhea! Look—I came to see if you needed...well...if you were in any...Damn it! I came to help!"

"And watched me on those field mags..."

They still hung on him. He blushed furiously, following my glance down at them, and I felt satisfaction despite my anger and embarrassment.

"But you obviously had it well in hand," he said.

I blushed at his unintended pun, which made him redden too when he realized what he'd said.

"But how was I to know," he continued with a grim smile. "How was I to know you were making a jagging good deal with him, *Frenchman-style*," he added sourly as if he'd eaten raw blenoid meat. "Then closed the deal with your *pocket* pistol, *Rhea-style*."

I had to look away. That was the part that had really bothered him. Serge thought I was a cold heartless assassin, who'd made out with Raphael for mere sport—to sucker him in—then killed him heartlessly after I got what I wanted. Keep it clean, uncomplicated, like an Enforcer. Raphael was obviously infatuated with me; he'd intended to come with us, after all—thanks to my performance. I'd been too convincing in my deception. I'd done it to fool Raphael's staff, to put them off looking for him; but I'd hooked Serge with my duplicity as well. And how could I dissuade him otherwise without revealing what I was? A creature of his loathing. God, I hadn't even told him about what I'd done to his sister yet.

I should have explained something; instead I asked, "What made you change your mind?" He looked puzzled at me and I added, "To come back, I mean?"

His brows drew together as he tinkered with the last ingredient then set the machine to brew his concoction. As it percolated and dripped, he said in a strained voice, "I always had the intention of staying." I knew he was lying. "But I guessed that Martinez had us monitored. He had to think I was really going, that I had a legitimate reason to leave you behind, so I made our argument convincing."

In actual fact, there had been no need to stage our squabble, I thought sullenly and still felt the bite of his harsh words. Our spat had been genuine and had erupted naturally like a lover's quarrel. And it had been a long time in coming. Ever since Serge had returned with V'rae, I'd been cold, churlish and rude with him, rebuffing his friendliness. My brazen and depraved behavior with Raphael in the dining hall had tipped Serge over the edge, sparking a lover's jealousy. But we *weren't* lovers, I considered with a lingering gaze at him as he tested his brew. Its aroma reminded me of the first time we'd been intimate. *"Good soyka should be black like the devil, hot like hell, and sweet like a kiss*—Hungarian proverb," I said rather snidely then escaped aft to change in the med/storage/bedroom.

We avoided each other after that and I wished yet again for a larger ship.

### ELEVEN

Autochthon and Elasippus turned out to be more than useful and very resourceful. They also served a reprieve for Serge and I, who weren't speaking to one another. Both Eosians were genuinely respectful but relaxed and friendly, which surprised me.

Autochthon graciously met Serge and I at the docking hatch aboard his flagship, the *Elyssia*. There we waited for Elasippus, who was docking one of *Boeotia's* shuttles. I noted the impeccable condition of the docking bay and associated stores. As I had suspected, Autochthon was an exacting officer.

Once Elasippus arrived, Autochthon ushered us to his tactical room where he made me a bergamot tea with milk. Elasippus slid the chair back for me to take a seat at the circular table. I blushed at the attention but understood; I was Raphael's beloved, after all.

The two Eosian commanders then took seats across from me and proceeded to discuss strategies for finding the two installations. As Autochthon and Elasippus fell into what I discovered later to be a familiar banter regarding some small issue, I sipped the hot and delicious tea that tasted of home and found my mind wandering.

Although I'd managed to glean some long-term knowledge from Raphael while inhabiting his form—thanks to his DNA inside me—most things eluded me. Like where he intended to send his two squadrons. It was possible, I considered, that even Raphael didn't know where the weapons factories were. That was something Ka wasn't likely to have shared, particularly with a non-*Nihilist*, unless he had to. It was more likely that Raphael would have sent Autochthon and Elasippus to a neutral location at the appropriate time, when the MEC fleet was complete, and from there, the Eosian commanders would have joined the new MEC fleet—

"Commander Hawke?" Autochthon regarded me expectantly. He'd stood up beside a colorful holo that showed a portion of the Milky Way. His hairless brow was raised in inquiry.

I realized that everyone was watching me and cleared my throat. "I'm sorry," I admitted, feeling my face heat, "I...drifted off. Could you repeat what you said?"

Elasippus threw back his head and guffawed. "Missing him already, eh?" Elasippus turned to Autochthon who joined him in a good laugh at my expense.

I noticed Serge, slouched beside me, practically glowering.

Elasippus cleared his throat. "What Autochthon was saying, Commander Hawke, is that the installations would most likely be in remote space, far from any traffic routes, but strategically placed for maximum attack efficiency of the major human colonies." He pointed to the holo. "These sectors."

I counted Iota Horologii, Gleise 876, HD70642, 55 Cancri, and HD28185 where Bastion's home planet was. That made sense. Major human colonies had established in these systems. But that still left a huge area to search. Which would take time; something we didn't have.

"We need more clues, Commander," I said, turning to Elasippus then back at the holo with a frown of concentration. "Information on large illicit Kappa shipments, for instance." I raised a brow, looking from one to the other. Serge averted my gaze and fiddled with something on the table. So, he didn't want to join the discussion. Fine. I didn't need him. To chaos with him, I thought. This wasn't his strong point, anyway. I focused on the two Eosian commanders.

Elasippus inflated his chest with a grin, uniform straining, and stretched back against the chair. I thought it might break. "What you need is someone with connections, Commander Hawke…Eclipse connections."

"And you know of such a person?" I asked, shifting forward in my seat.

He grinned at me then glanced at Autochthon, who laughed.

Autochthon offered, "Elasippus soiled his hands with Eclipse once."

"I wouldn't call *dust* soil, Auto," Elasippus quipped. "One feeds plants and the other bakes your brain."

Autochthon ignored his colleague and continued, "Before Barbariccia went to Sekmet, Elasippus intercepted a shipment of *dust* intended for a Spor colony in the 55 Cancri system. Apparently Barbariccia's men stole it from Eclipse, who'd stolen it from the Badowins during an illicit shipment to Fomalhaut."

"What happened?" I asked Autochthon with a sidelong glance at Elasippus. I noticed Serge intently listening for a change.

"Elasippus made a deal."

"You made a deal with Eclipse?" Both Serge and I said at once. We exchanged an awkward look then I turned back to Elasippus. "Are you joking?" I said. He was crazier than I was. I wondered if Rafael had known about this side of Elasippus.

"It wasn't exactly a deal," Elasippus said with a smirk.

"He gave them Barbariccia—"

"I'll tell it," Elasippus cut Autochthon off then turned to me and leaned forward, clasping his great hands on the table. "One of my crew used to belong to Eclipse. How he got with us is another story, but he'd told me that Eclipse have wanted Barbariccia and Dark Sun shut down for a long time. I suppose they were competition. I found a contact through my man and told them that I'd set up Barbariccia with the *dust* I intercepted and have him put away. Eclipse and I have been on semi-good terms ever since."

So, Elasippus had been the one who'd helped put

Barbariccia on Sekmet. I curbed the urge to glance at Serge even though I felt his burning gaze on me. At one time I'd thought Serge had been the snitch; there had been a large reward posted for any evidence leading to Barbariccia's capture. I let my gaze drift to the holo of the systems, mind brushing memories of Sekmet and Barbariccia to life. Of course I now knew that Sekmet was ironically where Barbariccia wanted to be, where he could oversee the operation of his precious *glitter* business while living like a king.

I found Elasippus watching me carefully. "You won't tell *Mon Seigneur*...will you?"

I gave him a tight smile. I hadn't expected that slightly naïve remark from him. "I won't tell Raphael," I assured Elasippus. "Whatever is discussed here in the tactical room remains between us."

I caught Serge's surly look. He was obviously disgusted with my feigned assurance. I wasn't going to tell Raphael because Raphael was dead, not because I was honoring some covenant of confidentiality among us here. I felt suddenly corrupt again and realized that every time I saw Serge looking at me I felt corrupt. I made a point of ignoring him from then on.

Turning to Elasippus with new intensity, I said, "I'd like you to make some discreet inquiries with your connections. Find out about any large Kappa shipments. Where they're going." He nodded. I then turned to Autochthon, "Benny will forward what he has on the specs of the Kraal weapons facility to your ship's com. Chances are the other two facilities are arranged like Kraal. It may help with your strategy for entry."

I then dismissed our meeting, thanking everyone, and without a glance at Serge or waiting for him to accompany me, I stood up and bid them farewell. I made my way directly back to Benny, still docked on *Elyssia*'s port side and wondered briefly if Serge would accompany me; or would he elect to stay aboard the *Elyssia*? I decided I didn't care. Then I heard his perfunctory steps behind me as he silently followed me back.

## TWELVE

The worst part was waiting. Days went by and, apart from communications with the *Boeotia* and the *Elyssia*, the silence aboard Benny was oppressive. There was so much between Serge and I. I couldn't bear the tension in the air. My tryst with Raphael on Lac Boivin followed by my cold-blooded murder had been the last debasement in my already questionable character. I thought how Serge already blamed me for so much: being a thoughtless, ruthless assassin in killing his family members—all of them now; never giving him the MEC but instead giving it to the *Nihilists* and the Guardians; my pathetic performance on Sekmet.

Whatever his personal feelings, he'd returned to *Solstice* to help me. Just like he'd returned to my diverse with a decision to remain at my side on a mission to stop the *Nihilists*. That was why he was here. But it was obvious he hated every moment of it. He'd obviously decided that I was competent—and ruthless— enough to achieve our goal of stopping the *Nihilist* annihilation of humanity.

On the fourth day of our journey, I sought him out. I didn't know what I was going to say, but knew I had to start. He'd taken to hiding himself in the brig; he'd made himself a cozy place in there with his few books and a small cot Benny had rigged for him. I appeared at the door and cleared my throat. He was reclined on his cot, dressed only in his t-shirt and shorts with his legs crossed at the ankle. He looked up from his book.

"I need to talk about Earth..." I began. He visibly tensed as I pushed on, "What happened with Raphael—"

He cut me off sharply, "Rhea, I understand." He snapped the book shut and sat up. "You were under the influence of the powerful *vishna*—at first, anyway, until you found your Enforcer's strength of will." His voice took on an edge. "Heck, even I wanted to make out with you when we were there," he said hurtfully. But he wasn't finished. "Too bad you had to leave your beloved behind, though. Jag 'em and leave 'em, eh?" His eyes narrowed with purpose and blazed into mine with a temper I hadn't counted on. "You used him, Rhea. In the worst possible way. And then you discarded him like a soyka gum wrapper."

My own temper got the better of me. "As if you never did that!" I retorted, thinking of how he'd lied to me about his feelings for me.

He ignored my snide remark. "The bastard was besotted with you, did you know that?" he said sharply. "You even made him cry." He hadn't forgotten my performance and I managed to appreciate the irony: those tears I'd cried as Raphael had been for Raphael. "He must have done something to piss you off, though. Like ask you to marry him or something," he scoffed. I swallowed. Raphael *had* asked me to marry him. "Seems like you're always trying to kill your suitors...Can't let them get too close to you...Like those dead—or brain-dead—colleagues of yours."

Then he turned back to his book. I had never considered him really cruel until then. I hated him right then, especially for speaking those malicious words about what I'd done to Bas. I wanted to flee. Instead I did what I usually do; I lashed out angrily, "Since when do you care who I love!...Or kill!"

His head snapped up and he stared at me. "Since—" He choked on what he was going to say and forced the rest out in breathless words, "...I thought you were a different person."

He'd reduced it to academic disappointment in my character. As if he cared a quintle. What was I to him except a botched mission and a dark reminder of the perfect woman he really loved—and who had probably deserted him for his twin. Was that what was really bothering him? Had V'rae abandoned him for Bastion? I studied his face as he glared at me with far more emotion than his words conveyed, and felt wounded anger boil up.

"You have no right to judge me," I seethed. "I'm not yours to forsake or to condemn. I may remind you of someone you care for, but I'm not her!"

"No," he agreed in a low voice of defeat. Then he bowed his head and opened the book to resume reading. "No, you certainly aren't."

Somehow, those words, delivered in sad resignation, cut deeper than his angry retort. As if needing to pour iodine on my own wound, I added, "But you *can* blame me for your sister's death."

He didn't even look up. "I know." I stared at him in stunned silence. He looked up, eyes cold. "Nice of you to finally tell me."

I blinked hard and stammered, "It was an accident—"

He turned back to his book. "With you, it always is."

I hurried away.

Ω

Serge occupied himself with infiltration strategy and pursued many discussions over the com with the two Eosian leaders, particularly Autochthon. Unfortunately this meant that I spent a significant amount of time out of the cockpit, which was my haven. I peevishly ascribed his obsession with ship-to-ship as a coping mechanism to keep him occupied, at my expense.

Near the end of his tenth long discussion on ship-to-ship, I prepared to rebuke him for taking up so much of the squadron leader's valuable time, and stomped forward from my aft bunk. I was at the entrance to the cockpit when I caught Autochthon's heartfelt compliment on the holo: "Serge, that's brilliant. I'd never have thought that. If you ever want a job as a tactician, give me a call. I know a few people who could use you."

Serge chuckled. I backed away quickly before he noticed I was there and returned aft to the storeroom/infirmary.

As I let myself drop to my bunk, I realized that I'd always underestimated Serge. I'd passed him off as an intellectual agent, a cocktail spy. He was, after all, a very elegant dissembler, a suave and charming interrogator and very persuasive politician. But I'd concluded that, intelligent and sly as he was, he'd lacked the skills for technical sleuthing. I'd forgotten how he'd managed to infiltrate Sekmet, a maximum-security prison from which no one escaped, or his sister's weapons making facility, or Raphael's heavily guarded estate on Earth. I'd half-convinced myself that he'd had Eclipse or *Nihilist* help in gaining access to Uma 1, Sekmet and Kraal. I knew now that he hadn't; he'd done it on his own. His sneaking into Raphael's estate had proved his skill. No one would have helped him there. I'd done him wrong: he had a flare for this game and far surpassed me in it, as it turned out. He'd just cleverly concealed his abilities under a cavalier arrogance. Where I managed to find and get into trouble well enough, he was able to get himself both in and out of it, the latter of which I had yet to learn.

Ω

Autochthon and Serge became good friends, exchanging long colorful discussions about all manner of things. As I furtively listened in on their cheerful discussions I realized that it was the only thing that brought some levity to my ship.

Within a few days, Serge tersely inquired if I wouldn't mind docking with the *Elyssia*, the flagship of Autochthon's *Daedalus* squadron and letting him off. He cited the need for prolonged strategic discussions with Autochthon as his reason and I didn't argue. Serge quickly gathered the few things he had and left me to my ship built for two but made for one.

Ω

Within a day of being left alone, I received a holo from Elasippus: his contact had disclosed to him several incidents of large and illicit Kappa shipments to obscure planets located near the Iota Horologii and Gleise 876 systems. I felt certain that these were the locations of the two weapons making facilities and gave the command to prepare for infiltration as soon as possible.

While Autochthon and Elasippus made preparations, I continued my search for Ka. I'd be left with a small contingent from each of the squadrons. We had no time to waste.

When it came time for the two squadrons to head for their respective targets, I wasn't surprised to find that Serge intended to remain aboard the *Elyssia*. He thought he'd be more useful there. He argued that he had no idea of how to help me track down Ka, and I'd know better how to sleuth him out. "You're the trained assassin," he reminded me coolly on the holo. "You know best. I'd just get in the way...like I usually do."

So we parted. And I didn't think I would see him again. I never did get a chance to explain why I'd killed Raphael. And I never got a chance to find out what he'd meant about V'rae heading for her beloved either. I didn't think I ever would now.

I was left with two ships from each squadron at my disposal, lead by a very young lanky Eosian named Gadeiros from the *Daedalus* squadron. Something about him, perhaps it was his naïve eagerness, reminded me of Bas, and endeared me to him instantly. Both Autochthon and Elasippus assured me that they would contact me via our agreed-upon code as soon as they'd reached their destinations and fulfilled their missions to destroy the weapons facilities. They were then to join me and assist me, if I still needed help with dispatching Ka. I knew that Serge would have departed for some wayside planet by the time Autochthon joined us.

Ω

Gadeiros turned out to be a lot more like Bas than I'd initially thought. As a result, I ended up spending most of my time in his friendly company with Benny docked to his *fugitive* ship. I found Gadeiros's irreverent humor both annoying and endearing at the same time. Once he realized that I was approachable and wouldn't bite, he relaxed and treated me like one of his own crew; respectfully, but not immune to his strange humor. He even had Bas's propensity for practical jokes. When I first came onboard, he offered me some specialty Eosian appetizers, a small flat pastry in the shape of a frying pan, with a pastry 'handle'. He raised a hairless brow at my hesitation and grinned at me in invitation. "It's called spart, after the jungle epiphyte we make the filling from."

I eyed the filo-like pastry then took a bite of the handle and chewed. The spikes of the pastry cut like glass in my mouth!

I ungracefully spit it out on the table with a choking cough and glared at Gadeiros.

"I thought you said you've eaten Eosian food before," he said, laughing hard with amusement, lavender skin deepening to purple. "You're supposed to suck it until it's soft."

"Right," I said, scowling at him with a swollen tongue as he continued to laugh. *"Each of us must sometimes play the fool—Yiddish proverb,"* I said, shaking my head with a chuckle. Once I did as he instructed, the spart tasted wonderful, a little like marzipan in sweet lemon pastry. Gadeiros then informed me that he'd made it himself from ingredients he'd brought on board and I smiled, impressed.

Gadeiros prided himself on being somewhat of a gourmet chef and liked to cook for his crew. Once he'd discovered my adventurous palate, he became eager to share the dishes of his culture with me and we shared many meals together, drinking Earth's wine and eating exotic Eosian food, spiced with laughter and stories about his world or those I'd visited.

It was after I leaned back, sated with one of his wonderful meals, a glass of wine in my hand, that Gadeiros introduced me to the strange fika fruit and the fascinating ecology of the Eos jungle. The fika resembled a large yellow gourd with the flesh of a cantaloupe and a strong nectar-like fragrance. He'd cut it in half and presented it on a plate that he placed in front of me.

I looked up inquiringly at him and found him smiling smugly. That meant I had to guess. Which usually meant something was amiss. I turned back to the fruit set before me and inspected it. It had a strong nectar-like fragrance with a firm fleshy part next to a thick tough husk with white and dark seeds— fertilized and unfertilized, I presumed—embedded in it like a watermelon and a softer core of fibrous material. I pointed to it.

"What's left of the flowers," he said.

I nodded but frowned in slight confusion.

"Go on," he urged with a conspiratorial smile and a wave of his hand at the fika fruit.

I pursed my lips and gave him a quick warning glare then took the fruit in my hands and bit into the fleshy part, slurping the juice that spilled out. It was delicious! Like mango, passion fruit and cantaloupe combined. I looked up and smiled at him. He watched in quiet appreciation as I took another bite and chewed and swallowed down the soft white seeds and harder dark seeds of the fruit.

Gadeiros nodded. "Good, eh?"

"Yes, very," I said, waiting for the blow.

It came: "Eosians usually spit out or poke out the insect adults—"

I choked mid-bite and threw down the fika on the plate. Gadeiros cackled. He took a chair beside me and leaned over the back of it with his arms. As I wiped my mouth and glared at him, he explained, "We only eat fika that have insects inside them. They make it edible. Otherwise it's very poisonous."

I leaned back in my chair and eyed him askance as I took my wine glass back in my hand, and ran my tongue over my upper lip.

"When the insects mate inside the fruit, they release a chemical that neutralizes the poison made by the fika to protect itself from being eaten before it's ready to spread its mature seeds, which are too small to see. This activity makes the fruit drop off the tree, so we only harvest fruit that have fallen to the ground. It starts with the female feek entering the fika fruit through its small hole, there." He pointed and I reluctantly looked, swallowing convulsively. "The hole is so small that the feek tears off her wings as she pushes through," he went on. "The first flowers are male and undeveloped still so she collects no pollen from them. Once she reaches the back of the fruit, where the female flowers are, she dusts them with the pollen from the fruit she herself grew up in. Then she lays her eggs and dies."

I swallowed, stomach clenching, and wondered how many little insects I'd just eaten.

"Male feeks emerge first," Gadeiros blithely continued. "They mate with the female hatchlings and enlarge the hole so the female feeks can leave without tearing off their wings. The male feeks then die soon after mating. While the female feek larvae grow inside the fika, it makes seeds that were fertilized from the pollen the adult female feek brought in. Meantime the male flowers develop so that the female insects can take pollen with them when they leave. This activity causes the fruit of the fika tree to fall, making it available to be eaten by birds and other animals, which spread the seeds through their feces—"

"Wonderful!" I managed. I clapped my hand over my mouth and ran for the washroom, hearing Gadeiros bark with unalloyed laughter.

## THIRTEEN

Serge was right; I did know how to find Ka. As a plan began to formulate in my mind, I found myself wandering to my clothes container and I absently pulled out Raphael's shorts and soft cambric shirt. For the life of me, I don't know why I'd kept his things. But right now, I was grateful. They would come in handy.

Ω

"Are you sure about this?" Benny posed in his usual skeptical voice of reason.

I smiled out of the side of my mouth. "Dead sure. Just take us right in, Benny." I'd already instructed Gadeiros and his four Class B *fugitive* ships to meet me at a pre-determined rendezvous point and await my further communications. I had to do this alone. Benny had earlier informed me that the MEC design file that I'd sent to Ennos no longer existed. It had been destroyed. That meant that he'd tried to transfer it. Benny had tapped all my messages with a tether signal to keep track of their whereabouts. While the original design destroyed itself in Ennos's office, its copy died in transit to the *Ulysses*.

"Why are you turning yourself in to the Iota Hor Precinct?"

"Who said I was turning myself in?" I quipped.

If Benny could shake a head he would have. Instead he answered noncommittally with that much used all-meaningful word, "Fine." He added, "Suit yourself."

Ω

I landed Benny in one of the Guardian hangers, knowing full well that I'd set off several alarms.

As I emerged from my ship, I saw half a dozen Eosians arranged in a semi-circle around Benny's hatch, all with *pocket* pistols aimed at me. I recognized Aeamon at the center. He was the leader of the precinct's security squad and we had never gotten along. He'd let me know in clear language that he thought me an arrogant and conceited bitch with no regard for his race; I'd thought the same of him.

I smiled wryly at him. "What were you expecting? A criminal?"

"Where's Rhea Hawke?" Aeamon demanded. I stood as Raphael in his shorts, cambric shirt and sandals. "This is her ship. Did you know that you're harboring a dangerous criminal who's wanted for murder and recently escaped from Sekmet?"

Ignoring the *pocket* pistol aimed at me, I turned my back to him and climbed down Benny's ladder. I then approached him with my long stride, and saw him draw back as I got to within touching distance of him. For once I was almost equal height to him; Raphael had been quite tall, I realized. I'd never liked Aeamon; somehow, he reminded me of what I used to be like. "She's my friend," I said. "But she's not here. I am. And you *will* take me to see Ennos."

Aeamon studied me for a moment, and then made a quick decision. He brusquely gestured to two of his guard to flank me and stepped back with his communicator. After a brief exchange in a low voice, he nodded to me. "Apologies. Ennos will see you. We'll kindly escort you there."

"Thank you," I responded evenly.

"Excuse me, Mr. Martinez," Aeamon said, "But we do have to check for concealed weapons." He patted me down, brushing his hands loosely over my body and I was glad I hadn't brought my *pocket* or MEC along. Satisfied, he nodded and led me out of the hanger.

It felt odd, coming back, I thought as I walked down the Great Hall. The last time I was here, Euaimon had intervened and surprisingly helped me get away.

Within moments, Aeamon ushered me into Ennos's office with a curt nod at the round Eosian and left. I stood alone with Ennos, regarding me with a guarded smile as he came forward to greet me.

"Excuse my casual dress but I was in somewhat of a hurry to get here," I said and offered my hand in greeting. Ennos took it in a loose handshake and at the touch of his hand, I felt an odd stirring below and realized to my astonishment that it was the beginnings of an erection! There was apparently enough of Raphael coursing through me to arouse his erotic sensations. I knew instantly that he and Ennos had been torrid lovers once. I'd guessed at Raphael's appetite for young boys; I hadn't expected this. From either of them.

"So, how's Rhea?" Ennos posed in a cool tone after letting go.

"She's marvelous, especially on her back." I gave him a churlish grin.

He wiped his sweaty brow in frustration and went to sit behind his massive gadpie desk. "Where is she?"

"In my pants these days," I quipped to his bewildered look. I grinned at my private joke as I slid, sprawling, into a chair. "Do you think I'm going to tell you where she is?" I added soberly. "You were ready to send her back to Sekmet."

Ennos pursed his lips in silent confirmation then sucked air through his teeth annoyingly. "She's well, I trust," he persisted, hands nervously tapping the desk.

"Of course she is," I said tersely. "She's with *me*." Was I lathering it on too thick? I gauged Ennos's response and noticed his look of disgust. He didn't like Raphael. They'd obviously had some kind of falling out. I couldn't access that memory, although I now knew for certain that Ennos was a Vos and had passed through the gate some thirty years ago as V'lem. He'd murdered the Outer Diverse Ennos and had taken his place. "I didn't come here to discuss my love life, Ennos. I came to find out why you've betrayed me."

He straightened suddenly, sucking in his barrel of a chest. "Betray you?" He looked surprised but I smelled his tension rise. His mauve skin deepened to violet. "How's that?"

"The list," I simply said.

He understood immediately and nodded to himself with a knowing smile. "Ah, the list, of course. You're wondering why you're on the list." The smile curved in private amusement. Ennos stood and came around the desk to approach me. I stiffened in the chair. "You'd never believe me if I told you, Raphee. Do you know who Rhea really is?"

My heart beat fast but I hid my apprehension under a casual expression. "Of course I do."

"No, you don't," he called my bluff, studying me with a sneer. "She's my *daughter*, creon." Something in my expression made him laugh. A short giddy bark of delighted amusement. "Even she doesn't know; her mother never told her," he added. I hadn't expected this and forced my breaths even. "This is bigger than you, Raphee. Bigger than saving your pathetic depraved fiefdom on Earth or letting you continue your precious movement."

So, that had been Raphael's ruse with Ennos and the *Nihilists*. He'd cleverly traded his apparent self-centered greed as a corrupt spiritual leader for the services of his Eosian guard. The *Nihilists* had obviously promised him that they'd leave him and his harem alone in exchange for the use of his elite guard. It was a cozy little ploy, until I'd messed it all up.

"You didn't think me capable of it, eh?" Ennos giggled like a girl. "Rhea's mother was stunningly beautiful." Of course she was, I thought, she was an Epoptes, even though she didn't know it. "Ten times more beautiful than her daughter, who's a bit of a looker herself, eh?" He winked. "The mother's still a beauty. Blessed Epoptes, I might have even married her, Raphee," he confided with an oily grin. "But she was a cheap harlot and I was moving up the ranks. I had no time for a whore and her brat."

"You were a man on a holy mission..." I said, holding back my anger with a cold sneer.

"That's right." He sneered back.

"For the *Nihilists*."

He sneered. "She's like *me*. You understand? Rhea's a Vos. She belongs to *me*—not to you."

"Oh, really?" I snarled, trembling inside with anger. "You let them send her to Sekmet, knowing she was innocent."

He fixed cold eyes on mine in a steady unrepentant gaze. "*Let* them?" He broke out into a peel of churlish laughter. Leaning his brawny hands on the arm rests of my chair, he shoved his face close to mine. "Sacred Universe, I made sure she went. I told them all about her misdeeds." I stiffened. "She had a job to do there."

Barbariccia. My face tightened in a losing battle to hide a wounded glare. So, *this* was my father. Not the hero, Mark Hawke, I'd idolized; but a cold-hearted *Nihilist* Vos who had gladly played and sacrificed his daughter to their selfish war. Then it dawned on me that perhaps Ennos was the legendary Nihilist agent, *the Rose*. He'd sent me to Sekmet to kill Barbariccia.

Ennos stared at me with a puzzled look. He'd obviously not expected the expression of pain that I couldn't hide. Certainly not the tears that forced their way to the surface. He shrugged. "Frankly, I don't see what you see in her, Raphee. She's a mean cold bitch."

*Thanks to you*, I thought.

"As for her, if she wants to jag around with a slime-blenoid like you, I actually don't give a quintle. It's her jagging life. But only on my terms."

"What do you want of me, then?" I managed to get the words out in a fairly steady voice. "My men are ready to help. My two best squadrons, the *Odysseus* and the *Daedalus* are waiting for your word to meet at the agreed rendezvous. But I need you to take me off the list. I don't trust you, Ennos, so I'll need reassurances from Ka himself."

Ennos straightened and raised his head up to sneer down at me with pursed lips and a hairless frown. "You get nothing from me until I know Rhea is all right. I want to talk to her."

I hadn't expected this and glared at him. How was I going to achieve that? My mind scrambled then lit as if on fire. "I can do better than that. You can see her too. Touch her, even," I grinned sinisterly. "Your *precious* daughter," I snarled.

Now it was his turn to look surprised.

I nodded. "Yeah, I hid her on the ship. She's with me. She goes everywhere I go. We're inseparable, " I ended with a mean smirk and before he had a chance to react I rose from the chair and snatched his sidearm. I had his *pocket* in my hand. "Just you and me, Ennos."

His eyes turned soft and lambent. I winced as he stroked my cheek like a lover. I felt revulsion roil with a remnant desire. It made me want to vomit. He'd caught my flinch. "We had something wonderful once, Raphee," he said in a maudlin voice.

I couldn't stand it and recoiled, pointing the *pocket* at his waist. "No funny business, Ennos," I said. "Let's go."

He shrugged then silently led me back to Benny without incident; I kept one hand in my shorts pocket, wrapped around the concealed sidearm. Ennos gruffly instructed the guard to let us inside Benny. I waved Ennos ahead of me and followed him inside. Once the hatch door closed, I rapped him on the back of the head with the gun, knocking him out cold. He fell with a thud. I stared down at him for a long moment.

My father. Who picked up strays...not to help them, but to manipulate them. I released a long breath at the thought. Then with a shudder, I stripped, took a deep breath and centered my mind to find my inner universe. After switching back to my human form, I put on my flight clothes, black trousers and charcoal grey top, and belted on my MEC. I tied Ennos's hands behind his back, then crouched beside him, MEC resting on my lap, and waited for him to awaken. What morbid thoughts swirled through me I can't say.

When he finally stirred and looked up groggily, I stood up with my MEC pointed at him. "Hello...*father*," I said, mouth snarling.

He sat up on the floor and rubbed his head, blinking up

at me. "Rhea...so, he told you."

A part of me really wanted to cry, but I'd never shed tears in Ennos's presence—as close to it as I'd come on many occasions—and I wasn't about to start now. I gathered up all my strength and growled, "Where's Ka?"

He smiled. "How are you? Is Raphael treating you well?"

"What do you care?" I snapped, voice as sharp as blenoid teeth.

"I'm your father." I didn't respond to that and Ennos searched the storage room. "Where is he? I want to thank him for this," he said, rubbing his head gingerly.

"He's resting."

Ennos fixed his gaze back on me and moved to get up. I twitched my MEC and raised my brows in response. He got the message and stayed put. Then he sighed and asked, "Why are you with him? He's a cruel degenerate who loves only himself."

"You should know, I guess," I said languidly. "How'd you meet? At a Virgil City parlor?"

"That was fresh, daughter," he chided. "But it's closer than you think. I was in charge of the investigation of his mother's strange death. We formed a...friendship. It went from there."

Good God! Was my father a pedophile too? Or did that relationship happen only later? How many more ways was I to find Raphael's and my life intertwined? This was too much!

"You've made an interesting choice, Rhea," he went on, studying me. "One I wouldn't have thought you'd make, but then it's your life. Raphael will be spared from the onslaught, of course; he's made sure of that with his deal." Ennos eyed me critically and shook his head. "In truth, Rhea, I'm astonished that you hooked up with him—or more to the point, that he hooked up with *you*. I could tell from my conversation with him that you're definitely his flavor of the month. How'd you manage to push his buttons? You must have learned something on Sekmet..."

I felt such an urge to strike him senseless; he'd casually referred to Sekmet as though it was a prep school. I fumed in silence.

He went on, "so, I suppose it's a better choice than going

121

with that loser you were hanging around with before...that Bastion punk—"

"Enough!" I let anger heat my face and surged forward, driving the MEC into Ennos's neck. "I asked you a question earlier," I snarled.

"Yes, the whereabouts of Ka," he said with forced casualness, violet eyes betraying a little fear. "You don't trust me either?"

"Not after the last time I was here," I said, breathing on his face.

He sighed again. I didn't think he was particularly skilled in the art of sophistry and waited cynically for his response. When it came, I was vindicated: "I had to do what was expected of me. The precinct watches my every move."

"You *are* the precinct," I retorted, drilling the MEC further into his neck. "Okay, you've seen me," I hissed. "Now, tell me where Ka is."

He grimaced and stared wide-eyed at me, breathing with difficulty. I was hurting him, cutting off his air. He'd called me a cold bitch; well, I considered, I could still be one.

"Rhea—you're hurting me—"

"Where!" I drilled in.

"He's on Cancri-4, a moon off 55 Cancri b," he choked out. "At least until the attack. After that I couldn't say."

"That'll do." I stood up, pursing my lips. He gasped in some air and rubbed his neck. I said, "Benny, start up engines. Ready on my mark for rapid take off."

"What are you doing?" Ennos said, betraying panic.

I sidled to the starboard-side window and watched a dozen Guardians assemble in the hanger, all with *pocket* pistols aimed at Benny. Then I caught a glimpse of Euaimon by one of the doors. "Don't worry...Father," I said, scanning the Guardian line, "I'm not taking you anywhere..." Then I saw it—a pulse-rocket. A land-to-air weapon for taking out a ship. Surely, they wouldn't do anything with Ennos still on board?

"On my mark take off, Benny!" I repeated, dashing over to Ennos and gruffly pulling him to his feet.

"Any time you're ready, Rhea," Benny gave the okay.

I flung open the hatch and shoved Ennos out. As he stumbled down the hatch ladder and sprawled on the floor, I yelled, "Now, Benny!"

Ennos stood up with a glance at me and I threw his *pocket* down to him. As he caught it, I saw Euaimon give the signal and I ducked behind the hatch as Benny rose in a roaring din of heat and exhaust; I didn't need to. The Guardians opened fire, but not on me. I watched, horrified with my face pressed against the window, as a dozen pulse waves sliced my incredulous father and seared him to shreds, *pocket* flying from his severed arm.

Euaimon and I stared at one another for an infinite instant. His brow line curved up and he gave me a mock salute. Then he smiled at my stricken face. A smile that I could not comprehend.

Benny screamed out of the hanger and soared straight up. "Stealth trajectory, Benny!" I commanded sharply, dumbly staring through the window at the receding town of Neon City. No longer my city. Or my home.

$$\Omega$$

To my confused relief we weren't pursued. When I reached our agreed upon rendezvous, I hailed Gadeiros and he bid me join him on his ship. Although he seemed relieved to see me, he looked pale and troubled. "What's the matter?" I asked.

"I'll tell you when you get onboard."

I didn't like the sound of that but kept silent and proceeded toward his ship for docking. He stood waiting for me at the hatchway once I did.

"Okay, I'm onboard," I said, eyes stern with expectation.

"I've had word from the squadrons," he responded darkly as he led me past his two crewmembers to the cockpit. I immediately stiffened. "I'll take over, Reamos," he said to the young Eosian in the pilot's chair. The boy briskly left and Gadeiros sat down, bidding me to sit next to him. As I glanced out at the vastness of black space ahead of me, he continued, "You'll be satisfied to know that they were successful in destroying both weapons facilities and most of the MEC *phantom* fleet with them. The *Odysseus* is expecting coordinates from you for the next rendezvous."

My shoulders sagged as the tension drained from me and I turned to face him with a hopeful smile. "That's good…isn't it?" Then I realized what he'd said. "What about the *Daedalus* squadron?"

Gadeiros didn't smile back. His eyes met mine and there was pain in them. "There were casualties, Commander."

"Oh." I blindly brushed my face with my hand, mind racing into places I didn't want it to go. I kept my voice steady, "What were the casualties?"

"Most of the *Daedalus* squadron…" He paused and took a big swallow. "Actually, with the exception of one ship, *all* of the *Daedalus* squadron. And the *Elyssia*, herself."

My heart slammed. "Oh, my God," I breathed, leaning forward. Serge was on that ship. Silence stretched before us, punctuated with the thrum of the ship's environmental system and the blinking console.

"Only one of the Class B *fugitives* got away to tell us and that was just because Benoît was on board and somehow got away," Gadeiros said. I looked up at him. Benoît was the only human in their squadron. The boy with flaming hair I'd noticed when Autochthon and Elasippus had first assembled their men before me. He was the only crewmember I'd noticed in a sea of anonymous mauve hairless faces. Forty-nine faces that I'd never remember, now gone.

"What happened?" I asked.

"Autochthon and Elisappus successfully destroyed the facilities on Theletus and Bythios-2. They got most of the MEC *seed phantoms* inside before the *Nihilists* even knew what happened. But, apparently a whole unit—eight MEC *phantoms*— was out doing drills when Autochthon's squadron bombed their facility. The MEC fleet ambushed them. They used the MEC wave to kill everyone, except Benoît, the only non-Eosian…"

And Serge, I added silently to myself.

"Then they destroyed the ships at will, like target practice."

"But the *Elyssia*—Serge was aboard. He isn't Eosian, so he could have..."

Gadeiros shook his head at me, his face a torment of silent pain. "He might have, but he didn't. Benoît saw it go. It's what gave him the chance to escape. When the *Elyssia* blew, the blast was blinding for a few seconds, letting off a blue-particle wave; it gave Benoît the chance to slip into stream. Even so, he was injured and his ship was disabled by the blast. The *Odysseus* squadron found him drifting in the 37 Geminorum system and he was barely alive."

My hand had flung involuntarily to my mouth at the shock of it. I was sure that the pain expressed on Gadeiros's face reflected my own. Serge was my beloved. But I wasn't the only one grieving for a loved one; Autochthon was Gadeiros's surrogate father. And the squadron was like a close family. Without thinking, I leaned over and seized him in a strong embrace and felt him shudder in silent grief beneath my arms. We embraced, both crying for several moments; soldier of the Elite Guard and trained assassin of the Galactic Guardian Enforcers. For those brief moments we were just two people grieving our loved ones.

Ω

We met the rest of the fleet off EpsEri b. I docked Benny to Elisappus's flagship, the *Boeotia*, and was met at the hatch doorway by Elisappus himself. He looked grave but calm as we greeted one another with the customary handshake, my small hand lost in his giant mauve paw. He then turned and beckoned someone forward and I noticed for the first time that we were not alone in the hatch-chamber. A human boy with flaming hair shuffled toward us, avoiding my gaze. I recognized him as the young lad in Autochthon's squadron, the only face I remembered in that now obsolete group of men.

"This is Benoît," Elasippus said sternly. "I thought you

might like to question him about the ambush, Commander Hawke."

I did. But one look at the boy made me regret my intention. I could tell he was afraid of me and wondered what stories had circulated about me. A year ago I might have forced him at attention and grilled him relentlessly. Now, I could barely look at him as he trembled beneath my gaze. He was no older than the acolyte, Jacques, with large round eyes of lambent green and curly hair that tumbled like molten fire to his shoulders. One of Raphael's beautiful flowers. And I wondered if Raphael had plucked him as well. Or had he spared the boy for this? Benoît's eyes shone up at me in a terrified gaze as I spoke. Trying to make my voice as gentle as I could, I picked my words carefully, "You were the only one who survived, Benoît..." Then I swallowed a lump in my throat as I watched him squirm and understood his incredible guilt.

"I should have stayed and fought," he stammered between halting breaths. "*Mon Seigneur* will—"

I silenced him with a stern look then placed my hands on his shoulders. It was typical of one still so inexperienced, to shoulder the guilt of the massacre. I recognized the feeling. As the lone survivor, somehow it seemed natural to blame oneself. "No, Benoît, *Mon Seigneur* would—" I cut myself off with a glance at Elasippus. "I know you did the right thing. You were one ship among many hostiles; you couldn't have done anything by staying, except get killed too. And we needed someone to come back to tell us what happened." I pressed his shoulders and added softly, "Don't blame yourself, Benoît. We're just glad you made it back," I added. I released him and straightened. "That is all." I turned to Elisappus. "I won't need to question him any further. Thank you."

Elasippus blinked at me for a moment, as if surprised. Then he turned to the boy. "You may go, Benoît."

I saw Gadeiros waiting at the doorway, smiling at the boy, and felt gladdened. If anyone could make him feel better it was Gadeiros.

"Come, Commander Hawke," Elasippus said gravely,

touching my arm. "We have matters to discuss."

I nodded and let him lead me to his private quarters.

## FOURTEEN

I found his quarters more opulent than I would have imagined for a military man like Elasippus. But then again he'd served for many years under Raphael, who was not known for modesty and stark design. I smiled in appreciation, scanning the bold paintings and tapestries on the wall—more nudes of human females, of course—the ornate and colourful furniture, thick shag carpet and lavish decorations. Souvenirs from exotic worlds he'd visited.

As my gaze swept the richly decorated room, I noticed a holo of Elasippus and Autochthon. It was a cheerful portrait taken recently and clearly demonstrated that the two men were close. I felt my throat close and swallowed down my guilt. I'd been responsible for that loss. And so much more; all those valiant young men—boys, who'd barely begun their lives. A sob tore up my throat and I quelled it with a half moan that I hid by clearing my throat.

"You were compassionate with the boy," Elasippus remarked behind me.

I gathered my composure and turned to him to meet his steady gaze. "He looked as if he thought I'd bite his head off," I said, offering a faint crooked smile.

Elasippus let his lips curl slightly in a wry smile. "He's heard the stories. We all have."

My gaze faltered and I lost the smile. "I'm not...that person anymore."

"So, it seems," he uttered quietly, drawing my gaze back to him. "Sit, sit," he instructed, waving a hand at one of the comfortable chairs. As I took a seat, he went to his small credenza and poured a drink then handed me a wide stubby glass with an amber liquid and two ice cubes. "Here." It smelled pungently of distilled alcohol and medicine. I accepted it and looked up at him with a faint inquisitive smile. "It's bourbon whiskey," he said. "Single barrel." He held up his own glass. "It's made on Earth from a grain called barley and the very best comes from a place called Kentucky." He then clinked his glass brusquely against mine. "Down the hatch, as they say." He drained his in one long draft and growled then blew out a loud exhale of appreciation. "Go on, it's the best thing for you." He waved his empty glass at me.

I took a large gulp of the vile-smelling stuff. It burned down my throat and took my breath away for an instant. Then warmed me through with the smoky taste of peat and alcohol.

He watched me with a smile of appreciation. "See? It's working already. It's put some color back into your cheeks." He looked away for a moment, wrinkling his hairless brow in a thoughtful frown. When he turned back to me, his eyes sparkled like amethysts. "I know what you're thinking, Rhea." He'd used my given name for the first time. "I know a lot more about you than you think too." He smiled enigmatically. I stiffened and searched for signs of maliciousness. I found only dedication and genuineness. "He might have left the ship prior to the attack."

"What?" I straightened in the chair and felt my neck tense, despite still feeling the heavy warmth of the whiskey weigh my shoulders down. "Who?"

"Your companion. Your man." I hadn't expected this from Elasippus either. He'd returned to the credenza and poured himself another drink. Before I could refuse, he poured more into my glass then sat across from me in a sprawl. He studied his glass for a moment, swirling the ice cubes, and let his lips curl in a faint smile. "You're much more fond of that companion of yours than you'd care to show. And he of you. I saw how he looked at you when you didn't know he was…a kind of sick puppy-blenoid yearning look." He chuckled, still studying the ice cubes in his glass. "Perhaps you'd had a silly lover's quarrel over some misunderstanding, eh?" He looked directly at me and our eyes clashed. "And you are feeling more than just remorse because you didn't have a chance to right it before you lost him." I swallowed convulsively but kept my gaze steady. He continued, "I know the feeling. I wish I'd settled a few things with Auto before he...Well, anyway..." He smiled sadly to himself then took in a long breath. "They stopped for some technical equipment on Remy 6, a forsaken little planet in Upsilon Andromedae with nothing on it, except for a tiny spaceport with a transportation link to the Galactic Shuttle Service."

"You think Serge might have gotten off there?"

"It's possible. That shuttle goes pretty well anywhere in the Galaxy." He pushed out his great belly and pointed at me with his glass. "Here's my thought: The MEC wave that instantly killed Auto's crew wouldn't have affected him. So, why didn't he pilot the ship away? Maybe because he wasn't on board." With that he tossed his whiskey down with an exuberant smack of his lips and sighed loudly with an appreciative glance down at his empty glass.

It was a convincing argument; one I'd already considered, and abandoned. I thought it unlikely for practical reasons: Serge had demonstrated himself as a valuable tactician, which Autochthon would have prized for his mission. Autochthon would have kept Serge onboard out of respect and I saw no reason for Serge to abandon the mission for safety reasons; whatever else he was, he wasn't a coward. I remembered the time I'd thought that Bastion had been killed by that genetic Q-bomb, only to hear that he'd survived. I refused to give in to that devastating kind of hope now for Serge.

Hope, compassion...they'd always been my undoing. I smothered a sob by forcing down more of the whiskey. It blazed a fiery trail down my throat, both raw and pungent with a lingering after taste of bog. Why didn't I feel him gone? I'd almost expected to feel a rift in my universe—Epoptes that I was—but there had been nothing. Even though we'd argued like two blenoids all the time, we'd always seemed to know what the other was doing, thinking, or feeling. There'd been a kind of bond that went beyond friendship, beyond anything I'd ever known, a kind of knowledge of home. He *was* my home. Where my heart resided.

I shuddered and buried my sorrow by gulping down the rest of the fiery whiskey, impressing Elasippus, who'd followed my gesture with wide appreciative eyes and a skewed smile.

I drew in a shuddering breath and proceeded to tell Elasippus in a rush of words of our new destination. Thanks to Ennos, I now knew where Ka was. "We should head there post haste, Commander. If we catch the quadrant five particle stream we can get there in three SG days, then—"

Elasippus cut off my nervous ramble with a stern gesture of his large hand. Then he stood up and startled me by pulling me up off the chair then sweeping me into a great bear hug. His brawny arms squeezed me in a crushing embrace.

"First we grieve," Elasippus simply said. "Me for my colleague and friend...and you for your beloved."

Shocked at first, I gave in to his soothing embrace and before I knew it, I'd buried my face in his chest and released my grief in shuddering sobs. When he finally let me go, Elasippus looked down at me with large tear-filled violet eyes and said with a faint smile, "The Rhea Hawke I heard about never shed a tear for anyone, including herself."

I tried to laugh. It came out in a strangled whimper.

"I won't tell the others that you cried, Commander, though it is not really a sign of weakness, eh? Your secret's safe with me." He smiled at me tenderly, wiping his own eyes with his fists. "Your love may have disembarked before the battle, Commander. He was, after all, a civilian. Autochthon might have insisted, even. He was that kind of person. Too damned full of integrity, that Auto." He shook his head sadly.

I nodded. It was possible but not likely, I thought. I met Elasippus's eyes and searched. Did he know the depth of my secret? He'd already confirmed that Serge was my love—not Raphael. He'd started the unraveling; I impulsively decided to finish it: "I'm not what you think I am," I said, fixing a steady gaze at him.

"Yes, you are," he said with a knowing smile and swept his large hand over his baldhead.

It was all the challenge I needed. "I killed Raphael...*Mon*

*Seigneur,*" I blurted out. The words had come out more easily than I'd thought. Perhaps it had been the whiskey. Something about Elasippus's look had drawn it out of me effortlessly. I'd needed so badly to unburden myself to these valiant men since I'd begun the deception. I might as well end it now, I decided. They'd achieved what I'd bidden them to do and I'd been responsible for too many deaths. If Elasippus chose to kill me now, I'd welcome it.

Instead he smiled. A wry smile that shocked me. "He was quite mad, you know," he said, absently swirling his ice cubes in his glass. Of all the things I'd expected this was not one of them.

My eyes narrowed with sudden understanding. "You...*knew.*"

Elasippus turned and lumbered to his credenza. I kept my gaze forward and heard the clink of more ice in a glass then the gurgling stream as he poured himself another drink. He liked his whiskey.

"I suspected," he said behind me after a gulp. "Autochthon and I discussed the possibility. We knew your reputation. I'd heard about some hit list and didn't doubt that *Mon Seigneur* was on it. He had many enemies, some justified. It was possible. We thought you might have dispatched him in the hanger between your talks...when he and you were supposedly...you know...saying your good-byes...you *were* wearing his clothes after all."

I turned to stare at him with the startled dawning of truth. He leaned casually against the credenza returning my gaze with an enigmatic smile. "You were expecting—no, *hoping*—I'd kill him," I said. "Why not just leave his service if you thought him an ill leader?"

"Because he *was* our leader and a very powerful man. We are a loyal guard, dedicated to serve and protect him. We must all walk the fine balance between loyalty and honor, Commander Hawke. I know your story very well. Former Guardian Enforcer. Wanted for murder. Inmate of Sekmet. All the myriad sides of it." I stiffened but he offered me a wry smile and added, "You walk it well, Commander, admirably well. We try also, perhaps not as successfully. In the end our allegiance was to our leader, to *Mon Seigneur*. No matter how bad or crazy he was, we were sworn to him, and to serve his madness as best as we could, ever mindful of striking that balance. Only *Mon Seigneur* could release us."

I let my gaze drop to the floor and studied the bright shag carpet—my feet sank at least three centimeters into it. I let my shoulders sag. I wanted to sink all the way into that soft forest of carpet and disappear. What would Elasippus think if he knew what his *Mon Seigneur* really was? An Epoptes, the very god his kind worshiped. Would he have condoned my killing Raphael so eagerly? When I looked up again I leveled a steady gaze at Elasippus. "What now? What will you do?"

He shrugged. "Nothing. We are yours to command, Commander Hawke. Raphael handed us to you in loyal service, until such time that you deemed fit to release us. It is, I believe, up to you; not to me."

Raphael had done no such thing; I had given the command, disguised as Raphael. "What will you have me do, Commander?" I asked.

Elasippus examined his glass for a moment, as if the answer lay in the whiskey inside. When he looked up at me, he was grave. "*Mon Seigneur* has been…difficult to serve. He was cruel at times and…depraved." I swallowed and thought of all the young boys who'd entertained him, some willingly, others not. "We have done things in his service that we are not proud of, I am sad to say. But this mission of yours carries honor and integrity. It has been both a pleasure and an honor to serve under you, Commander Hawke. My men feel the same, though some of them are still afraid of you," he ended with a wry grin.

I swallowed down turbulent emotions. I hadn't expected this response and felt truly overwhelmed. "Because of me, half of your fleet is gone, and your esteemed colleague, Autochthon, is dead."

"Because of you, I think we may have averted a galactic tragedy," he said with a slight nod at me. "As for my esteemed colleague and friend, he died valiantly in battle, serving a most honorable cause. That is the way any of us would wish to go,

Commander."

Emotion swelled up my throat and I blinked back tears. "Then I would be honored if your guard would accompany me on the next leg of our mission, Commander Elasippus," I said, trying to keep my shaky voice level.

He nodded with a warm smile. "It will be my pleasure, Commander Hawke. But," he then added as if in afterthought, "might I suggest that I deploy part of my squadron in pursuit of this lone MEC unit?"

I blinked in surprise. "To what end? How would you find them, let alone fight them if you did? Elasippus, the MEC weapon is brutally fast and lethal. I should know..." I couldn't help a glance down to my own MEC holstered on my right thigh.

He drained the last of his third glass of whiskey and stepped forward from the credenza, hands placed loosely on his hips in cavalier confidence. "Let me explain something of our weaponry and tools, Commander. Our Class A *fugitive* ships are all equipped with blue-particle screens. If a ship is destroyed, the blue particles are discharged at great speed with a radius sweep of at least ten kilometers. The particles embed in any foreign material and can be tracked by our sophisticated scans. That's how we found Benoît. When Autochthon didn't contact us within the specified time period, we went on a search and found Benoît drifting in the 37 Geminorum system. The boy was injured and must have jagged off-stream. He's lucky to be alive."

I nodded and folded my arms under my breasts, hugging myself. "You're saying that you can track these lone MEC *phantoms*?"

He smiled like a wolf. "I propose that two thirds of my fleet return to the location of the ambush then set out in search-vectors to find the lone MEC *seed phantoms* and dispatch them. Benoît counted eight of them. Shouldn't take too long to find them."

I nodded then brought a hand to my face and stroked in concern. "But there's still the problem of the MEC wave."

Now he was grinning, having anticipated my challenge. "We'll travel with a skeleton Eosian crew of officers and induct help from other species on one of our port-of-calls..." His grin turned into a leer and his eyes sparkled like amethyst. "I have a few favors to call in and I know some good men."

He'd thought it through well. I nodded. "It's a sound plan. Let it be done, then. I don't need too many men for my mission," I said. I'd be on my own for that one, I decided.

"Excellent," he said, slapping his hands against his thick thighs with close to glee. "I will leave you Olomos and two ships at your disposal. I will take Gadeiros and Benoît with me—they would be devastated and shamed if I did not—and we will stop on Remy 6 to drop off ancillary crew and gather our new multi-species crew. It will be a good short reprieve after the assault. I might ask around at the Shuttle Station about a certain human." He smiled wryly. "And you?"

I thought of my trajectory. I'd be passing the neighborhood of Scandia. If Serge was still alive he might have returned there. I tilted my head at Elasippus, thinking of his previous advice. "Perhaps I'll take your suggestion and also take a short break to gather my wits." *And inquire about a certain human,* I added privately to myself.

He nodded approval. "You have something in mind?"

I pushed a smile. "I do."

$$\Omega$$

I saw them off with mixed feelings. I made a point of speaking to each of the twenty-five crewmembers that was partaking in the mission and committed them to memory. I hugged Gadeiros and he made some ribald joke. I laughed and had to fight hard to keep my sobbing gasp that desperately wanted release in check. Gadeiros then gave me a small package and instructed me not to open it until I had returned to Benny. I took it with a nod of appreciation then moved on to shake Benoît's hand with a warm smile of shared loss. "You are very brave, Benoît, and I am proud of you," I said to him. "You are saving our world."

He stood at attention and looked at me with pride, if not

a little fear. I smiled at him with a glance at Gadeiros. Then I stood before Elasippus, gazing up past his massive chest to his kind face.

"Come back," I said and fought down tears. This was no time for crying.

Elasippus smiled tenderly and took my hand in a firm grip then placed his other hand over it. He tipped his face down to speak in a low voice. His brows furrowed in a stern expression but his eyes danced with the glee of the hunt. "You will spoil my reputation, Commander, never mind yours," he chuckled, referring to my expression. Then he pressed my hand in his. "We'll come back because an angel is sending us."

I stared up at him and nodded with a tremulous smile. "Then God speed and God keep you."

With that I returned to my ship and disengaged from the *Boeotia*, accompanied by two small *fugitive* ships. When I opened the package Gadeiros had given me, I found a dozen sparts and only then burst into tears.

**FIFTEEN**

I saw them both long before they noticed me approaching. They were working in the front garden together.

V'rae was teasing Bastion with some joke and he responded by smacking her on her rump.

V'rae spotted me first. "Rhea! What a surprise!" she said happily as I reached the garden gate.

Bastion turned and smiled. I tried to smile back. I'm not sure what came out. I saw him search past me, looking for Serge.

"Come inside and I'll make some tea," V'rae offered and led me inside their modest house to the dining room as Bastion cleaned up.

I noticed a bowl of dried *vishna* petals on the table and before I realized it, I shrank back. V'rae noticed my reaction with a puzzled face. To her, they were a novelty, a wonderful aphrodisiac. But the *vishna* were not my friends. Those sentient souls had conspired against me, torn me from my true beloved and compelled me to desire one of their own...one like *me*, I reminded myself...*my twin*...I pondered the irony with misery. It was Serge who had liberated me, and released what I'd repressed for so long. *Awoken my senses*, he'd once said to me. The very senses the *vishna* had prayed upon; the very ones that had disgusted him so entirely—no, it was my apparent cruelty afterward that had totally offended him. He might have forgiven me all if not for that.

Not knowing what to make of my reaction, V'rae stuttered out an embarrassed laugh and, quickly removed the bowl to a far shelf then added self-consciously, "I hope no one minded that I took some with me..."

I forced a smile of conciliation. "No, I'm sure no one did. I doubt anyone would have noticed."

Sensitive to my dark mood, V'rae grew sober and sat down at the table. "What's wrong, Rhea? Why have you really come to see us?"

I sat down across from her. Forcing my voice steady, I said, "Is Serge—I mean V'ser—did he come by recently?"

She frowned in confusion at me. "I thought he was with you."

I shook my head, no longer trusting my voice. The news hit me harder than I'd thought. I'd foolishly let down my guard...and hoped.

"What happened?" she asked.

I couldn't answer and shook my head with a bridled sob. I was coming apart in front of her. She came beside me and drew her arms around me, holding me in a warm embrace. It was enough to release my dam and tears spilled out. Without knowing the cause of it, V'rae soothed me with long strokes as I sobbed loudly in unrestrained guilt and sorrow.

"But he came back for you, didn't he?" she posed.

I nodded, still sobbing.

"Didn't V'ser tell you?" she asked. I swallowed hard and

sniffled at her, suspending my tears for a moment. "He and I...well, I have Serge now..." She trailed at my expression.

I found my voice. I then told her everything; everything that I hadn't told Serge. About Raphael's seductive power over me, our commingled history and strange energy link. I told her of Raphael's treacherous plan—I even included his greater plan for his own kind, the Epoptes, but left out my true identity. I told her why I had to kill him, but not how. Then I described Serge's reaction and his apparent fate aboard the *Elyssia*. By the time I finished I was sobbing again.

Bastion came in with some tea for me and I flinched, reminded of Serge—V'ser, that is. I couldn't look at him and turned away to sip my tea after a murmur of gratitude.

"Well, he might still show," Bastion said hopefully and passed me a handkerchief.

I blew my nose and looked up with a thankful smile. I was better off not hoping, I thought eventually. After another long sip of tea, I stood up. "I must go. I just came to...in case..." I let the words fade. Elasippus had suggested that I take some time to grieve and relax. I'd foolishly let hope interfere and now realized that I felt more miserable than I had before I came.

V'rae seized my hand. I stared into her eyes. They glinted at me with determination and hope. I saw myself, another version of me. The light in her eyes sparkled with love and peace. That had never been my fate; not since I'd killed a man with my eyes when I was five and began the ruin of a family; two families, I amended—mine too. Yes, I'd given Serge back the love of his life but at the cost of his whole family. Had it been worth it? The irony hadn't escaped me: now that his beloved had rejected him for his twin—and she never would have met Bastion if Serge hadn't brought her here to help me—It was only fitting that I'd caused his death as well. I'd entirely decimated his family.

God...*my* God, was an unforgiving god. He'd condemned a path for me that didn't include love and peace. I was glad V'rae had found hers. She'd been an innocent victim in the intrigue V'ser and his family were involved in; the same with Bastion, who'd lost his family to the *Nihilists*; I was glad they'd found peace and love—true love—in each other's arms.

"Stay with us for a while," V'rae urged, squeezing my hand and searching my eyes. "It'll do you some good."

"I can't," I said too emphatically and tightened my lips in a curt false smile. "I have a fleet of Eosians waiting for me." And a mission to complete. I owed it to those who had contributed their lives or worse: Asphalios, Bas, Autochthon and his men. Even Raphael. But mostly Serge. My one and only beloved, I thought, glancing briefly at Bastion. Then I took V'rae's other hand so we were gripping both hands and squeezed them. Her eyes glistened with tears and I felt my own well up. "Thanks for listening. I'm glad you're happy." And I meant it.

"You'll come back?"

"Sure," I choked out and hastened outside, eyes avoiding Bastion. It hurt too much to look at him. I wasn't sure I would come back.

Ω

Olomos was waiting for me at the spaceport. "Commander," he said with a curt nod as our eyes briefly met. He stood in stiff confusion as I climbed Benny's hatch ladder.

I threw a glance back at him. "We're leaving now, Olomos," I said brusquely. "Next stop is the 55 Cancri system. Where I have an old friend to meet."

"Very good, Commander," he said and turned for his *fugitive* ship.

## SIXTEEN

I stretched back in my pilot's chair and hugged myself then brought my arms up to inhale Serge on the wool sweater I was wearing. I seemed to be wearing it a lot these days, I concluded. The smell of him on that sweater was all that I had left of Serge now and I realized that even that was fading. I laughed, a sob catching in my throat, at the thought of what might have been in some other universe perhaps, then shook my head to clear it and checked telemetry readouts.

Benny and I were headed for Cancri-2, the icy moon off 55 Cancri b, a Jupiter-like planet 5.5 AU from the star. I was reminded of Uma 1 in the 47 Ursae Majoris system. Ka appeared at home on icy planets. Well, perhaps I was too.

Ω

Ka was still eating his meal at a large table when I was ushered in like a welcome guest by the taciturn Eosian guard. The guard then left, closing the mammoth door behind him and I stood facing my grandfather.

Ka looked up from his plate and his beak-like mouth curled into a genuine smile when he saw me. I was in the form of Raphael, wearing Brother Luc's robe and flip-flop sandals. They were a little short and small on me but fit well enough. I approached Ka in my best boy's long stride, feeling the MEC tucked into the waistband of my shorts, well hidden beneath the cloak; the reason I'd chosen to wear the cloak over Raphael's other clothes.

"Ah! My dear Raphael!" he sang out cheerfully. "I've been expecting you."

He had? I didn't let the remark unsteady me and held my smile.

"It took you a while, eh?" His amber eyes smiled.

"*The difficult is done at once, the impossible takes a little longer*—French proverb," I quipped.

He tilted his head at me with some amusement. "There's so much of Rhea inside you already," he remarked.

He had no idea how true that was, I thought with some amusement. "She rubs off..."

"Ah, yes..." Ka nodded. "Here, see, I have your favorite off-world ale, *Szider's Bite*." He pointed to where a pitcher of amber liquid, thickly topped with foam, sat on the table. Two glasses sat beside it. It seemed that he had indeed expected a guest. *Szider's Bite* was a rough-tasting bitter made by Creons—their only claim to fame in the universe—I wouldn't have thought that it suited Raphael's more refined taste.

I approached the table and poured ale in both glasses then handed one to Ka. He nodded to me and stood up with the drink in his feathered hand then raised his glass up to me.

"To all our worlds, Raphael."

"To them all," I echoed and watched him take a hearty gulp as I raised my glass to my lips then gulped down the bitter pungent drink. It coursed like a siege and left a strong metallic aftertaste in the back of my throat; *Szider's* was certainly not *my* favorite off-world ale. I suspected from my grandfather's betrayed attentiveness that the ale was drugged. Alas, I felt compelled to drink or raise undue suspicion. At least I experienced no immediate effects and felt the consolation that whatever the drug was, Ka had imbibed it as well. Then I remembered the shallick oil; my grandfather was willing to subject himself to a lot in order to achieve an end.

Ka drained his glass and put it down on the table then wiped his beak-mouth with a napkin and threw it down. He moved away from the table. I followed, still holding my ale, as he led me toward a large door that opened to an exotic garden, with tiled archway. It reminded me of the passage in Pyramid City that we'd strolled along when I'd first met him.

When we entered the garden, aching with the scent of home, my grandfather reached over to a rose bush and snapped off a blooming stem. Was it my imagination or was everything so much brighter than I'd anticipated? Everything vibrated with garish color and painfully sharp contrast. Even Ka's purple robe was rough with detailed filigree. Studying the blood-red rose in his hand, my grandfather spoke, "Theletus and Bythios-2. That was your doing, wasn't it?" He hadn't turned to face me and had asked his question calmly, more like a curious strategist than one who'd just lost his entire army.

I forced my stuttering steps to continue and nodded with an enigmatic smile, "Yes," and pretended to drink.

"You tamed that unruly Eosian guard; gave them something real and meaningful to do for a change. A mission with integrity and honor." He nodded to himself, absently picking off the thorns from the long rose stem, de-clawing it. "Admirable."

I stared at him, puzzled. I'd stopped walking before I realized it. Why would he say that to Raphael? Unless....

Ka tipped his raptor head sideways to eye me with some curiosity. Feeling rather unsteady, I felt compelled to play my card early and shape-shifted in front of him. When I stood before him as Rhea Hawke, quickly cinching in Raphael's shorts so they wouldn't fall off, I winced at Ka's expression. I'd expected surprise at least. Astonishment, even. He simply nodded in appreciation, though openly impressed.

"You...knew..." I breathed out and began to feel queasy. Damn it, he *had* drugged the ale. And now that I was in a smaller form, I was feeling it more acutely.

"More than you realize, young one. I suspected your lineage," he said, now smiling with memories and twirling the de-thorned rose stem in his hand. "I suspected that Genevieve Dubois was an Epoptes. But I was never sure. I met her once, did you know?"

I shook my head, unable to respond, and felt a dizzy sickness overtake me.

"It was before Azaes was murdered and she escaped the government authorities. In fact, I helped her escape."

My mouth gaped open in astonishment. I'd hoped to astonish Ka. What a fool I was! That remained clearly in his domain.

"It was important to save her child, your grandmother," he said with a curling smile. Of course, I thought. She was to be his mate. "Good thing too," he added with a conspiratorial grin, and pointed at me with the rose. "Or you wouldn't now be here listening to my story. And doing what needs to be done." He chuckled. Despite the reprehensible things Ka had done, I found his laugh lyrically attractive. He was still my grandfather.

His sage-like face swam in and out of focus and I blinked hard to clear my vision. My mouth began to water and I smelled the cloying metallic stench of blood in the back of my throat. What had he given me? The glass slipped out of my hand and fell with a crash on the tile. I felt the cold wetness of ale on my bare feet.

He smiled at my struggling face of growing terror. "It's better for you if you don't fight it like the last time, granddaughter. Give in to its God-wisdom, Rhea, and it won't kill you..."

*Glitter!* Oh, my God! He'd *dusted* me!

I stumbled back in shock and he seized my arm to steady me. I shook him off and stumbled, wavering on my feet and nearly falling, then knocking over a three-tiered plant stand. It crashed and spilled soil and uprooted plants over the tiles. I did a staggering dance to keep from falling.

Ka folded his feathered arms over his rounded chest, and appraised me as I felt the first *dust* shudder overwhelm me. I grasped at a nearby table for support and missed. It sent me staggering like a drunk to regain my balance. "Give in to it, young one. Let it take you on your journey..." I stared at his face, glowing with neon colors. "Everything you have done was orchestrated by me, young one. Every life you took, every man you jagged...every friend you betrayed..."

"No..." I refused to believe that and felt a cloying wave of uncertainty shiver through me. I kept swallowing down the saliva pouring into my mouth. *My* life...*my* destiny...*my* mistakes...

"Why do you think Raphael Martinez remained on the list after striking his deal with the *Nihilists*?" Ka said. "That list was meant for *you*, Rhea. It was *your* hit list."

I gasped.

He smiled. Then he handed me the rose. I blinked at him and, without thinking, accepted the flower in my shaking hand.

"You're *the Rose*."

The shock struck me like lightening. The force of it shook me and buckled my knees. Ka, the room, my whole world, spun into a wide arc and I fell. The rose fluttered out of my hand, spilling to the ground in a spatter of blood red petals. I must have blacked out because the next thing I knew I wavered with hands and knees on the tiled ground, blinking up at Ka. Violent spasms shuddered through me in chaotic waves as my hands slid over the slimy petals, smearing red over the tiles. My grandfather looked down at me with liquid amber eyes, swimming in and out of focus.

Ω

"Now, young one, you begin to finally understand," Ka said, voice soft and cruelly caressing. I pieced together the path I'd taken and it all made sense. I saw it all too clearly and wondered how I hadn't seen it before: it began with Amphalios's ease in breaking into A'ler's system to retrieve the hit list in the first place. He already had the code; and he was a Vos, after all, even if he wasn't a *Nihilist*. Ennos, I surmised, had taken his orders straight from Ka and had briefed Asphalios on how to break in, with or without A'ler's knowledge—I suspected the latter; she didn't know I was *the Rose*. Every move had been planned and choreographed for me to dance through: Asphalios retrieving the hit list; Bas ensuring that I got it; even Ka's blatant hint to me about the music of the spheres to help me break the encryption. Ka had produced an elaborate treasure hunt for me, which led right here.

"Ennos was delighted that his own daughter would play such an important role in our mission," Ka went blithely on as I shivered and twitched uncontrollably on the floor. "He was the only person, besides me, who knew you were *the Rose*." I saw the irony; even I hadn't known. "It was easy for Ennos to instruct Asphalios to infiltrate A'ler's system, masquerading as *the Rose*, and access the vault, Eclipse's encrypted inner file system that only three of us in the organization could access," he continued. The vault that Shle had wormed into and paid dearly for. "The vault was where the hit list was kept. And it's the only place where your precious MEC design now resides. That was very clever of you, by the way...what you did with your design." Ka smiled like a grandfather, proud of my accomplishment. "You embedded some dual code right into the design to destroy it upon

143

transfer without its code-mate, didn't you?"

Ka was no slouch, I thought, trying to control my chattering teeth and keep from biting my tongue.

"We couldn't move it or do anything to it once we'd entered it into our secure system," he went on. "Ennos learned that pretty quick. Alas, when we tried to move the design that I'd put into the vault, it too destroyed itself. I had to physically download the information from my memory into each local com system." He shook his head with an annoyed but impressed smile. "After a time, alas—I am getting old, young one—my memory grew faulty and I could no longer rely on it to provide the design. By then there were only three copies, two of which you'd destroyed already. Of the three of us who could access the vault, two of us are now dead, thanks to you..." he ended, raising a feathered brow at me to emphasize his point.

"Ennos and A'ler," I stuttered out through chattering teeth, still on my hands and knees.

"Which leaves *me*, young one. Thanks to your destruction, the only intact MEC design is now secure in the vault—accessible only by me—and inside your own head."

All I needed to do was kill my grandfather and the MEC design was safe from Eclipse and the *Nihilists*. Could I do it before the *dust* overtook me? Except I'd also sent the design to Euaimon. *One step at a time, Rhea*, I told myself. *Or you aren't going anywhere.*

"Does that make your choice easier?" My grandfather smiled recklessly. I stared up at him. A wave of violent shudders overcame me and sent me sprawling on the cold tiles. But he was not through astonishing me; I saw his whole body shiver then blur and understood that he was shape shifting. When he was finished, I gasped. He looked the spitting image of Raphael! There were a few differences but they were minor. I surmised that Raphael had adopted this familiar angelic form of the Epoptes and that Ka had obviously touched one long ago.

Ka's robe, obviously made of smart material, had adapted to his new form perfectly. I suddenly recalled my grandmother's description: *He was the most beautiful man I'd ever seen...too beautiful.* I now understood my grandmother's obsessed infatuation. "Now, perhaps, my young Epoptes-Vos, you finally understand." Ka bent down to help me up.

Unthinking—mesmerized by his beauty—I let him, and forgot to shudder, as if the *dust* effects had suddenly lifted. Ka's hand was warm and firm around mine as he pulled me to my feet. I stared up into that stunning face that had been my undoing before, violet lambent eyes piercing my soul with an ancient wound, and felt an incredible yearning—not aching desire like with Raphael but a deep longing for *wholeness*.

"The Vos have forgotten what they are; but I remember. In ancient times we were alike, Epoptes and Vos. Twins," he informed me. I thought of Raphael's words: *nous sommes pareils.* "Twins, meant to complement one another in a metaverse held together with love. That is what the ancient souls had in mind for us. That is the key to the music of the spheres and the music that sings through everything."

Twins. Raphael's prophesy sprang to my mind: *the destruction of an old world will be signified by the joining of twin soul mates who will herald the coming of a New Age.* I was certain that, like Raphael, Ka had figured me into that prophecy as well as himself.

"Always have two plans, young one," my grandfather went on blithely. "One for darkness and one for light. I truly believed that darkness would prevail, but I also pinned my hopes on *you*...we—Vos and Epoptes—were one long ago. Now we are again...in *you*."

My hand, still in his, trembled. I then realized that all of me was trembling. But not from *glitter*. What did Ka mean? And what was his intention? My mind raced with thoughts as I searched his nebulous gaze for meaning. Did he mean *me*, as in I represented the merging of Vos and Epoptes, or *in me*, as in the answer lay literally *inside me*? Was he referring, after all, to what Raphael and I had done? I recalled Raphael's words in the aftermath of our lovemaking, words I'd refused to heed. But they came back to me now: *First you'll bear my child—the one I've just seeded you with.* Oh, God! Was I carrying Raphael's child?

My grandfather smiled; warm, solicitous, and caring. Like a patron god, a beautiful god. As if to verify my fearful thoughts, he placed his free hand on my belly and caressed it. I stared into his nebulous eyes, drawn in to that fluid gaze that swirled like the universe itself.

"Did you know, young one, that Rashomon promoted the use of *glitter* to experience God, knowing full well the dangers, particularly to weaker species like humans, of its prolonged use; he knew that they would become addicted and that it would eventually drive them mad and blind and then kill them. For an enlightened man, he was undeniably cruel in his secrecy, don't you think?"

I found it hard to think of Rashomon as cruel. But then again, I'd found it hard to consider my grandfather cruel too; and yet he'd brutally destroyed the mind of my one true friend. He'd done things of incomprehensible cruelty.

"How do you think that Rashomon alone was not killed by the poison gas on Uma 1?" my grandfather asked me. "Because he was there, you know, along with all the others." I'd certainly wondered that very thing. In fact, I remember asking Ka the same question before and receiving no answer. My grandfather smiled bitterly at my expression of curious wonder then added, "He was an Epoptes, Rhea."

I stared at my grandfather. He smiled at me now like I was a child. "He dissipated himself. You—Epoptes—can do that, I'm told. Then your soul reconstitutes the rest of you back. We, Vos, require a device to help us achieve the frequency." Yes, the device Serge had mentioned for absorption. "You already have it inside you, given to you supposedly by the ancient souls. The music of the spheres…"

"B-but," I stammered, thinking of how I'd caught Raphael off guard and melted him, "when I—he must have willingly—"

"He knew it was his time, young one. I give them that. Epoptes always know when their time has come to be re-absorbed into the primordial womb of the galaxy."

"B-but…why…" I trailed, unable to continue. It didn't make sense. Raphael had let me destroy him? And why would an Epoptes promote the use of *glitter* to hasten humanity's awakening? I thought they'd shared the same repugnance for humans as the Vos *Nihilists* and wanted also to keep the two diverses separate.

My grandfather sighed and looked into my eyes with a sadness I couldn't understand. "Ah, the hubris of the gods..." He shook his head. "Epoptes are making the same mistake they made eons ago when they created Atlantis, young one. Many now think they should connect the worlds and rule them both. Now they have their warriors, the Eosians, to do their dirty work for them. They want humans to awaken early, before they are wise enough to know what they are really doing. Then the Epoptes intend to seize and rule both realms, and reign them into order."

I stared, incredulous. The hubris of gods...I thought of what Raphael had said to me on Earth: he'd intended to let the *Nihilists* destroy all humans to keep the diverses separate, then he intended to destroy the *Nihilists*. "But Raphael would have let the *Nihilists* destroy humans with their MEC ships," I challenged.

My grandfather nodded with a sad smile. "Ah, Raphael..." He shook his head again and pursed his beautiful lips. "Raphael was different. A rebel. A narcissist with a different vision of the world. He had other plans..." Yes, I knew them. Ka went on, "He was obsessed with the *vishna* trees and his kin locked inside them; he wanted to free them, but at the expense of many others, too many others."

I blinked up at my grandfather, who looked so much like Raphael. I agreed with my grandfather: Raphael's price of freedom had been too high.

"Let me tell you a story, young one." Still holding my hand in his, Ka's liquid violet eyes seized mine and I stood transfixed like a child, raptly listening to his beautiful voice and watching his beautiful face. "Over ten thousand years ago, after haphazard meetings between diverses, the Vos and the Epoptes, understanding that they complemented each other, agreed to attempt a joining of inner and outer diverses for the benefit of all. They found a species that could evolve into "portals" with the help of Vos in dreams and Epoptes in intellect."

The *Great Experiment* that Serge and Raphael had

mentioned: humanity.

"Together, we awaited 'the Awakening' of humanity," Ka went on. "But some grew impatient for perfection. Seduced by the naïve and beautiful humans, the Epoptes procreated with them. They created the Atlanteans and then became convinced that it wasn't necessary to join the two diverses. They decided that it was too risky, after all, to join with the Vos; and unnecessary, now that they had their super-race, their evolved race, guided by the *joining* of an ancient soul, the *vishna*. So, being great material-energy manipulators, the Epoptes caused the Great Rift, trapping many Vos in the outer diverse with no way to return to their loved ones. One of these was the *Ancient One.*"

Ka bowed his head to me, acknowledging that it was he, and continued, "Not only were we trapped, but the Epoptes blamed us of sedition. They blamed the Vos for instilling in the Atlanteans the hubristic ambitions of greatness that eventually brought about the downfall of Atlantis. The Epoptes then caused the Great Flood on Earth and left with choice members of their super-race for Eos to start all over again with the tree of wisdom, the *vishna*. The *Ancient One*, abandoned with the primitive humans, and separated from his loved ones in the inner diverse, eventually made contact with an ancient nomadic race of bird-like aliens who had harmonic powers and knowledge..."

"The Khonsus," I said.

Ka nodded to me. "They'd come to Earth and I became their leader," Ka continued. "They were revered as gods by the primitive humans. I worked hard at hastening 'the Awakening' of the humans, but soon became disillusioned with them, finding them as shallow and feckless as the Atlanteans, only weaker, more primitive and warlike. The Khonsus spoke of a place that had a great mind-power that transcended time and space. An ancient soul they called Horus. I went with them in search of Horus. I helped them find it around 2,000 years ago and there we found the coupling of the ancient soul of the planet with the migratory tree. Wherever old and new meet there is music, Rhea. The Khonsus learned to sing and recognize the music of the spheres. That was when they achieved the mind-probing power."

He sighed. "Many years passed. I came to realize that this outer diverse was replete with shallow greed and power mongering. I saw that eventually 'the Awakening' would occur and the two diverses would be joined at last. By then it was the last thing I wished to see happen while the Epoptes began to think otherwise. I saw how the Epoptes seduced the great religious leaders into cheating by using the dangerous mind-altering drug, *glitter*; its prolonged use would cause the 'Awakening' to happen earlier than it should. I grew disillusioned and hateful, Rhea. Through my soul-drifting, I formed the *Nihilists*, a group of young Vos terrorists both in the inner and outer diverse, who were devoted to annihilating the evil elements of the outer diverse and regaining control of the gates between the two diverses. Some Epoptes, like Raphael, agreed to the annihilation of humans, though not with the *Nihilist's* larger mandate to also annihilate Eosians, the Epoptes's cherished guard."

That sure amounted to an awful lot of killing, I thought. I remembered Ka's emphatic censure of the Eosians before he turned Bas into a brain-dead vegetable.

"Most Epoptes wanted to keep the gate open and wished to hasten the 'Awakening' of humanity to provide a conduit between inner and outer diverses. Not to let the Vos *out*, but to let the Epoptes and their cherished warriors, the Eosians, *in*."

Ka squeezed my hand, beautiful eyes diving into mine. "So, here we are...on the brink of humanity's false 'Awakening' and a potential war between *Nihilist* Vos and Epoptes, both of whom care not a wit about humanity. If the latter win, which is most likely, what are the potential repercussions to the inner diverse, now open to one and all through the gate? The inner diverse is so vulnerable," my grandfather lamented in a voice close to anguish. "Innocent and ignorant, like naïve children, Rhea." I suddenly thought of V'rae, her gentle callow face, so different from my cynical mask. "You have a responsibility, young one. The *Suntelia Aeon* is upon us. A New Age is dawning...you have seen the ouroboros. You're part of it, part of the great music of the spheres. You can orchestrate it, Rhea. You...and yours..." He stroked my belly.

My grandmother's words rushed, unbidden, to me and filled me with dread: *The music of the spheres is the key to all things, good and evil. Ka is a master of its music and an impeccable dissembler. He's both your key and your doorway. But don't let him rule you!*

Ka looked at me with new intensity. "You can save us all...with my help," he ended, shifting back to his Khonsus form, and before I thought to jerk my gaze away, he'd caught me in the iron grip of his liquid amber pools and penetrated deep, singing his terrifying song of seduction. He combed effortlessly through the familiar territory of my oddly welcoming mind—he'd been there before and knew the way—and penetrated to the depth of me before I even thought to resist. Then my mind, filled with tortured raptness, sang back my grandmother's words: *There is no victory in resistance; only in yielding without surrender.* But surely this was surrender—then I felt him seize my soul with his and gasped.

It was the last thing I remembered of my mundane surroundings. What followed I cannot describe. Mostly sensations: of sparkling galaxies coiling and flowing in a black sea of infinity to a celestial music like I'd never heard, both exalting and humbling in its divine beauty. Like its own galaxy, memories of my whole life flowed past me, carrying me on their cresting wave to the present. And there, with Ka standing resplendent before me, a purpose resonated within me so sparkling and blindingly clear that I cried out with it.

Ω

When I was next conscious of my surroundings, I was hunched on all fours with my forehead resting on the cold tiles, as if abeyant, before Ka in his Khonsus form. I sobbed with the release of...I wasn't sure what. Surely, I'd forgotten something. What was it?

I raised my face to his and found him smiling wisely at me. What did I feel? What had happened? I could not tell. Only that he was pleased. And that I felt a glow of pleasure in it.

"You've done well, young one. You've had a long

journey, traveled far from that churlish brat I met a year ago on Horus. And you have taught me a great lesson."

I'd taught *him*?

"Who would have guessed that a distrustful loveless loner could rally the loyalty and devotion of the most misguided Eosian guard in the galaxy then inspire actions of integrity from brutal men. The apophus, Sekmet, even Raphael have taught you well. Prepared you for me. Made you wise and yielding. And ready for my final lesson. You and I traveled the spheres together. Did you hear it?"

I tearfully nodded. Was I grateful or horrified?

"You have fulfilled the destiny I handed you."

No, destiny didn't have to be that way, I thought, forcing clarity into my giddy mind. I groped for a memory, something Serge had said: *I don't believe in that kind of destiny, Rhea. You are master of your own life...My* life; *my* destiny...I scrabbled for Serge's image, the compass of my heart, the foundation of my mind—

Ka's voice surged like a rushing wave, smashing over my rebellious thoughts, obliterating them: "You obediently let the hit list take you on your journey here to me. Now there is one more thing you must do..."

What was it? I wanted to ask but my mouth wouldn't work. Still on my hands and knees with my face upturned, I stared into those golden pools in desperate silence.

"You'll know when the time comes, young one," he said as if in answer. "I've given it to you." Then his huge feathered arms swept out in a grand gesture of benediction. "It is only providence that Vos and Epoptes have equal party in you, our creation: Raphael penetrated you with seed; I penetrated you with mind."

I wanted to feel horror and revulsion at his words but could only muster discomfort as bile rose in my throat. What had Ka done to me? Oh, dear God...*my* God is a fearful wretched and manipulating god. Ka had infiltrated me, traveled to the depths of my mind and put something there. Something fearful. And terrifying.

In a moment of insane terror, I scrambled up to my feet

and shrugged off the robe to seize my MEC. I pointed it shakily at him in a two-handed grip.

"Go ahead, young one," he said, dismissing my action with a wave of his feathered hand. "Is that not why you came?" He stepped forward and I held my position with difficulty. "I can finally rest now. My work is done. I've lived far too long. My age has come to an end...*you* must usher in a New Age of hope, granddaughter. You are my avatar, my queen of the New Age." Raphael's words. "You will not fail me. You haven't yet..."

"Stop saying that!" I screamed. The MEC slipped out of my hands and nearly fell. What did he mean? I couldn't hang on to my MEC, just as I couldn't hang on to my thoughts. They raced in a febrile haze, chasing themselves, chasing circles around Ka who smiled beatifically at me.

"Go out and mother-in a New Age, a New World."

I couldn't pull the trigger. I knew it. He knew it.

Ka took two steps and seized my hands, turning the MEC so it was pointing up at me; to my chin. He was so strong; my struggles were in vain. He applied slight pressure on the trigger— it was on the universal setting for kill. I stared, face upturned, fixed on his golden eyes. They shone with a strange light. "Not the MEC," he whispered hoarsely. "Your eyes, young one. You must do it with your eyes."

"No!" I cried in a half-sob. I tried to back away and he held me in a vice grip, MEC still pointed up at me, poised to shoot. My heart slammed as I felt that familiar uneasy sensation burn inside me. A heat that begged release or it would consume me.

"Do it! Or I will kill *you*," he commanded sharply. I sobbed and resisted the seething flame with all my strength. Staring into his lambent eyes, I thought of what he'd said to me the last time I'd confronted him: *You weren't born to kill, you were born for love...*

"This is different," he commanded softly as if he'd read my mind, his own mind stoking that sparking fire. He pressed the trigger a little more. "For love, Rhea. This is for love...Do it! For love! NOW!"

I did. Oh, precious God, I released the fire that blazed

inside me in a scintillating bolt. It steamed through my tears, flashed out of my eyes and lit Ka on fire, so close to me that I felt the heat on my face. He let go of me and swiftly melted, glowing with an eerie greenish light, then coalesced into a molten pile that oozed around my feet.

I stood, in a moment of stupor, transfixed, not noticing at first that I still gripped the MEC pointed up at my head. Hands suddenly shaking, I lowered them and let the MEC drop to the tiles in a clatter. The last thought I had, before everything blacked out, was to wonder if Ka had introduced the thought of me killing him during his mind merge. Then I was falling and darkness claimed me.

## SEVENTEEN

You see the Gate on Borrias, its orifice shimmering with sudden life, vibrating. Then hundreds of small spaceships the shape of elongated teardrops burst through the Gate. They fly low over the planet's surface then arc up into the blackness of space. Dread grips you even though you are only vapour, watching without eyes, feeling without a body. You know what they are and where they are bound. *Nihilist* suicide ships bound for your home.

Is this a *glitter* nightmare? It is too vivid, too painfully real. And you know too well what will happen…Wake up! You command yourself to wake but it goes on….

…You are commanding one of the *teardrops*…at least you feel his body. Feel his heart pumping with adrenalin and his short breaths, shallow with fearful exhilaration; you see his sweaty hands, human hands, feel them tremble as they manoeuvre the controls with the fervent determination of a fanatic.

The ship has just jacked the particle stream, and you recognize the Iota Horologii system. The massive red giant, Iota Horologii b, lies ahead. The pilot manoeuvres the ship alongside its other squad ships into formation and you head toward the far side of the gas giant where Iota Hor-2, your home, orbits like a loyal servant in quiet serene beauty. It looks so much like Earth. Your maudlin thoughts breathe through you like a silent fleeting wind.

The pilot barks over the holo-com to the command ship: "Our squad is approaching target," he snarls. You hear the response: "All other squads are in position at designated targets." You know them: Gleise-12; Moner 7; Beleus; Ogium 9; Uma 1, Upsilon 2…Earth…"Commence attack on my mark…"

You feel his thrill of anticipation as the obsessive iron will of duty grips you. You see your hands—the pilot's hands— readying the instruments for lethal trajectory; for a crash landing. The console, once set, locks so the pilot cannot pull out in a last panicked moment of recoil, preventing the suicide bomb. Upon impact each of the ten ships will detonate a particle bomb that will engulf the planet in lethal radiation, which will kill all life.

The ship is locked into its deadly trajectory. You feel it abruptly list into a suicide angle. You see several of the other *teardrops* ahead of you in formation. They will impact on the ground first, the particle bomb causing such a forceful explosion that several ships will detonate in the upper atmosphere, ensuring maximum radiation coverage. Total annihilation. This is worse than your MEC could ever be.

You scrabble at your own terror and anguish, elusive like vapour, but swirling about you in a perfume of horrible inevitability. How can you stop this atrocious thing? You are a ghost without form or substance, without a mind to bend another's. You feel the pilot's abject fear. He fears death; yet he agreed to this mission. He thinks of his little brother…his two dead parents…of the small town he grew up in…

If this is a dream, you think, now is a good time to wake up…you do not wake up.

Iota Hor-2 rushes toward you. One of the ships explodes prematurely in a white flash; Athena, the defence/research space station shot a missile. Your ship shudders briefly but punches through the debris. Within moments it and the other ships are beyond Athena's range and far too close to the moon's surface for the Athena to risk another shot. Nine ships; nine particle bombs. More than enough to unleash a sufficient amount of deadly radiation to devastate an entire planet and all life upon it.

Ω

You are your mother...on Gleise. She sits across from a blank-faced Bas in the outside courtyard of the hospital. She holds a book in one hand, reading outloud to him, and holds his hand with her other. You sense her placid ignorance of what is about to happen.

You feel helpless urgency. She looks up, drawn by the comet-like suicide ships hurtling toward the planet. They chose their time well, when the atmospheric shield was temporarily down. You feel her slight alarm. Staring at the projectiles careering toward her, she drops the book and grips Bas's hand more tightly.

NO!

Deafening smash. You're torn apart. Blinding white flash and searing heat. A hard molten cut through your chest. Blood spurts up into your face—

You man the controls of an Epoptes ship with the purple hands of a giant Eosian. Your squadron bursts through the Gate into the Inner Diverse.

Oh God! You glimpse telemetry and recognize the target: Earth!

...You gaze at the orange tones of sunset bathing English Bay from your flat in Vancouver. You are your mother, in the Inner Diverse. In a Vancouver unravaged by the Vos attack. You feel her serene passion as you stand in her studio, applying metallic blue on a canvas landscape.

A brief snap-crackle precedes a blinding light. Before the sound reaches you, the melting heat tears through your body in a ruthless instant made eternity.

Ω

The galaxy sprawled before me with harmonic brilliance. I was awareness. I was light. Energy. Purpose. I was here…where souls are born and reborn…

Why was I here?

I finally knew; I was serving my grandfather's redemption. He'd lived for so long without hope and love. Empty and soulless. I could give it back to him. Me. His granddaughter. Incomprehensibly, inconceivably me: the dark twin. The heartless assassin.

I was *the Rose*.

It was no coincidence that I'd been born the same year that my grandmother had left him and abandoned his soul, her twin…Epoptes and Vos. Twin souls. Twin Aeons. How many twin partnerships had I already formed in my short lifetime? I was Raphael's Akhana. Elasippus's angel. Bastion's sister. Bas's mother. Ka's salvation. Serge's…What was I to him?…I knew what he was to me: my twin heart, my twin soul…my soul-mate…my home and hearth.

My grandfather, the *Ancient One*, had relented. My own transformation had given Ka hope. He'd watched me find my heart and my soul and fill it with love. Yes, I was his avatar, queen of the New Age. I knew what needed to be done. I'd unknowingly already prepared the way by fulfilling my grandfather's hit list. I'd prevented an early Awakening by stemming the flow of *glitter* to the Gnostics. I'd accomplished this by hastening the death of Barbariccia, and unfortunately even that of Raphael and Rashomon, both heavy distributors of *glitter* to enlightened humans. And I'd further averted Raphael's plans by absconding with his elite fleet, the one intended to help *Nihilists* slaughter humanity and then, in turn, slaughter *Nihilists*. Now all I needed to do was close the gate, letting humanity awaken at the pace they were meant to. I knew how to close the gate without killing off all humans. I just needed to soul-drift into each of the surviving spiritual leaders, now in the inner diverse, and mass-hallucinate them into closing the gate they'd once opened. Finish what my grandmother had started.

This outer diverse was rougher and edgier than the inner diverse. The outer diverse had Eosians and Epoptes. Good and bad. There were Epoptes who had decided they should rule the metaverse with an ordered benevolent hand. Then there were those, like Raphael, who just wanted freedom to feel and engage in all the sensuality the human form offered them. Neither really understood what love was. I hadn't until now either. Yes...my grandfather had pegged me right: I was not born to kill; I was born for love. And for love I would do this last task that he'd set before me. But I would need my grandmother's help...

I focused on her and found her there, in my 'mind'.

>*Ah, you now know what you are...young one...*

Yes, I know it all now, grandmother.

>*Did I not tell you he was beautiful? Do you forgive me all?*

*I do.* And knew that I truly did.

>*You now know your mission...*

Yes. *To undo what you did.* But who would undo what I'd done?...

>*That is good. You will redeem both your grandparents with one act. It is meant to be, young one. Then we can both rest in peace. You are our savior.*

Who would be my savior?

>*You will need your twin self to become whole, young one...*

My twin self...my twin sister! Could this be what the prophesy *really* meant? V'rae and I? Twin souls? I'd forgotten all about V'rae. In my recent thoughts of matching twins I'd somehow forgotten about my inner diverse twin, my true *twin soul*. I remembered what Serge had said to me before: *she is your other self, your inner self. And you're her outer self. Together, you make up the whole like two beating parts of a single great heart.* Surely she was my *twin soul*...It was she and I who would enact the prophesy: *a joining of twin souls to usher in a New Age.* She and I would join to close the Gate.

*Oh, V'rae, how could I have forgotten you, my sister soul!* I focused on her and found her easily. She was already there.

>*I'm here, sister! Where are we?*

*I think you're asleep. So am I, in a manner of speaking. Sister, we need to find all the spiritual leaders who dreamed of the Gate and make them close it. We must do it together.*

>*I will help you!*

## EIGHTEEN

I stirred awake as if out of a very long slumber, feeling extremely heavy. As though heavy gravity was pushing me down on the ground and the cold wetness of the ground was sucking away my strength. I forced my eyes open and saw that I lay on the cold tile of Ka's private garden, in a pool of sticky goo. It took me a moment to realize that it was all that was left of my grandfather.

The rose he'd given me lay tattered on the tile before me, petals scattered around it. A shadow descended over me. Shaking, I looked up and saw the kind face of Elasippus. He bent over me, stretching out a brawny arm, then deftly picked up the rose and grasped both my hands to pull me up, innocently handing me the rose like a gift. Weak and trembling, I wavered on my feet and clutched the rose and his arms. I stared into his violet eyes.

"You...came," I said hoarsely.

"It's what friends do." He smiled kindly. It was what Bas used to say to me. "You're done here, I think," he said, looking around and finally gazing at the sticky pool on the tiles that also covered my face and body.

I followed his glance to what was left of Ka then met Elasippus's gaze with a wary look of guilt.

"You melted him, didn't you?" he said.

I nodded, biting down on my lip and trembling anew.

"I mean Raphael. That's what you did, wasn't it? At the lake..." I stared into his eyes with sudden alarm. But the eyes that gazed at me were kind. "Autochthon guessed that you were an Epoptes. I wasn't totally convinced. But I am now."

I swallowed. "You are?"

He nodded. "Only another Epoptes could kill *Mon Seigneur*. Because he was an Epoptes too."

I stared.

He laughed at my expression. "Rhea, we aren't fools. Raphael did things that no human was capable of. His powers of seduction, his perfect beauty, a body that swiftly healed, never aged."

"And you still wished him dead, condoned my killing him? He's one of your gods."

"He was a monster. Not all gods are good or deserve to rule." Then he ignored Ka's sticky goo on me and put his arm around me to steady me and gently lead me away with a sidelong appraising glance and comment, "so you like to wear men's clothes? I have a wonderful pair of Umy trousers that would look splendid on you."

Despite the situation, I laughed and Elasippus guffawed beside me.

No, not all gods were good, I thought with a last glance at what remained of my grandfather. I dropped the rose over his remains and snuggled in Elasippus's warm embrace.

But *my* God was....

Ω

We walked the strangely empty hallway back to the hanger where Elasippus had taken port. Though I was not visibly injured, my strength ebbed swiftly from me like water spilling from a broken dam and by the time we reached the *Boeotia* I'd grown totally incapable of walking or standing. It was as though I'd suddenly become porous and was bleeding out my life-force. As though the galaxy was reclaiming me, sucking out all that I was to broadcast me into space. My legs wouldn't hold me and I sank in his massive embrace. If he'd let go, I'd have collapsed like a rag doll; but Elasippus held on to me.

Once inside the *Boeotia*, he apologized then swept me up into his brawny arms and carried me to sickbay; it was a lot easier than dragging my limp body down the long corridor, he explained to me. Once in sickbay, he laid me on one of their firm beds for his doctor to examine me. I looked up, weakly grasping his hand like a child. He nodded to me and squeezed back, understanding; he would not abandon me.

"This is Doctor Poseidos," he said, glancing up at an older Eosian who came beside him. The doctor, a stern large man with rough features but kind eyes, grunted a terse greeting then brusquely ordered me undressed with an expectant glance at Elasippus. Elasippus hesitated only briefly then helped the doctor strip me of Raphael's clothes. He grasped my hand again after the doctor threw a loose sheet over me and without any further word attached several sensor pads to my skin. He set immediately to probing me gruffly with a large device. So much for his bedside manner, I thought.

As he studied the monitor behind me, the doctor made several sounds of exasperation. He then turned gruffly to Elasippus. "Sacred Universe, Commander! What are you doing to your crew?" He obviously didn't recognize me. Neither I nor Elasippus corrected him as he went on, "This human is in severe shock. Fluids and chemistry are off kilter. Her pineal gland is pumping out triptamines like there's no tomorrow. Her pituitary is releasing endorphins…the angular gyrus is very active. There's an incredible anomaly in overall temporal-lobe function. And, look." He pointed over my head at the monitor I couldn't see. "Glutamate is flooding her system. Look at this." He leaned toward the monitor and squinted his eyes. "Good chaos, she's totally misaligned. Even her bones! I'm not sure how that happened or what it all means…In fact, she shouldn't be…Wait—" He stared at his monitor. "Blessed Epoptes, it's correcting itself," he breathed out in disbelief then glanced pointedly at me with narrowed eyes. The question was obvious: *what are you?*

*You don't want to know,* I thought. I gave him a lame smile in response and glanced at Elasippus. He grinned then winked at me. I was an Epoptes.

"She's going to be just fine," he said to the doctor, grinning with confidence.

"And who's the doctor here, Commander?" Doctor Poseidos said brusquely, hiking his naked eyebrows up at Elasippus. Then he turned to me and said, "You're going to be just fine." He turned back to Elasippus with a sharp glance.

Elasippus ignored him and looked down at me, patting me with his free hand. As the doctor administered a nutrient solution into my arm, Elasippus said eagerly, "Commander, I wanted to tell you that we took care of our wandering MEC ships. Not one is left now." He grinned like a boy. "There are, no doubt, still some *Nihilists* scattered about, but they've slunk into the shadows like bugs under a rock, I'd wager, and not likely to emerge for a while. You've done it, Commander."

I squeezed his hand. *"We've* done it, Commander," I corrected him in a hoarse whisper. It was only then that I fully realized that we *had* done it...Yes, I'd willingly closed the gate—no doubt Ka's last command through his mind-probe. But Elasippus's and Autochthon's Eosian guard had saved humanity from the *Nihilist's* scheme to destroy them. I managed a thought at the irony; the Eosian guard had done the opposite of what they'd originally been charged to do. Closing the gate had isolated the few remaining *Nihilists* from inner diverse recruitment and averted any potential attacks in either direction, I reasoned. I thought of Ka and what he did. I remembered his oddly unresponsive reaction to my disclosure of the destruction of his two weapons facilities. I knew he'd changed his mind about destroying humanity but the machinery had gotten away on him. Taken a vicious life of its own. He needed my help, his secret weapon, *the Rose.* Secret even from me. Now my work was done...

"...And I have someone here who wishes to see you..." Elasippus's voice sounded as if from far away. "...Rhea?...Rhea?..." Even though the readings on the instruments suggested there was nothing wrong with me, I felt my strength swiftly drain. I could no longer speak, even as my mouth moved. Then it too refused to respond. Elasippus stared down at me with alarm and I caught a glimpse of the doctor's bemused face, gaze jerking from the instruments to me. I was breaking apart. The music of my body was jagging off stream. I found myself sinking into darkness and looked up at Elasippus as if from a long tunnel, watching him and the light slowly recede.

What was happening to me? Then I knew...

Elasippus disappeared and darkness enclosed me. My grandfather had said it: *Epoptes know when their time has come to be re-absorbed into the primordial womb of the galaxy.* It was my time, I realized...I'd done enough. I'd righted my wrongs. All but one...

I had ushered in a New Age, fulfilled Raphael's prophesy. I'd slowed down the 'Awakening' by making *glitter* much harder to get and had destroyed those who promoted it; I'd saved humanity from *Nihilist* destruction by destroying the weapon I'd given them and I'd stemmed their onslaught by decapitating their movement. There was something I was missing but my mind refused to grasp or summon it...No matter...My mother and my baby brother were safe; so was Bas, who sadly would never know the difference. Bastion and V'rae were safe too. And so was the inner diverse. I had ushered in a New Age, full of the light of hope and peace. But I'd done it through killing and causing death. Killing those I'd felt great compassion for, those I'd dearly loved. All my twins...I still belonged to the Old Age, the dark cynical age of my grandfather, Raphael and the others, who were all dead...as I would be soon...

I thought of my old world, the outer diverse, its immense and dark expanse of strange and bizarre astrophysical creatures: black holes, pulsars, quasars, magnetars and dark energy. In truth, the Milky Way had not changed much; yet somehow it had become a richer, friendlier, warmer place. I thought of Elasippus and his Eosian guard, invigorated with renewed pride and purpose. There was my mother and my little baby brother, sharing an enthralled life of wondrous discovery. And there was V'rae and Bastion, bathed in the warm mantle of new and passionate love. They were content and whole, twin souls living in a world safe from oppression. I'd righted my wrongs. All but one...

My twin soul...I thought of what Serge had said to me the last time we'd made love: *I believe that when two souls are meant to be together, no matter where or when they're travelling in our infinite wrinkled universe, they'll find each other. Each time, in each life. They'll recognize each other somehow, every time.* My twin soul-mate, my love...I wanted to believe that we would find one another somehow and I could make it up to him, make his soul happy. Perhaps in that place where souls were born—

But that's not where I ended up...I felt an exquisite softness against my lips that tasted of home and drew me elsewhere...

...I was floating, without a body above myself as I lay in the *Boeotia*'s sickbay bed, pale, with my eyes closed. Serge was bent over me, kissing my parted lips. I could feel his lips on mine, like sweet nectar. The instruments whined and the electroencephalogram flattened. No heart beat. No brain activity. I was dead. Serge looked up from my body to the instruments and cried out. He seized my limp face and drew it close to his, rocking slowly and weeping in spasms. I wanted to cry with him.

Then I realized that I was dreaming. I knew that I'd always imagined him crying for me the way he had for V'rae. I was spinning a last fantasy for myself, my final spark of coherent thought before I splintered and dispersed in the galaxy. My form faded in Serge's arms. I was breaking up. He stared then let out a gasping cry of anguish that clenched my heart.

"NO!" he wailed. "Not like this!" Serge then turned sharply and looked up. He stared right at me! His thunderstorm eyes blazed into me and I inhaled sharply—

My body on the bed seized in a gasping breath and the monitors beeped to life. Then darkness claimed me.

$$\Omega$$

"...I have someone here who wishes to see you..." Elasippus's voice sounded as if from far away. "...Rhea?...Rhea?..."

I wasn't sure how to leave the darkness. Then I thought of opening my eyes and forced my heavy lids open. Elasippus's concerned but smiling face swam in and out of focus. I saw him as if through a long dark tunnel and felt his great hand still clasping mine. Had I dreamed it all in a few blinks? I must have dreamed about dying, about Serge kissing me and weeping for me.

"You scared us for an instant. You flat-lined for ten seconds. But you're here now. Welcome back. And I have someone here who wants to see you." Elasippus let go of my hand and stepped back to let someone else step forward.

I stared. Serge's face swam into view.

His eyes braced me like an ocean breeze. Then that beautiful mouth I so longed to kiss smiled. I wanted to reach up to him and fold my arms around his neck, but my body wouldn't move. I had just enough strength to give him a weak smile.

"Hi," he said quietly, sitting in the chair next to the bed and bending close to take my limp hand in his.

"Hi," I whispered back in a sigh, feeling his warm hand clasped around mine. I stared at his beautiful thunderstorm eyes. "You're...alive..."

He grinned. "So are you." His eyes glowed with warmth. "Elasippus told me that everyone thought I'd died with Autochthon and his squadron in that MEC *phantom* ambush." He looked grave for a moment. "I didn't hear about what happened until much later...Elasippus told me the whole story." He turned to Elasippus and smiled gratefully at the large Eosian. When he turned back to me, his face tightened with repressed emotion. "I'm so sorry...I didn't know about...I wish I..." he trailed and swallowed, squeezing my hand. "Well, I'm glad you're okay."

I was glad too. Then I remembered: I'd closed the Gate, severed the link between our two worlds. I'd done exactly what he'd been trying to prevent.

Elasippus tapped Serge's arm. "I think we better let her sleep. She still looks exhausted and needs to rest."

Serge let go of my hand, to get up. His eyes, still focused on mine, caught my expression. Whatever it was, it made him sit back down and grasp my hand again. "I'd like to stay," he said to Elasippus. Then he turned back to me and said, "I won't leave you." Our eyes locked and I felt a hundred silent apologies pass between us. Serge placed his other hand on mine. "You need some rest, Rhea. Sleep," he urged. "Sleep. I'll be here."

I sighed at his words of reassurance and let my heavy eyelids close. I didn't want to sleep; I didn't want to dream. But I was so tired and his voice soothed my mind into quiescence. Within a few heartbeats I fell asleep.

## NINETEEN

When I flinched awake from a dreamless sleep, Serge was no longer holding my hand. But he was still sitting beside me, slouched in his chair. His head was thrown back and he snored lightly with his mouth open in blissful sleep. I stared at him for a while, studying every feature. He looked so beautiful.

I gave the room a quick appraisal. There was no one else here and I had no idea what time it was. The room had no viewport and I saw no chronometer. My own watch had been removed along with my clothes—Raphael's clothes, that is—which lay draped on a dresser nearby.

Some of my strength had returned and I realized that I could sit up. I pushed myself into a sitting position, letting the sheet fall from my naked body, and realized that I was famished. Careful not to awaken Serge, I pulled off the monitor tabs from my arm, head and chest then swung my legs over the side of the bed and hastily dressed. I gratefully found the MEC that I'd dropped in Ka's garden. Someone must have picked it up and put it in its holster on my belt. After putting the belt on and cinching it tight on my waist—now feeling complete—I walked unsteadily out of the sickbay room in search of food.

Instead I found the doctor in the outer adjoining office. He gave me a gruff glance then nodded brusquely to me. "Don't go too far, Crewmember."

"I won't," I assured him. "Can you tell me where your cafeteria is?"

"Straight aft to Hall B, turn right," he said, pointing to the door of the office. "Return here for inspection, Crewmember so I can dismiss you."

I didn't bother to correct him about being a crewmember and just nodded then left, flip-flops rhythmically slapping against my bare heels as I shuffled along the corridor.

Ω

I found Elasippus in the cafeteria, seated alone at a table, nursing a soyka. As soon as he saw me, the giant Eosian surged to his feet and stomped toward me, arms outstretched like a big bear. I sank willingly into his massive embrace.

"You're looking much better, Commander," he said once he disengaged, eyes appraising me with a warm smile. "Come." He motioned toward the food synthesizers. "You must be hungry."

"I am."

"Sit, sit! Let me get you something. Perhaps an Earth dish...or would you like to try one of our Eosian meals?"

"Earth is fine," I said and took a seat across from where he'd been seated. I'd had enough adventurous meals for the time being. Right now, I felt that I couldn't stomach anything but a familiar taste.

"Any preferences?" he said, now standing in front of one of the synthesizers.

"A hamburger, please. Just plain, with cheese."

When Elasippus returned with my not-so-plain hamburger and a cup of damsel juice, he silently watched me bolt it down and smiled in amusement. I couldn't believe how good it tasted. I felt some dressing dribble out the side of my mouth and unthinkingly slurped it up with my tongue before I realized it with a flush of embarrassment. I immediately thought of the times I'd eaten in front of Ka, Father Uriel, Raphael, even Serge. It seemed that I was fated to always satisfy an urgent hunger with questionable table manners under the critical eye of someone I should otherwise be impressing. I then decided that Elasippus no longer needed to be impressed. We'd gone way beyond that stage in our relationship—friendship, I corrected myself.

Still grinning, Elasippus leaned forward, placing his thick arms on the table and asked in his gruff voice, "Where's your man?"

I nearly choked on my last mouthful and forced a smile. He wasn't exactly *my man*, I reflected, but I thought Elasippus sweet for saying so. "Still asleep. He looked so peaceful. I didn't have the heart to wake him." In fact, I didn't have the heart to confront him.

He nodded, misunderstanding. "Ah, love…"

Love…Did Serge love me? Maybe. But it was a misplaced love…a substitute love, an injured love, a betrayed love. One that I couldn't face right now. "So, you found him on Remy 5?" I asked.

He nodded with a grin. "Six. Remy 6," he corrected. "He was waiting for us. So, I was right after all, Commander. Auto did let him off there."

I curbed a frown and gazed past Elasippus's grinning face to think. I wasn't sure why but that didn't seem to make sense. Serge wouldn't just leave Authochthon's squadron and further more, Autochthon wouldn't let him go. Serge wasn't a coward; he would have insisted on staying to fight and Authochthon would have respected his wish.

Elasippus leaned back and folded his massive arms across his enormous chest. "So, Commander, what are your plans now?"

I wiped my mouth with the back of my hand and took my drink then looked up at him gravely. "I hadn't thought that far yet." Actually, I had started to think about it and where my mind was going the rest of me didn't much care for.

"Well, I've thought a lot about the future," he said. "And I've discussed things with my entire squadron. We are unanimous in this. I know that you have not yet dismissed us of our obligations to you but in anticipation of your thinking to do this in the near future, let me say this to you now, Commander Hawke: the *Odysseus* squadron has declared itself in your service until perpetuity."

I jerked up in my seat, stunned. Had I understood him correctly? "What?"

Elasippus guffawed loudly and leaned forward again.

"Rhea," he said, softening his voice, "we would rather work for you than for anyone else. We are yours to command. Don't worry, you don't have to pay us; I know you have no funds. We can supply our own needs. I still have many contacts in the galaxy and most of us are capable of obtaining additional wages through other pursuits. But our fleet is yours whenever and for whatever and for free." He then gave me a great big self-satisfied grin and leaned back again.

I brought my hands to my mouth and blinked at him. He was obviously waiting for me to say something. When I could trust my voice, I said, "Commander, I'm incredibly honoured."

"Good! Then—"

"But I can't accept."

He eyed me sternly. "Why not?"

"Commander, I'm still a fugitive, an escaped convict. I'm charged with several murders, some of which I *did* commit. I escaped the galaxy's maximum security penal planet, and I—"

He waved me down. "You're not alone, Commander. We are also wanted, or will be shortly." I frowned at him, not understanding. "For the possible kidnapping and murder of Raphael Martinez. In short order Étienne and Eumulus will report him missing—if they haven't already—along with our failure to return. The rest of the *Orichalkon* will likely be pursuing us. We are in this together, Commander Hawke."

I stared at him. Then I burst into tears.

Elasippus pushed himself off the chair with a loud scrape and swiftly glided over to me as if his considerable mass weighed nothing. Within a heartbeat he'd seized me in his great arms again, pulling me up off the chair inside his massive bear-hug. "I know what you're thinking, Commander," he said as I sobbed all my released tension out, face buried in his chest. "You blame yourself for all this. But I think of it differently." He placed his giant hands lightly on my shoulders and looked down at me with a stern expression. But his eyes sparkled and he said with soft intensity, "You've released us from a prison, Rhea. We are now free for the first time to do the right thing, to claim our honor. Each of us decided and we all made the same choice. No one wanted to go back. Not one."

I stared up at him, blinking, and unable to say anything. Then I managed to smile back at him, both humbled and exalted.

Elasippus straightened and released his grip. "I'll leave you then to your thoughts. No doubt you have many right now." He nodded and started to walk away then had a second thought and turned, appraising me up and down. "Oh, in case you're interested, I still have those Umy trousers. They'd look better on you than on any of us!" Then he left, chuckling.

I smiled back then sat down with a sigh.

$$\Omega$$

I hunched over my drink and rested my head in my hand. Elasippus was right. I had a lot to think about. During my dream-voyage to the inner core of the galaxy, whether real or not, I'd sensed that I'd neglected something. I now knew what it was: two loose items required my attention before I could feel that I'd completely ensured a galaxy safe from further *Nihilist* attacks and from an Eosian-mediated invasion of the inner diverse.

I hadn't forgotten what Serge had told me about the Guardians simply letting the Rill sell the wakesh root to Dark Sun to manufacture into *glitter*. It was just another example of the Guardian's self-serving attitude and their less than honourable treatment of a society. I found it ironic how they'd sanctioned the Rill's illicit drug dealing on Sekmet with Dark Sun on the one hand and on the other supported the Rill's enslavement by the Legess on their own home planet. The Guardians had sent me, after all, to crush their rebellion.

With Barbariccia gone, Dark Sun had no direction and Eclipse would likely seize the *glitter* market with tacit sanction from the Guardians. My grandfather suggested this meant that the *glitter* previously available to Gnostics would vanish. But, it was no guarantee and I had to stop it all somehow. Particularly since I'd been responsible for Barbariccia's death, which would presumably bring the market to Eclipse. And I didn't want to see what Eclipse would do with such a windfall. I either stopped it at the *glitter*-making stage on Nexus, or at the wakesh root collection stage on Sekmet. Neither choice was good and I had to choose one. Then I managed a wry smile. At least I wasn't alone; Elasippus and his squadron would help me.

That was task number one. My second task was to ensure safety from further *Nihilist* attacks. Elasippus had reassured me that the *Nihilists* were all but demolished, scattered across the galaxy. However, Eclipse, the enclave for *Nihilists*, still existed and from few there could arise many again. My MEC design needed to be eradicated from all Eclipse and *Nihilist* sources. According to my grandfather, the vault could only be accessed by one of three people. They were all dead now. But the vault still existed. I had no idea how I was going to access a heavily encrypted system that only three people had previously accessed, all of which were dead. Then there was the small matter of Euaimon who now also had my design. Where did his allegiances really lie?

I was so busy with my thoughts that I didn't notice someone enter the cafeteria until he sat across from me. I flinched and quickly straightened. It was Serge.

He greeted me with an awkward smile. Apart from his rumpled brown shirt and his usual tussled hair and young stubble, he looked refreshed from his sleep.

"Hi," I said with a guarded smile.

"Hi."

The silence that followed grew thick. Now that the crisis was over, we were back to that, I concluded, feeling the strain that interfered with my ability to breath.

Serge stood up then moved over to the synthesizers to make himself a soyka. He turned and was about to ask me if I wanted one then checked himself and pulled out a steaming cup from the slot. Leaning against the synthesizer, he turned to me and said, "The doc told me you were here."

I nodded to him. Did he have something he wanted to

share with me? I both longed for and dreaded a topic I knew neither of us dared bring up.

"*A cat pent up becomes a lion*—Italian proverb," he winked at me with a slanted smile. Jag me, was he picking up my bad habit too? Then he launched his first scud missile: "Elasippus tells me you executed the *Ancient One*."

I nodded. Did he think me cold-hearted for that too?

"Must have been hard to do," he said soberly "His being your grandfather, I mean."

I was examining the wood grain on the table and nodded again. I heard him taking small sips of his hot soyka and raised my eyes in a furtive glance.

His eyes caught mine and blazed into me with a strange mixture of emotions. "Listen, Rhea, about Earth and Raphael—"

Oh, God! Not this! "I think we've covered that topic sufficiently," I said, hiding my dread under a brusque manner. I spilled some of the damsel juice from my cup in my jerky reaction and hastily wiped the table. It gave me the excuse not to look at Serge. "You summed it up pretty nicely before." I didn't look up. Whatever he was going to say, I'd stemmed it. Thinking only to swiftly change the subject I looked up and blurted out violently, "I closed the Gate."

"What?" He gaped at me. I was always doing that to Serge—unbalancing him.

"I closed the Gate," I repeated stonily, bracing for his anger. He just blinked at me. It gave me a chance to explain. "I had a vision...a *real* vision of a possible future...The inner diverse *Nihilists* have been busy building too; they plan to re-invade with conventional ships and weapons using the Gate, which is big enough to let them through. Kamikaze one-man *teardrop* ships..."

Serge nodded and rubbed his hands along his stubbled cheeks, betraying his knowledge of these vehicles.

"Suicide ships," I continued soberly, "equipped with simple particle disintegrator bombs. They're being built as I speak. Hundreds of them. It would be a devastating war out here, Serge. Millions of innocent lives would be wiped out, entire planet ecosystems destroyed. Particle bombs are an ancient and non-discerning weapon. They cause a horrible death to every life form; they're a sign of desperation." I sucked in a long breath before continuing, "If that's not enough, the Epoptes and their loyal Eosians have already been contemplating an invasion into your diverse. If this last *Nihilist* attack in my vision were to happen, the Epoptes would strike back. And they'd win, Serge. They'd defeat the *Nihilists* and take control of both diverses." I broke my gaze and looked down at the cup shaking in my hands. "I couldn't let that happen. Any of it. So, V'rae and I soul-drifted into the minds of all those spiritual leaders who'd willed the Gate open and made them will it shut." I looked up into Serge's bewildered face. "It was that simple. So, now we're back to waiting for humanity's natural 'Awakening', which will create a safer connection between the diverses again; not some massive Gate that war machines can pass through. By then we'll all be ready for it— humanity included."

He looked away and pursed his lips in thought. "I see," he said. I couldn't fathom what he was thinking and he didn't offer his opinion. He just tapped his cup and studied what was inside, as if all the answers lay there. I turned back to my cup and endured a long silence.

I looked up finally with questioning eyes and broke the silence. "Elasippus told me that he found you on Remy 5—"

"Six," he corrected. "Remy 6. I'd just returned. I'd gone to see V'rae…"

Of course. His beloved. "How is she?"

"Good. I missed you by a day, it seems." He smiled sideways. So, he knew I'd been there. What else had she said to him about me?

We both nursed our drinks in silence. I finished my damsel juice and rose then approached the synthesizer next to him to get another. As I made my selection, I glanced sidelong at him and hiked my brow. Then I asked the question that bothered me: "Why did you leave the *Elyssia* on Remy 6?"

Serge smiled knowingly and studied his cup of soyka for a few moments before answering. "I had somewhere to go."

"To see V'rae?" I asked in a voice thick with scepticism.

He smiled sideways. "No—well, yeah, I did drop by, but on my way somewhere else." I waited several moments for him to tell me. "To the *Ulysses*."

I stiffened and found my eyes searching his. "To the *Ulysses*," I repeated. Obviously not to see A'ler...so, why?

He nodded at me with a strange smile, like he knew what I was thinking. Then he fished in his trouser pocket and held up an info-pod. "I went to get this."

I glanced from the pod in his outstretched palm to his enigmatic face and felt my heartbeat increase. "What is it?"

"Your MEC design. The only copy that presently exists."

I stared at him. I'm sure my mouth gaped open. I wanted so much to trust Serge. But every time I relaxed and gave him more of my trust, he did something to undermine it. Like now.

I seized him in a vizion grip, pulling his body up against mine, and pressed my MEC against his neck. He yelped in painful surprise. His cup fell and clattered to the floor, spattering scalding soyka over the floor and my bare feet. He didn't struggle.

"I don't know how you managed to get on board the *Ulysses*," I snarled, breathing harshly on him. "I don't know how you cracked the vault and retrieved a file that's booby-trapped to self-destruct on transfer without knowledge of a code—a code *only* I know. And I don't know how you just waltzed out of there after you did...The only thing I know for certain is that you aren't *the Rose*, because I'm *the Rose*." I heard his sharp intake of air and had to smother a bitter smile at his astonishment. "Now tell me the truth for once," I said, tightening my grip.

Serge annoyed me by relaxing under my hold, which relied on the tension of the victim. "Rhea..." I could hear the smile behind his voice and smelled the spice of his attraction for me. It didn't mean that he liked me though. "It's nice to have you back," he said. "I was getting a little worried...you were so...well, I missed your blenoid temper."

Just as he let out a laugh, I let go and pushed him off with an exasperated exhale.

He turned to face me, grinning like a pirate. A hot flush swept up my face and I grew angry at myself for letting him affect me this way. I kept my MEC pointed at him. He shrugged. "Listen, I can explain....although I think I first deserve an explanation of how you're *the Rose*..."

"It's a long story that you don't need to hear." I leaned back against one of the synthesizers, gazing at him with narrowed eyes and crossed my arms under my breasts, MEC still pointed on him.

"But if you're accusing me of lying and being cushy with *Eclipse* then..." he trailed, pointing loosely at me; his inference being that I sure looked like I was a prime *Eclipse* member myself, being the infamous *Rose*. He had a point.

I let out a sigh and forced out the words, "My grandfather used me." I swallowed down the memories and pushed on, "He created the hit list for me, without me knowing it. I did his bidding each time either through my own stupidity or through some kind of elaborate set up, like with Rashomon. I was Ka's secret weapon in every way; I mean *every* way, as in secret even from me. He just had to point in the right direction and I automatically did what was required," I ended bleakly. "I was the obedient granddaughter to the end when I killed him. He was the last one on the list." I shrugged and examined the floor then gazed up through my eyelashes at him.

Sure enough, he was staring at me with a look of pain on his face. Did he think me abhorrent? Whatever he thought of me, I'd already thought it for him. But his gaze softened. It was worse than his look of initial horror because it melted away my defiant anger and tapped a spring of tears. They swelled up my throat and heated the backs of my eyes. But I was damned if I was going to let him see me cry, I thought, as I bridled them in.

"I'm sorry, Rhea," he said gently. "I wasn't sure if you'd be successful in your mission. I wasn't sure you'd make it out alive even." He waved his hands at me with a shrug. "Chaos, Rhea, I was almost right. You were actually dead for ten seconds back there. I couldn't let them have it, especially without us having it..."

I felt a convulsive hysterical laugh swell inside me. After everything we'd done and said to one another, it was all still about the MEC. My free hand flung up to my mouth to stifle the insane laugh. If I released it I'd be lost.

"Autochthon and I discussed it," Serge explained calmly, apparently unaware of my rising hysteria. "We kept it a secret from Elasippus because of his affiliations with Eclipse; we didn't want to compromise him or his contacts. The less he knew the better off everyone was." Serge hadn't bothered to mention me in his equation of secrecy; it was obvious what I would have thought of his little plan. "How did I get into the vault?" He itemized my points on his fingers. "Shlsh gave me an access code last time I was there." Of course. "As for retrieving your MEC file unscathed...do you remember when I told you that I learned a lot about you through V'rae? Your transfer self-destruct code was one of them. A lock-and-key code. The one you use for your important files. The one only you know...well, not quite." His smug smile stabbed like a knife. "V'rae, your twin, also knew — through her dreams. She told me innocently. She'd intuitively revealed it as a suggestion for an encryption on a puzzle I kept bringing up to prompt her sub-conscious mind. When she suggested a lock-and-key code, I knew she'd tapped into your mind. It was both simple and elegant and surprisingly difficult to decipher. When I asked her to suggest one, she came up with two tetragrams: *True Love*. It says a lot about her...but it says a lot more about *you*." He grinned at me and I felt like my insides were being ripped out of me. "Once I knew the paradigm," he continued blithely, "I could search for any corresponding ciphers. I guessed that the lock you'd embedded in the design corresponded to *True*. Sure enough, I found it in the form of a numeric anagram of an old Khonsus mathematical progression that described the planetary motion of Venus in Earth's solar system. All I needed to do was substitute the corresponding Khonsus ciphers for *Love* and input them. *Voila!* I could liberate the file for transfer." He gave me a self-pleased smile and I felt sick.

The hysterical laugh threatened and I choked it back with a kind of repressed sobbing sound. *True Love*. I remembered when I'd come up with it, thinking it a joke, something that had eluded me for so long that I no longer sought it. I'd thought it a particularly safe code for me to use as my safety-catch for any of my valuable communications. For anyone who knew me it was as unlikely a combination as any. The irony was that the one man I might have considered as my true love had used it to get his precious weapon design—out of mercenary motives. True love was a fictional idea that resided only in my head. Whatever Serge felt for me, he was foremost still an *anti-Nihilist* agent on a mission. That was why he came back; that was why he was here now.

"As for just waltzing out of there," Serge continued more soberly, "I'm still V'ser, a member of Eclipse. A'ler never blacklisted me. I can come and go as I please. I'm her brother still, after all. What ever else we were to each other, we were always family."

A family of murderers that I'd murdered one by one. All but him. Another sound escaped my mouth and I felt my throat close convulsively in an effort to stem the tide of hysteria. It was a losing battle. My MEC began to shake in my hand and an insane laugh bubbled up my throat.

Serge broke the spell. He reached out to hand me the info-pod with a sad remorseful look on his face. I flinched and recoiled at his movement then stared down at the pod in his hand. "I'm sorry, Rhea," he said as I met his eyes fleetingly. "It's yours. Do with it what you want, what you need to do. Just know that I destroyed the original MEC design in the vault. This is now the only existing copy."

I couldn't move. We stared at one another, eyes locked in a sad embrace of regrets. Remorse for what we'd done to one another, how we'd abused each other and inexorably distanced ourselves from what we might have been together.

Ignoring the MEC still pointed at him, he gently placed the pod on the table then turned and left the cafeteria.

### TWENTY

Elasippus, Serge and I sat around the cafeteria table, discussing our next move. Thanks to Serge, my MEC design was safe in my head and pocket…and, for the moment, with Euaimon, who'd done nothing with it so far. We were all clear that controlling the *glitter* trade was our greatest but most imminent challenge. With the added danger of an Eosian/Epoptes attack on the inner diverse, we all agreed—even Serge—that closing the Gate had been the right thing to do. Serge had grumbled his agreement to the logic of it, although he'd given me a sidelong glare as he did. We also agreed that preventing an early 'Awakening' was paramount to keeping both diverses safe, particularly the inner diverse from an Epoptes/Eosian invasion. That meant doing something about *glitter*.

"The way I see it," I began, "we have two choices for stemming the *glitter* flow. One is to destroy Dark Sun's main *glitter*-making facility on Nexus—"

"Where've you been, Rhea?" Serge cut in. "Eclipse now runs that *dust* manufacturing plant. They took it last month. Dark Sun is no more."

I stared at him briefly, astonished at his news, then continued, "And the second choice is to stop *glitter* distribution at the source, stop the export of wakesh root."

"Like that's even possible," Serge quipped. He folded his arms over his chest and leaned back with a frown. He thought either choice ridiculous, obviously.

Undaunted, I glanced briefly at Serge who was studying some marks on the table and continued, "Given Dark Sun's demise, export will now go to a disparate number of clients, including Eclipse…" I drew in a breath and pointed my gaze away from Elasippus and Serge, "so I think we're best off taking Sekmet."

"Are you jagging insane?" Serge turned on me with a look of appalled disbelief; like he couldn't believe that such stupid words had come out of my mouth.

I frowned at him in stubborn determination and folded

my arms across my breasts, offering no objection. I glanced briefly at Elasippus; he met my gaze with a contemplative though enigmatic look.

Serge surged to his feet and paced the room. Then he raked his hands through his tussled hair the way he always did when I rattled him. He looked infuriated as his eyes flashed into mine. "That's suicide, Rhea. The security is outrageous there."

"*If you can't dance, you'll say the drumming is poor—* Jamaican proverb," I said.

Ignoring me, he ranted on, "Have you forgotten what it's like? Your experience there? I'd have thought that Sekmet would be the last place you'd want to return to—"

"What I like and don't like isn't the issue here," I cut him off and stood up myself. "This isn't a pleasure cruise. What's important is to decide where we'll make the most difference. Besides, *you* got in nicely enough last time." I gave him a pointed look.

"That'll only work once," he defended sullenly. "Besides, Sekmet is a Guardian installation with Guardian ships arriving almost daily. It would be like trying to infiltrate a Guardian precinct. That's just plain stupid!"

"I don't think—"

He flung his arms up at me. "You might as well just go in there handcuffed and turn yourself in, for creon's sake!"

"You're over-reacting."

"Am I? They'll recognize you right away and feed you to the sobeks!"

"I'll disguise myself—"

"You were their jagging *mevlani*, for creon's sake!"

"They won't recognize me!"

"They *will*! You're not easy to forget." Serge turned away and raked back his wild hair into submission. When he turned back to face me, his eyes blazed. "When will you come to your senses, Rhea, and stop trying to kill yourself!"

"Stop being my mother!"

That stopped him briefly. I'd shocked him. He had to take in a long breath to collect himself before he replied, "I'll stop when you stop needing one!"

I shrieked back, "I'll stop needing one when you get out of my life!" I saw him wince. I'd gone too far, I realized with sudden regret. I hadn't meant it. But I couldn't take it back.

I glimpsed Elasippus, the only one still seated, watching our argument quietly with an expression of fascination. His gaze had bobbed from side to side like he was watching a Grease Ball match and I was reminded of the quarrel Serge and I had had on Earth with V'rae looking on. Elasippus's expression was similar to hers; a look of bewildered interest.

Serge finally turned to him with a desperate look of expectation. "Tell her, Commander. Put some sense into her head. She listens to you."

Elasippus cleared his throat as I turned to look at him. "Only on matters concerning Bourbon Whiskey, actually," he said. "On sleuthing issues I must defer to her," he ended with a cursory glance at me before swinging his gaze to the ceiling. I caught his lip twitch in an effort to hide a smile.

Serge glared at Elasippus with a shocked expression of disgust. I hid a vengeful smile. I had to admit, as I glanced at Elasippus with some bemusement, that I thought his flippant remark rather inappropriate to the present situation. It then occurred to me that he'd cleverly taken himself out of our surly argument. I also knew right at that moment that Elasippus would never question my decisions and choices and I wondered with alarmed puzzlement what I'd done to earn the undying loyalty of this seasoned warrior.

Serge, on the other hand, was another matter, I thought, watching him pace again and utter a growl of frustration. He knew I was right. Elasippus knew I was right. None of us liked it but we all knew. We just had to agree and get on with it. For some reason Serge was fighting it with more passion than I could understand. Serge glared from me to Elasippus. "She's mad, you know. Blenoid mad, and she's going to get us all killed."

"Yes," Elasippus agreed rather heartily with a half-grin. "I know."

Serge threw up his hands and waved them as if pleading

to some invisible god. Then he dropped his head to stare at the floor in defeat. When he turned to me, the fire in his eyes had died; they now gleamed cool and calculating. "What's the plan?"

I met his hard gaze with a lame half smile. "I haven't gone that far yet."

"You haven't gone that far yet!" he exploded, taming back his unruly hair with wild movements of his hands. "When were you going to?"

"I just know that's what we—*I*—have to do," I said.

"Well, when you finally figure it out I'll be in my quarters," Serge said, throwing a glare from me to Elasippus, like he was a traitor. Then he stormed out of the room.

Elasippus caught my eye. He gave me a big grin. "I think he likes you."

## TWENTY-ONE

"This is Elasippus, Captain of the *Boeotia*. Requesting permission to land my shuttle on Hades. I have something of yours that you...eh...lost." Elasippus's lip curled slightly in an amused half-smile. He sat in the Command Centre, facing the large communication screen.

"What of ours could you possibly have?" Sekmet tower responded. There was no image except an automatically generated shot of Hades floating on Sekmet.

"We're returning one of your prisoners. Rhea Hawke," Elasippus said, glancing at me as I stood outside the view of the monitor.

Serge stepped in front of the monitor, dressed in my Great Coat and looking like an Eosian. "Guardian Enforcer Meenos here. Elasippus was kind enough to alert me when he ran across her stinking scent," he said with a sneer. "We captured the bitch...but only after she killed seven of our men..."

I tilted my head and gave him a hard look. I mouthed

*seven*?!

His mouth twitched slightly but he kept his gaze forward. "There better be a reward…"

"Bring her in, Meenos," the tower responded. "We'll be happy to see her."

They cut communications.

"Well, that was…*happy*," Elasippus quipped, turning to me with a grin.

Serge turned to me with a quizzical look. "Recognize the voice?"

I shook my head and frowned.

We had two plans; neither one good for me, I considered. I was the bait, after all. Plan one was to get the Rill to cooperate by convincing Mayling, probably at my expense. Plan two was to blow up the facility if the Rill didn't cooperate, which implied that I'd been dispatched in some way.

I glanced through the ship's porthole to Sekmet's blanket bog, shimmering below in the afternoon light. I spotted Hades, floating on the bog like a giant *shadow* freighter with smoke stacks billowing. It left a muddy trail in its wake. My whole body tightened with an imperceptible shiver. Memories of my ordeal there cloyed and twisted in my gut: the torture and humiliation; the drugs, the games. Barbariccia, Bondar, Iris and her cronies…Mayling… Oh, God…

My body couldn't stop shaking and a kind of sick longing wormed its way amidst the trembling revulsion that clutched my belly. I wondered with dread if I was succumbing to remnants of the wakesh root still inside me. Was I an addict still or was I simply going mad? They say that no one ever truly leaves Hades; that its grip is fatal. Perhaps, I thought at length, they were right. Could I handle this? Or would I fall apart and "die" all over again once I set foot inside that jagging place?

I caught Serge staring at me with an odd expression. I kind of sick curiosity, I thought. I glared at him and left the Command Centre.

## Ω

I slowly climbed down the shuttle ladder, handcuffs clattering on the rungs. Elasippus waited for me on Hade's open landing-bay platform, eyes locked on the entrance of the penal colony. Flanking the entranceway were two statues of Egyptian gods: Anubis, the judging god and Sekhmet, the goddess who gave the planet its name. She had the face of a lion. She was dressed in a blood-red robe and bore a solar disk and uraeus. Considered the goddess of justice and order she was called "the one before whom evil trembles". Why was I trembling?

*The only Zen you find at the top of the mountain is the Zen you bring with you*—Zen proverb, I thought with irony.

The overpowering stench of methane, sulphur and ozone assaulted my nose. I remembered standing on this very platform "eons" ago and watching an escaping Azorian inmate run past me and dive into the open bog behind us. He'd tried to swim away. He didn't get very far. Hade's defence system had peppered him full of holes five seconds into his swim. I remember watching his dead bloated body roll in the black bog as the giant floating prison chugged away.

Serge hopped down behind me and gruffly seized my arm. A little too gruffly, I thought, feeling the hard pinch of his hand. We all knew about the surveillance cameras, so acting our part from the beginning was crucial. But his vice-grip was going to leave red pinch marks. I knew he was nervous. And, damn it, he was hurting me. It didn't take any acting for me to try to shake him off. He just responded by gripping me tighter.

It didn't help, I thought with a sidelong glower at him, that he was wearing my Great Coat. As logical as it appeared—it made him an obvious Enforcer—I felt uncomfortable with it. It's not that I didn't trust him; it just felt as though I'd given a piece of myself away. That wasn't the only thing that bothered me: my precious MEC was holstered to *his* thigh—not mine.

That was not to say that I had no weapon; I was dressed in a slim black top and pants. My *pocket* pistol was tucked neatly into the small of my back. So, to a casual observer I carried no obvious weapons. It wasn't my precious MEC though.

Serge was sweating. "This isn't going to work," he finally hissed, slowing his pace with second thoughts. Elasippus glanced at us both with a frown of concern. Was our plan falling apart before it even began?

I pulled him forward. "Yes, it is," I hissed back. "Just do *your* part; get me close to Mayling."

"*They* aren't Mayling," Serge grumbled under his breath as two hulking Veniks lumbered through the Hades gateway onto the shuttle platform.

"Stick with the plan," I said, feeling my own body tense.

For a moment I contemplated the irony of my action. I was the prisoner and I was dragging Serge forward to give me to those animals. Who was the Mevlani now? It didn't matter; he— or she—had ordered these hulks to greet Meenos and take me into their lair. Within moments I would be inside my own Hell. What *was* I doing?

"Remember, you have the MEC," I added. "It's set to stun a Venik." I'd known who would greet me, I thought, glancing at the two bare-chested reptilian hulks in bright lumipants. And I knew Serge well enough that he wouldn't use the MEC to kill. The Veniks looked ridiculous and treacherous at the same time. Veniks were massive thugs with thick legs, six poison-clawed arms, Rotweiller heads with six mouths filled with razor-sharp blue teeth. Add a kind of dull-wittedness and predatory tendancy to that mix and you had a species generally despised; but not openly, of course. They were the bullies of the universe. Any sharp-witted criminal—like Barbariccia or elite members of Eclipse—could and did make great use of these soldier-bullies.

My comment about the MEC seemed to reassure Serge and he straightened. His grip tightened on my arm and he pulled me forward in a strut.

"Here's the bitch!" He shoved me violently forward. I squeeked in surprise and staggered. I lost my balance and did a stumble-dance to keep from falling until I was wavering metres from Hade's gates and the two Veniks.

They laughed in a chortle, beady eyes bright with dust.

Serge demanded, "Now, where's my reward?"

I made a cursory study of the Veniks, salivating in front of me, and concluded that I did not recognize them. Too much time had passed since I was here, I decided. Hades inmates were like blood cells in a body; they didn't last long. Between the games, Cerberus, murders and back-breaking work, the life-cycle of an inmate was pretty short. Days for some; months to a year for most. I'd be lucky to recognize anyone, I thought. Just as well.

"Ah, fresh meat," one of the Veniks said in a multi-timbral voice. "Mevlani will be happy."

"Actually old meat," Serge corrected the Venik. "She's just being recycled. Do with her what you like." He stepped right behind me and pulled me back gruffly. "But not until I get my reward. You promised."

"We did not," the same Venik growled. "We just told you to bring her."

I quelled a smile of amusement despite the situation. They were right; the tower had not openly confirmed his request.

"You're an enforcer. It's your job to bring her here," the Venik added.

Serge drew out my MEC and pointed it at the Venik who'd spoken. The Venik recoiled. "Talk to your Mevlani," Serge commanded. "Meantime, I'll keep her here." He seized me from behind with his arm and pressed the MEC against my head. I seized in a breath of surprise. He was starting to enjoy himself, I decided as I choked under his tight grip. "I think your Mevlani will find her quite the prize. Go tell him!"

"*Her*, slave!" the Venik corrected. "Mevlani is a woman!"

"Take us to her, then," Serge ordered.

The Veniks looked at each other.

"Let me spell it out for you...*slave*," Serge said. "I don't give a creon's ass whether this piece of meat is alive or dead when she comes to you. But if your Mevlani finds out that I toasted her right here and now because you didn't give me my reward, I guarantee you that your Mevlani will be majorly jagged about it. And she'll have you so jagged that you'll wish you were born on Upsilon 3 and jagged by the blenoids when you were just a child."

The Veniks glanced at one another again.

Ω

The two Veniks led Serge and I through the great hall where inmates, drunk on mash, lingered and drank themselves into oblivion. I glanced at the Eosians, a Badowin and some Azorians lying prostrate in the huge room, sucking on mash or just comatose in the stupor of drugged satiation. My breaths stuttered at the smell and I felt an involuntary shiver run through me. I glanced at Serge. He was studying me without turning his head. Our eyes met briefly before I broke off and focused on the long hallway where the Veniks were taking us.

I knew the way. I'd been Mevlani for several weeks, after all. They were taking us to the Mevlani's great chambers. Who was it? A woman they'd said. Would she be as ruthless and wild as I'd become when I sat on the Mevlani's chair?

As we approached the large chamber, the shivers returned and I felt ill. My steps faltered and Serge harshly pulled me forward. "Come on, murdering bitch!" he growled. Stunned by the intensity of his words and actions, I flinched and stared at him. His face twisted with real anger. My heart plummeted. Was he feeling regret? Then a chilling thought numbed me: Serge had both my Great Coat and the MEC in his possession; two things he'd coveted from the moment we'd met. Then I had another dark thought: had he played with the controls? Was the MEC set to kill a species? As if to mirror my suspicions, he ranted in a cruel voice, "You've caused me too much grief already, killing my colleagues and loved ones! I'll get my reward and you'll get yours now, slave! Let's go! To your keeper!"

Realizing that I was losing it, yet powerless to stop myself, I felt hot tears sting my eyes and grimaced to keep in the torrent of emotion that fought to escape.

He shook me violently, like a rag doll.

The Veniks chortled. One opened the great door with a flourish. "Here is your new prisoner, Mevlani!" he announced. "Rhea Hawke!"

My knees gave out and I would have crumpled to the floor if Serge had not held me up. He shook me again. "Bitch! Stay on your feet! Face your fate with honour—or at least a pretence of it!"

He dragged me toward the shadowy figure seated in the Mevlani's chair.

She finally came into view and I stopped, this time pulling Serge to a halt. At the same instant as I stopped, the Mevlani began to laugh. A cackling mean laugh that chilled me from inside.

The Mevlani was Mayling!

Ω

"Well, looks whos the fakes Guardians broughts in... Rhea Hawkes!" she snarled as Serge pushed me forward. Mayling bristled with obvious rage.

I recoiled and backed into Serge. What did she mean by *fakes Guardians*? Had she guessed our play? I wasn't so sure myself, feeling the tension in Serge's hold grow painful again. Trembling with rage, he drew out the MEC from the folds of my Great Coat and jammed the barrel against my head. I felt the pressure of cold metalloid against my temple.

"All I want is the reward," he said darkly. "I deserve that reward. She's all yours then. And good riddance!"

"So, youz haves her Great Coat and MECs too, eh?" Mayling observed cooly.

Serge quipped, "Part of my reward. She won't be needing them here."

"Theyz comes with her and therefores belongs here, with us," she argued back. "Besides, youz are a fakes..."

"I don't think so," Serge said. The Veniks had crowded forward. He swung the MEC and shot in one smooth motion. Both Veniks tumbled on the floor. His swing ended on her, the MEC pointed fully on her disdended belly. "Quite the genuine article, Mevlani," he ended with a slanted smile.

I elbowed him hard in the gut and Serge doubled over

with a grunt of surprise. I grabbed the MEC as it fell out of his hand and wacked him over the head with it. I winced at the hard clunk and watched him drop to the floor like a metatron-weight. I kept doing that, I thought: knocking him out. I shrugged, deciding that he now had several good reasons for being angry at me. *"Be careful what you wish for; you're apt to get it*—old Chinese proverb," I said as a smirk curled itself on my lips. I turned to Mayling, visibly cringing in her seat. *"She who has been bitten by a snake fears a piece of string*—Persian proverb," I said. "Hi, Mayling." Then, much to her surprise, I handed the weapon to her.

Ω

Serge growned and stirred on the floor. I nervously glanced from his crumpled body to the MEC in Mayling's playful paws, and pulled in a breath, about to launch into my argument.

Mayling fiddled with the settings of the MEC, pointed at Serge and shot.

I flinched and fought the urge to rush to him. I was about to scream at her when she said calmly, "Don't worryz. I just stunned hims. He cans still help makes yourz babies..." She swung the weapon to point at me.

I recoiled slightly and raised my hands.

"What do youz wants, Hawkes?"

"To make a deal."

"Youz haves nerves, Hawkes. Comings back heres. Theres no deals weez cans makes with youz."

I leaned forward. She responded by pointing the MEC closer to me. I froze.

"Hear me out, Mayling," I said evenly. "Yes, I'm with him." I pointed to Serge, lying on the floor. "You guessed right; he's not an Enforcer. Neither am I anymore. But our mission is a noble one; to save the galaxy from the devastating effects of dust and its use by dark forces intent on killing the entire human race."

"Likes I cares..."

I blinked at her. I hadn't expected her to be that harsh. So, that was how she intended to play it. My eyes narrowed with hard intent. "You *should* care. We're the ones who can help you the most—or hurt you the most," I ended with a hard look at her. "I know how you Rills got this gig on Sekmet. You made a deal with the Guardians…" Then I tossed out my wild guess: "But only a select few of you know, eh? The rest of the Rills think they have no power, that they were sent here to Sekmet to serve out the rest of their lives as inmates, oppressed by the current Mevlani and other wakesh users."

I saw from her expression that I'd guessed right. I could never totally swallow what Serge had told me about the Rills running the place. I'd seen too much genuine suffering and killing. I thought of all the mutilated inmates, many of them Rills; Iris, Orchid, Hyacynth, and April…Sure, it was a ploy, part of the job; but the irony for most of the Rill was that they weren't in on it. "Your deal with the Guardians involved export of wakesh to the crime lords and *rein*-rich peat to Zeta Corp—in return for certain favors."

I saw her grow more agitated and uncomfortable, confirming my suppositions. I ruthlessly went on; I was on a roll. "Rills quietly oppressing other Rills, eh? How is it that you're the Mevlani now? Do the other Rills even know?" She was squirming now. "I'm guessing they don't. Just like most of them don't know that an elite Rill group actually run the place, determine who the Mevlani is and do commerce with Dark Sun and the Galactic Guardians. Wouldn't it be a shame if they found out that one of their own now runs the jagging place?" I leaned forward and said in a quiet voice, "I think you might have a little revolution on your hands, at the expense of wakesh and *rein* production…"

Her bulbous eyes shivered and she growled, "What do youz wants?"

I finally had her full attention, I thought and suppressed a smile. I leaned back and folded my arms across my chest. "I want you to stop production."

### TWENTY-TWO

"In exchange for desisting your wakesh root export and for abandoning this facility, we would give you what you most want."

"What could youz possibly gives us that weez would wants more than this?" she scoffed.

"A home," I said. "*Your* home."

Mayling turned all three tube-eyes to me in quiet rage. We stared at one another for several moments, eyes locked in mutual challenge. Although the fury aimed at me was blistering, I refused to surrender.

It was Mayling who finally broke off. She lifted her bulbous head and spat out a chilling laugh, rippling with anger. "Youz already destroyed us once. Youz single-handedly destroyed our dreams to be a freez peoples. Weez were almost theres. Youz destroyed our chance to beez a prouds and honests peoples in our own homelands. Youz tooks away our identity."

Yes, I'd been a monster. I'd done to them what the Eosians had done to my people and my home. I'd taken their dream and their home. Crushed their spirit with haughty hubristic righteousness. Of all the atrocities I'd committed, this had been the worst. But ironically, this one I could undo. I couldn't bring back Serge's family. Couldn't undo what I'd caused to happen to Bas. Couldn't unkill Asphalios or all the others I'd sent to chaos. But *this* I could do. And I meant to succeed.

I met her challenging gaze with fierce determination and breathed out hoarsely, "I wish you would reconsider, Mayling." The words came out in a rusty tremulous voice, but I forced myself on. "I'm offering you the chance to regain your home and freedom for your people. To be the proud, honest and hard-working people you are destined to be. A people who deserve to be recognized this way by the galaxy. I offer myself, and those with me, as the champions of your cause...if you'll have us." I'd finally found my voice as sincerity coursed through me. I straightened and let the rich tones of my clear voice carry my message with new confidence. "We *will* get your home back for you." I thought of my MEC. "And we'll keep it safe from Legess and Guardians alike." I thought of Elasippus's guard with close to smug satisfaction. "This I can guarantee you." I felt my body drain of tension and my shoulders relax. "And after…" I searched deep into her sad eyes with my own sad gaze. "Afterward, you can do with me as you please."

"As weez pleases?"

I swallowed at her menacing look and nodded.

Mayling seemed to contemplate for a moment. I felt my heart quicken in the stillness of anticipation. Mayling said in a softer voice, "No one has ever stood up and fought for the Rill like you did on Sekmet." She contemplated some more in a long silence as I unblinkingly endured her stare. Then she finally leaned forward. I fought the instinct to recoil and mimicked her action instead. "We'll accept your offer to redeem yourself, Hawke," she said.

I seized her hand gratefully but she pulled out of my grip and drew it back.

"You chose well, Mayling."

"I hope so," she grumbled, handing me back my MEC.

## TWENTY-THREE

Slouched in my captain's chair with one leg parked on the console, I peered down through Benny's porthole at the convex horizon of Omicron 12. Slick brown streaks meandered through its rough grey-green surface—worm tracks left by the huge peat-harvesting ships as they scoured the planet's surface layer. It reminded me of the old images of the planet Mars in my home solar system and those "pesky" *canali*.

I glanced at Benny's console and asked him to continue his string of statistics. He happily obliged: "Omicron 12 is a bog-planet with a mass of $5.2 \times 10^{24}$ kg, a density of 5633 kg/m$^3$ and diameter of 12,204 kg..."

I nodded slowly.

"This backwater planet orbits Beta Canum Venatorocum or Beta CV, otherwise known as Chara, a G-type main-sequence star in the northern constellation Canes Venatici of the galaxy's Alpha Quandrant." Chara meant joy in Greek, I recalled. Together with the bright star Cor Caroli, the pair formed the 'southern dog'.

"Omicron orbits Chara at 35 km/s with a period of 225.8 days and inclination of 3.3," Benny continued. "It has no rings but possesses a global magnetic field." Something that—along with water, which it had plenty of—appeared as important in promoting diverse life forms as a viable atmosphere.

"Aside from the Rill, the bog-planet is also home to over six million species that vary from Protista to plant-like and animal-like creatures including the peeka, a key creature in helping to form and maintain Omicron 12's unique peatland," Benny continued.

Until the Rills got their gig mining Sekmet, they'd made Omicron 12 the top vendor of peat. It was interesting, I considered darkly, that two of my most significant life-changing experiences involved peat. And Rills. Our destinies seemed inexorably entwined. When I singlehandedly quelched the Rill uprising on Omicron 12 with my MEC, I set into motion a number of ironies— for the Rills, the Legess and ultimately for me.

"The peatland of Omicron 12—like Sekmet—is part of an ancient blanket fen that developed over thousands of years," Benny went on. "Rain seeps down through the iron-rich soil and forms a thin impenetrable iron pan, which waterlogs the soil above. Lack of oxygen prevents the bacteria and fungi from decomposing the dead plant material, helping to form the much sought-after peat."

"Yes," I said with a scowl, "much sought-after indeed." I gazed down at the rolling tapestry of exotic epiphytic and parasitic plants; the rust and blue-green patchwork covered most of the planet's soggy surface.

Omicron 12's open marshlands were home to the peeka, a small monotreme whose principle diet was *güçlüvesağlam*,

Omicron's most common marsh plant. Thanks to its unique digestive system, the peeka's feces accelerated the process of peat formation, making Omicron 12 one of the richest sources of renewable peat.

"Peat," Benny went on, "is the source of many products throughout the galaxy such as medicines, therapeutics, textiles, filters and fuels." Lots of planets had bog ecosystems that created peat and peat moss, I reflected. What made the peat of Omicron 12—and Sekmet, for that matter—unique and valuable to the Guardians, was that these two minerotrophic peatlands were both rich in *rein*, a compound that, when purified, could be transformed into a highly efficient crystal fuel for several Zeta Corporation ships such as the *alpha* class *twin-V wing*, *scythe-wing*, *beta* class *dauntless* and the *shadow tracker*.

That was why the Guardians harbored an interest in Omicron 12 and Sekmet. And who ran these planets, I considered. The Guardians obviously favored the Legess. I remembered Vuk, the Head Legess, telling me two years ago: "Rills are an undisciplined and vulgar race who, if they are not kept busy mining for us, are copulating for themselves. They are animals who must be managed by a good husbandry program." That wasn't why the Guardians supported the oppression of the Rill; the Guardians simply preferred doing commerce with the slimy Legess instead.

I shook off dark memories and sat up with a jerk. Today was the Day of the Rill.

Quelling the urge to pop a soy gum into my mouth—I'd stopped chewing that vile stuff since Sekmet—I ruffled my hair and leaned forward, blinking at Benny's readouts on his console.

"How are we doing, Benny?"

"Good, Rhea. I believe our old Enforcer code is still in good standing. It will secure us a landing permit to Mantis City."

I nodded with relief. "Thanks, Benny. And Elasippus?"

"He reached his allocated orbit half an hour ago. Stirring up a little trouble already, Rhea."

I nodded with a sly smile.

"The Legess have reacted to the presence of the *Boeotia*,"

Benny went on. "They've haled it several times."

"Without acknowledgment?"

"That's right, Rhea."

"Good." I sat back. They were nice and scared. Just the way I liked them, I thought with an ill-humored sneer. Something about the tall insectoid green bodies of the Legess reminded me of the *credula*, a plant-like mycoheterotrophic parasite. A social parasite, the *credula* "cheated" by first sharing then singularly taking from its established supposed symbiont.

The Legess were not known for their compassion, empathy or generosity. They were shrewd tradesmen, conducting their commerce with quiet, ruthless—and soulless—precision. Appearing like benefactors, they preyed on the weak and desperate, securing favors in the shadiest places. Hoarding ill-gotten riches collected through slavery, the Legess held themselves with lofty haughtiness in the galactic community. While many species expressed admiration for them as clever and astute, the very same likely feared them for what the Legess knew and held over them. They were the credula of the universe. *Dress a monkey in silk and it is still a monkey*—Argentinian proverb.

When a significant number of the Rill from Omicron 12 were sentenced to Sekmet and then proceeded to make it the prime peat—and wakesh—trade location in several galaxies, the Legess burst into a rage. They'd have retaliated with trade embargoes at least or more likely a mercenary raiding party; except they were dealing with a maximum-security galactic prison. The very facility that imprisoned the Rill protected them.

It was the ultimate irony: in punishing the rebel Rills by sentencing them to Sekmet, the Legess had given the Rill the best chance to rob them of their primary trade. Sekmet was, after all, a rich bog planet, much like Omicron 12.

I'd served as the prime vector. In "helping" the Legess, I'd actually provided a great opportunity for the Rill; particularly considering what Serge had confided in me. According to Serge, the hard working Rill pretty much ran the penal colony. And they ran it at a huge profit. But they still served a life of indenture and still suffered the risks of being in a lifer prison. Well, all that was about to change, I considered with a small smile of victory.

Today was the Day of the Rill. Today the victims of the universe would prevail. Today the arrogant would be humbled. Today a killer would be redeemed.

I released a deep sigh and straightened in my seat. "OK, Benny. Seems everything is in place. How's our passenger?"

"Resting," Benny replied.

"Good. Alert our guest. You're ready for my signal, right?"

"Right."

"Let's do it. Hail the Legess."

"Right, Rhea."

Ω

Benny set down on one of several dozen floating ships that resembled old Earth aircraft carriers. Each ship was a massive flat platform that housed buildings and a landing area for airships. Several dozen of these floating ships congregated in a loose fleet, forming migratory communities that drifted randomly over the planet, harvesting peat and other amenities. The ship I'd landed on housed the principle governing body for the Legess.

Hades had been designed after successful Legess floating cities, I considered. The nomadic model suited the lifestyle of the Legess, who needed to keep moving to harvest new peat. It was like rotating crops in Earth's old agricultural industry; only the Legess were the ones who "rotated".

"Remember what I said, Benny," I mentioned as I threw on my Great Coat and checked the settings on my MEC.

"Yes, Rhea."

I smiled. Like I had to remind Benny of anything, I thought; it was usually Benny who did the reminding.

"Prep our guest."

"Copy, Rhea."

Once my guest arrived, cloaked from head to foot, at the doorway, I opened the hatch and felt a clammy freshness on my skin. The cool breeze lifted my hair in a cruel carress and brought with it the pungent scent of oily bog. It smelled of darkness and unease. I blinked away dark memories and let my gaze sweep over the ship's platform to the endless rusty waves of rolling bog.

As I stepped down Benny's ladder, I glimpsed Vuk, approaching from the adjoining building in a loping gait. I hopped down with a light spring and turned to face the eight-foot tall Legess as my guest lumbered down the ladder.

"A pleasure and an honor as usual, Officer Hawke," he greeted me in the high-pitched obsequious voice that I found annoying and extended a claw to me in greeting.

I took it briefly and nodded. I craned to make eye contact. He was a good two feet taller than I was, even with that typical slight stoop. And he stood too close, crowding me. I thought of a turkey vulture on Earth and felt my hand itch toward the MEC holstered on my thigh.

I matched his look up to the cloaked figure slowly descending Benny's ladder. "My assistant," I explained. "And they could use some fresh air," I added, thinking that ironic; to me the pungent air seemed anything but refreshing.

My guest finally made it to the ground with a thump.

Vuk glanced with what I interpreted to be a frown at the stranger, then straightened and turned to me with an intake of air. "As you requested, the high council is assembled in the com centre," he informed me and swept a claw toward the building he'd come out of. "This way."

I had to scramble to keep up with his long steps as he clacked across the platform into the building. I glanced back a few times to ensure that my guest was following. We entered a spacious hallway with arching transparent ceilings.

"It is quite fortuitous for us that you chanced to be in the vicinity just as you did," said Vuk.

If that was an invitation for me to elaborate, I certainly wasn't about to accommodate him. "Yes," I simply said and nodded soberly.

"What do you think these pirates want?"

I curbed a smile; he'd already decided Elasippus and his crew were pirates. Perhaps he was right, I considered. "Peat, probably. Rein, most likely," I said. Did the Legess really not know about the bounty on me? Or was Vuk playing me to get what he wanted? I didn't trust him.

We stopped at a large door, attended by two guards with *nokerig* pistols holstered on their hips, and entered a tall chamber with a long table; a dozen or so Legess were seated around it, obviously waiting for us. I felt like a pigmy among them; even seated, they were imposing. On quick inspection, I recognized the high council of the Legess supreme government. They were all in this room, I thought. What a convenience.

I fought from glancing at my hooded guest, body concealed beneath the bulky cloak and face veiled by the hood.

I slid my Great Coat aside and poised my hand loosely on my hip beside my MEC, gunslinger style. Their beady eyes had all turned to us with expectation. I registered a few glinting eyes aimed at my impressive weapon and curbed a snarling smile.

The Legess weren't warriors, I considered. Just the thought of a pirate ship hovering over their planet made them more than uneasy. I was hoping for that very sentiment and decided to rest my twitching hand by letting it settle on the holster of the MEC in plain view.

"This is Galactic Guardian, Rhea Hawke," Vuk announced. He glanced dismissively at the hunched figure beside me and decided not to bother continuing the introductions.

"Gentlemen." I nodded to them. They were clearly expecting some kind of rescue; they weren't going to like what I had to say. "Thank you for assembling on such short notice." I then turned to my guest and nodded with a sly smile.

The hood came down and the council stared at Mayling. I heard a few intakes of air.

Vuk puffed up his insect-like frame. "What is the meaning of this!" he huffed and swung an arm out to direct his guards inside. "Guards!"

I cleared my throat loudly and he turned to my MEC pointed at him. "By all means, bring them in, Vuk," I said in a quiet voice. "Have your guards place their weapons on the ground and step away from them," I commanded, then added,

"Slowly, if you please."

The guards entered and I closed the door behind them, keeping the MEC pointed at them. They removed their *nokerigs* and placed them down then stood away.

"Thank you." I smiled politely and kicked the guns to the side. I then turned to the committee. "This is Mayling. You may recall sending her to Sekmet a while ago for inciting a rebellion—"

"Again, I say, what is the meaning of this?" Vuk cut in. "What do you want?"

"Justice," I replied.

"Why do you bring this murderer here now?"

"Yes, what does that *thing* have to do with justice?" another committee member piped up: an elder, whose weathered shell had already tarnished from chlorophyll green to grey.

"Everything, actually," I said.

Ω

"The Rill are the natives of this planet. Before you came along, they pursued a simple agrarian lifestyle. They made an honest living...until you enslaved them—"

"We did no such thing!" that same Legess said from the table. He was definitely an elder of the committee; small creases in his outer green shell provided telltale signs of a withering exoskeleton. A bit of a hothead too, I thought, letting my eyes narrow at him. He went on in that Legess-typical simpering voice that I decided I really hated, "We found them living in squalor in the swamps, dirty and malnourished and without the means or ambition to improve their sorry lot—"

"But weez werz *happy!*" Mayling countered. Her body shivered with rage. "We didn'ts needs youz to makes us into somthings else thans whats weez werz."

"Bah!" the Legess scoffed. "You were half-alive. We gave you a purpose in life and some amenities."

"Amenities!" Mayling's eyes bulged more than they already were.

I thought they might pop out of their protuberances. Luckily, I anticipated her next move — to rush the Legess elder and clout him on the head and barged in front of her. The Legess reacted by rising.

"Enough, Zok!" Vuk shouted. "This is getting us no where!" Then he turned to me. "What *do* you want? Why are you here?"

"I'm here to give the Rill their home back."

This time it wasn't just Zok who reacted with outrage. The entire committee got rowdy. I decided to stem a nasty scene and discharged my MEC into the ceiling. I'd swiftly set it to percussion. The glass ceiling popped and smashed into thousands of pieces. They rained glittering shards on us, followed by a brisk wind and the pungent spray of Omicron mist.

"You will do this," I said simply. "And I'll tell you why. Because an interstellar ship, full of the galaxy's best and most ruthless warriors is now orbiting your planet, awaiting my orders. No one will help you; certainly not the Guardians — who know what I'm doing right now and have already made a deal with the Rill..."

They hadn't yet, but I knew they would. They were typically awaiting my success here. Playing it both ways. The Legess didn't need to know that little detail, though, I thought.

I went on, "The Guardians are prepared to give the Rill amnesty from Sekmet — so long as they provide them with what they need from Omicron 12." That part was true; I'd spoken briefly with Euaimon on this. I let that settle in the minds of the Legess. They were quiet for a change. They knew they were in trouble now. "The Rill have a reputation as the very best harvesters of rein peat." Of course the Legess knew that; they'd been trying to mess with Sekmet for years.

"You have pretensions of grandeur," I continued. "You want respect? You have the chance to earn it — finally."

"You expect us to just give this place back to those *beasts* after we've made it into a successful enterprise?" Vuk said in a scoffing tone. He glowered briefly at Mayling with disgust. "You expect us to just leave? You're a fool and a naïve idealist, Rhea

Hawke. And you haven't a clue how this world works." His sly eyes gave him away; I knew he'd secretly alerted his outside guard before the door slid open.

I'd already reacted and pounced on Mayling, knocking her to the ground, as six guards burst into the room, Q-guns out. I shot from the floor and caught them all. I'd been expecting this. Maybe I did have some clue how this world worked, after all—

The crack of lightning struck and I realized as I fell that it was the sound of something making contact with my skull. As I reeled to the floor, MEC clattering to the ground, I caught the blurry image of Zok, leering down at me, peat shovel in his claws. Then the darkness of pain took me.

Ω

I eased painfully out of the darkness to a harsh light. I was looking up from the floor, where I'd fallen. My head pounded like a metratron weight. I saw Mayling's body lying beside me and felt my breath hitch in terrified misgiving. Had they killed her?

"It's useless, Hawke," Vuk said in a squeaky growl, something I hadn't thought possible. It grated on my ears like a cobal's squeal. He peered down at me with insect-eyes, MEC pointed at me.

As I rose shakily to my feet, he recoiled in obvious fear but kept the MEC pointed steadily at me. "We've alerted the national guard," he said smugly. "Three squadrons will be here in moments and your ship has been impounded."

It was an empty threat, I convinced myself. Benny had closed himself off like a kepry and was impregnable. I hoped.

Mayling stirred with a groan and I took heart in the fact that she wasn't dead.

"We won't take orders from a rebel Guardian, an Ex-Guardian," he said. So, they did know. "We'll take our chances with the *real* Guardians. As for your pirate friends, they'd do well to stay away or receive reprisals from the Enforcers of the Galaxy."

I'd had enough.

"Okay, Benny," I barely breathed out over my tooth-mic. "It's time." Was it too late already?

A sound by the door made me flinch. Jag me! The Legess guard was already here! I saw it in the smug faces of Vuk, Zok and the others. I was toast and Mayling might already be dead.

The door slid open.

A dozen Eosian guards, armed with stun sticks, surged inside, led by Gadeiros. He spotted me right away and nodded, intense eyes speaking volumes. Benoît was right behind him. His face flushed in the excitement of the hunt; he stood out as the only human of an entirely Eosian *Orichalkon* guard.

Elasippus entered followed by Serge, clutching his pocket pistol with both hands high in the *och's* position of fencing.

"I'd put that MEC down before you hurt yourself," Elasippus commanded in a booming voice. He pointed his stun stick at Vuk and cocked his head with a slanted smile. I thought him magnificent looking, dressed in his steel-blue *Orichalkon* uniform, stun stick outstretched in the crook of his arm like it belonged there. "Just try your luck," he added.

The Legess, true to his race, dropped the MEC and cowered back.

Elasippus nodded to me as I picked up my MEC. I noticed to my amusement that the setting hadn't changed from stunning a Legess; if Vuk had shot me I wouldn't have felt a thing.

"The national Legess guard have been dispatched and we've secured the ship," Elasippus reported to me. I must have made a funny face in my puzzlement because he smiled sideways and added as explanation, "Benny tipped us off a while ago, Rhea."

Ah, my smart ship...still rescuing me, I thought with a brief smile.

Serge knelt beside Mayling, who was already rousing. At my look of concern, he said, "She's ok. Just a bump on the head."

She growled out some nasty invective and struggled to her feet.

It was time to finish this, I decided, turning back to Vuk, now shrunken in the corner with the other Legess. Even Zok looked totally defeated. The gray of his chitinous skin had paled even more than its insipid gray.

I gingerly touched my head, where his shovel had made contact and felt the stickiness of blood. A huge bump had reared itself on it. After a glance at Mayling, I addressed the Legess leader, "Here's the deal: the Rill are returning from Sekmet, every single one of them. They will take over the running of these ships and the business of harvesting and selling peat to the Guardians and others. You will enter into a cooperative partnership with them and help them run the business. You are welcome to stay…" I glanced at Mayling, who was rubbing her bulbous head with her hand. She didn't look too happy with this arrangement but the pragmatist in her had agreed that it made sense. "Any Legess who can not see themselves entering into this egalitarian arrangement, can leave," I added. "We will keep a squadron of the Orichalkon here for the next five years to help in the transition and to ensure that all runs well—particularly for the Rill."

I turned to Gadeiros and waved my arm at him with a nod. "This gentleman will lead the armed contingent."

Gadeiros bowed to me and gave the Legess and Mayling a nod of acknowledgement.

"He is yours to command, Mayling," I added.

Gadeiros and she exchanged greetings.

I studied the Legess for a moment. "Anyone who thinks they will get support from the Guardians against this arrangement is in for a surprise; the Guardians are fully behind this."

I let my gaze rest on Zok, who looked humble for a change. The sight of the Eosian guard had changed everything for them. Good, I thought, noting that the old Legess didn't look so bad now. His former harsh appearance had vanished. A little humility sat well with him.

I pointed to Mayling beside me. "Mayling is now your new leader. You will accord her your complete respect. She was the successful Mevlani who ran Hades on Sekmet and has been running their peat business, which outcompeted yours, for years. You would do well to respect her wishes and ideas."

Vuk nodded and uttered quietly, "Yes, Officer."

I didn't bother to correct him. I was no such thing. No matter, I thought. The rest was up to Mayling and the Legess. They had much work to do; she, with the help of the Orichalkon and the cooperation of the Guardians, would retrieve her colleagues on Sekmet and reassemble the Rills, scattered here on Omicron 12.

It was time for me to go. I was suddenly very tired.

"I'll leave you all to it, then," I finished and turned to go, thinking only of Benny's snug pilot's chair.

Ω

Serge caught up to me and came beside me.

"I'd like to ride with you," he said.

I blinked. Why did he want to ride with me? I must have betrayed puzzled surprise.

"You're going my way," he explained. "To Scandia," he added quickly. Somehow, it had come out like a lame excuse and I wondered what his real motive was. I stopped and frowned at him. I was about to rebuff him when he added in a soft voice I couldn't gauge, "You handled them very well, Rhea." He smiled at me. "You showed compassion." Then he added with sincerity, "You were amazing."

I felt blood rush to my face and started walking again to hide my expression. A furtive glance revealed that he was still watching me. I couldn't stand it. I turned and practically growled, "Ok, you can come along in Benny; just don't get in my way," and left him there.

## TWENTY-FOUR

The door swung open and Serge burst into the washroom with an urgent expression on his face. He was breathing hard and his eyes gleamed like star clusters.

I started and flung my towel over my naked body.

"Serge!" I barked out my surprise in a sharp tone of rebuke to hide my thrill. I was ready to be alarmed, then swiftly registered that it wasn't danger but feral passion that lit his dark eyes. "Get out!"

"I'm in love with you!" he announced in a halting voice.

"I know," I said. "You mean V'rae. I just look like her."

He looked suddenly flustered. "You're not listening. I said I'm in love with *you*. Rhea Hawke. Rhea, *cherie*..." I hadn't heard that endearment in a long time and flushed at hearing it. "I want to spend the rest of my life with you, preferably in your arms."

Stunned, thrilled and appalled in quick succession, I backed away and secured the huge towel around me by rolling its edge with trembling hands. Was he drunk? His breath reeked of bourbon. He and Elasippus had been drinking again, I concluded.

His smile faltered but he moved forward, matching my retreat. "Oh, Rhea. I've finally come to my senses. Is it too late for us?"

"What about V'rae, your beloved, the one I brought back...for *you*."

Serge let out a breath and smiled sadly, ironically. "You saved her so she could find her true love. But it isn't me. V'rae discovered her soul-mate in Serge Bastion. They clicked like she and I never did. You would have noticed too if you weren't so busy saving the world." I *had* noticed. I just didn't think Serge had. "When she left Earth on that shuttle she asked for her freedom and gave me mine. She's moved in with him, at his place on Scandia—but you already know that. They've already made plans to wed. Bastion and V'rae are a perfect match for one another, Rhea." He moved forward, gazing at me with sudden eyes, until he was almost touching me. "Just like you and I are."

I stared at him.

"It's you I've *always* loved. Rhea Hawke: renegade Galactic Guardian Enforcer; rough around the edges, escaped-convict of Sekmet; fiercely devoted and noble warrior for justice and truth. And above all, the most ferociously beautiful, exciting and sensual woman I've ever met. I love you." He'd kept inching toward me until I felt his intoxicating breath on me.

I backed away, clutching the towel around my body more tightly, even though it was secured. I stammered, "But you *hate* me..."

He shouted out an unalloyed laugh that made me flinch. When he settled himself, he gazed at me longingly. "Oh, Rhea...I was wrong about so much. I was convinced that *you* hated *me*. After Martinez, I was still in love with you. V'rae explained everything to me when I visited them on Scandia. She told me what happened and why you did...what you did. And most importantly, that you still had feelings for me. Which gave me hope. I realized that I'd misjudged you terribly. I should have known better, should have had more faith in you. Martinez needed to be stopped. And you did it the only way open to you, which meant killing him after, well, after..." he stumbled. "Even if you did like him just a little..." He gave me a strange crooked smile of inquiry. "Did you?"

I lowered my gaze with an ironic smile. "I did feel sorry for him, though..." I trailed off. Then I murmured to the floor, "I thought you'd left...for good."

"But I came back!" He leaned in to kiss me.

I twitched my face aside, confused and needing to breath. I stammered out some nonsense: "But you and V'rae—you fell in love at first sight. I...you and I...we never really...and we always argued..."

"It's the other way around, Rhea. The love-at-first sight that she and I shared was prompted by your and my feelings for one another. V'rae and I didn't share as passionate and deep a bond as you and I, so you and I weren't compelled to fall in love instantly. Yes, I love her, but *you're* the one I fell head over heels in love with when I first met V'rae. It was you inside her that I fell for. She was your image but it was your spark, your nerve, your fierce heart that excited me. Those parts of you that I kept catching only glimpses of in her. Like your feral passion, your incredible smile, and even those sharp and nasty insults. Then, when I met you, I knew it was *you*. It was *you* I was making love to that last night before she was attacked by my brother. You were there, weren't you?"

I felt my face heat in confusion and nodded—my recurring dream. I backed into the sink and blurted out, "You abandoned me on Uma 1, when I crashed."

"No I didn't," he said, leaning into me and sending my heart thumping. "I called in your position—"

"Then took off."

He looked directly at me, eyes focusing deep, touching my heart. "I waited for them and the necessary equipment to arrive then I shifted into an Azorian and helped them get you out. I held you in my arms and carried you to the emergency vehicle then I laid you inside the emergency vehicle's healing tank. I so longed to kiss those pale lips of yours but there were too many meds around so all I did was make sure the tank was operational and you were on your way to healing. *Then* I took off."

I blinked in astonishment and stumbled on, "You told me that you only rescued me on Sekmet for the MEC design. And when I refused to give you the design, you agreed that it would have been better to have left me there."

His face softened and those thunderstorm eyes blazed into mine, drowning me. "Oh, Rhea," he said with obvious emotion. "Do you remember—and believe—*everything* I say?" He firmed his lips with memories. "I was angry—"

"At me."

"No—well, yes. But mostly at myself for being such an arrogant fool. I was dead certain that I could prevent you from giving the *Nihilists* your MEC design. So jagging sure I'd get it from you instead. That was my mission, Rhea. I was so confident of my powers of seduction over you, I thought it would be a quick play getting the MEC and its design and keeping you away from Ka. But you proved unswayable. Everything I said to you on Benny after Sekmet I was really saying to myself." He dropped his gaze briefly and let his shoulders sag, backing away a little to give me some room. When he looked up again, his eyes sparkled like galaxies. "You did nothing wrong, Rhea. You acted out of compassion for Bas and everything you did on Sekmet was more than admirable, particularly considering your physical and mental condition. You behaved with honour, compassion and mercy toward a group of sick murderers, none of whom would have accorded you the same. And what you did for the Rills, even though it wasn't what they needed, touched them with compassion for you. I know, Mayling told me."

"She did?" I was close to tears. She certainly hadn't given me any impression the last time I was with her.

He gave me a kind smile, guessing my thoughts. "Yeah. And that was *before* this last trip to Omicron 12. She's proud. Ironic, huh? Considering what most think of them, the Rill are actually very proud folk. She could never tell you to your face how much she was moved by your actions for her and the others on Sekmet, never mind what you just did on Omicron 12. You totally redeemed yourself in their eyes. Even that old cow, Iris. You gave them back their pride."

I laughed and flung my hands to my mouth to keep the rest from bursting out.

"They told me some of the things that happened on Sekmet, before I got there and saw for myself." His face grew dark and pensive. "I'm so sorry..." He leaned his head against mine and I felt my heart swell with memories. "When you recovered onboard Benny and I found you awake in sickbay, I wanted so much to just give in to my feelings for you. But I had a mission, one I was failing miserably because you refused to let me sway you. In fact you made it clear right then what you thought of me. From that moment on I convinced myself that you really didn't like me and I'd ruined our chances together by being such an arrogant blenoid. I was more devastated by that than my failed mission. And then—"

I lunged forward and stared into his eyes with a crazy manic grin. The kind I knew drove him crazy. "Oh, shut up and kiss me!"

He stared at me for a silent moment, registering what I'd just said. Then his storm cloud eyes lit into mine and he seized me in a tight embrace. I leaned into him and we kissed.

I'd found home at last.

Ω

With sudden urgency, he tugged off my towel and let it drop to the floor. After a deep inhale as his dilated eyes drank in my body, Serge gruffly lifted me off my feet and carried me to the shower stall.

"No, there!" I pointed out of the bathroom.

He rushed us through the door and practically threw me on the infirmary table with a frantic swipe of his hand on the table to make room. Equipment flew off in a clatter then he swiftly pulled off his sweater.

"I meant the bed!" I gasped in a half-laugh.

"Huh?" he grunted, mid-way through sliding out of his trousers. He grinned like a boy and scooped me up then deposited me more gently on the bed and finished pulling off his trousers. I hadn't seen him naked in a long time and inhaled sharply at his magnificent physique, drinking in every inch of exquisite maleness. From his long chaotic curls of silver-brown hair, his roughly hewn imperfect aristocratic face, down his powerful torso, marked by exquisite blemishes and scars, and his thickly corded arms and legs. And then finally to the dark froth of hair that crested his manhood. Already swollen and erect. Waiting, begging for me and stirring me to wetness.

Serge moved onto the bed and kneeled astride my hips. My belly flamed and I felt my heart pulsing between my thighs, hungry for him. It had been so long that I'd wanted to touch him intimately. Now I was frantic with uncontrollable passion for all of him.

He bent low, warmly pressing, until I felt his hard organ trail against my skin, and flushed. A wild rhythm beat inside me. His hands moved over my breasts, kneading and teasing my nipples hard. A painful ecstasy welled up in a tide of wet arousal as I hungered for him to fill me. I pulled him franticly close, felt his young stubble brushing my cheek, heating my face. I took his face in my hands, kissed his slippery lips and invited his tongue inside. His penetrating kiss sizzled through me like a shaft of lightening.

Tongue and phallus charged in deep. I gasped in a flush of sudden coming and struggled to hold back from climaxing, waiting for him. But in bridling it in, the longing pain became almost unbearable and sent me into a plaintive trembling wail, bucking into him with urgency.

He thrust hard, ricocheting in throbbing waves of aching desire. Up through my trembling body until, feeling him crest and ejaculate, I released my tide of coming. It pulsed out of me with a shuddering, unrestrained scream to his growling bellow. He continued to throb inside me with echoes of his love as I shuddered out my release in waves, like the aftershock of a tumultuous earthquake.

I seized him close in dreamy effervescence, and kissed his whole face hungrily, possessively. He responded with wild kisses then finally drew my face next to his, cheeks touching, in quiet love. Still joined, he coaxed us into lying sideways, and we remained entwined in rapt silence, drifting into a half-sleep.

I woke from my doze, aroused, with arms and legs entwined in Serge's. Feeling him still deliciously inside me and aching for more, I ran my finger along the crease between his buttocks and thighs and murmured, *"Mon cherie..."*

He roused with a low moan and abruptly throbbed inside me, firming in waves. It sent a pulsing charge through my loins.

"Ah, *ma cherie...*" he whispered hoarsely then brushed his lips and tongue against mine.

I gasped into a moan of wanton desire and arched into him.

"I'm all yours," I breathed out in a husky voice. "Take me again."

"I think I already have you," he laughed hoarsely, now lazily pumping me. I met his escalating rhythm, undulating with him and climbing slowly toward another apex.

"You know what I mean."

"Tell me. Exactly," he teased, giving me his sideways rakish smile, and slowing his motions to my frustration.

"*Jag* me!" I grunted out urgently, bucking into him and grabbing him by the hair. "Damn you! Will you *jagging jag* me!"

Ω

Serge was leaning on one elbow and lazily drinking me in with his dark lustrous eyes. His fingertips languidly trailed the smooth curve of my torso, hip and leg as I lay nude on my back beside him. "She knew even before we did, you know," he quipped.

"Who?" I turned to face him.

"V'rae. She knew from the beginning. But it wasn't until our big spat at Martinez's estate that she understood how besotted I was with you...and understood why."

Martinez...Raphael. It brought back memories and responsibilities I'd briefly forgotten.

"Before she left Earth on the shuttle, V'rae told me that you were in love with me but I didn't dare believe her..." Serge blithely went on. "She told me to go to you as she was going to her true love. She beat me to it, Rhea. I told you the truth before: I never intended to leave you on Earth. I was going to put V'rae on the shuttle, after telling her that I intended to stay. Only, she beat me to it, told me that she knew I was in love with you as she'd fallen in love with Bastion." He grinned like a boy. "We set each other free."

I smiled askance. "Only you hadn't counted on..." I trailed.

"Raphael...When I saw you with...*him*...doing..."

I put my finger on his lips and thought of Raphael. My Epoptes twin. "It wasn't love," I said softly then kissed Serge. He leaned into my kiss and wrapped himself around it like a mantle, gripping my face with trembling hands. He knew he had my love, all of it. But he sensed there was more. Something I wasn't sharing with him. Raphael would remain between us, a mystery, until I unfolded the truth. A truth I wasn't willing to share just yet.

"I know," Serge said when he drew away. Eyes suddenly sparking into an intense gaze, he abruptly seized my arm. "You know that I have to go back to my diverse to prepare against the *Nihilist* revolt."

I stared into his storm-cloud eyes in confusion. "How will you go there; the Gate's no longer open."

His eyes crinkled in a crooked smile. "I'm sure you could help me there, being a soul-drifter." Then his eyes blazed like a star cluster and his mouth opened to a gleaming open smile. "I could use some help in the inner diverse...So, will you come back with me? Join me there?"

Totally unprepared for his invitation, I stared at Serge and opened my mouth without saying anything. He touched my lips with his fingers.

"Marry me, Rhea."

"Serge...I..." I squeaked, now overwhelmed. When I finally found my voice I knew what I had to say. I turned on my side to face him and mimicked his position of leaning on my elbow. "I belong to this world, Serge, the outer diverse. I might have a few clues as to how it works after all...thanks to you and my good friends." I thought of Elasippus, Gadeiros, and my loyal Eosian Guard. "I can't give up on the outer diverse now." I swallowed down my emotions and pulled away from him to sit up. He followed and sat up with me, legs crossed and listening intently. "I *want* to marry you," I said. "But—" I kept swallowing convulsively as I forced out the rest, "I can't. It wouldn't be fair to you. You need to be in your diverse and I'm still needed in mine." I thought of Raphael and the rest of the renegade Epoptes. I couldn't abandon my Eosian Guard, not after what they'd done for this diverse, for *me*.

"What about the law?" He said in obvious frustration. "You're still a sought-after Sekmet convict, Rhea, by both the Guardians and local PDs. If they ever catch up with you, you're dead. Plus Eclipse is still after you and the rest of the *Nihilists*."

Not to mention the other renegade Epoptes for killing their leader. "I'll be fine," I said.

"In my diverse you'd have a fresh start. You could take V'rae's identity. She's staying here with Bastion. You could try a hand at art. I know you studied it when you were young. And you have an interest in book collecting. You could make a fresh start, have a normal life..." Then he added with a mischievous understanding smirk, fingertips trailing a path along my leg, "on the side, that is."

To live my unrealized dreams. It was an opportunity most people didn't get, I reflected. And it was very tempting. But impossible for a number of reasons, several I could not tell Serge. How far from that place I'd traveled, I considered.

"I can still do a lot of good here," I finally responded. "I know too much not to share that knowledge with those who need it. I have a responsibility, Serge. Dangerous as it might be. The Galactic Guardians aren't what I thought they were. What they used to be. And with Ennos gone, Euaimon is in charge of the Iota Hor b Precinct." And I had a score to settle with him. "I have to stay. This world needs me even if they don't think they do." I didn't tell him about the Epoptes and my obvious role in dealing with them. That would come later.

I'd watched his expression change from hopeful confidence to dismay then sad acceptance. I knew he understood. I'd spoken from the heart. Serge bowed his head for a moment. When he looked up again, there was pain on his face. "What about *us*. What about our love for one another?"

I dropped my gaze to my fidgeting hands.

He seized my hands and forced me to meet his fiery gaze. "We can't do this to each other, Rhea. We belong together. You know we do," he said in a hoarse voice. This was too much. Burning tears threatened and tightened my face in an effort to keep them from flowing. "From the moment we met, there was fire between us," he went on. "Rhea, we're so good together. In every way. We work so well together."

I nodded with a swallow. He was right. We made a good team. We complemented each other and seemed to share an uncanny ability to sense the other's need. I cleared my throat and gave him a hopeful, imploring look, pushing out words of compromise, "We could have long visits together in each diverse...Take turns." I found my lips quivering in a smile. "We'd be the first inter-diverse couple, the first metaverse travellers." I saw his eyes light up with hope. "We could divide the year into quarters: first quarter together in your diverse; next alone in our original diverses; then third quarter together in my diverse; then last quarter alone in our original diverses. And so on."

Serge responded with a sad chuckle. "Oh, Rhea, you know I'll take you any way you want and anything you offer me." Did he really mean that? "I just can't get enough of you. When you aren't with me I'll be longing for you with every sighing breath. But when you're with me, I'll be celebrating every part of you with all my being…starting with now…" He leaned in and folded his arms around me then pulled us down on the bed, mouth embracing mine.

When his mouth finally pulled away it was only to whisper in an insistent tone, "Marry me anyway. It'd be the first inter-diverse marriage. Marry me, Rhea!" And clamped his mouth back on mine before I could answer. I smiled, mouth still connected to his, and assented with my eyes. *Yes!*

## TWENTY-FIVE

"Leave us," Euaimon said gruffly to the Eosian Guardians that held me at the door of his office in the precinct. The security men let go of me and shuffled out the door, leaving me alone with Euaimon.

After a long studious gaze at me, Euaimon turned to pour himself a glass of red wine from his personal bar and eyed me in inquiry, raising his glass to me. I shook my head. He crossed to one of his comfortable chairs and sat. "Please," he said, motioning to a chair facing him. As I sat down, he continued with a crooked smile, "I hear that the galaxy's most talented independent Eosian guard, the *Orichalkon*, now calls itself *Hawke's Men*."

I glanced down at the floor with a faint smile of amusement. It was Elasippus's idea to rename their guard, especially now that they'd foresworn any further connection with

Raphael's Hermetic Order. Despite my objection, he'd gone ahead and chosen something he'd thought more appropriate, much to my embarrassment. Of course, I felt honoured. Elasippus told me the day I presented him with a crate of original Kentucky-made *Buffalo Trace Bourbon* bottles I'd managed to find on Ogium 9. I'd never seen a happier man.

"I hear they've sworn to serve only one person," Euaimon said with a growing smirk. "You." He aimed a steady gaze at me. "Apparently they follow you everywhere. What do you say to all that?"

"It's true," I said with an enigmatic smile. "They're orbiting Iota Hor b right now."

He leaned back in his chair and studied me in silence for a moment, then asked in a quiet voice, "Why have you come, Hawke?" He'd decided to be direct with me and I appreciated it.

It gave me the chance to be equally direct with him. "You killed my father."

"Ennos, your father?" Euaimon stared at me for a moment then laughed sharply in unalloyed humour. "He couldn't be anyone's father; he couldn't sire a blenoid if he tried. Besides the fact that he normally preferred men, he was impotent." He pointed gruffly to his holo-com. "Check the medical records. Use you ship's AI; I know it has successfully tapped our confidential files." I felt my face heat at the truth. Then, he leaned forward with alarming intensity and astonished me with his next statement: "*I'm* your father, Rhea."

"You couldn't be!" Was he a Vos?

Euaimon smiled indulgently at me. "You're thinking about your inner diverse twin...yes, of course I know about her. I'm her father too. You were a lot alike; V'rae even has your penchant for sweets, chocolate, especially, eh? If you check her right knee you'll find the same scar you have when you crashed at twelve in that *Whip* race and didn't bother to nuyu it away. She got hers in a fall doing *Vedallic* skydance. I watched her grow up, put her through school. Alas, with your mother, such a free spirit, it was a little different. Off to the next one, eh? When she and you disappeared off Earth, I lost you for a while. I never stopped looking, you know. Both Ennos and I moved up the ranks and ended up at the Iota Hor Precinct. Then I found you on Ogium 9 and I convinced Ennos to take you on."

I thought he was smoking hedon. It was my weapons designing that got me in. "You were the main one protesting my inclusion," I challenged.

He shrugged. "I had to object." He leaned forward with a sideways smile. "You don't know Ennos that well, do you? It was my intense objection that solidified his decision to take you on." He grinned. "A bit of reverse psychology."

I couldn't stand it and surged to my feet, swinging my arms up in exasperation. Tears of confused frustration weren't far away but I kept them at bay. "I don't care who my father is!" I said gruffly to hide my other emotions and paced the room. "Ennos, you, Donald Duck…None of you were there…It doesn't matter to me anymore—"

"It should," he said. "Because I'm an Epoptes." With that he stood, body shifting from deep mauve to human flesh colour and into the beautiful angelic form I'd learned to associate with an Epoptes. He looked a lot like Raphael, I considered. "I'm one of a few Epoptes that made it across to the other diverse."

I gave him credit; he stood in calm silence, giving me time to recover. I managed to counter, "That doesn't alter the fact that you shot my—my—your superior officer for no apparent reason."

He shrugged, eyes still casually regarding me as though we were discussing the upcoming tournament of Galactic SpaceBall. "He was aiding a known convict of Sekmet, accused of murder and terrorism…He'd just emerged from your ship, unscathed, with you about to escape and you'd just thrown him his weapon. What was I to think?"

"Thinking and doing are obviously two different things for you," I remarked dryly.

He sighed out a wry grin and sipped his wine. "I knew what Ennos was, Rhea. A *Nihilist* terrorist, besides being a bastard and a most appalling bureaucrat. You gave me an opportunity I couldn't neglect."

I gave him a steady gaze. "*Never cut what can be untied—*

Portugese proverb."

"*A little help is better than a lot of pity*—Celtic proverb," he rejoined and raised a brow.

I nodded and persed my lips in sad acknowledgement. He was probably right, I considered, thinking I'd slung enough proverbs to everyone to deserve a few back. Even from Euaimon.

He drained his glass and set it down on his bar then turned back to me, eyes glinting with a new topic. "You've done well, Officer Hawke." He'd returned to his official tone. "You rid us of those vicious *Nihilist* Vos terrorists—they've scattered and are all but lost without their leader; you averted a nasty galactic catastrophe and closed the Gate to keep the rest out. Now we have our tidy peaceful world back." He sat back down, crossing elegant legs. "I've reinstated you to full Enforcer status. It's yours—if you still want it, that is. In any case, I've wiped your record clean. I'm not feeding you blenoidshit, Rhea. Have your pesky AI check out the files." He grinned. "No more vigilante squads, bounty hunters or nasty head-hunters following you. You're free to go wherever you wish. But you're more than welcome here. We could use your special skills and your unique resources. Welcome back."

I stared at that beautiful Epoptes face and willed myself to sigh with relief. I was free. And home at last...or was I?

## TWENTY-SIX

I felt my heart swell inside me as I strode beside my mother down the Gleise 12 hospital hallway. My little brother flopped across my chest in my arms. His head rested on my shoulder and he sighed in the bliss of sleep. I inhaled his sweet scent—ginger and clove with a touch of juniper—and couldn't help a grin of unalloyed joy. I'd seen far too little of him, I considered. He kept growing so much!

"I thought it was a stroke of genius, Rhea." My mother leaned into me as we approached the Rill at the reception desk.

She was no doubt referring to my recent donation to the hospital of a certain furry creature.

My mother looked beautiful, I thought, as I briefly studied her in her elegant tocanai skirt and jacket and her newly shaped hair. It made her look so much younger, I decided. I felt proud to be her daughter. She had no idea what she really was and I wasn't about to tell her. Maybe one day. But not today.

"That tappin of yours is quite a character," she added with a wink. I nodded with a self-pleased smile. I'd given Jaz to my mother for Bas, if the hospital allowed it. They did. My mother had reported that Jaz was a hit with the other residents and she thought she'd recognized a reaction from Bas to the charming tappin. Jaz was happy in his new home. They'd built a small door for him so he could come and go and do his tappy things like roam the neighborhood at night and hunt for drens and mice; then return in the early morning and curl up at Bas's feet, paw draped over him like a prize.

"Rowling, this is my daughter," my mother introduced me to the Rill, who checked me out with his extended eyes. "She's—"

"Rhea Hawke," Rowling finished for her. My chest tightened at his recognition. "Rhea Hawke, who freed the Rills," the Rill added.

I blinked hard at him, overwhelmed.

My mother grinned. "We're here to see…"

"Yes, Bas," Rowling finished for her again. "Please go ahead. An honor to meet you, Rhea Hawke." Rowling nodded respectfully to me.

A kind of warmth coursed through me and I felt a smile blossom. "Thank you, Rowling," I said.

My mother led me to where Bas lived and after a gentle knock, she opened the door to his room.

We entered and I saw Bas, sitting on his bed with that blank face I hadn't forgotten. That blank expression that had haunted me since I'd brought him here. He stared ahead as if to a distant shore, to a place only he could see. Jaz lay curled up against him on the bed.

Then a miracle happened.

That blank face softened. The glaze in his eyes lifted and he focused on me and my baby brother, now stirring in my arms.

Then an inkling of a smile lit his face and his hand moved gently over the cat in a soft caress.

I stared and felt tears spring to my eyes.

"Welcome home, Rhea," my mother said gently. *"There are many paths to the top of the mountain, but the view is always the same*—Chinese proverb," she offered.

I barked out a laugh amidst my tears—more because it seemed that everyone was offering me my own medicine of wise proverbs—even my sweet mother.

She looked at me in bewilderment, not sure how to gauge my reaction.

"It's OK, Mom," I reassured her. "I agree." Then my eyes lit with my own piece of acquired wisdom. *"Knowledge is learning something every day. Wisdom is letting go of something every day*—Zen proverb."

My mother laughed with joy. "Yes, my wise daughter. Yes, indeed…"

We both turned back to Bas, his smile now in full bloom, watching us with clear eyes as he patted the purring tappin.

*The acts of this life are the destiny of the next*—Eastern proverb.

## EPILOGUE

*I'm an Epoptes. To be sure, I still don't know what that really means to me. I never believed they existed until I discovered that I was one. You're never quite sure what you are until circumstance throws you a curve ball. I look, feel and talk like a human. But I'm so much more—so my apophus grandmother told me. Indeed, to most humans—and certainly to all Eosians—Epoptes are regarded as gods...the Watchful Ones, according to the ancient Greeks. I'm certainly no god...and yet I am capable of god-like feats. Does that make me a god? My devoted Eosian Guard seem to think so. It makes me feel so...responsible.*

*The esoteric books claim that in seeking enlightenment our souls venture on a journey of great distance only to return home, finding it there. My journey of discovery has been a long and tortuous one. It has taken me to the farthest spiral arms of the galaxy. Yet, nowhere have I encountered more challenging or enlightening aspects of my journey than when I came 'home', to Earth, where I grew up as a child...and had to face the violence I'd committed, which I'd let define the rest of my life.*

*The psychology books say that prejudice results mostly from fear of an unknown and guilt in one's known faults. They claim that to lose both, you need only do the one thing: accept. I used to despise Eosians, then my mother told me that I was partly Eosian. I hated and feared the Vos, until I learned that Vos blood coursed through my veins and what it meant to be a Vos. I then discovered that I was the very being whose existence I'd denied as myth all my life. An Epoptes. I'd become my own myth.*

*The Bible—the greatest book of them all—claims that "there is no fear in love; but perfect love casts out fear." I'd so long practiced the illusion of strength in aloofness and force that I'd forgotten the genuine thing in compassion and love. In the end, it was my grandmother who gave me the most important lesson of my life when she told me to yield but not surrender. I never understood until the very last, when I yielded to Ka and closed the Gate and brought us back to the point from which we had begun. I used to think they were the same but they are the opposite. To surrender is to give up; to yield is to give in. One is an act of defeat and the other an act of faith. To yield to that which we do not quite understand is to faithfully embark on a journey that will lead us home; in moments like the reciprocity of the blenoids in the desert, or uncalled for compassion from a ruthless assassin...*

*I haven't told anyone that I'm an Epoptes, or that I carry one inside me; not even my dear beloved and betrothed, though I think he suspects something. When I do find the courage to tell him, I pray that he'll forgive me and understand. I'll explain why I think that a Vos like him and an Epoptes like me—mortal enemies in principal, but twin soul mates in a Metaverse held together with love—can together usher in a new age of peace and harmony. I pray that our love for one another and for the worlds we live in will carry us through.*

*Because God...my God is a loving god.*

# Lexicon of "Splintered Universe"

**Ae•on (also Ai•on)** \ Æ-ôn \ *n* : in Gnosticism, a divine power or nature emanating from the Supreme Being and playing various roles in the operation of the universe

**Ae•on Sun•tel•ia** \ Æ-ôn sün-tel-iä \ *n* : **1** : the End of the Age according to the ancient Greeks, described by Plato as a cycle of catastrophe; the sun rising out of the mouth of the "ouroboros" or "serpent eating its own tail" of the Milky Way; **2** : a prediction made in 207 SGT by Raphael Martinez, leader of the Hermetic Order, of a violent end of an age; according to the prophet Martinez, the destruction of the old world *"will be signified by the joining of twin souls who will herald the coming of a New Age."*

**al•tru•ism** \ ôl-trü-ism \ *n* : the principle or practice of unselfish concern for or devotion to the welfare of others; a motivation to provide something of value to a part other than oneself; pure altruism consists of sacrificing something (e.g., time, energy, possessions) for someone other than the self with no expectation of compensation or benefits, direct or indirect

**al•tru•is•tic** \ ôl-trü-is-tik \ *adj* : describes the action of *altruism*

**am•mut** \ am-mət \ *n* : a large invertebrate that makes its eggshells of swamp detritus. During their larval stage, they are extremely carnivorous and will devastate the swamp wildlife. They hatch and swarm during the season of the dead on Horus. The ammut eat the young *apophus*. As adults they become vegetarian and serve as food for the *apophus*

**an•ti-Ni•hi•list** \ an-tē-nī-a-list \ *n* : someone who opposes either philosophically or through action the activities and philosophy of the *Nihilists*.

**a•po•phus** \ A-pô-fəs \ *n* : a gigantic snake-like creature known through local myth that inhabits the *Boiling Sea* in the *Weeping Mountains* are of the planet *Horus* (47 Uma a) in the 47 Ursae Majoris system

**A•the•na** \ A-thē-nä \ *n* : 1 : Greek goddess of reason, intelligence, arts and literature; 2 : defence / research space station orbiting Iota Hor-2

**A•zor** \ A-zór \ *n* : a planet in the 55 Cancri binary star system 40 ly from Earth that orbits 55 Cancri b, a Jovian planet; principle inhabitation on Azor is Phla

**A•zor•i•an** \ A-zór-ē-ən \ *n* : a tall, heat-loving lean-limbed biped species with tough sand-paper hide, long snout and ferret face from Azor in the Beta Hydri system

**Bad•o•win** \ bad-ō-in \ *n* : a small, very strong, gnarled and hairy biped species of often ill-repute, originating on the planet Nexus in the M103 star cluster

**bar•khan (also bar•chan)** \ bär-kən \ *n* : cresent-shaped migrating sand dunes that are wider than long. These dunes form under winds that blow consistently from one direction and may move over desert surfaces with remarkable speed, particular to Upsilon 3.

**bas•tet** \ bas-tet \ *n* : a genetically produced mammal that displays aggressive co-evolution and wiped out the domestic cat population and Earth's large feral cats.

**Be•le•us** \ be-lē-əs \ *n* : an Earth-size moon, colonized by humans, which orbits the gas giant planet HD28185b that orbits the G class main sequence yellow star HD28185

**Be•le•us Ci•ty** \ be-lē-əs ci-tē \ *n* : the principle human inhabitation on the Earth-size moon Beleus

**Ben•ny** \ ben-nē \ *n* : Rhea's sentient ship; see *corvette*

**bio•mi•me•tic** \ bīó-mi-me-tic \ *adj* : the application of biological methods and systems in nature, particularly in living organisms, in the design by sentient beings of houses, engineering structures, vehicles, etc.

**blan•ket bog** \ blan-ket bôg \ *n* : **1** : an extensive peatland (wet spongy perched water ecosystem) formed in a climate of high rainfall and low level of evapo-transpiration, allowing peat development not only in wet hollows but over large expanses of undulating ground; an ecosystem usually consisting of hummocks and pools with specifically adapted plant and animal life; an extensive bog-fen landscape; **2** : principle ecosystem of the planets Sekmet and Omicron 12

**blen•oid** \ blen-óid \ *n* : **1** : a ferocious and supposedly dull-witted four-legged dog-like animal with three sets of razor sharp teeth, massive head with three eyes and tough red hide; indigenous to Upsilon 3 in the Epsilon Endari system; **2** : term used for a person with these traits : CRAZY; MAD

**bless•pep•per wine** \ bles-pep-ər wīn \ *n* : a mood-altering alcoholic beverage made from the fermented drupe-like fruit of the blesspepper tree, favored by the Scandi, who show a particular sensitivity to its effects

**Bo•eo•tia** \ bō-e-tē-ä \ *n* : the flagship of the stealth squadron *Odysseus* in the *Orichalkon*; a Class A *fugitive* interstellar ship crewing 100 men and commanded by Elasippus, a leader of the Special Operations Unit of the Eosian *Orichalkon*

**Bo•bo Bar** \ bō-bō bär \ *n* : a snack bar comprising of chewy bobouris fruit jerky and artificial chocolate

**Bog** \ bog \ *n* : form of wetland mire characterized by acidic conditions, low mineral content and usually dominated by sedges, shrubs and *Sphagnum* moss; major ecosystem that contributes to peat formation; see also *fen*

**Boil•ing Sea** \ bóēl-ēng sē \ *n* : term used for the great convoluted inland sea surrounded by the *Weeping Mountains,* on the planet *Horus* (47 Uma a); characterized by a surface scum of *shallik oil,* a narcotic oil produced by microbes in the *Weeping Mountains*

**Borr** \ bōr \ *n* : **1** : four-legged gentle species, indigenous to the planet Borrias and extirpated by the Vos Nihilists; **2** : a shape-shifting species thought to be from Borrias

**Bor•ri•as** \ bōrēass \ *n* : a planet in the Perseus Arm, home of the Borrs

**bu•ma** \ bü-mä \ *n* : the inside muscle of the buiuma's digestive tract that sloughs off as the *buiuma* inverts itself. This event occurs twice a year, during *kelm,* the wet season of the Eosian jungle. It is considered an Eosian delicacy.

**Cer•ber•us** / sər-bər-äs / *n* : **1** : a multi-headed dog or "hellhound" that guards the entrance of Hades in Greek and Roman mythology; **2** : the term Rhea coined for the tall cylinders that dispensed the drugged nourishment on the penal colony of Sekmet : *"Each cylinder with its swollen bulbous reservoirs, resembled a three-headed cyber-beast, with flexible teets suckling its deformed young."*

**cha•os** \ kā-ôs \ *n* : **1** : the confused unorganized state existing before the creation of distinct forms; **2** : complete disorder **syn** confusion **3** : common expletive to denote less than optimal to utterly calamitous or disastrous conditions **syn**

"hell"

**co•bal** \ cō-bôl \ *n* : a small vole-like burrowing rodent native to the deserts of Upsilon 3 and the mainstay prey of the blenoid

**cor•vette** \ cōr-vet \ *n* : mid-sized intersteller ship manufactured by Tangent Shipping, owned and operated by Fauche ship-builders on Bedar 9 in the Sigma Draconis system; **1** : *ray* class is a two-man hybrid with organo/nano technology that uses brain waves (in REM sleep) as a source of power; a sentient ship with folding wings and fuel scoops that retrieve particle energy from gas giant upper atmospheres where Kappa particles concentrate; Rhea Hawke's ship, Benny **2** : *hawke* class is a four-man interstellar ship

**co•zu shrub** \ cō-zü shräb \ *n* : a silver-green small shrub with thorns, and "popping" seed pods, indigenous to the desert of Upsilon 3

**creel** \ crēəl \ *n* : a fungus from Omega 6 that grows naturally into a metallic burnished hard surface and used by biomimetic architects on Horus to build their floors.

**cre•du•la** \ credülä \ *n* : a plant-like mycoheterotrophic parasite, native to Eos. Considered a "social parasite", given that it initially provides a beneficial nutrient only to ultimately consume its host once the host reproduces.

**cre•on** \ crē-ôn \ *n* **1** : an individual of the main species from the planet Creos in the 55 Cancri system; known for their laziness, lack of good judgement and imagination; **2** : term used to indicate an individual with these traits : FOOL; IDIOT; DULLARD

**Cre•os** \ crē-ôs \ *n* **1** : a planet in the 55 Cancri binary star system with dust disk; Creos orbits 55 Cancri b, a Jovian gas giant, in an orbit around the G8V class yellow-orange star; **2** : used in expletive to denote idiocy or unlikely chance (as in *"what in Creos were you thinking?"*)

**daunt•less** \ dônt-less \ *n* : beta class 10-passenger interstellar entirely AI-run ship manufactured by Zeta Corp Aeronautics

**De•le•ne•an** \ Də-le-nē-ən \ *n* : simple furry creatures with six appendages, native to Mar Delena in the Fomalhaut system. This species is subservient to the AI community that runs Mar Delena

**di•verse** \ dī-vərs \ *n* : a term that describes the notion of the existence of two parallel and divergent universes that comprise an infinite metaverse; twin paradoxical worlds, outer and inner diverses, connected through black holes, quasars, dreams, intuition and déjà vu

**dool blade** \ dül blād \ n : a large scythe-shaped Class D weapon manufactured by Anglebush Industries and used by Venik slave traders.

**drec•ca•line** \ drec-cä-lēn \ n : a non-specific highly potent nerve poison that kills all life

**du•en•de** \ Dü-en-de \ *n* : an old Spanish word that describes a heightened state of emotion, expression and authenticity, loosely meaning "having soul"; promoted and discussed by Spanish poet Frederico Garcia Lorca as an inner transcendent emotional response and spirit of evocation with roots from Spanish mythology

**dust** \ dəst \ *n* : a psychoactive drug that produces mild euphoria and drowsiness in most sentient species; refined from the *wakesh root* that grows in the blanket bogs of Sekmet; see also *glitter dust*

**Elyssia** \ elisia \ *n* : **1** : a place the gods go to when they die; **2** : the flagship of the stealth squadron *Daedelus* in the *Orichalkon*; a Class A *fugitive* interstellar ship crewing 100 men and commanded by Autochthon, a leader of the Eosian Special Operations Unit of the *Orichalkon*

**en•do•rhe•ic** \ en-dō-rē-ik \ *adj* : pertaining to a closed drainage basin (a lake) that retains water and allows no outflow to other external bodies of water such as rivers or oceans; a self-enclosed system equilibrated through evaporation

**E•os** \ Ē-ôs \ *n* : ringed jungle Planet in the Pleiades Nebula, where Eosians settled from Earth; original home of the vishna tree; principle city is Uruk

**E•os•i•an** \ Ē-ōs-ē-ən \ *n* : principal sentient being from Eos in the Pleiades Nebula; originally from Earth (Atlantis) and responsible for establishing the Galactic Guardian force in the Milky Way Galaxy

**E•pop•tes** \ Ē-pôp-tes \ *n* : **1** : shape-shifting god worshipped by the Eosian species, and from whom the Eosians presumably take their instruction through dreams; **2** : a master mason and seer in the Eleusian Mysteries, one who has the vision sublime; an initate into the highest, the 7th degree of the Mysteries (epopteia) who has attained spiritual clairvoyance and is at one with his inner divinity

**Fauche** \ Fōsh \ *n* : an ungulate-like biped species with very long ears, wide frequency hearing and large lustrous eyes, originating from Bedar 9 in the Sigma Draconis system

**Fen** \ fen \ *n* : one of the six main types of recognized wetland and one of two types of mire (the other being a *bog*); usually fed by mineral-rich surface water or groundwater and characterized by neutral or alkaline water with high dissolved minerals and few other plant nutrients, dominated by grasses and sedges and mosses; distinguished from bogs, which are acidic, low in minerals and usually dominated by sedges and shrubs, and Sphagnum moss

**Fisk** \ fisk \ *n* : large herbivorous ungulate, native to Moner 7, over-hunted to extinction by the natives after they were introduced to new weapons technology

**fok** \ fôk \ *n* : excrement from a blenoid

**Fo•mal•haut** \ fōmǝlhōt \ *n* : **1** : "fishes mouth" in Arabic; **2** : bright lone star 25 ly from Earth below the Galactic North Pole with the mass and size of Sol and a dust/gaseous disk surrounding it

**fu•gi•tive** \ fügitiv \ *n* : class A 100-crew interstellar ship built by Zeta Corp Aeronautics; a class B *fugitive* is a smaller version; see *Orichalkon*

**gad•pie** \ gad-pī \ *n* : **1** : a tree indigenous to Horo-2, the moon of Horologii b; **2** : the wood of the gadpie tree

**gam•ma ray** \ gamä rā \ *n* : photon packets of electromagnetic energy, denoted by Greek letter ; extremely high frequency and high-energy electromagnetic radiation that have no mass and no electronic charge; pure electromagnetic ionizing radiation that cause visible auroras and are biologicaly hazardous

**ghost** \ gōst \ *n* : a person acting as a *portal*, capable of recalling aspects of the other *diverse* through their other soul-half in a déjà vu experience. If they are capable of soul-drifting—locking into someone else's dream or trance—a ghost can manipulate both the dreams and real aspects of that other person's life in the other diverse, usually in the form of a lengthy déjà vu

**ghou•roud** \ gü-rüd \ *n* : **1** : Original French term for moving dunes; **2** : fields of moving dunes (barkhans) resulting from shifting sands, particularly found in Upsilon 3; as in the West Ghouroud

**Gleise-12** \ glēss-12 \ *n* : a moon of the gas giant planet Gleise 876b in the star system of Gleise 876, where a human colony established in Phoenix City; the star system's copious debris bombards the planet and its moon, resulting in a constant sunset

**Gleise-876b** \ glēss-876b \ *n* : a gas giant planet, locked in a 1:2 harmonic orbit with its sibling, Gleise 876c, around the Class M4V dim red dwarf star Gleise 876

**glit•ter** \ glit-tər \ *n* : **1** : a psycho-active drug used by Gnostics to see God; **2** : a refined form of *dust*, glitter is obtained through the major drug cartel of Dark Sun, run by Barbaricca on Sekmet; also known as *glitter dust*; also see *dust* and *Wakesh root*

**Gness** \ ness \ *n* : a gentle wolf-like species with translucent skin from the 61 Ursae Majoris system

**Gno•sis** \ nōs-sis \ *n* : knowledge of God

**Gnos•tic** \ nôs-tic \ *n* : a follower of Gnosticism; *adj* : pertaining to a follower of Gnosticism

**Gnos•ti•cism** \ nôs-ti-sizəm \ *n* : a belief system based on early Christianity, Helenistic Judaism, Greco-roman mystery religions, Zoroastrianism and neoplatonism, which teaches that some esoteric knowledge (gnosis) is necessary for salvation from the material world, created by an intermediary (demiurge; considered evil or merely imperfect) to God

**Gnos•tic Hermetic Order of Québec** \ nôs-tic hər-met-ic or-dər of qā-bec \ *n* : an order devoted to Gnosticism. Founded by Rafael Martinez, the Hermetic Order is based on Earth but has several outposts throughout the universe

**Gnos•tic Schiss Order** \ nôs-tic shiss ōr-dər \ *n* : a very small Hermetic order devoted to Gnosticism with mostly non-human members. Targeted by an *Eclipse* assassin, the Schiss Order was nearly extirpated. Its remnants is currently based on Uma 1

**Great Coat** \ grāt cōt \ *n* : part of the uniform and weapons arsenal of the Galactic Guardian; millions of thixtropic nano-sensors incorporated into its durable yet flexible fabric let it respond to any number of internal and external stresses, providing its wearer with a shield from the cold or from a weapon's discharge; see *thixtropic*

**Great Galactic Library** \ grāt galactic lībrerē \ *n* : the largest and most comprehensive collection of knowledge, culture and learning, located in Pyramid City on 47 Uma a and administered by the Khonsus

**gü•çlü•ve•sağlam** \ güchlü-ve-sôlam \ *n* : **1** : the most common marsh plant of Omicron 12 and main staple of the *peeka*, whose feces accelerate the process of peat formation and the formation of *rein* **2** : derived from Turkish for 'strong and sturdy'

**he•don** \ hē -dən \ *n* : **1** : a mildly euphoric recreational drug that is inhaled and produces a pungent yellow smoke; **2** : used colloquially to indicate incredulity (as in *"you must be blowing hedon")*

**Helsig 2** \ helsig 2 \ *n* : a planet in the HD168443 system, where the deep fever virus, carried in a shipment of damsel squashes, originated

**Her•metic Or•der** see *Gnostic Hermetic Order*

**hes•i•um fuel** \ hēs- ē-um feü-əl \ *n* : a highly inflammable and incendiary rocket fuel used by most Zeas Corporation ships

**Hor•us** \ hor-əs \ *n* : **1** : Egyptian god of knowledge and wisdom, who's head resembles an ibis; **2** : common name for the planet 47 Uma a, coined by the colonizing Khonsus, after the Egyptian moon god whose curved beak is the moon's crescent; orbits star 47 Uma (47 Ursae majoris in the constellation Ursae Major). The planet's indigenous inhabitants include *migratory trees, ammuts,* and the *apophus*

**i•ga•po flood** \ ē-gä-pō fləd \ *n* : very sudden and devastating flood event in Eos's swamp jungle, with tidal heights of over twenty feet

**in•ner di•verse** \ in-nər dī-vərs \ *n* : the world or existence comprised within the inner twin universe of the metaverse and linked to its twin existence, the *outer* *diverse,* through transitional phenomena such as black holes and intuition

**I•o•ta Hor•o•lo•gii** \ ī-ó-tä hōr-ó-lo-gē \ *n* : a class G0V yellow-orange main sequence dwarf star, 56 ly from Earth in the Constellation Perseus

**Iota Hor-2** \ ī-ó-tä hōr -tü \ *n* : Earth-like moon of Jovian gas giant Iota Horologii b; location of Galactic Guardian precinct

**jag** \ jag \ *vb* **1** : the act of straying off the space-time stream of faster-than-light travel and often accompanied by dangerous ship stress; **2** : used colloquially to indicate a serious misjudgement (as in *"he jags up all the time"*); **3** : slang swear word for copulation

**jag•ging** \ jag-gēng \ *vb* : **1** : describing a ship that is straying off the space-time stream; **2** : *vb; adv* : used as an expletive to describe a person, concept or action that lacks sense or causes harm, embarrassment or discomfort (as in, *"he's jagging with your mind"* or *"she's so jagging stupid"*)

**jagged** \ jagd \ *vb* : **1** : past tense verb of straying off the space-time stream of faster-than-light travel; **2** : *adj* : colloquial expletive term for a serious error or bad circumstance; SCREWED, MESSED UP (as in, *"we're jagged");* **3** : slang swear word for having copulated (as in *"he jagged me good")*

**join** \ jóēn \ *vb* : **1** : the metaphysical joining of two entities such as souls, spirits, or otherwise; the joining with an Epoptes ancient soul is mediated by the ancient vishna tree of Eos through the sexual act of inter-species "copulation" **2** : in reference to the prophesy by Raphael Martinez that *"the destruction of our old world will be signified by the joining of twin soul-mates who will herald the coming of a New Age."*

**kap•pa par•ti•cles** \ kap-pä pär-ti-cəlz \ *n* : energy particles that concentrate in the upper atmosphere of several gas giants; retrieved by Fauche *ray* class sentient ships for fuel using specialized fuel scoops

**kelm** \ kelm \ *n* : the wet season on the planet Eos

**kep•ry** \ kep-rē \ *n* : a flying crustacean-like creature on Sekmet that lives in the dung piles left by the sobek. Sobeks, in turn, lay their eggs in the dung and when they hatch, the young feed on the kepries; see *sobek*

**Khon•sus** \ kón-səs \ *n* : tall, feathered biped creature with raptor head, wings, and liquid amber eyes able to mind-probe, origin unknown but currently in the 47 Ursae Majoris system; hawk-like people who achieve powers through a symbiotic interaction with the planet's energy and forces; known as seekers of knowledge and truth, masterful librarians and database keepers, who run the *Great Galactic Library*

**Kraal** \ kräl \ *n* : icy moon that orbits HD222582b in the HD222582 G3 star system in the Constellation of Aquarius; location of Eclipse weapons making facility

**Kres•lid** \ kres-lid \ *n* : a small crustacean-like plankton that inhabits the toxic Beleus Sea on Beleus

**Le•gess** \ lə-gess \ *n* : tall, slim praying mantis-like invertebrate creatures who colonized *Chara* and enslaved native *Rills*

**Long Gun** \ lông gən \ *n* : a Class B side arm made by Bodek and Lamb with an extremely accurate narrow-barrel and used for years by Guardian Enforcers. When Guardian Enforcers started trading open enforcement for stealth operations, accuracy was exchanged for secrecy, and the Long Gun was abandoned in favor of the smaller less obtrusive *pocket*. It is illegal for non-Guardian citizens to carry a weapon that is designated Class A or B

**L'Ordre de l'Arbre Sac•ré** *n* : see *Order of the Sacred Tree*

**man•da•la** \ man-da-lä \ *n* : an ornate, highly detailed geometric design made of colored sand and symbolic of the universe. Used in a sacred ceremony by Tibetan Buddist monks, it is painstakingly created over many days and represents their sacred world of balance held together by spirit. Once the work of art is finished and revered in a short ceremony, it is destroyed

**Mar Ci•ty** \ mär ci-tē \ *n* : principle town on Mar Delena, run by artificial intelligence

**Mar De•le•na** \ mär de-le-nä \ *n* : planet in the Fomalhaut system, run by AI community whose principle inhabitants are the Delenians, a simple furry creature with six appendages and subservient to the AI

**MEC** \ mek \ *n* : acronym for Magnetic-Electro Concussion pistol, created by Rhea Hawke, which uses electro-magnetic wave energy to focus sub-atomic quintle particles into resonance with specific DNA

**met•a•tron** \ met-ə-trôn \ *n* : **1** : a very dense tetrahedral crystal with fiery light-radiating properties, first discovered on Sedna in Earth's solar system **2** : an archangel in *Judaism* and the highest of the archangels, he serves as the celestial scribe (of the akashic record). According to Jewish medieval apocrypha he is Enoch, ancestor of Noah, transformed into an angel and the keeper of the ultimate secrets of the universe.

**met•a•verse** \ met-ə-vərs \ *n* : a term that describes the composition of all matter and energy encompassed by divergent twin diverses; a whole quantum cosmos that includes all that was and will be

**mev•lan•i** \ mev-län-ē \ *n* : term used on Sekmet to describe the leader of the penal colony, Hades

**mi•gra•tor•y trees** \ mī-grə-to-rē trēz \ *n* : a tree known in myth to migrate from one location to another in the *Weeping Mountains* area of the planet *Horus*; according to myth, the Khonsus inhabited the trees in ancient times

**min•e•ro•tro•phic** \ min-ə-ró-tró-fic \ *adj* : soils and vegetation fed by stream or spring water usually rich in nutrients and dissolved chemicals with reduced acidity; in contraxt to ombrotrophic environments that get their water mainly from precipitation and are low in nutrients and more acidic

**mire** \ mīr \ *n* : **1** : an area of wet, soggy, spongy, muddy ground; swampy or boggy ground; *peatland*; dominated by living peat-forming plants

**Mo•ner 7** \ mo-ner 7 \ *n* : a moon of the planet Tau c in the Tau Gruis star system, 100 ly from Earth; a place where artists such as Binder Hapaan flourish

**Ne•on Ci•ty** \ nēôn ci-tē \ *n* : principle inhabitation of Iota Hor-2, a planet colonized by humans in the Iota Horologii star system; location of Galactic Guardian precinct

**Nex•us** \ nex-əs \ *n* : planet in the M103 star cluster system, 8,000 ly from Earth in the constellation Cassiopeia; location of major Badowin *spice* mine and smelter

**Nex•us Ci•ty** \ nex-əs ci-tē \ *n* : principle inhabitation of the Badowin race on Nexus in the M103 star cluster system

**nex•us por•tal** \ nex-əs pór-təl \ *n* : a person who enters the state of acting as a portal with ease through meditation or a self-induced trance. See *portal*

**Ngu** \ nü \ *n* : a photosynthetic amoeboid creature with protuberances as sense organs; they live in close aggregates symbiotically with AI-machinery on Virgil 9 in the 70 Virginis system

**Ni•hi•list** \ Nī-ə-list \ *n* : **1** : a member of a militant splinter group of the Vos; **2** : a specially trained death squad of shapeshifter assassins on the Vos payroll

**No•ke•rig** \ Nó-kə -rig \ *adj* : a Class D pistol of unknown origin and used by Eosian guards; an ancient ballistic weapon with projectiles that fester in the body wherever they embed

**Nu•yu** \ nü-ēü \ *n* : a nano-chemical mixture, imbibed as a liquid, that acts at the genetic level to temporarily change small aspects of outer appearance such as skin, eyes, hair; used as make-up

**O•gi•um 9** \ ó-gē-əm 9 \ *n* : a planet inside the orbit of the Jovian planet Ogium around the bright star HD70642, 90 ly from Earth, in the Constellation Puppis

**Om•i•cron 12** \ óm-i-crôn 12 \ *n* : a planet in the Chara star system whose principle native inhabitants are the *Rill*, bulbous short bog creatures with tube eyes and webbed limbs adapted to semi-aquatic life; colonized by aggressive commerce race, the *Legess*

**O•pus 9** \ ó-pus 9 \ *n* : a planet in the Sagittarius Arm, 2,500 ly from Earth, where the deep fever virus spread, in Obsidian City

**Or•der of the Sa•cred Tree** *n* : a closed membership in Quebec on Earth, devoted to the divine nature of the *vishna* tree, considered the tree of life and knowledge and the answer to achieving the balance of all things. The Order believes in the notion that a messiah, connected to the tree, will bring balance and begin a new age of enlightenment and peace

**O•rich•al•kon** \ ó-rich-äl-kon \ *n* : **1** : the durable alloy that the mythical Epoptes bestowed to the Eosians in Atlantis; **2** : an elite guard of five squadrons of highly skilled sleuth Eosian warriors (squadrons include *Cadmus, Odysseus, Prometheus, Perseus* and *Daedalus*) dedicated to guard Mon Seigneur Martinez and his Hermetic Gnostic Order

**O•gi•um 9** \ ó-gē-um-9 \ *n* : a planet of mixed colony (concentrated in Splendid City) in the HD70642 system

**ou•ro•bor•os** \ ü-rō-bōr-us \ *n* : **1** : a mythical serpent eating its own tail; **2** : connected with the *Suntelia Aeon* that refers to the serpent of light residing in the heavens (the Milky Way); **3** : the ouroboros symbolizes an Aeon

**ou•ter di•verse** \ ou-tər dī-vərs \ *n* : the world or existence comprised within the outer twin universe of the metaverse and linked to its twin existence, the inner diverse, through transitional phenomena such as black holes and intuition

**Pa•ra•dise Ci•ty** \ paradīs ci-tē \ *n* : principle inhabitation of a mixed colony on Uma 1, an icy moon of Horus; location of Schiss retreat and mystery school; see *Uma 1*

**peat** \ pēt \ *n* : a type of soil with high dead organic matter, mainly plants that have accumulated over thousands of years; an accumulation of partially decayed vegetation dominated by *Sphagnum* moss in histosol and formed in wetland conditions, where flooding obstructs flows of oxygen from the atmosphere, slowing rates of decomposition; *mires*, particularly *bogs*, are the most important source of peat with less common being *fens*; also called turf

**peat•land** \ pēt-land \ *n* : an area where peat is found; an ecosystem of peat bogs and some fen, consisting of a layer of peat at the surface, which has accumulated over thousands of years

**pee•ka** \ pē-kä \ *n* : a small monotreme creature that lives in the marshes of Omicron 12, the peeka feeds almost exclusively on Omicron's principle marsh sedge *güçlüvesağlam* and its feces help maintain the unique fen peatland rich in *rein*

**pee•wee** \ pē-wē \ *n* : small open two-seater flying vehicle resembling a motorcycle (available as convertible or hard top), made by local shipbuilders, *Beleus Boats & Air*

**Phoe•nix Ci•ty** \ fē-nics ci-tē \ *n* : main human inhabitation on Gleise-12; shielded from stellar debris and in constant sunset; location of Galactic Guardian precinct

**play•a** \ plī-ä \ *n* : a dry desert lake that contains water for a short while after a sudden downpour, causing a flood; an endorheic lake that is smooth hardpan most of the time

**plock nec•tar** \ plôk nectər \ *n* : **1** : a tasty nectar that is normally a mixture of juices from various planets with 50% of the juice made from the plock root of Scandia; **2** : 100% nectar from the plock root, known for its medicinal properties

**poly•synth fi•ber** \ pôlē-sinth fībər \ *n* : nano-strings that resonate with matter

**po•cket** \ pôk-et \ *n* : acronym for PulsOniC Kinetic Energy Tracker, a small Class B pistol created by Rhea Hawke and manufactured by Bodek & Lamb; used by the Galactic Guardian force; the pistol tracks a target once the gun has identified their signature

**pock•ta** \ pôk-tä \ *n* : a highly nutritious leguminous plant from whose giant seeds a rich thick soup is made

**poi mash** \ pói mash \ *n* : a substance like tobacco that is either smoked or chewed.

**Portal** \ pór-təl \ *n* : **1** : a person capable of entering into the other diverse and through their experience capable of seeing into the future of their current diverse; **2** : a person in the act of said action; **3** : a person, when acting as a portal, during dreamtime or meditation, may open a *gate* to the other diverse.

**pro•max•in** \ pró-max-in \ *n* : a sleep drug activated by metabolism

**pul•son wave** \ pəl-sôn wāv \ *n* : **1** : an electromagnetic green energy wave emitted by a long range stun cannon to disable a ship; **2** : a wave discharged by a weapon used in ships of Tangent Shipping design

**PSR 1257 + 12** \ *n* : a millisecond pulsar approximately 1,000 ly from Earth in the constellation Virgo; a "neutron star" and one of 9 known in the disk of the galazy, likely formed through supernova recoil; orbited by three terrestrial planets and an outer asteroid belt and planetoid with ionized gas clouds

**PSR 1257 + 12C** \ *n* : Earth-sized planet that is regularly swept with *gamma radiation* from the pulsar, energizing its atmosphere and causing auroras and bathing it in green light

**Pyr•a•mid Ci•ty** \ pir-ä-mid ci-tē \ *n* : major inhabitation of planet 47 Uma a, known as *Horus*, by *Khonsus* of the 47 Ursae Majoris system; a city known for its culture, philosophy and learning; site of the *Great Galactic Library*

**quin•tle** \ qəin-təl \ *n* : **1** : dark energy particle found in everything; **2** : destructive energy discharged from a weapon (e.g., Q-gun, created by shape-shifters) that resonates with matter to dematerialize an object; **3** : used colloquially to express something of importance (as in: *"who gives a quintle about spice?"*)

**Q-gun** \ kiü-gən \ *n* : a side arm of unknown origin and manufacture that discharges quintle waves, which resonate and dematerialize matter

**Q-gel** \ kiü-gel \ *n* : an amoebic blue-green explosive gel with nano-bots inside it that can be programmed to detonate within a specified distance from a specific object

**rein** \ rīn \ *n* : **1** : a mineral component found in the *minerotrophic* peatlands of Sekmet and Omicron 12, transformed via purification techniques into a highly efficient fuel used by Zeta Corp interstellar ships **2** : "pure" in German

**Rill** \ ril \ *n* : a short, stout and smelly bog being with tube-eyes, webbed limbs, large genitals and sloughing outer skin from Omicron 12 in the Chara system

**sab•kha** \ sab-kä \ *n* : a liquid-like desert feature of Upsilon 3 resembling "quick-sand", in which the sand worm hides while waiting for prey

**Scan•di** \ skan-dē \ *n* : a lizard-like lean-limbed biped with remarkable healing abilities; indigenous to the Upsilon

Andromedae system

**Schiss** \ shiss \ *n* : a hermetic order of peaceful Gnostic priests, devoted to the use of dream-meditation, particularly lucid dreaming, to achieve transcendence and evolve closer to God and the universal consciousness; several of its older founders experienced the Gate Hallucination; targeted by Eclipse and massacred into near extirpation during a meeting in Paradise City on Uma 1; see *Gnostic Schiss Order.*

**Scimitar class shuttle** \ simitär class shutəl \ *n* : Ten-passenger mid-sized interstellar ship

**Scythe-wing** \ sīth wing \ *n* : Four-man Badowin interstellar ship with wings that curve toward bow like a scythe and cockpit like an insect head; manufactured by Zeta Corp Aeronautics

**Seed phantom** \ sēd fantəm \ *n* : 1-man short-range ship with conical bow and flexible mid and aft; borrowed from ancient alien technology; manufactured by Zeta Corp Aeronautics

**Sek•met** \ sek-met \ *n* : bog-fen planet that orbits the KO star HD177830, 186 ly from Earth and inside the orbit of Jovian planet HD177830b; characterized by bog-fen landscape of mostly wet blanket bog, muskeg, distrophic lakes and ponds; location of penal colony Hades

**SGT** *n* : Standard Galactic Time; based on a decimal system from the basis of the Earth 24 hour diurnal cycle, with ten days equal to one month and ten months equal to one year; zero SGT is set at the moment of first alien contact with Earth

**sha•dow** \ shadó \ *n* : *delta* class 80-passenger & 10-crew interstellar freighter manufactured by Zeta Corp Aeronautics

**sha•dow trac•ker** \ shadó trakər \ *n* : mid-size short-range stealth ship manufactured by Zeta Corp Aeronautics

**shal•lik oil** \ shäl-lik óil \ *n* : an oil that possesses natural narcotic properties that numb the nervous system of those in contact with it and make them docile; the oil is produced by microbes indigenous to the Weeping Mountains area of the planet Horus; when ingested, the oil will make one very ill

**shape•shifter** \ shāp-shiftər \ *n* : a being able to change his or her physical appearance and associated physiology into several other forms; considered an ability possessed by the Borr species from Borrias

**skip•boat** \ skip-bōt \ *n* : a two-man vehicle with skates/skis that is able to move rapidly over water, ice and snow; used by settlers of Uma-1

**slave** \ slāv \ *n* : **1** : a derogatory term indicating one of lesser standing, often in actual indentured status : **2** : a term used by crime lords to their own hirelings or any considered lesser being

**sling rif•le** \ sling rīf-əl \ *n* : harpoon-like Class F weapon developed and made by Anglebush Industries and used by hunters, primarily those hunting blenoid on Upsilon 3. The sling's sharp harpooned projectile seldom kills. *"Killing wasn't its objective; maiming, injuring and demobilizing was the intent. The sling was popular with hunters and gamers looking to satisfy their brutal sport of tormenting lesser beings."* – Rhea Hawke

**so•bek** \ sō-bek \ *n* : a fierce over 20-foot long crocodile-like native of Sekmet that digs underwater tunnels in the peat and drowns its victims

**soul-drift** \ sōl-drift \ *vb* : the practice of entering another's dreams, even one's own, and change "reality" through them

**soy•ka** \ sói-kä \ *n* : a soy-based warm drink like coffee made with

L-theanine; stimulant

**Spice** \ spīss \ *n* : a mild psychoactive drug in common usage; see also *dust*

**Splen•did Ci•ty** \ splen-did ci-tē \ *n* : the principle inhabitation of mixed colony of humans and other sentients on *Ogium 9* in the HD70642 system; a very wealthy city run by crime lords

**Spo•ri•an** \ spó-rē-ən \ *n* : a very tall, pear-shaped lanky greenish species with elongated head and leather-like skin, long limbs and large bulbous eyes from the planet Spor in the 18 Scorpii system

**stun stick** \ stun stik \ *n* : a high-energy unclassified weapon that resembles a staff. Of unknown origin and manufacture, it is used by the *Orichalkon*, an Eosian elite guard of Mon Seigneur Martinez assigned to guard his Gnostic order in their various outposts in the universe. The weapon is wielded like a staff in Tai Chi movements and discharges an energy wave that stuns all that it contacts

**Sun•tel•ia Ae•on** \ sün-tel-iä Æ-ôn \ *n* : **1** : the End of the Age according to the ancient Greeks; see *Aeon suntelia*

**synth•flesh** \ sinth-flesh \ *n* : real skin molecules and synthetic materials combined by nano-technology, used in synthplast

**synth•plast** \ sinth-plast \ *n* : prosthetic made of a combination of real skin molecules and synthetic flesh using nano-technology

**Tan•gent Ship•ping** \ Tan-gent Ship-pēng \ *n* : the name of a Fauche ship building company. Maker of the *ray* class corvette, *falcon* class ship, *speeder* class viper, *speeder* class peewee, and *hawke* class corvette.

**tat•suk** \ tat-sək \ *n* : **1** : original Turkish Earth term meaning prisoner **2** : used by the galactic crime sub-culture, particularly Black Sun, to designate someone under indentured servitude; **3** : slave

**tap•pin** \ tap-pin \ *n* : a small domesticated cat-like mammal with fangs and three tails, indigenous to Iota Hor-2

**¹teck** \ tek \ *n* : a permanent genetic change induced through nano-technology developed by Eosians by acting at the DNA level

**²teck** \ tek \ *vb* : the act of applying a teck, usually done by a qualified nano-genetics doctor

**thix•tro•pic** \ thiks-trô-pic \ *adj* : describes the intelligent nano-sensors incorporated into the durable yet flexible material of a Great Coat, which respond to ongoing environmental stresses that protect its wearer from a range of assaults including disease, weapon discharge, extreme temperature, etc.; see *Great Coat*

**to•can** \ tō-can \ *n* : a rare insect-like creature indigenous to the Upsion Andromedae system from whose larvae a natural protein fibre is spun to create the shimmering tocanai fabric used in the creation of expensive suits

**to•ca•nai** \ tō-can-aē \ *n* : the name given to the fabric produced from the fibre spun from the tocan larva

**Tree Cult of Earth** \ trē cəlt of ərth \ *n* : see *Order of the Sacred Tree*

**Twin-V wing** \ twin-v wing \ *n* : *alpha* class four to eight-man double-set movable winged interstellar craft and official stealth vehicle of Guardian Enforcers. Manufactured by Zeta Corp Aeronautics

**U•ly•sses** \ eü-lis-sēz \ *n* : an interstellar space station built by Zeta Corp Aeronotics of Earth; a self-sufficient long term agrarian colony in the vein of an O'Neill Colony with a set of large rotating cylinders many kilometres long and thousands of meters across with large gimballed mirrors; the station maintains a circular motion of 1 rpm to create artificial gravity

**U•ma 1** \ ü-mä 1 \ *n* : ice moon of 47 Uma b (47 Ursae Majoris
b) orbiting the yellow-orange main sequence dwarf star
47 Ursae Majoris, 46 ly from Earth in the Constellation
Ursa Major; the moon's great seas are covered in ice;
principle settlement is Paradise City, used by the Schiss,
a spiritual sect, as a spiritual retreat and mystery school

**Up•si•lon 3** \ ü p-si-lôn 3 \ *n* : moon of Upsilon b, a ringed gas
giant in the Upsilon Andromedae star system 44 ly from
Earth. An arid, planet with heavy gravity and hot,
fluctuating temperatures, mostly red sand and scrub,
inhabited by the *blenoid*, abandoned by an ancient
civilization

**Ve•nik** \ Ve-nik \ *n* : a large reptilian-like scaled black-blooded
creature from the HD177830 system with indolent eyes,
several sets of arms with poisonous claws, and several
"mouths" or orifices; Veniks are known for their violent
and unprincipled nature; they are one of the few species
that still actively trade in slaves

**Ve•nika** \ Ve-nikä \ *n* : the home planet of *Veniks*

**Vir•gil Ci•ty** \ vər-gil ci-tē \ n : the principle inhabitation on the
moon Virgil 9 by the *Gnu*, an amoeba-like race

**Vir•gil 9** \ vər-gil 9 \ *n* : a moon, whose rotation is locked by the
tidal forces of the Jovian planet 70 Virginis b (Goldilocks),
creating widely fluctuating "day" and "night"
conditions; located 59 ly from Earth in the 70 Virginis star
system in the Constellation Virgo; inhabited by the *Gnu*

**70 Vir•gin•is** \ 70 vər-gin-is \ *n* : a G4V class, yellow-orange
main sequence dwarf star with a circumstellar dist disk,
generated by collision s between Kuiper-Belt objects

**vish•na** \ vish-nä \ *n* : a species of tree with thorns and violet
flowers, thought to be sentient and linked to an ancient
soul, of unknown origin but currently found as the major
component of Eosian and Earth forest ecosystems. The
tree forms the basis of the belief by the *Order of the Sacred*

*Tree of* the coming of a messiah who will bring balance needed to begin a new age of enlightenment and peace

**viz•ion** \ viz-ēôn \ *n* **1** : a small very strong and tenacious mammalian creature of unknown origin *adj* **2** : a term used to describe a powerful grip based on the animal

**Vos** \ Vôs \ *n* : presumed extragalactic war-like species of which very little is known

**Weapons class** \ wepônz class \ *n* : all weapons are classified according to their use; it is illegal for anyone except a Guardian to carry a weapon that is designated Class A or B

**wa•kesh root** \ wä-kesh root \ *n* : edible root, indigenous to the planet Sekmet, with strong psychoactive properties; source of *dust* and *glitter*

**Weep•ing Moun•tains** \ wēpēng mountənz \ *n* : extremely steep and jagged mountains, covered with shallik oil-producing microbes, that define and surround the *Boiling Sea* of the planet Horus (47 Uma a). The microbes that cover the surface of the *Boiling Sea,* excrete a narcotic oil (*shallik oil*) that numbs and hypnotizes prey

**Xhix** \ ziks \ *n* : a chameleon-like species with multiple eyes capable of wide wave-length vision and changeable skin according to mood, indigenous to the 37 Geminorum system

**Zar•zo•za** \ zar-zō-zä \ *n* : the name for the Gnostic Sanctuary of the Hermetic Order of Québec on Upsilon 3

**Zeas Cor•por•a•tion** \ zēss cōr-pōr-ā-shən \ *n* : a galactic trading company specializing in exotic foods and merchandize

**Ze•ta•Corp Aer•o•nau•tics** \ ze-tä-cōrp ā-rō-nô-tics \ *n* : a galactic ship builder from Earth. Maker of *alpha* class twin-V wing, scythe-wing, *delta* class shadow, shadow tracker, *beta* class dauntless, Class A and B *fugitives*, seed phantom, and *scimitar* class shuttle.

**Zi•bar** \ zi-bär \ *n* : an ephemeral desert town on Upsilon 3, where blenoid traders congregate to hunt and process blenoid meat for export

Phonetic symbols based are on *Merriam Webster's Collegiate Dictionary* and the *Dictionary of Pronunciation* by Abraham Lass and Betty Lass.

# Vehicles in the Splintered Universe

| Ship-Builder | Make & Style | Details |
|---|---|---|
| ZCA | *alpha* class *twin-V wing* | Four to eight-man double-set movable winged interstellar craft and official stealth vehicle of Guardian Enforcers: *Bas and Raekwan's ship* |
| ZCA | *scythe-wing* | Four-man Badowin interstellar ship with wings that curve toward bow like a scythe and cockpit like an insect head: *stolen by V'mer* |
| ZCA | *delta* class *shadow* (freighter) | 80-passenger & 10-crew interstellar freighter: *run by Eclipse for smuggling; Rhea and Bas board to kidnap Ka* |
| ZCA | *shadow tracker* (stealth) | mid-size short-range stealth ship: *used by Eclipse for stealth operations* |
| ZCA | *beta* class *dauntless* | 10-passenger interstellar entirely AI-run ship: *used by Guardians to transport criminals to Sekmet, Rhea taken to Sekmet in one* |
| ZCA | Class A *fugitive* | 100-crew interstellar ship: *used by elite Eosian guard, the Orichalkon* |
| ZCA | Class B *fugitive* | Smaller version: *Gadeiros's and Olomos's ships* |

| Ship-Builder | Make & Style | Details |
|---|---|---|
| ZCA | *Seed phantom* | 1-man short-range ship with conical bow and flexible mid and aft; borrowed from ancient alien technology: *Nihilist suicide squad* |
| ZCA | *scimitar* class shuttle | Ten-passenger mid-sized interstellar ship: *Ka's shuttle; stolen by Serge* |
| UN | skipboat | Water/ice/snow 2-man speed vehicle: *Rhea commandeers one on Uma 1 to chase Serge* |
| TS | *ray* class corvette | Two-man hybrid organic/nano-tech with folding wings and fuel scoops — interstellar capability: *Rhea's ship* |
| TS | *falcon* class | Four-person mid-sized interstellar ship, once used by Guardian Enforcers, now replaced by twin-V: *Enforcers chase Rhea* |
| TS | *speeder* class *peewee* | Small open two-seater flying vehicle resembling a motorcycle; *Rhea and Bastion steal one to escape a med-facility on Beleus* |
| TS | *speeder* class *viper* | One-man air vehicle (not inter-stellar): *stolen by Rhea on Horus* |
| TS | *hawke* class corvette | Four-man interstellar ship: *Ka's earlier ship (stolen by Diana Wood)* |

ZC = Zeta Corp Aeronautics (Human); TS = Tangent Shipping (Fauche); UN = unknown technology and builders

**Nina Munteanu** is a Canadian ecologist and novelist. In addition to nine published novels, she has authored award-winning short stories, articles and non-fiction books, which have been translated into several languages throughout the world. Recognition for her work includes the *Midwest Book Review Reader's Choice Award*, the *Delta Optimist Reader's Choice Award*, finalist for *Foreword Magazine's Book of the Year Award*, finalist for the *Science Fiction Writers of Earth Award*, nominated for the *Gaylactic Spectrum Award*, the *SLF Fountain Award*, *Ecata Reviewers Choice Award*, and the *Aurora Award*.

Nina served as assistant editor-in-chief of *Imagikon*, a Romanian speculative magazine and is currently co-editor of *Europa SF*, an ezine dedicated to informing the European science fiction community. Nina regularly publishes reviews, essays and articles in magazines such as *The New York Review of Science Fiction* and *Strange Horizons*, and serves as staff writer for several online and print magazines including *Amazing Stories*. She currently teaches writing at the University of Toronto and George Brown College in Toronto, Canada.

Nina taught ecology, limnology & environmental education for over twenty years at colleges and universities in Canada. She has published numerous papers in scientific journals and gives workshops on scientific & technical writing. Nina provides personal coaching and group workshops for writers on all aspects of writing and publishing in fiction and non-fiction venues. Her guidebook *The Fiction Writer: Get Published, Write Now!* is used in schools and universities across North America and forms the basis of many of her workshops. *The Fiction Writer* was translated and published in Romania by Editura Paralela 45. The next in the guidebook series, *The Journal Writer: Finding Your Voice*, was released in winter of 2012 in both Romanian and English. Her award-winning blog *The Alien Next Door* hosts lively discussion on science, travel, pop culture, writing and movies.

Nina shares her time between Toronto and Vancouver, Canada, where she teaches writing. Visit www.ninamunteanu.com for more information on Nina.

**Costi Gurgu** is an internationally acclaimed digital artist and designer and an Aurora Award finalist. He has illustrated book covers, magazine and newspaper covers and feature editorials for a variety of publications since 1999. Costi served as art director, designer and illustrator for clients from Romania, France, Italy, England and Canada. He helped design the French fashion magazine, *Madame Figaro*, and served as the art director for *Playboy* and *Tabu* magazines.

Drawing inspiration from Rene Magritte, Gorgio de Chirico, Neville Brody, Dali and H.R. Giger, Costi became the creative director of MediaPro Group, the largest publishing company in Romania. He currently resides in Toronto, Canada, where he writes, teaches digital design and creates graphic designs and illustrations for various media through his company Super Pixel Design.

Costi is a celebrated award-winning fiction writer in Romania, where he has sold five books and over forty short stories and won over twenty awards.

His first short story collection, *The Glass Plague*, was released in 2001 through ProLogos. Since then he published two more books, and edited three anthologies. His short stories can be found in the Daw Books' anthology "Ages of Wonder", Wildside Press' anthology "Third Science Fiction Megapack", Danish anthology "Cratures of Glass and Light", Millennium Books' anthology "The Second Revolution" and "Voices—New Writers from Toronto", a literary anthology.

# Other Books by Nina Munteanu

## Fiction:

The Cypol (2006, *eXtasy Books*)

Darwin's Paradox (2007, *Dragon Moon Press*)

Angel of Chaos (2010, *Dragon Moon Press*)

Outer Diverse, Book 1 of The Splintered Universe Trilogy (2011, *Starfire World Syndicate*)

Inner Diverse, Book 2 of the Splintered Universe Trilogy (2012, *Starfire World Syndicate*)

The Last Summoner (2012, *Starfire World Syndicate*)

Collision with Paradise (as Kate Wylde) (originally published in 2005 by *Liquid Silver Books*; re-issued in 2013 by *eXtasy Books*)

Natural Selection: a Collection of Short Stories (2013, *Pixl Press*)

## Non-Fiction:

The Fiction Writer: Get Published, Write Now! (2009, *Starfire World Syndicate*)

Scriitorul de Ficţiune. Fii Publicat, Apucă-te de Scris! (2011, *Editura Paralela 45*)

The Journal Writer: Finding Your Voice (2013, *Pixl Press*)

Scriitorul Jurnal: Descoperirea vocii interioare (2012, *Editura Paralela 45*)

Water Is...The Meaning of Water (due 2015, *Pixl Press*)

Find these books at a quality bookstore near you and at Amazon (Nina Munteanu's Amazon profile, http://www.amazon.com/Nina-Munteanu/e/B002MO6ZOW)

Enjoy *The Splintered Universe Trilogy* in audiobook format through Audible.com.

www.ingramcontent.com/pod-product-compliance
Lightning Source LLC
Chambersburg PA
CBHW020830260626
47169CB00003B/919